"Do You Know How Badly I Want to Kiss You, Daphne?"

Her eyes grew wide with an intoxicating combination of fascination and uncertainty. "I-I-I . . . don't . . ."

"Very badly. So badly it's unendurable." Pierce brushed Daphne's lips lightly with his. "I need to taste you. Will you let me?"

"You're asking me?" Her breath was tantalizingly warm against his lips, but Pierce could feel her tremble as she balanced on this new yet exhilarating threshold.

"Yes, I'm asking you. I'd never take what you didn't willingly offer."

Wonder and something painfully akin to relief flashed in her eyes, softening Pierce's hunger into something achingly tender as it melded with a wave of blind protectiveness. He wanted to enfold her in his arms, shield her from anything—or anyone— who tried to harm her.

"Kiss me, Daphne," he whispered. "Let me show you how safe you can be."

An Outpouring of Praise from Booksellers for
Andrea Kane's Magnificent Romance

SAMANTHA

"This has to be the best book I've ever read! I loved it!"

—Adene Beal, House of Books

"Andrea Kane at her best—an all-nighter. Pure pleasure!"

—Shelly Ryan, 1001 Paperbacks

"Be sure and put *Samantha* on top of your Christmas list—Andrea Kane is a literary Christmas angel!"

—Linda Wilson, Linda's Book Exchange

"Words cannot really express the writing style of Andrea Kane. *Samantha* is a story of dreams, reunions, as well as a hero to die for. A great writing accomplishment!"

—Jenny Jones, The Book Shelf

"*Samantha* lets you discover the end of the rainbow with intrigue, faith, love and a young woman with a heart of pure gold. Andrea does it again!"

—Judy Spagnola, Waldenbooks

"If love truly makes the world go 'round, then we need someone like the precious Samantha to be its navigator."

—Susan McConnell Koski, The Bookworm

"Outstanding! Andrea Kane has joined the ranks at the top!"

—Mary Bracken, Book Depot

Books by Andrea Kane

The Last Duke
Samantha
Echoes in the Mist
Masque of Betrayal
Dream Castle
My Heart's Desire

Published by POCKET BOOKS

ANDREA KANE

The Last Duke

POCKET **STAR** BOOKS

New York   London   Toronto   Sydney   Tokyo   Singapore

An *Original* Publication of POCKET BOOKS

 A Pocket Star Book published by
POCKET BOOKS, a division of Simon & Schuster Inc.
1230 Avenue of the Americas, New York, NY 10020

ISBN: 0-671-86508-0

First Pocket Books printing June 1995

10 9 8 7 6 5 4 3 2 1

POCKET STAR BOOKS and colophon are registered trademarks of Simon & Schuster Inc.

Cover art by Brian Bailey
Stepback art by Gregg Gulbronson

Printed in the U.S.A.

The Last Duke is dedicated to my extraordinary editor, Caroline Tolley, whose unrelenting faith in my writing and enthusiastic commitment to her craft command that she stand alone. Thanks, CT.

Acknowledgments

Love and gratitude go to the following, who, each in his own way, enabled me to tell Daphne and Pierce's story:

Brad and Wendi, who are, quite simply, the loves of my life and the best of the best.

Plunk, who still never permits me to give anything short of my best, and who has patiently waited four years to see the words, "The last duke was dying. . . ."

Pat, who offers her invaluable friendship with an open heart, a quick mind, a ready ear, and an interesting cup of tea.

Helen, who tirelessly helped me research everything from foxes' dens to Victorian workhouses.

Clare, whose friendship and support lift my spirits, and whose sympathy meals feed my family at deadline.

Professor George Ford, who introduced me to the world of Charles Dickens and who taught me that writing is a gift to be ever savored, enhanced, and given free rein to fly.

The Last Duke

Prologue

Leicester, England
1828

"PLEASE, PAPA, DON'T MAKE ME GO IN THERE."

The child hung back, tugging to free herself from her father's iron-clad grasp. Terrified, she stared up at the dingy brick building, the rotted sign heralding The House of Perpetual Hope looming over her like some odious monster.

"This inexcusable behavior is precisely why you're accompanying me." Harwick Wyndham, the Marquis of Tragmore, scowled down at his eight-year-old daughter, determined that once their visit to the dilapidated workhouse was concluded all semblance of nonsensical tenderness would be forever erased from the delicate features now tilted imploringly up at him. "Come," he ordered. "'Tis time you saw the unsalvageable waste that is allowed to drain the strength of our country and squander our tax money. Then perhaps you'll save your pity for those more deserving."

Purposefully, he dragged her along, ignoring her frightened protests, until they reached the heavy wooden door. There, he knocked.

"Wot ye want? Oh, it's ye, sir."

A vile stench accompanied the soot-covered man who

1

admitted them, his sunken eyes dilating as he recognized the marquis. "Mr. Barrings wasn't expectin' ye, m'lord. I'll tell 'im ye're 'ere."

"No need. The Duke of Markham and I aren't scheduled to meet with Mr. Barrings until Thursday. I've come today merely to show my daughter about."

The man gaped. "But, sir."

"That'll be all. You can return to your duties."

"Yes, sir."

Tragmore pivoted to face his daughter. "Daphne, I've decided to be kind and spare you the horrors of the dead and diseased rooms in the hopes that the debauchery you'll witness right here will be enough to set your mind straight. However, if need be, we'll visit every nook and cranny of this workhouse in order to harden that foolish heart of yours."

Daphne's little fists knotted in her gown. Assailed by an unimaginable dread, she dragged her shocked gaze from the peeling walls that encased her to the rotted floor beneath her feet. "Please, Papa, I . . ."

"Did you see the man who greeted us?"

"Yes, Papa."

"And what was your impression of him?"

"That he needed a bath, Papa. And a new set of clothes."

"Is that all?"

"I wondered if we might find a way to give him those things."

"We're already giving him far too much," Tragmore growled, "and it's time you realized that." Scanning the hallway, he gestured toward the far corner. "Look over there."

Daphne looked, spying two ill-kempt women on their knees, alternately scrubbing the floor and wailing undistinguishable sorrows to each other.

"Filthy trollops," the marquis muttered. "Foul vermin who breed disease and immorality. They're given a place to live, food to eat, and yet look at them, Daphne. Look well. They do naught but deplete what we provide them and then demand more. To what end, I ask you?"

Silently, Daphne stared at the two women. "They're in pain, Papa," she said at last, her young face filled with anguish. "Perhaps they're ill. See the smaller one? She can scarcely catch her breath. Why is she scrubbing? She should be abed."

Tragmore's jaw clenched so tightly he felt it might snap. "Any illness she possesses she herself caused and is now spreading to others."

"Are you acquainted with her, Papa?" Twisting a strand of tawny hair about her finger, Daphne kept her voice even, devoid of sentiment. Her father despised emotional displays; were she to give in to one now she would doubtlessly feel the weight of his hand.

"Of course not!" Tragmore spat out. "Where would I come to meet such a person?"

"Then how do you know she caused her own illness?"

He gaped in stupefied silence.

"In any case," Daphne continued, "she needs medicine. And rest. Then she'd be quite fit. With a bath and a mended gown, she'd actually be lovely."

The marquis sucked in his breath, coughing violently as the foul air permeated his lungs. Daphne's observation, her untenable feelings of compassion, were a disturbing echo of the past.

Rage pumped through his veins.

"Your mother once spoke as you do," he ground out through gritted teeth. "Had I permitted it, she would have squandered my fortune aiding vermin such as these." He glared down at Daphne, fire blazing in his eyes. "I revised her opinions in whatever manner I deemed necessary. Do I make myself clear, Daphne?"

"Yes, Papa." Daphne's lips trembled. Lowering her lashes, she fixed her frightened gaze on the toes of her slippers.

Tragmore stifled a curse. He'd brought the little chit here for a purpose, and he intended to make certain that purpose was realized.

Mentally, he counted to ten.

"Perhaps I've chosen poor examples, things beyond your

comprehension," he reasoned aloud, trying a new tactic. "After all, you are a child. Very well, then. A child is what you will see."

So saying, he steered Daphne forward, down the hall and beyond, until he reached the rear door of the workhouse. Flinging it open, he gestured toward the garden. "Look."

Five or more scruffy urchins milled about, a few tugging idly at the weeds, others cupping their hands beneath the spout of the water pump, peeking furtively about as they drank.

Daphne opened her mouth to comment on how bedraggled the children looked, how torn was their clothing, then thought better of it and snapped her mouth shut. She was in the process of devising what she hoped her father would consider an appropriate response when one of the children, a little girl of about the same age as she, glanced up from the weeds.

Her gaze locked with Daphne's.

The bleak pain reflected in the child's eyes caused a tight knot of sorrow to form in Daphne's chest, driving home an ugliness until now vast but intangible.

Unable to bear it, Daphne looked away.

"Appalled, are you?" the marquis asked, satisfaction gleaming in his eyes. "You have reason to be. Rather than tend the garden and pump the water as they've been assigned, these unwanted bastards are frolicking about, taking in the sun. They should be beaten until fear impels them to work. And, should that prove unsuccessful, they should be thrown into the streets to starve, thus ridding England of their poisonous influence." Staring at his daughter's averted head, Tragmore demanded, "Now do you see, Daphne?"

"Yes, Papa. Now I see."

"Good. In that case, we can thankfully take our leave. This place sickens me."

Guiding her back through the hallway, the marquis tripped over an object in his path. Stifling an oath, he kicked it aside.

"It's a doll, Papa!" Daphne exclaimed, stooping to retrieve the toy. Wiping soot from its cheek, she held it out in

4

delight. "Why, she looks just like Juliet, the doll Mama gave me for Christmas!"

"Are you mad? Don't touch that . . . thing!" Tragmore ordered. "Lord alone knows what disease it carries!" Lunging forward, he struck the doll and sent it crashing to the floor, where it lay in a tattered heap, its torn dress tangled about its disheveled mane of hair.

"No, Papa! Don't!" Daphne begged. "She's too beautiful to be diseased!"

"She mine!" a trembling voice rang out from the rear. In a flash, the little girl dashed through to the hallway, snatching her precious treasure from the floor. Terrified, she stared at the well-dressed strangers, quivering as she faced them. "She's mine! Ye can't 'ave 'er!"

"Nor do we want her, you odious, impudent creature!" Tragmore spat. He drew back his hand, glowering as he poised to strike the white-faced child. "Do you see, Daphne? This is what I've been trying to tell you. These people are animals; loathsome parasites. You must harden yourself to the truth and act accordingly."

"I will. Oh, Papa, please don't hit her," Daphne whispered pleadingly. "What point is there? I've learned all you wanted me to. Please. Can't we just go?"

Her words struck their mark.

With a shudder of revulsion, Tragmore turned on his heel. "Very well. Come." Striding to the door, he prepared to depart.

Daphne started after him, then hesitated, her sober gaze returning to the little girl who cringed before her, clutching her doll to her chest.

It was the little girl they'd seen in the garden. Daphne recognized her immediately, from the moment she'd darted into the hallway.

She was as lovely as her plaything, despite unkempt hair and worn clothing. Beneath a thin layer of grime her coloring was fair, her eyes huge and thickly lashed.

Once again, those penetrating eyes met Daphne's, wide and unblinking.

A chill encased Daphne's heart as she stared into those eyes—dark, fathomless eyes—nearly black in their color and intensity. Their hollow depths were filled with fear and sadness and something far worse than either.

Futility.

Acting on instinct, Daphne took a step toward her.

"Daphne!"

Tragmore's thunderous summons cracked through the hall, striking Daphne with all the force of a whip.

"Coming, Papa." Instantly, she complied, helplessly bolting from the dingy workhouse walls and the haunting gaze of the little girl.

But it wasn't over, nor would it ever be. For the image of that child and her doll were forever engraved in Daphne's mind, profoundly etched in her heart.

Why can't Papa see? an inner voice cried out. *They'd both be so very lovely.*

All they need is a bath and a change of clothes.

1

Northamptonshire, England
October, 1840

THE LAST DUKE WAS DYING.

Dragging shallow breaths into his lungs, the sixth and final Duke of Markham cursed the fates for snatching him so quickly and himself for not foreseeing how imminent was his end. His legacy lay in fragments, shards of immortality he could no longer ensure. Markham itself, the perpetuation of his title, both would be beyond his protection, lost to the hands of strangers.

He needed time.

He had none.

Moistening his lips, the duke reached for the bell pull beside his bed, summoning the valet he'd only just dismissed.

"Your Grace?"

It was that blasted doctor who entered, and impatiently the duke waved him away. "Bedrick. Send Bedrick." He dissolved into a weak fit of coughing.

"Of course, Your Grace." The doctor gestured for the uniformed valet to enter.

"Get—out." The duke gasped at his grim-faced physician. "Bedrick—alone."

7

With a curt bow, the doctor complied.

"You sent for me, Your Grace?" Bedrick frowned at a loose button on his coat, his demeanor as calm as if he planned to assist the duke in shaving, rather than stand by his deathbed.

"Pen—paper—"

"Certainly." Bedrick provided both.

With a shaking hand, the duke scrawled a name and a few words on the page, barely managing to fold the paper in two. Utterly spent, he fell back against the pillows. "To my solicitor," he whispered. "I've made provisions. He'll know what to do."

"I understand, Your Grace."

"Immediately. As soon as I'm gone."

"At once, sir. Will there be anything else?"

"Pray, Bedrick. Pray it's not too late."

"As you wish, sir." Dutifully, Bedrick slipped the note into his pocket and moved away.

The dying man stared after him, drifting into a world where the past flowed forward, melding into a soothing haze with the future.

Then the last duke closed his eyes.

"Give me back my wallet, you filthy urchin!"

Red faced and sputtering, the gentleman waved his cane at a cringing lad. "I said, hand it over!" Violently, he thrust his gloved hand forward.

None of the hundreds of people flocking into Newmarket's Rowley Mile Course paid the slightest heed to the ongoing confrontation. Bound for October's Champion Stakes, they had little time to witness a common pickpocket being apprehended.

"You heard me, you wretched bandit! Return my money. Instantly. Or else I shall haul you off to the local magistrate!"

"I . . . I . . ." The lad wiped a muddied sleeve across his forehead, his eyes wide and frightened.

"Excuse me, sir. I believe there's been some mistake."

The nobleman whipped around. "I beg your pardon?"

Stiff with outrage, he glowered at the stranger who towered over him.

"I said, I believe you're mistaken," the newcomer returned, his tone as hard as his features. "This lad didn't take your wallet."

"He most certainly did. I witnessed the theft myself."

The enigmatic stranger shook his head. "What you witnessed was an unfortunate coincidence. The wallet fell from your trousers. This boy merely had the bad luck to be in the wrong place at the wrong time. He didn't steal anything."

"Why, how dare you. I'm positive—" The elder man stopped in mid-sentence as the stranger flourished the missing billfold in his face.

"I saw it fall to the ground and retrieved it," the stranger explained. "I was about to return it when you wrongly accused this poor lad." He patted the boy's shoulder and extended his other hand. "Your wallet, sir."

"Why I was sure—that is, I spied—at least I thought I spied—" The nobleman drew a disconcerted breath as he took the proffered billfold. "Thank you for restoring my property and alerting me to the facts," he amended with stilted dignity.

"You're welcome."

"I don't believe we've been properly introduced. I'm Lionel Graband, the Earl of Caspingworth. And you are?" He paused expectantly.

"Thornton."

"Lord Thornton." The earl bowed politely.

The stranger didn't. "Not *Lord* Thornton," he corrected brusquely. *"Thornton.* Pierce Thornton."

Caspingworth blinked. "My mistake. Thornton." Smoothing his mustache, he assessed Thornton's tall, powerful frame, the expensive cut of his clothing. "I'd like to offer you a token of my appreciation."

"Don't. Instead, offer an apology to the boy."

A sharp gasp. "Apologize? To this riffraff?" Caspingworth glared disdainfully at the grimy-faced lad who was inching away. "I assure you, if I wasn't his intended victim today,

9

someone else was. He's a common pickpocket. He should be tossed into prison where he belongs. Good day, Thornton." With exaggerated offense, the earl turned on his heel and strode off.

Pierce stared after him, a muscle working in his jaw. Simultaneously, his hand clamped down on the retreating boy's shoulder. "Wait."

"Wot do ye want?" the boy asked, white faced.

A corner of Pierce's mouth lifted as he regarded his quarry. "You look bewildered."

The lad dropped his gaze, kicking the dirt with his toe.

"Your eye is good, but your touch is heavy," Pierce instructed quietly. "You also made an inexcusable, often fatal, error. You allowed yourself no path by which to flee."

"Wot?" The urchin's chin shot up.

"You chose your target well, and positioned yourself perfectly. Then you ruined it with a clumsy execution and no planned means of escape."

"I . . . Ye . . ." The pickpocket swallowed. "Ye saw me take th' wallet."

"Of course."

"How did ye get it?"

Pierce's grin widened. "My touch is light and my execution is perfect."

"Ye pilfered it from me?"

"Under the circumstances, it seemed prudent." Pierce extracted a few shillings from his pocket. "Here. Take these. Buy yourself something to eat. Then go home and practice what I've taught you. A light touch and a well-thought-out plan. The advice will serve you well."

The lad looked from the coins to Pierce and back again. Then, with an awed expression, he bolted.

Keenly satisfied with the results of his handiwork, Pierce resumed his course. Slicing his way through the crowd of enthusiastic racegoers, he scanned the grounds, easing past beer-drinking men and fortune-telling Gypsies, past the tents where loud betting was taking place, toward the pavilion where the fashionable crowd readied themselves for the first race.

Just outside the stands he spotted his mark and bore down on him.

"Tragmore. What a surprise."

The marquis turned, his face draining of color when he saw Pierce. "Thornton. What the hell are you doing here?"

"Why wouldn't I be here? The Champion Stakes are exhilarating to behold. Besides, I'm feeling incredibly lucky today. How about you, Tragmore? Are you feeling lucky as well?"

An angry flush spread up Tragmore's neck and suffused his face. "Don't toy with me. If you've sought me out, it's for a reason."

"Why do you assume I've sought you out? Perhaps our encounter is no more than mere coincidence."

Tragmore wiped beads of perspiration from his forehead. "When you're involved, there are no coincidences." He lowered his silver-white head, his voice dropping to a whisper. "It was you who bought that bloody note, wasn't it?"

"Which note is that?"

"The only one of mine you had yet to acquire, damn you. The one held by Liding Jewelers."

"You owed Mr. Liding a considerable sum. Not to mention the fact that you were three months late with your payments. Liding was on the verge of calling in the full amount." A sardonic smile twisted Pierce's lips. "Perhaps you should view my purchase of the note as your salvation."

"I view it by another name." Tragmore's fists clenched. "Why have you come here today, Thornton? To gloat? To remind me that you own me, body and soul?"

"Harwick? The horses are lining up." A woman's tentative voice reached their ears. "You mentioned that you didn't wish to miss the onset of the race, so I thought perhaps—"

"A moment, Elizabeth," Tragmore fired over his shoulder. Tight-lipped, he turned back to Pierce. "My wife and daughter accompanied me today. Therefore, if you'll excuse me."

"Excellent! I'd enjoy meeting your family." Pierce squinted, ignoring the marquis's furious sputter. "Is that the marchioness over there? The lovely woman with the flowered hat who's waving in our direction?"

"Thornton, Elizabeth knows nothing about—"

Withdrawing his pocket watch, Pierce declared, "We have just enough time for an introduction." Snapping the timepiece shut, he strode through the congested pavilion to the box where Tragmore's wife and daughter awaited.

Left with no option, Tragmore swallowed an oath and followed.

"Lady Tragmore?" Pierce asked, inclining his head in her direction.

"Why, yes. Do I know you, sir?" The woman who stared solemnly at Pierce, her fingers alternately gripping and releasing the brim of her hat, had obviously at one time been extraordinarily lovely. It was evident in her still-smooth skin, the fragile lines of her features. But, like a small broken bird's, her beauty was faded, her eyes listless and surrounded by lines of suffering and sadness.

Both of which had been caused by the brutality of one heartless bastard.

Pierce's gut gave a savage twist.

"Elizabeth, this is Pierce Thornton." The marquis was reluctantly performing the introduction. "Mr. Thornton is," an uneasy cough, "a business associate of mine. Thornton, may I present my wife, Lady Tragmore."

"Delighted, Madam." Pierce bowed.

"And my daughter, Lady Daphne." Tragmore reached out to guide his daughter from behind the eclipsing wall of her mother's headpiece.

"Lady Daphne, 'tis a pleasure." Pierce caught a glimpse of tawny hair and readied himself, with more than a touch of curiosity, to inspect Tragmore's only child.

His inspection was limited to the golden brown mane that flowed gracefully down her back.

Head averted, Daphne appeared to be scrutinizing the grounds, as if thoroughly fascinated by something or someone in the crowd, and was thus oblivious to her father's introduction.

12

"Daphne!" Tragmore snapped, his fingers biting into her arm.

Like a frightened rabbit, she jerked about, her face draining of color. "I'm sorry, Father. What were you saying?"

"I was performing an introduction," Tragmore ground out, indicating Pierce's presence. "This time I suggest you listen. Carefully." Fury laced his tone, blazed fire in his eyes. "Pierce Thornton, my meditative daughter, Daphne."

"Mr. Thornton, I apologize." Turning in Pierce's direction, Daphne bowed her head, the pulse in her neck accelerating with the blow of her father's reprimand.

"I should hope so," the marquis berated. "Thornton, forgive my daughter's behavior. At times she is inexcusably—"

"No apology is necessary." Pierce raised Daphne's gloved hand to his lips, revealing none of the rage that coiled within him like a lethal spring. "In truth, I can guess just what dilemma occupies Lady Daphne's thoughts."

Instantly, Daphne's fingers went rigid in his, her lowered gaze unconsciously darting to her father, gauging the degree of his anger. "No dilemma, sir. I was merely watching. That is, I was wondering—"

"Which horse to choose in the first race," Pierce finished for her. "The choice is a difficult one, isn't it, my lady?"

This time Daphne's head came up, her brows arched in bewildered surprise. "Why, yes, it is."

Pierce's first unimpeded view of Tragmore's daughter was a dazzling revelation.

Small and fine boned like her mother, but with a vibrancy clearly lacking in the marchioness, Lady Daphne was exquisite, emanating, not the glittering beauty that filled London's ballrooms, but the classic beauty of a rare and priceless painting. Her hair, like rich honey, cascaded over her shoulders in a tawny haze—all but those few tendrils that had broken free and now trailed stubbornly along her cheeks and neck. And those eyes. The most amazing contrast of colors—a kaleidoscope of soft greens and muted grays with luminous sparks of burnished orange; delicacy offset by strength.

"The contenders are exceptional." Pierce held Daphne's hand a fraction longer before releasing it. "Perhaps if we compare notes we can together arrive at the winning candidate."

A faint, uncertain smile. "You're very gracious, Mr. Thornton."

"Yes, you are." The marchioness sounded vastly relieved. "Look, Harwick, the horses are lining up." She urged her husband toward his seat. "Come."

Apparently convinced that no irreparable damage had been done, Tragmore gave a curt nod. "Very well."

"Mr. Thornton?" Elizabeth turned to Pierce. "Please, won't you join us? Unless, of course, you've made other arrangements."

Seeing the immediate opposition on Tragmore's face, Pierce made a swift decision. "No, I have no other arrangements. I'd be delighted to join you."

"Wonderful. We have an empty chair directly beside Daphne. I'll take that seat myself, so you and my husband can discuss your mutual business dealings."

"I wouldn't hear of it," Pierce declined. "The race is a social event. Your husband and I share a wide variety of interests, all of which promise to be ongoing for quite some time. Isn't that right, Tragmore?"

"Indeed." The marquis had begun to sweat.

"Good. Then tomorrow will be soon enough for us to arrange a meeting. For now, I insist you sit right up front beside your wife. I shall take the empty chair beside Lady Daphne. And, in the unlikely event that I think of a matter too pressing to wait a day, I'll simply call out to you between races. How would that be, Tragmore?" Pierce's smile could melt an iceberg.

"Uh, fine. That would be fine, Thornton."

"Excellent." Pierce gestured for Tragmore and his wife to precede him. "After you, then."

The marquis seized his wife's elbow and steered her into the box.

"Lady Daphne?" Pierce extended his arm.

"Thank you." Daphne paused, her quizzical glance swerving from her father to Pierce, where it lingered.

"Is everything all right, my lady?" Murmuring the question for Daphne's ears alone, Pierce held her stare, deftly tucking her arm through his.

Her smile came slowly, an action rooted in some private emotion more fundamental than cordiality or amusement. "Yes, Mr. Thornton. I believe it is."

"Good." Pierce guided her to her seat. "Then let us get down to the serious task of selecting the winner."

"Us?" Daphne looked startled.

"Certainly us. I did promise to assist you in this arduous task, did I not?"

"Well, yes, but I know very little about—"

"Have you attended the races before?"

"Of course, many times. But—"

"Surely you must, on occasion, have had a feeling about the potential of a particular horse?"

"I suppose so. Still—"

"Trust your instincts, then." Pierce gestured to where the horses and their jockeys were poised for the first race. "In your opinion who exudes an aura of success?"

Hesitantly, Daphne leaned forward to study the contenders. A moment later her eyes lit up, reluctance transforming to eagerness. "Why, Grand Profit is running today! She's that magnificent chestnut mare whose jockey is in green. I've seen her race several times before. She's fast as the wind and graceful and—"

"That has little to do with whether she'll win or not, my insipid daughter," Tragmore snapped over his shoulder. "Thornton, pay no attention to Daphne's inane meanderings. She has her head in the clouds, with no knowledge of the rules of the turf." His voice dropped to a mutter. "Rumor has it that Profit's jockey has instructions to fall behind in this race."

"Really?" Pierce crossed one leg nonchalantly over the other. "And have I your word on that, Tragmore?"

"You do."

"How reassuring." Pierce rose. "In that case I feel ready to place my wager."

"My money is on Dark Storm," the marquis hissed.

A mocking smile. "I'm pleased to know where *your* money is." Pierce turned to Daphne. "Will you excuse me?"

"Of course." Daphne's nod was gracious, but the light in her eyes had gone out.

Swiftly, Pierce conducted his business, returning to his seat in time to see the horses speed around the first stretch.

"It appears Grand Profit has a considerable lead," he commented.

"Yes." Daphne sat up a little straighter, staring intently at the magnificent horse who was several yards ahead of the others.

"Dammit!" Tragmore leaned forward, hands tightly gripping his knees. "Hell and damnation!" he bit out long minutes later as Grand Profit crossed the finish line.

"A problem, Tragmore?" Pierce asked with apparent concern.

"Just a bloody poor informant." The marquis slumped in his chair. "Sorry, Thornton."

"It's your money, Tragmore," Pierce reminded him. "Remember?" Without awaiting a reply, Pierce eased back in his seat, turning toward Daphne.

What he saw made him grin.

Daphne's eyes were sparkling, her chin tilted proudly in his direction. She looked exuberant and thoroughly pleased with herself.

"As I suspected," Pierce murmured, brushing his knuckles across her flushed face. "Your instincts are quite good, my lady."

She stared at his fingers as they caressed her skin. "I'm sure it was luck."

"Perhaps. But good luck, nonetheless." He ran his thumb across her soft lower lip. "Congratulations."

Her breath broke in a tiny shiver. "I'm sorry you lost."

"Ah, but I didn't."

"Pardon me?"

"Your enthusiasm was contagious, as was your logic. I placed my bet on Grand Profit."

"You placed your . . ." Daphne shook her head in amazement. "All because of what I said?"

"A good gambler trusts his instincts. Always remember

that." Pierce winked. "Now, shall I choose the next winner or shall you?"

Daphne's lips quirked. "I don't believe in pressing my luck, Mr. Thornton, good or otherwise. I believe I'll leave the rest of the day's wagers to you. I suspect you are far more proficient at this than I."

"As you wish," Pierce agreed.

The remaining races were exhilarating, as was the extraordinary sum he won, but seeing Daphne blossom like a newly opened flower filled Pierce with more satisfaction than all his winnings combined.

That, and one thing more.

The sheer triumph of watching Tragmore squirm as his losses compounded, plunging him deeper and deeper into debt.

The indications of the marquis's agitation were subtle, but, having survived thirty years on wits alone, Pierce knew just what to search for. He took in each bead of sweat on the marquis's brow, each nervous quiver of his unblemished hands, each uneasy glance over his shoulder as he waited for the axe to fall, for Pierce to publicly expose him to the world.

No, you bastard, Pierce thought grimly. *That would be too easy and too painless. Sweat. Die inside. Wonder if you'll survive. Just the way I did.*

Beside him, Daphne shifted. Pierce turned in time to see her peering over her shoulder, searching the crowd.

"Have you lost something?" he asked, leaning toward her.

Daphne started, pivoting around in her seat. "No."

"I don't devour innocent women."

Those amazing eyes widened. "Pardon me?"

"You needn't look so terrified. I'm harmless."

Another hesitant smile hovered about her lips. "Are you? I think not, Mr. Thornton. In fact, I'm unsure why, but harmless seems the least likely word to describe you."

Pierce acknowledged her assessment with a dry chuckle. "Uninteresting then? Given the fact that, since our introduction, I've spent an inordinate amount of time viewing your back."

She flushed. "Forgive me."

"And you've done nothing but apologize."

"I—"

"Don't." He covered her hand with his. "Just don't."

Daphne twisted a loose strand of hair about her finger, glancing nervously toward her father's seat. "Is it unusually warm today?" she blurted out.

"I don't know," Pierce responded quietly, making no move to pull away. "Is it?"

Yanking her hand from beneath his, Daphne swept her hair up to cool her nape. "Perhaps it's the excitement of the race."

"Perhaps." Pierce didn't bother reminding her that neither of them had been watching the horses run for the past quarter hour. Further, although he felt her confusion, her discomfort, it was his own myriad emotions that intrigued him: compassion for the fear that clearly imprisoned this enchanting young woman, hatred for the man he was certain inspired it, and something more, an odd combination of fascination and attraction.

Following the movement of Daphne's hair, Pierce's gaze fell to her throat, exposed now, and bare but for a small strand of pearls.

"Beautiful," he murmured.

"What?" Daphne dropped her tresses as if they were lead.

"Your necklace. The gems are lovely."

"Oh. I thought—I apologi—" She caught Pierce's eye and broke into unexpected laughter.

"Your laughter is lovelier still."

"And my parents are ten feet away."

"I'm sure they already know of their treasures."

Daphne's laughter faded and Pierce had the irrational urge to coax it back, to make her glow the way she had when she'd chosen the winning horse. The vulnerability of her smile, the honesty of her laughter, were as tender as a child's, but the resignation in her eyes was old, sad, tempered only by a small spark of inextinguishable pride. The combination was stirring, and Pierce, whose knowledge went far deeper than Daphne imagined, found himself strangely moved by Tragmore's daughter. It was the first time he could remember feeling such empathy for a blue blood. In this case, however . . . Pierce's gaze drifted slowly over Daphne's delicate features, the alluring curves concealed by the modesty of her day dress. Lord alone knew what she must endure with Tragmore for a father.

The thought left him cold.

"Mr. Thornton, you're staring."

A corner of Pierce's mouth lifted. "Am I? How boorish of me. I'm usually far more subtle in my approach."

"Your approach? What is it you're approaching?"

Again, he leaned toward her. "You."

"Oh. I see." She moistened her lips, venturing another swift glance at her father, sagging with relief when she saw he was absorbed in the last race of the day. "Tell me, Mr. Thornton, are you always so direct?"

"Yes. Tell me, my lady, are you always so naive?"

She considered the question. "Yes."

A rumble of laughter vibrated in Pierce's chest. "How old are you, Daphne?"

If she noted the informality of his address, she gave no sign. "Twenty."

"And why is it, if I might be so bold as to ask, that no worthy gentleman has yet whisked you down the aisle?"

"I don't know, Mr. Thornton," she replied with artless candor. "I suppose none has found me pleasing enough to pursue."

If her tone had not been so solemn, Pierce would have dismissed her comment as being intentionally coy. "You truly believe that, don't you?"

"Yes. However, in their defense, I've done little to encourage them."

"I see. And why is that?"

"Many reasons." Another furtive glance at her father, who was now heartily congratulating himself on a huge win in the final race. "Suffice it to say, I've been preoccupied with other matters."

Pierce noted Tragmore's glee from the corner of his eye. "Too preoccupied to seek a life of your own?"

Daphne paled at Pierce's softly spoken question. "I'm perfectly content with my life, Mr. Thornton. But I thank you for your concern."

If Pierce hated Tragmore before, the stark terror on Daphne's face multiplied his enmity threefold. With visible effort, he retained his composure, settling back in his chair. "I fear we've missed quite a bit of the—"

At that moment Tragmore stood. "We should be taking our leave now." It was a command, not a request.

Instantly, Daphne and her mother rose.

Slowly, Pierce came to his feet. "We have winnings to collect, I believe."

"Uh, yes, we do."

Pierce turned to the marchioness. "Your husband and I will settle our accounts and order your carriage brought around. Should I not see you again, thank you for your kind hospitality, my lady."

"You're quite welcome, sir."

"Lady Daphne." Pierce bowed, acutely aware of Tragmore's presence beside him. "You've been most gracious, not to mention an astute wagerer. 'Twas a pleasure to enjoy the races with you."

"And you, Mr. Thornton." Daphne's smile was genuine, although, once again, her curious gaze darted from Pierce to her father.

Striding off with Tragmore, Pierce waited only until they were out of earshot. "How fortunate for you the last race turned out as it did. No need to collect your winnings, though. They belong to me."

"What?" The marquis stopped dead in his tracks.

"Interest, Tragmore, remember? You owe me quite a bit."

"You miserable son of a—"

"Careful," Pierce warned quietly, "else I might be forced to ask why a man who is one step from the gutter can afford to provide his daughter with so costly a necklace."

Sweat broke out on Tragmore's brow. "It's an inexpensive copy of—"

"On the contrary, the pearls are very real. And very valuable. Had Lady Daphne a shred of your loathsome nature, I wouldn't hesitate to remove them from her neck and count them among my day's profits. But it so happens she's charming, as is your wife. Therefore, consider the necklace a gift from me to you and your family. Surprised?

20

Don't be. On occasion, even I have a heart. To those who deserve it, that is." Pierce plucked the marquis's winning ticket from his hands. "I'll take this. You go summon your coach. My solicitor will contact you tomorrow to arrange a meeting. See that you make it. Unless, of course, you want the entire world to know just how penniless you are." A biting smile. "Enjoy your comforts, Tragmore. For now."

2

THE SUN WAS SLOWLY MAKING ITS ASCENT. THE CHURCH PEWS were still shrouded in shadows when a solitary figure eased her way through the wooden door.

"Vicar, I'm here."

The announcement echoed through the silent church, summoning Alfred Chambers from his quarters. Adjusting his spectacles, he emerged, shaking his head in indulgent worry as he watched the spirited young woman who was hastening down the aisle toward him.

"So I see," he returned, scowling. "And before dawn, no less. Daphne, my dear, I doubt even the lark has sung his first note." The reprimand was halfhearted, the lines about the vicar's eyes soft with warmth and tenderness. "How many times have I warned you that it is unsafe to roam the streets of the village before day has broken?"

"Countless." Calmly, Daphne halted before him, easing the huge basket she carried to one side and slipping her hand beneath the hem of her petticoat to extract a six-inch blade. "But you have nothing to fear. See? I'm well protected."

"How comforting. And precisely how many times have you used your lethal weapon to defend yourself?"

She gave him a dazzling smile. "None. I haven't had

occasion to. Which only goes to show how safe the village truly is." With a flourish, Daphne restored the knife to its original hiding place. "In any case, I didn't come here to argue with you, my dear friend. Today is too special for that. Besides, you didn't really expect that I would shut an eye last night, did you? Not with our morning visit to the school tantalizing my thoughts. Why, I could scarcely stay still through yesterday's Champion Stakes. All I could think about was the children I'm finally to meet. Which reminds me." Triumphantly, Daphne held up her basket. "Wait until you see what I've brought." Oblivious to the dust that settled on the fine layers of her morning dress, she sank down onto her knees, swiftly removing her treasures, one by one.

"Mrs. Frame made a huge side of mutton last night. No one could finish it, not even Father. So I brought all that was left with me. There's enough for at least a dozen portions." Carefully, she set aside the food. "I also pilfered two mince pies from the kitchen. I don't think Mrs. Frame saw me, but even if she did, she'd never tell a soul." Daphne sat back on her heels, her eyes glowing. "Now for the best part. Look!" Joyfully, she held up a neatly folded pile of clothing: pants, shirts, dresses, and aprons of various sizes and design.

"Where on earth did you get these?" the vicar asked in amazement, reverently touching the gingham frock atop the pile as if it were gold.

"I made them," Daphne confided in a whisper. "Mama ordered material from town so the maids could sew new uniforms for themselves and the footmen. The materials were sent for while Father was in London on business." Daphne gave the vicar a secret smile. "Mama made certain the order was a substantial one."

"God bless Elizabeth," Chambers murmured, his voice laden with emotion. "And God bless you for your hard work."

"'Twas no work, but a blessing," Daphne countered with a mischievous grin, rising to her feet. "You know how much trouble I have sleeping at night. My lantern and I worked most efficiently until the sun's light arrived to offer its assistance. Just think how many children will benefit from this, Vicar." She seized his forearms. "And there's more. A delivery of coarse wool is due at week's end, to make blankets for the horses. Their old blankets have quite a bit of wear left in them so I'll be able to make shawls to protect the children through the winter." Daphne's brows knit in a frown. "I haven't yet devised a way to get boots for them, but that is the only problem I have yet to surmount."

"I beg to differ with you, child." The vicar enfolded Daphne's fingers in his, his gentle features taut with worry. "You have a much larger, more daunting problem to face, as does Elizabeth."

Daphne's lips quivered. "Father."

"If he should find out—"

"He won't."

"But if he should, child, there would be no limit to his wrath."

"I cannot allow myself to dwell on that." Daphne turned away, her expression set in that familiar contradictory blend of resigned determination. "Mother and I both know the risk we're taking. But it's something we must do, each to the extent that we're able."

"At all costs?"

"Yes."

"Snowdrop." Lapsing into the familiar term of endearment he'd given Daphne as a child, Chambers placed work-worn hands on her shoulders. "Your mother has endured one and twenty years of pain and fear. I remember her as she was—a radiant, vivacious young girl. But she's weakened now. Her strength is gone. I fear she's withstood all she can."

"Don't you think I know that?" Daphne replied with quiet resolution. "Should Father learn what we've—*I've*— been doing, I will deny that Mama had any knowledge of my actions. The responsibility and the consequences will be mine to bear."

"Lord alone knows what Harwick will do."

"All he can do is beat me. He can do nothing to my spirit. He expended that power years ago."

"I'll do everything I feasibly can to prevent—"

"No. You'll do nothing." Daphne pivoted to face her

friend. "He's my father. By law, you have no right to interfere with his treatment or his punishment of me. Please, don't endanger yourself or your role in the parish. The village needs you too badly." Briefly, Daphne lay her hand on the vicar's jaw. Then, she stooped to repack her basket. "The sun is up. The schoolroom awaits us."

With a deep sigh, he nodded. "Very well. Let's go, my tenacious snowdrop. At the very least you can see the joyful faces of the children your generosity is nurturing. My only prayer is that you're not gambling with consequences too dire to withstand."

An enigmatic smile touched Daphne's lips.

"And what, might I ask, is so amusing?"

Daphne rubbed her palms together, a gesture the vicar had long-ago learned indicated there was something significant on his young friend's mind. "Well?" he prompted. "I voice concern that you perpetually risk discovery by your father and you find my worry humorous?"

"No, of course not. Your worry is loving and sensitive, and I'm deeply grateful for it. It was just your choice of the word gambling. It reminded me of something. Someone," she amended softly.

Chambers blinked in surprise. "Is this someone a gentleman, by any chance?"

Daphne's lips twitched. "I think not. A gambler, a rogue, and a charmer. But definitely not a gentleman." Recalling the way Pierce had restored her dignity following her father's censure, she amended, "Except those times when he chooses to be."

"I see. And where did you meet this complex stranger?"

"At Newmarket. He joined Father for the races."

"He's a friend of your father's then?" The vicar couldn't keep the dismay from his voice. He'd hoped that someday Daphne would meet a man worthy of her, not a cad of her father's ilk.

"No, I wouldn't say they were friends." Daphne chewed her lip thoughtfully. "According to Father, they're business associates."

"You sound dubious."

"It's silly, I suppose." Daphne shrugged. "I have no

reason to doubt Father's explanation. It's just that he and Mr. Thornton seem so mismatched—in age, in background, in manner."

"In other words, this Mr. Thornton is young, unpretentious, and lacking in social position."

Daphne smiled at the vicar's accurate insight. "He's about thirty, I should say. Definitely untitled. My guess is, unpampered as well. While he's obviously well-to-do, he has a hard edge that leads me to believe his wealth is not inherited but earned, probably through a keen set of wits."

"You're right. He doesn't sound like someone your father would choose to associate with. However, lack of breeding might dim in comparison with shrewd business acumen."

"Perhaps." Daphne hesitated, her brows drawn together in a frown. "There's something more, though—something odd. Father acts so skittish around Pierce Thornton, uncharacteristically off balance and accommodating. I have the strangest feeling that Mr. Thornton has some kind of hold over him. It's nothing I can prove—just an instinct." Another faint smile. "According to Mr. Thornton I should look away from those who would thwart me and trust my instincts."

"Ah, a good man." The vicar's relief was evident. "He was giving you spiritual advice."

"No, actually he was giving me gambling advice. I was placing my wager in the first race."

"Oh." The vicar removed his spectacles and began to vigorously clean them with his handkerchief. "It sounds to me as if excitement over our forthcoming visit to the school was not alone in distracting you from yesterday's races."

"And what does that mean?"

"This Mr. Thornton appears to have made a strong impression on you."

"Yes, he did. Not because of his gambling, if that's what's concerning you," Daphne assured him with a twinkle. "But because he's such an interesting embodiment of contradictions—composed and sure of himself, yet intuitive and compassionate. You must admit that is a rare combination, least of all in a gambler."

The vicar shoved his spectacles back on his nose, his penetrating blue eyes searching Daphne's face. "How did you learn so much about the man in one meeting?"

"If you watched the way he assessed the horses, realizing his goals time after time without batting an eyelash nor expecting anything short of total victory, you'd understand what I mean by the composure."

"And the insight? The compassion?"

An uncomfortable pause. Then, "Father chastised me in public. Mr. Thornton must have sensed my embarrassment. He very intentionally extricated me from what might have been an ugly episode."

"You're right. That is both insightful and kind." Chambers did not belabor the point, knowing how painful Daphne found her father's bouts of cruelty. Besides, in light of Daphne's revelation, another, far more interesting, avenue required his attention, and he intended to pursue it, as subtly as possible. Concentrating on the task of adjusting his sleeves, he asked, "What does this Pierce Thornton look like?"

Daphne twisted a lock of hair about her finger, visualizing the man who'd preoccupied her thoughts since yesterday's races. "He's tall and dark haired, very impervious looking, almost as if he wants to warn you that he'll extend himself just so far and no one had better trespass beyond that point. He's definitely not what you'd call classically handsome. His features are hard, severe, even a trifle forbidding. I sense he's struggled somehow, and I detect the same in his eyes, which are the darkest green I've ever seen, almost like a forest at midnight. Still, beneath that fierceness . . ."

"Lies the heart of a saint, no doubt," the vicar chuckled. "Is there no one you cannot find good in, Snowdrop?"

The engrossing memory of Pierce Thornton vanished, instantly eclipsed by the ugly answer to the vicar's question.

"Daphne, have you been providing charity to those worthless urchins again?"

"No, Father."

"Then why did Lord Weberling spy you in the yard of the parish church, with that bloody clergyman?"

"The vicar is my friend, Father. I was only—"

"I'd best not discover you've disobeyed my orders, Daughter. For if I should learn you've given a single shilling of my money to street scum, your punishment will exceed severe. Do you understand what I'm saying, Daphne?"

"Yes, Father, but I—"

"Perhaps you need a small taste of what I mean. Perhaps then you'll think twice before squandering your time—and my funds—on the vicar's futile causes."

Even now Daphne flinched, feeling the sting of her father's blows as sharply as she had the week before.

Was there anyone she couldn't find good in?

"Yes," Daphne whispered, tears clogging her throat. "God forgive me, but yes."

Chambers went to her then, gathering her hands in his. "Don't, Daphne. In some men, the good is so deeply buried that one must spend a lifetime digging in order to find it. As for you, no forgiveness is necessary. For, despite this lapse of faith to which you allude, your belief prevails and your search for Harwick's goodness continues." He kissed her forehead. "Come. Let's be off to the school. While we walk, you can tell me all about this mysterious Mr. Thornton. And I shall regale you with the latest deeds of your Tin Cup Bandit."

Instantly, all else was forgotten. "Tell me," Daphne demanded, nearly bouncing with excitement. "What has the bandit done now?"

A hearty chuckle. "I thought perhaps that would capture your attention. Now, mind you, it's still only hearsay."

"I know, it's always hearsay. Yet, all the stories turn out to be true, and each and every one of the bandit's exploits is recounted in the *Times* day after day. So, tell me, Vicar, whose manor was invaded this time? Through which window did the bandit enter? What jewels did he take? How much money did the stolen gems yield? Which stone did the bandit leave behind from the collection he pilfered from the Earl of Gantry's estate four nights ago? Which workhouse benefitted from the theft?"

Chambers threw back his head and laughed. "Gather up your basket, Snowdrop. I'll fetch the pile of books I've collected for the school and we can be on our way. I shall do my best to answer all your questions while we walk."

Minutes later, Daphne and the vicar trudged purposefully through the village streets.

"I'm not certain precisely what was stolen or how the bandit gained his entry," the vicar began. "But I do know that the theft occurred the night before last."

"Somewhere between two and three A.M.," Daphne supplied in a reverent whisper. "That's always when he strikes."

"Yes. Well, this time it was the Viscount Druige's estate."

"I knew it! Remember I told you about the garish ruby-and-diamond necklace the viscount bought for his wife? According to Mama, the entire *ton* was buzzing over it. She said the poor viscountess could scarcely keep her head erect, so heavy were the jewels. The bandit must have heard the gossip—or perhaps he saw the piece himself. Vicar," Daphne's voice rose in baffled wonder. "Who is he? How does he know just whom and where to strike?"

"I honestly don't know. I only know that, because of your bandit, dozens of hungry children will be fed, clothed, and offered hope where none previously existed."

"Which workhouse received the money?"

"The one in Worsley."

"Oh, thank God," Daphne breathed. "That was the workhouse you planned to visit this week, the one in dire straits."

"Exactly. The poor headmaster there had contacted every parish for miles, begging for assistance. His funds were gone; there was no food. Within weeks, innocent children— little more than babes—would have been forced into the streets, or begun starving to death."

"The headmaster himself sent you word that the bandit had been there?"

The vicar smiled. "Evidently, your brazen bandit left his tin cup right on the headmaster's desk. He came and went before dawn, silent and unseen."

"How much money did he leave them?"

"Just shy of five thousand pounds."

An awed gasp escaped Daphne's lips. "The man is a savior."

"The man is a thief," the vicar reminded her gently.

"How can you say that? You of all people must see what he's done for—"

"You needn't defend him to me, Snowdrop. I bless the man each and every day. Still, facts are facts. And, in answer to your earlier question, the Earl of Gantry's diamond cuff link was found in the tin cup placed upon Viscount Druige's pillow—a tin cup that was identical to the one placed on the desk of the Worsley headmaster."

"Just as always—a jewel from the previous theft left at the scene of the crime. Two identical tin cups, one at the crime, one at the chosen workhouse." Daphne glowed. "The bandit is brilliant. Not to mention generous and crafty. And I, for one, hope the authorities never catch him. I can hardly wait to read of their stupefaction in this morning's newspaper."

"Can you contain yourself long enough to distribute your treasures?" the vicar chuckled, coming to a halt before the village school. "The children are eager to see you."

"Oh! I didn't realize we'd arrived." Daphne scurried forward to peek through the window. "They appear to be immersed in their studies," she murmured, her voice laden with disappointment. "Does that mean we must delay our visit?"

"Miss Redmund, their teacher, is expecting us. I suspect she'll be more than delighted to abandon her lessons." Scowling, the vicar knocked, leaving Daphne no opportunity to question his apparent disapproval of the school mistress.

"Yes? What is it?"

Seeing the tight-lipped woman who filled the doorway with her ample presence, Daphne's questions vanished.

"Oh, pardon me. 'Tis you, Vicar. Come in." Miss Redmund's frigid tone was as unappealing as her demeanor. Stiffly, she stepped aside, gesturing for the vicar to enter.

Her reproachful gaze fell on Daphne.

"Miss Redmund," the vicar interjected, guiding Daphne ahead of him. "May I present Lady Daphne Wyndham."

Miss Redmund's frosty stare became positively glacial.

"Wyndham? Are you, perchance, related to the Marquis of Tragmore?"

Daphne raised her chin. "The marquis is my father."

"Look around if you wish, but I'll save you the trouble. If one of your tenants's children is missing, he isn't here."

"Pardon me?"

"I assume your father sent you. Tell him there's no need. I haven't allowed anyone from Tragmore into this school since the marquis ordered me not to. Much as I dislike teaching these ruffians, I need my position. So assure your father I'm adhering to his wishes."

"Miss Redmund," the vicar began.

With a gentle shake of her head, Daphne silenced her friend. She understood the significance of the school mistress's assumption—as well as her father's tactics—only too well.

"I'm not here as my father's messenger, Miss Redmund," she refuted, trying to keep the quaver from her voice. "Were I to have my way, all the children living at Tragmore would be among your students. Unfortunately, I have no say in my father's decisions." Tentatively, she held out her basket. "However, I am trying to make a difference, in whatever small ways I can. If you'll allow me, I've brought the children some food and clothing."

"Oh." Miss Redmund's mouth opened and closed a few times. "I see. Well, naturally I assumed . . . Forgive my impertinence, my lady." The flabby cheeks lifted in a more cordial, if not actually warm, welcome. "Come in." She turned, her voluptuous bosom nearly knocking Daphne to the floor. "Children, we have guests."

Two dozen pairs of curious eyes stared at Daphne.

"If we're interrupting your lesson—" Daphne began.

"Nonsense," the teacher broke in hastily, as relieved by the interruption as Chambers had predicted. "Put your slates away, children. The vicar has arrived. And he's brought a very special visitor, Lady Daphne Wyndham. Say how do you do to Lady Daphne and the vicar."

Two dozen mumbled "'ow do ye do's" followed.

Swiftly, Daphne assessed the boys and girls who filled the benches surrounding the classroom's long wooden desk. Ranging in age from approximately five to thirteen years old, they were all terribly thin, all dressed in worn clothing,

ANDREA KANE

and all staring at Daphne as if the portrait of Queen Victoria
that graced the schoolhouse wall had just come to life before
their very eyes.

The familiar ache tugged at Daphne's heart.

"Would you like me to introduce you, Snowdrop?"
Chambers asked, acutely aware of Daphne's distress.

"No. Thank you, Vicar." Daphne shot him a quick,
grateful look, telling him without words that she was
determined to obliterate this particular wall on her own.
"I've awaited this day for a long, long time."

"Very well." The vicar nodded sagely, praying she would
accomplish all she sought, praying that his presence could
give her the strength she needed to bridge these long-
established class lines.

Daphne turned and walked toward the children. "You
have no idea how much I've wanted to meet all of you," she
admitted with a shy smile. "The vicar has spoken of you so
often I feel we're already friends." Deliberately ignoring the
ponderous silence, Daphne searched the sea of faces.

Her eyes fell on a lad of about ten. "You must be Timmy,"
she guessed, taking in his freckles and unruly black curls,
swiftly matching them with the description Chambers had
provided. "I hear you have a lizard."

Meeting the boy's astonished stare, Daphne held her
breath, counting each endless second until he replied.

At last, the freckled face thawed. "'is name's 'enry,"
Timmy supplied. "I used to bring 'im to school, but Miss
Redmund made me stop."

"That's probably because she was afraid Henry would
distract you."

"No, it's 'cause she was afraid 'e would bite 'er."

"I see." Daphne stifled a smile, feeling Miss Redmund's
glare bore through her back. "Tell me, Timmy, do lizards
like mince pie?"

He rolled his eyes in exasperation. "No. They like bugs."

"Oh." Daphne's brows drew together as she pondered
that dilemma. "Well, Timmy, I didn't bring any bugs with
me, so it's just as well Henry's at home. You'll have to take
care of his feeding yourself. However, I did bring some pie.

And, since Henry's not here and wouldn't enjoy my dessert if he were, would you like some?"

That got the reaction she sought.

A brilliant smile illuminated Timmy's face. "I sure would!"

"Ye 'ave mince pie in there?" another boy piped up.

"I sure do." Daphne grinned. "What's your name?"

"William."

"William . . . William." Daphne tapped her chin thoughtfully. "As I recall, the vicar told me you carried the most firewood of anyone in the class last winter."

The frail boy of eight sat up proudly. "I can carry a pile taller 'en me from th' woods to th' school without restin' once."

"That's extraordinary! And all the more reason you need to keep up your strength." Daphne went to the basket and lifted its cover. "I have enough pie for everyone. There are also healthy portions of mutton, which I want each of you to take home to your families."

As she began to unpack the food Daphne felt a small hand tug at her skirts. Looking down, she saw a tiny, blue-eyed girl gazing up at her.

"I'm Prudence," the tot offered. "What else did ye bring?"

Scrutinizing the child's frayed dress, Daphne reached into the basket and extracted a gingham frock. "I've brought this lovely new dress. Would you like it, Prudence? I think it would fit you perfectly."

The blue eyes grew huge. "Ye're givin' it t' me?" she whispered.

"It's yours."

Reverently, Prudence touched the edge of the hem. "It's so pretty."

"So are you." On impulse, Daphne knelt, hugging the child to her. "And pretty girls need pretty dresses. But you've got to promise me one thing. Promise me you'll wear the dress for my next visit so I can see how lovely it looks on you."

An awed nod against Daphne's shoulder.

"Very well. Then take it home."

"That's all I 'ave to give ye? Just a promise?" Prudence drew back, eyeing Daphne with the blind hope of a child and the ingrained doubt of deprivation.

"That's all you have to give me," Daphne assured her tenderly. She watched Prudence snatch the dress, clutching it as if it were a priceless treasure.

Daphne had seen that poignant possessiveness before.

A never-forgotten memory sprang to her mind of the dark-eyed girl in the House of Perpetual Hope gripping her tattered doll with the same hollow desperation as Prudence now gripped the dress.

Tears clogged Daphne's throat.

"Prudence," she blurted out. "Do you have a doll?"

The child winced, but she raised her chin bravely. "I 'ad Martha, but she's not mine anymore. Mama gave 'er to Jane, so she'd stop cryin'."

"Jane?"

"My little sister. She's only two. And Mama can't get the baby to sleep if Jane cries all the time. So she gave Martha to 'er. Now Jane don't cry so much."

"That was very kind of you, giving so precious a friend away."

Prudence shrugged. "I didn't want to. Mama made me."

"Prudence, I know Martha means a lot to you, but would you be willing to love a new doll?"

"Mama says we can't pay for a new doll."

"Let me tell you a secret." Daphne leaned conspiratorially forward. "I saw the most beautiful doll in the window of the village shop. She has hair the color of spun gold and a pink satin gown with a velvet bow. She also has a terrible problem."

"What?" Prudence stared, transfixed.

"No one wants her. She's been in that window for months now, and no one has taken her home. I suspect she's very frightened. After all, Christmas is a mere two months off, and I can't think of anything more dreadful for a doll than spending Christmas alone in a store window. Can you?"

"But why don't anyone want 'er?"

"Most little girls are not as unselfish as you. Most of them

34

refuse to give up their old dolls to love a new one. Thankfully, your heart is bigger than theirs. So, if I brought that new doll with me next time, would you be willing to take her home and love her as you did Martha? You'd be making her incredibly happy."

"I sure would! I'll take real good care of 'er and love 'er a whole lot, I promise."

Daphne smiled, stroking the smooth soiled cheek that was tilted earnestly toward her. "That's two promises, then—to wear your new dress and to love your new doll. You've more than repaid the cost of the garment. I have but one more favor to ask, and that is for your help. You see, Prudence, I think I've brought enough dresses for all your classmates. But I need someone to help me sort out the various sizes and match the right dress with the right girl. Do you think you could manage that?"

Prudence glowed. "I know I can. I'll match 'em all, Miss—Lady . . ."

"Daphne. My name is Daphne. Sort of like daffodil, only shorter."

"But th' vicar didn't call ye daffodil. 'e called ye some other flower."

Daphne grinned. "Snowdrop. The vicar has called me by that name since I was even younger than you."

"Why?"

"Have you ever seen a snowdrop, Prudence?" Chambers asked, coming to stand beside them.

"They're white. And pretty."

"Yes they are," he agreed. "They're also delicate—so fragile you fear they'll never survive, particularly in the dark part of winter when they first emerge. And yet, not only do they survive, but they flourish, fighting their way from the bleakness of the cold earth, opening their buds to the heavens, standing steadfast and proud, and offering the world an extraordinary beauty that none can equal and few can appreciate."

"Are ye really like that?" Prudence asked Daphne in wonder.

"Only in some ways," Daphne answered with an impish grin. "I'm stubborn and I'm proud."

"Yer also pretty. So's yer name."

"Which one? Snowdrop or Daphne?"

"Daphne. I like it. And I like ye," Prudence concluded decisively.

"I'm glad. I like you, too." Daphne swallowed past the lump in her throat. "Now, shall we distribute the clothing and the pie?"

A chorus of enthusiastic yeses greeted her request.

Two hours later the basket was empty, the pie was gone, and the atmosphere in the classroom bore no resemblance to the somber aura preceding Daphne's arrival.

Sitting among the children, Daphne elicited peals of laughter with her recounting of the summer the Tragmore pond creature had terrorized her, its deep, eerie summons permeating her bedroom in the darkest hours of night.

"'ow old were ye?" Timmy demanded.

"Five. I was convinced that a horrid monster was dwelling in the pond, just waiting for the right opportunity to carry me off."

"Did ye tell yer parents?"

A shadow crossed Daphne's face. "No."

"So what'd ye do?"

"I finally got up enough nerve to investigate on my own. I crept to the pond after dark, armed with the largest piece of firewood I could carry. My teeth were chattering so loud, I could scarcely hear a thing. But at last I heard my monster begin his terrifying chant. I was torn between confronting him and fleeing when, all at once, he jumped out at me. Or rather, *they* jumped out at me." Daphne grinned. "My dreaded monster was nothing more than a family of frogs."

Timmy let out a whoop. "Did ye feel dumb?"

"Very. It was the last time I allowed an animal to get the best of me. Although recently another came close."

"When?"

"This past summer."

"What 'appened?"

"Tragmore acquired a mysterious thief who, night after night, would emerge from the woods unseen, make off with all our berries, and disappear without a trace."

"I guess, whoever 'e was, yer thief's belly was full," William chortled.

"Maybe 'e wasn't eatin' the berries. Maybe 'e was bringin' 'em to someone who's poor and hungry, just like th' Tin Cup Bandit does," Timmy suggested.

Daphne rumpled his hair. "A lovely thought, Timmy. But, in this case, untrue. The Tragmore bandit was very much a four-legged creature whose motives were not nearly as selfless as those of the Tin Cup Bandit."

"Ye found out who it was?"

"I did. Actually, the berry thief found me. He was fleeing from a pack of hounds who were most anxious to hunt him down. I gave him sanctuary, named him Russet, and we've been fast friends ever since."

"Is Russet a fox?" Prudence asked.

"Yes. He was a tiny cub when I found him, but now he's nearly six months old and very independent. His home, as it turns out, is a well-concealed hole at the edge of Tragmore's woods—a spot that happens to be near both my bedroom and the bushes with the plumpest berries."

"Will ye bring Russet with ye the next time ye come?"

"I'll try." Daphne smiled. "Russet has very much a mind of his own. But, despite his arrogance and cunning, he is a most loving pet. For a bandit."

"'ave ye ever met *him?*" Timmy asked, his eyes wide as saucers.

"Who?"

"The *real* bandit. The Tin Cup Bandit. Do ye know who 'e is?"

"No, Timmy. No one knows the identity of the Tin Cup Bandit. But, whoever he is, I think he's wonderful."

"My father says 'e's smarter 'n all the blue bloods 'e robs."

Daphne's lips twitched. "Thus far, the bandit seems to be proving your father right."

"'as 'e ever robbed ye, Daphne?"

"I? Well, no, I can't say that he has."

"Why not? Ye're rich. 'ow come the bandit 'asn't been to yer 'ouse?"

It was a question Daphne had asked herself time and

again, with a mixture of relief and disappointment, each time she read an account of the bandit's most recent crime. Tragmore was indeed a likely place to strike, given her father's wealth and blatant enmity for the poor and the bandit's propensity for targeting both. Inevitably, the philanthropic thief would strike her home, and the prospect left her both terrified and exhilarated.

"Daphne?"

"Hmm?"

"Do ye think the bandit will rob yer 'ouse?" Timmy repeated patiently.

"I honestly don't know, Timmy."

"Would yer father be real mad if 'e did?"

"That's a dumb question," William retorted. "Of course 'e'd be mad. It's 'is money, ain't it?"

Eagerly, Timmy climbed over William to sit closer to Daphne. "If the bandit does rob ye, will ye tell us about it the next time ye come?" A worried pucker formed between his brows. "Ye are comin' back, aren't ye, Daphne?"

"Of course." Daphne gave Timmy's shoulder a reassuring squeeze. "Very soon. And, to answer your question, in the unlikely event that the bandit should visit Tragmore between now and then, I promise to relay all the details to you."

"We'd best be going, Snowdrop." As if the mere mention of Tragmore had cast an ominous cloud over the morning's jubilation, Chambers stood, frowning as he checked his timepiece. "It is fast approaching midday. Miss Redmund has barely enough time to complete her lesson."

Daphne knew it wasn't the conclusion of Miss Redmund's lesson that worried the vicar. It was Daphne's prolonged absence from Tragmore—and her father's reaction to it.

"I suppose you're right." Amid moans and protests, Daphne arose, rumpling Prudence's hair. "Your slates await you, my young friends. As my chores do me. But we'll visit again next week, if it's all right with Miss Redmund?" Daphne inclined her head questioningly at the schoolmistress.

"Of course." Reluctantly, Miss Redmund abandoned the relaxing hearth of the fire, facing her students with all the enthusiasm one would expect from a prisoner facing a firing squad. "We shall look forward to it, shan't we class?"

A roomful of eager nods and a chorus of yeses.

"Good. Then we'll see Lady Daphne and the vicar one week from today."

"And Russet," Timmy added eagerly.

"Yes—and Russet." Miss Redmund echoed with a distasteful shudder. "Now, say good day, children."

"Good day," the class responded.

"Oh! And Daphne?" Timmy scooted around the teacher, rushing up to tug at Daphne's skirt.

"Yes, Timmy?" Daphne paused, waiting.

"If ye should 'appen to see the Tin Cup Bandit, would ye tell 'im we think 'e's an 'ero?"

A soft smile touched Daphne's lips. "I most certainly shall, Timmy. If I should happen to see him."

3

"RUSSET, YOU SHOULD HAVE SEEN THEIR LITTLE FACES—SO SAD, so lonely, so hopeless."

Daphne stroked Russet's silky head, staring off into the surrounding woods. "How many times have I seen that look of futility? And still I can do nothing. Dolls and dresses won't fill their bellies and a side of mutton can't sustain them indefinitely. So what will become of them, Russet? Will Timmy, William, Prudence, and all those other precious children grow up to be like the men and women I saw at Newmarket yesterday? Oh, not like the ones in the fashionable boxes, but like the Gypsies telling fortunes in exchange for food and the homeless picking pockets to survive. Is that how they're destined to live?"

Obviously lacking an answer, Russet stood, pacing in an impatient circle around Daphne.

With a tender smile, Daphne broke off her impassioned speech. "Yes, love, I know it's nighttime and you're feeling alert and vigorous." She stifled a yawn. "But I've had a long, tiring day. Any prowling you do this evening, you do on your own."

Rising from the cold grass, Daphne shivered a bit, wishing

she'd brought her shawl with her. In the hour she'd spent in the woods, dusk and twilight had melded and were gracefully giving way to darkness. The air had chilled, and Daphne's already depleted body now ached from a long day fraught with turbulent emotions: self-doubt upon facing the children, anguish at seeing their deprivation, fear that her overtures would be rejected, and ultimately, joy when she'd earned their acceptance.

And with every step back to Tragmore, her apprehension had grown.

What would she say to her father? How could she explain her prolonged absence? Could she fortify herself to withstand the beating that would doubtless follow?

God must have taken pity on her. The marquis was blessedly away from Tragmore at a day-long business meeting in London. Given her welcome reprieve, and with no intention of looking a gift horse in the mouth, Daphne spent the duration of the day in her room, venturing out only after she'd heard her father return, take his evening meal, and retire for the night.

Only when she was safe.

Intent on capturing Daphne's attention, Russet shook out his luxuriant tail and waited, his features sharp.

"I know you'd prefer company," Daphne acknowledged with a smile. "But I'm truly exhausted. Moreover, I already evaded Father once today. I don't want to tempt fate yet again. You know how he feels about my nocturnal strolls. So, sleepless or not, I'd best go to bed. Now be off, and enjoy your explorations."

The fox blinked his comprehension, then turned and sauntered into the night.

Thirty minutes later, Daphne slid between the sheets, knowing even as she did that sleep would elude her. It always did, no matter how tired she was. Night after night, she tossed and turned, her mind refusing to succumb to the blessed relief of slumber, fretting over the world and all its inequities.

And tonight, there was the additional lure of her unsatisfied curiosity.

Waiting only until her maid's footsteps had disappeared down the hall, Daphne rose, lit a taper, and dragged the copy of the day's *Times* from beneath her mattress.

The headline was just as she'd expected: "Notorious Tin Cup Bandit Baffles Authorities."

The article went on to describe the robbery that had sent the Viscount Druige into a rage and reduced his viscountess to an attack of the vapors from which she'd yet to recover.

With an exasperated sigh, Daphne skipped past the silly details of the victims' distress, focusing instead on what she found most enthralling, the bandit's methods.

Evidently, he had entered the manor through the conservatory door, cutting a square of glass large enough to reach around and open the lock. He'd taken only the finest pieces of silver from the pantry, a strongbox containing five hundred pounds in notes and coins from the library desk, two heirloom bracelets with matching brooches from the viscountess's dressing table, and, of course, her flamboyant necklace, recently purchased by the viscount for the enormous sum of one hundred ten thousand pounds. Nothing else in the manor was disturbed and no one in the household knew the crime had been committed.

Until dawn, when Viscount Druige awakened to find the symbolic tin cup upon his pillow—a cup containing the Earl of Gantry's diamond cuff link, a remnant from the bandit's most recent theft. And then, four hours later, the Worsley workhouse's headmaster entered his office to find a tin cup containing five thousand pounds on his desk.

Leaning closer to read the final paragraph of the article, Daphne silently celebrated the fact that the authorities had no clue as to the bandit's identity nor were they any nearer to unraveling the mystery than they were months ago. "As the *ton*'s outrage grows, so do the accolades of the working class," the *Times* reported. "And through it all, the Tin Cup Bandit thrives, and no one seems able to predict where he will next strike, nor stop his series of extravagant crimes."

With a heartfelt sigh, Daphne put down the newspaper and extinguished her candle, raising the unlit taper in tribute. Then, satisfied that her avenging hero was righting the world's wrongs in a way she could not, she climbed into bed and closed her eyes.

Her final thought was of the beautiful doll she'd purchased before returning to Tragmore this morning—a doll that was now carefully concealed in her wardrobe. Somewhat appeased, Daphne drifted off to sleep, trying to visualize Prudence's forthcoming joy.

And fervently wishing she could make it last.

The thin blade slipped between the window sashes, forcing back the catch. The jemmy followed, prying the decorative shutters open just enough to admit the hooded figure in black.

Noiselessly, the bandit lowered himself onto the parlor floor, his eyes gleaming as he surveyed the dark, deserted room. As was his custom, he waited, although, in this case it was mere habit that compelled him to do so. No one was about, and no scrutiny was necessary. After numerous nocturnal visits to these grounds in particular, he knew Tragmore's late-night routine like a well-read book. The servants, the family, and the marquis would all be abed by midnight.

Ironic that he'd chosen this, of all homes, to invade, when everything in it already belonged to him.

Ironic, but infinitely appealing—for many reasons.

Slipping the jemmy and file into his coat pocket, the bandit swiftly removed his shoes. Then he lit a single taper and began his work.

The drawing room yielded no surprises, the only worthwhile items being a few pieces of silver plate and a silver soup ladle. Pilfering those, he made his way to the library.

The marquis's desk offered not the slightest challenge. The expected cash box was there, although he hadn't anticipated quite so much as he found: fifty pounds in silver and seventy-five pounds in gold. With a shrug, he reached to the back of the drawer, carefully feeling his way until he found the secret panel he sought. With a little help from his file, the panel came away, revealing a gold pocket watch, two antique rings, a dozen five-pound notes and twenty ten-pound notes.

For a destitute man, Tragmore was doing quite well.

Not for long, the bandit thought with a smile.

Deftly he stashed his booty in a sack he kept tucked inside the lining of his coat. Then he eased open the doorway and slipped into the hall. The corridors were dark. He crept to the foot of the stairs. Silently, he ascended, treading only on the inside edge of each step so as not to evoke even the slightest creak.

He reached the second-floor landing.

As always, he headed first for the mistress's bedchamber.

The marchioness was deeply asleep, her door unlocked. The bandit worked swiftly, taking only the dressing case of jewels and the gold locket that lay beside it.

Closing the door behind him, he moved across the hall to the marquis's room.

Gloved fingers on the door handle, the bandit paused, gazing down the corridor to the bedroom he knew to be *hers*. In his recurrent nightly scrutiny, he'd seen her light extinguished time and again. Hers was always the last room at Tragmore to lapse into darkness.

What was it that kept her awake? Was it a book? A worry? Thoughts of a man?

The questions erupted in his mind, along with another, more compelling one.

How would she look in slumber? Would she sleep curled on her side, her hair primly braided, her body ensconced in a chaste white nightgown buttoned to the neck? Or would she be unreserved, her hair unbound, her nightgown sheer and deeply cut?

After yesterday, he had to know.

Before he could rethink the foolhardiness of his actions, the bandit veered away from his original mark, and headed toward her chamber. There was no excuse for his behavior, and he knew it. He should be rifling the marquis's chambers, leaving his symbolic gem, and taking his leave. To divert from his customary methods was risky, insane. Unprecedented.

Until now.

Finding the door unlocked, the bandit eased inside, keeping his taper close and low so as not to awaken her.

She was breathtaking.

The dim glow of the candle flickered across her face, giving her an ethereal beauty unrivaled in its impact. Sprawled on her back, with her hair fanned over the pillow like a tawny waterfall, she was a golden angel, all captivatingly innocent and excruciatingly seductive.

And far from prim.

The tangle of sheets was caught about her waist, giving the bandit an unimpeded view of her body. Transfixed, he watched her breasts rise and fall softly above the low cut of her bodice, her bare throat and shoulders exposed, inviting his touch.

Sweat broke out beneath his mask, desire exploding in his loins like cannon fire, as startling as it was fierce. He wanted her. It was that simple. Only years of self-discipline kept him from acting on his impulse and taking her where she lay.

He was a bloody thief, for God's sake, and he'd come to Tragmore to divest the marquis of his possessions.

Instead, all he wanted to divest the marquis of, was his daughter.

Silently, the bandit fought the hunger raging inside him, a hunger rooted in too many emotions to explore, and utterly unthinkable to indulge. He had to leave Tragmore—now.

He made no sound, of that he was certain.

Yet all at once her lashes lifted, fluttered, then lifted again.

"Oh!" She sat bolt upright, all semblance of sleep vanishing in a heartbeat.

Lightning quick, the bandit reached into his pocket, his fingers closing around the handle of his pistol. Cursing himself for his careless stupidity, he withdrew it slowly, praying she wouldn't force him to use it.

"Don't scream. I don't want to have to hurt you."

The raspy command elicited a bone-melting smile. "You're he, aren't you?" Daphne whispered, climbing from her bed. "You're the Tin Cup Bandit!"

His gaze swept her scantily clad body, then, with the greatest of efforts, returned to her face. "Did you hear me?"

"I was wondering why you hadn't come to Tragmore

before now. I racked my brain trying to think of how I might send you a message, suggesting that you visit us."

He started, desire checked by disbelief. "Do you understand who I am? Why I've come?"

"Of course." Daphne shrugged into a robe, seemingly oblivious to her state of undress. "You can put your gun away. You won't be needing it." Tucking a wisp of hair behind her ear, she crossed the room, gathering up the strand of pearls and exquisitely crafted cameo from her dressing table, and thrusting them at the bandit. "Here. Unfortunately, they're all I have. But Mama has a jewel case filled with lovely gems. I'm sure she'd want you to have them. She's a fairly deep sleeper, so I wouldn't worry about disturbing her. Father, on the other hand—" Daphne broke off, frowning. "Before we resolve that problem, did you retrieve the cash box from the library? I'm certain Father keeps additional funds hidden away elsewhere in that room, but I'm not sure precisely where. I do know that he keeps absolutely nothing of value in his bedchamber." A wry grin. "Fear of burglary, you see. In any case, don't waste your time searching there. Also, I understand you always restrict yourself to jewelry—and money and silver, of course—but we do have a few paintings that would yield a decent sum, as well as some fine fabrics that were terribly expensive. Do you think your contact would be interested in them? If so, I'd be happy to—"

"Stop!" the bandit exclaimed. Dazedly, he shoved his pistol back into his pocket and took the jewelry from her hand. "One of us is mad. I'm just not certain which."

Daphne inclined her head quizzically. "Why?"

"Why?" He had scarcely enough presence of mind to keep his voice in that unrecognizable rasp. "Because you're not only unruffled by my presence, you're aiding me to rob your home—despite the fact that you obviously know who I am."

"It's *because* I know who you are that I'm helping you. It's also the reason I'm unafraid." Adoration shone in her eyes. "A man who sustains hundreds of needy children wouldn't harm one innocent woman. No, sir, I feel no fear in your presence."

Surprisingly, her praise evoked irritation, rather than pleasure. With brutal candor, he threw her description back at her.

"Innocent woman? Tell me then, little virgin, do you make it a practice to entertain men in your bedchamber?"

"Pardon me?"

He indicated her scanty attire. "I only wondered why a beautiful and *innocent* woman would so blithely display her attributes before a veritable stranger."

Daphne winced as though she'd been struck, glancing down at her sheer nightgown and open robe as if seeing them for the first time.

Her bewilderment, her pain, were like blows to his gut, and the bandit's anger dissipated as quickly as it had come. She had no way of understanding the complexity of what he was feeling. Hell, he didn't even understand it himself.

Soberly, he watched her draw the edges of her robe together with trembling hands, and shame and remorse converged inside him. She was as artlessly naive as a child, possessing not a shred of experience at seducing men. It wasn't her fault that he wanted her beyond reason, that she stripped away an iron control he'd spent thirty years building. The weakness was his, and he had no right to torment her for it.

"Forgive me," he murmured, "that assault was inexcusable. You owe me no explanation."

"Nevertheless, I'd like to offer you one." Self-consciously, she crossed her arms over her breasts. "It isn't that I'm unduly immodest. 'Tis only that I didn't realize—that is, I don't think of you as—I mean, I *know* you're a—but I never imagined . . ." Twin spots of red stained her cheeks.

"You mean you never thought of me as a man?" The bandit stepped closer, lifting her chin with one gloved forefinger. "I assure you, Daphne, I'm very much a man. And you are very much a woman."

"You know my name," she whispered.

"Your name—and a great deal more."

Those incredible hazel eyes searched his face, as if seeing clear through his mask to the man beneath.

"You're wondering who I am." Gruffly, he read her mind.

"I'm wondering many things. I have so many questions."

He slid his hand around to caress her nape. "Ask, then. Anything but my name. Ask."

She wet her lips with the tip of her tongue. "My head is spinning. I can't seem to think." A tiny smile. "I'm sure I'll berate myself in the morning. But, be that as it may, you dare not tarry longer, for our servants are instructed to arise before dawn. Whatever questions I have must remain unanswered. Nothing is more important than your leaving Tragmore undetected."

He stared at her mouth, possessed by the nearly uncontrollable desire to tear off his hood and kiss her.

She seemed to feel it, too, for her breath came faster, and the pulse in her neck began to beat rapidly. "I'll pray for you," she whispered.

"I don't believe in prayers."

"But you must. You answer them." Tentatively, she brushed her fingers across his masked jaw.

A low groan escaped his chest. "Ah, Daphne." Touching her in the only way he could, he sifted his fingers through her hair, wishing he could feel its silky texture. "Pray for me then."

She smiled. "I always do."

If he didn't leave now, he never would,

"Good night, Daphne."

"Wait—" She stayed him, blurting out her request as if it required all her courage. "I know it's none of my business, but unless you have a specific workhouse chosen to receive tonight's profits, would you consider donating them to an establishment I know to be especially needy?"

He said nothing, still combatting the fire in his loins.

"Please?" she repeated softly.

"What is this workhouse?"

"It's located in Leicester and is called the House of Perpetual Hope." Daphne gave a hollow laugh. "'Tis anything but."

The bandit went rigid, his hand tightening reflexively on her nape. "Why this house in particular?"

Daphne paled, but she didn't flinch. "I visited there once,

as a child. I've never forgotten." She swallowed, hard. "It would mean a great deal to me. Please, sir, it's all I ask."

"You ask very little." Another pause. "What would your father say if he knew you were aiding me—to rob your own home, no less?"

Daphne didn't hesitate. "He would beat me senseless."

The bandit's hand relaxed, shifting to idly stroke her cheek. "You are extraordinary, my lady. Truly extraordinary. I only wish—" He broke off, lowering his arm to his side. "Go back to bed, Daphne. Go back to bed and pretend none of this happened."

"I'm afraid I can't do that."

He started. "Pardon me?"

"Sir, I assume you've brought some jewel from your last robbery and that your intention is to leave it in your customary tin cup upon my father's pillow. Is that right?"

Beneath his mask, the bandit smiled. "Quite right."

"Well, didn't you hear what I told you? My father is a very light sleeper. He will surely awaken. And then—" she shuddered, a spasm of pain crossing her face. "Suffice it to say that your mission would fail and you would fall victim to his rather formidable temper."

"I appreciate your concern. But, at the risk of appearing immodest, I'm excellent at my craft. Rest easy, your father will not be awakened."

"You're wrong, sir." Daphne gripped his coat sleeves. "But don't let that deter you. Give me the jewel and the tin cup. *I* shall place them on my father's pillow for you."

"And if he awakens?"

"I have a far better chance of explaining away my presence in Father's bedchamber than do you."

"But if he is as volatile as you say, don't you risk inciting his anger?"

Her smile was resigned. "I'm accustomed to bearing the brunt of my father's hostility. Moreover, I am but one person. Your cause protects many. 'Tis worth the gamble."

Tenderness constricted the bandit's chest. "And are you so proficient a gambler, my lady?"

A flicker of something flashed in her eyes. "So I'm told,

sir. I'm also quite a bit smaller than you and extremely light on my feet. So, indeed, the odds are with me."

"Very well." He found himself extracting the small tin cup and the ruby from his sack and handing them to her—yet another unprecedented action. "Here."

Daphne glanced down and grinned. "The stone is from that monstrosity of a necklace belonging to Lady Druige."

"It was garish, wasn't it?" the bandit agreed.

A current of understanding passed between them.

"Go, sir," Daphne instructed softly. "I'll finish your task. Only please, give the funds to that workhouse in Leicester, if at all possible."

"Consider it done."

"Thank you." Daphne's voice shook. "Meeting you was an honor, sir." She turned and hastened to her bedchamber door. "Oh." Pausing, she looked back over her shoulder. "I have a message for you. The children in the village school asked that, should you and I ever meet, I make certain you know you're their hero. Which, given the vast potential of their loving hearts, is a most glowing tribute."

"Now it is I who am honored."

"Good night, sir. God bless you."

"Good night, Daphne."

He watched her go, assailed by a wealth of feeling as unexpected as his desire. Slipping out after her, he waited only until he'd heard her enter her father's chamber before he followed, determined, with or without Daphne's knowledge or consent, to ensure that she remained safe, undiscovered and unharmed.

She was impressively light on her feet, he noted, flattening himself against the wall outside Tragmore's room and watching in admiration as she tiptoed across to her father's bed. And her timing was impeccable. She executed the placement of the cup precisely as he would have, waiting until the marquis was drawing an inward breath, when he would be least apt to notice her whisper of a motion. Then, she acted, her touch as light as her step.

The bandit grinned. He'd learned at a dismally early age that in order to succeed in life one needed to possess three traits: cunning, skill, and instinct. Armed with all three, one's future was ensured, one's possibilities limitless.

Fortunately, cunning and skill could be taught.

Unfortunately, instinct could not.

Like compassion, instinct was a gift to be born with, not acquired.

Daphne Wyndham had been born with both.

He wasn't surprised. He'd told her as much just yesterday.

When she'd placed her first wager at Newmarket.

4

Damn, he was tired.

Pierce shut the front door of his house against the mid-morning sunlight, wearily extracted the folded mask from his coat pocket, and stuffed it into its customary hiding place beneath the floor planks.

His night's work was now complete.

He'd waited only until an unsuspecting Daphne had tiptoed back into her room before leaving Tragmore, riding the ten miles from Northampton to his home at a breakneck pace. Arriving in Wellingborough at half past three, he'd awaited his contact's arrival, prepared to leave the instant he and Thompson completed their transaction in order to reach Leicester and return before dawn.

Thompson arrived moments later, unnerved by Pierce's hasty summons—delivered by messenger to Thompson's shop just before closing time—altering their customary meeting place from London to Wellingborough. Swiftly but expertly he inspected the jewels, then muttered, "Thirty-five hundred pounds."

"Done." Pierce didn't question the offer. Over the past five years, he and Thompson had routinely concluded numerous successful and unorthodox business transactions in the back room of Thompson's Covent Garden jewelry shop. Thompson was too smart to try something as rash as swindling Pierce.

Once Thompson had gone, Pierce combined the thirty-five hundred pounds with the marquis's notes and coins. In total, it added up to just over four thousand pounds.

Pierce then sweetened the pot—more than usual, given the circumstances.

The tin cup he left at the Leicester workhouse contained ten thousand pounds.

Daphne would be pleased, he reflected, although she had no notion that her touching sentiments had stirred feelings long suppressed, that she'd forced him to confront a time and a place he'd sworn never to revisit—his past.

It had been eighteen years since he'd left those detested walls behind, but the painful memories remained, hovering just below the surface, needing only one glimpse to trigger their return.

They'd accosted him full force the moment he'd stepped inside the House of Perpetual Hope.

Every rotted corner was as he remembered it, every crack in the ceiling as vivid as it had been years ago when he'd lain awake, staring up and praying fervently for a miracle. The blistered plaster seemed to taunt his naiveté, squelching those boyhood prayers, and teaching him that prayers were for the haves, self-reliance for the have-nots.

Pierce could still recall the day he'd approached his mother with those all-important questions: Who was his father? Why weren't they living with him? Why did he allow them to stay in this horrible place?

Cara Thornton had answered her five-year-old son with tears in her eyes. His father was a wealthy, married nobleman. She'd been a tavern maid until her pregnancy was discovered, at which point she'd been discharged. She'd gone to Pierce's father, but, because of his wife and his social position, his hands were tied. To acknowledge their child was impossible. Surely Pierce could understand.

Pierce understood perfectly.

His father was a have. He and his mother were have-nots.

Two years later, Cara Thornton died, succumbing to a racking cough and a defeated heart.

Prayers would not bring her back.

Nor would prayers punish the heartless bastard who'd thrown her into the streets when she'd told him she was carrying his child.

It was on that day that Pierce made two irrevocable decisions.

As a have-not, he would ensure his own future, never leaving it in fate's unpredictable hands. And never again would he fall victim to the power of the nobility.

Somehow, some way, *he* would victimize *them*.

Tonight he had done himself proud.

Heading upstairs to bed, Pierce reflected on how damned good it had felt to place the tin cup of money right on the headmaster's desk, to brazenly invade the bloody sanctuary he hadn't dared enter as a child—not if he wanted to live. Not when it was Barrings's domain.

Thankfully for the current workhouse occupants, that scum had died five years ago, and his replacement was reputedly a compassionate sort who would use the money to better the workhouse, rather than to line his own pockets and the pockets of the two corrupt noblemen who'd ensured his position.

*Noble*men.

Dropping wearily to his bed, Pierce gritted his teeth, recalling the first time he'd overheard those unscrupulous blackguards talking with Barrings.

Hunger pains had awakened him that winter night, gnawing at his gut until lying down became an agony impossible to bear. He'd slipped from the sheets, the cold air invading his blood, causing his eight-year-old body to shake uncontrollably. But still, he'd stolen down to the kitchen to pilfer some food.

Taking a shortcut back to his bed was a mistake, for it led right by the headmaster's office. By the time Pierce spied the light burning through the crack in Barrings's door, it was too late to retreat, and the cold in his bones was replaced by terror. If the headmaster found him up and about, and with stolen bread, no less, he'd whip him mercilessly.

Inching past the door, Pierce prayed that Barrings had fallen asleep at his desk.

"Here's a hundred pounds more, Tragmore."

The headmaster's voice dispelled that hope.

"Excellent. And the rest?"

The sound of a fist slammed on the desk. "Dammit, Tragmore! The local vicarage only donated three hundred pounds. Certainly you don't expect me to give all of it—"

"I most certainly do," Tragmore interrupted. "Three hundred pounds, divided equally between Markham and myself."

"And what of me?" Barrings snapped. "What do I gain from this little arrangement?"

"What you always gain. The opportunity to retain your upstanding position as headmaster. Isn't that right, Markham?"

"Fine, Tragmore. Right." The third man's chair scraped as he rose to his feet. "Now let's end this meeting and be on our way."

Taking advantage of their noisy preparations to depart, Pierce had bolted, not stopping until he'd reached the safety of his bed.

But all night he was plagued by memories of that conversation and its implications — implications even a child could understand.

Once again, the haves were prospering at the expense of the have-nots.

Dragging himself back to the present, Pierce swore softly, rubbing his eyes, wishing he could just as easily rub out the memories. He half wished he'd never promised Daphne he'd go to the House of Perpetual Hope. The other half of him, however, felt a smug and overwhelming satisfaction that the money he'd provided to aid this particular workhouse was pilfered from the very nobleman who'd exploited it for so many years: the despicable Marquis of Tragmore.

Pierce doubted not that the funds would be wisely spent. He'd ensured that by adding a little something to the money in his tin cup: a note that read, *Use this endowment for the workhouse, or I'll be back.*

A sudden thought sprang to mind, making Pierce chuckle, despite the night's fatigue and emotional upheaval. Daphne would approve of that additional touch. Doubtless she would applaud the bandit for his cleverness and integrity. He wished he could see her face when she read the details in the newspaper.

Daphne. Just the thought of her made Pierce smile. She was the most bewitching, complex enigma he'd ever encountered.

He could see her as vividly as if she stood right there in his bedchamber, shy and withdrawn, intelligent and tenacious, principled and compassionate.

And so bloody beautiful that she stole his breath and his reason, prompting him to take a risk that might have meant his downfall.

But Daphne would never betray him.

How the hell he knew that, he wasn't certain. He just did—and had, even before she'd awakened, looked up at him with those melting eyes, and helped him rob her home. There was an intangible but implicit understanding between them, a commonality rooted in something deep and meaningful. He'd felt it at Newmarket, then again in her room—tenderness, affinity.

And desire.

Desire so powerful it had nearly brought him to his knees.

The combination was intriguing as hell; fascinating, exciting . . .

And, for many reasons, terrifying.

Because it was a combination Pierce innately understood would touch him in ways he'd never been touched, render him vulnerable in ways he couldn't refute, couldn't master.

Couldn't allow.

For thirty years he'd lived, worked, and prospered alone, and he had no wish to alter that reality. To him, autonomy meant survival. Oh, he cared deeply about those who needed him, about his cause, about many.

But never about one.

Yet she was the Marquis of Tragmore's daughter.

Pierce laced his fingers behind his head, accosted by a question he'd tried desperately to elude.

What did that bastard do to her?

Visions crawled into Pierce's mind like odious insects, too heinous to be ignored. How many times, during his workhouse days, had he borne witness to the marquis's vile temper? How many children had Tragmore tormented? How many others had he thrashed?

Dear lord, did he beat her?

Pierce felt his insides twist.

She'd implied as much to the bandit. But for God's sake, how could he? Daphne was his only child. She was small and delicate and beautiful.

And I'm thinking like an insipid fool, Pierce chastised himself bitterly. Who could be more fragile and unprotected than starving workhouse children? And if he brutalized them . . .

Frantically, Pierce recalled tonight's burglary, reliving the moments he'd spent with Daphne. No. He'd seen no welts on her neck or shoulders, no bruises on her slender arms. Of course that didn't mean anything. Tragmore was a smart man, too smart to leave such damning evidence unconcealed.

She was terrified of her father. Pierce had seen it, felt it, at Newmarket.

What prompted that fear? Was it Tragmore's violence?

Protective tenderness surged inside him, and Pierce tightened his grip until his knuckles turned white. Daphne needed him. It was that simple. And, whatever the risk, he would be there for her.

Would she welcome his presence?

That sudden, ironic thought inserted itself, and Pierce shot to his feet and began pacing the length of the room.

His lack of title and position wouldn't deter her, not Daphne. Just as he deemed her heritage an accident of birth, he instinctively knew she would view his background in much the same light. But how would she feel when she learned of Pierce's enmity for her father, of the vengeance he was determined to exact?

Because taking Tragmore's money was only the beginning. Pierce intended to see him in hell.

And whether Daphne feared her father or not, whether Tragmore were the most contemptible of scoundrels, Daphne was too fine a person to forsake the man who'd sired her, especially to walk into the arms of the enemy who sought to destroy him.

Which left Pierce—where?

Rife with questions; short on answers.

All but one.

Daphne's true loyalties were clear and irrefutable. Like him, she sought to protect those less fortunate than she, as well as those in danger.

Tonight, she'd protected the Tin Cup Bandit.

Grinning at the memory of Daphne's outrageous actions, Pierce felt more than a spark of pride. Heedless of her own safety, she'd spared him from Tragmore's ruthlessness, taking the ruby to her father's chambers so the bandit could escape undetected.

Her selflessness, her cunning, her earnest need to help, the inner beauty that melded with her physical radiance, made him want her all the more.

And she wanted him. Badly.

Or did she?

Pierce halted in his tracks.

Yes, she'd sat by his side at Newmarket, tested her daring, trusted her instincts. Yes, she'd thawed in his presence, joined in his banter, shivered at his touch.

But the true awakening of Daphne's sensuality, the exquisite unfurling he'd glimpsed, the longing and the exhilaration she felt, had occurred tonight.

And it was not for him, but for the Tin Cup Bandit.

Daphne was infatuated with a man who didn't exist, a romanticized champion of the poor who was more a god than a man.

What were the odds of combatting such a fantasy?

Not good, Pierce decided, tapping his chin thoughtfully. Not good at all. He'd provided himself with a unique and near-impossible challenge, one that required cunning, skill, and instinct.

To hell with the doubts and questions.

Veering to his desk, Pierce extracted a sheet of paper and a pen.

This was a high-stakes gamble in the most dangerous of territories.

Fortunately, he was one hell of a gambler.

Daphne pushed her food around on her plate, keeping her gaze firmly fixed on her fork.

"My lady, you must eat something." With a worried frown, Daphne's lady's maid hovered over her mistress. "I promised the marchioness I wouldn't leave this bedchamber until you did."

"I know, Emily, and I appreciate it, truly. But I'm just not terribly hungry today."

Emily winced as the sound of the marquis's bellowing emanated up from the first floor. "I understand your distress. Last night's robbery has upset all of us. Why, the entire house is in turmoil. But it's after noon and you do need to keep your strength up. Please, my lady, won't you just eat a bit of Mrs. Frame's pudding? It's your favorite."

The last thing Daphne wanted was pudding. But what she really wanted—to be alone with her thoughts—would be impossible unless she complied with Emily's wishes. "Very well, a bit perhaps."

Beaming, Emily watched her nibble three or four less-than-enthusiastic spoonfuls of pudding and take a great gulp of tea. "There, my lady. Now don't you feel better?"

"Much better, Emily." Daphne pushed the tray away. "But you're right about the house being in chaos. All morning long the authorities were here, the servants were scurrying about, and Father was agitated. It's taken its toll on me. I do believe I need to rest."

"Of course you do," Emily crooned, gathering up the tray. "You lie down and I'll make sure you're not disturbed."

"Thank you."

Daphne slid between the sheets and closed her eyes, relieved to hear the door shut behind Emily's retreating figure. At last, solitude. Solitude to relive last night.

He'd been every bit as dashing as she knew he'd be—tall

and broad and powerful, swathed in black from head to toe. She'd felt his strength when he touched her, even through the barrier of his glove. Never had she felt so vital and alive as when he'd loomed over her, murmuring her name, gazing into her eyes.

He'd offered to answer anything she asked, anything but his name. And what had she done? Stared blankly up at him like some lovesick schoolgirl, when all she really wanted was to blurt out a million things at once: Where did he come from? What spawned the incredible compassion he possessed? How did he choose the recipients of his funds and the victims of his robberies? Did he loathe life's injustices as she did? How could she help him? What more could she do for the ill and the needy?

Would he ever come to her again?

That possibility made her heart pound frantically. He'd seemed to like her, even seemed pleased by her cooperation. His eyes—the only unconcealed part of him—had spoken volumes, as had his carefully disguised rasp. And, at that moment, she would have gone anywhere, dared anything he asked of her.

If only he'd asked.

"This is an outrage! Find that bandit, whoever the hell he is, and do away with him."

Daphne cringed, pressing her palms over her ears to block out her father's shouts. She'd have to go down and face him sometime, but right now she couldn't bear it. Nor could she be a convincing enough liar, not only to act shocked and outraged, but to feign ignorance of the theft. It was easier to plead upset and remain in her room.

Her mind resumed its wild racing.

She could almost see the rejoicing that was doubtless taking place in the Leicester workhouse right now. Exactly where had the bandit left his tin cup? Who had discovered it? How much money had it contained? When would the details reach Tragmore so she might privately celebrate the bandit's success? And, when the news did arrive, how on earth would she manage to repress her joy and convincingly console her father?

What would he do to her if her efforts failed? What if he suspected the way she felt, or worse, what she'd done?

A knock interrupted Daphne's shuddering thought.

"Yes?"

"May I come in, dear?" Daphne's mother opened the door and tentatively poked her head in.

"Of course, Mama." Drawing her knees up, Daphne patted the bed. "I thought you were with Father."

"No, your father is in his study with the magistrate."

"The magistrate!" Daphne paled. "I thought only the constable was here."

Her mother sighed, closing the door and crossing the room to sit beside her. "Harwick wasn't satisfied with the constable's efforts to recover our property. He demanded to see the magistrate. Unfortunately, I don't think we know any more now than we did then." Lowering her eyes, she fidgeted with the bedcovers.

"Mama." Daphne leaned forward, touching her mother's hand. "Are you all right?"

Nodding, Elizabeth squeezed Daphne's fingers. "Your father's anger appears to be directed only at the bandit and at those who cannot unearth him—at least for the moment."

Silence hung heavily between them.

"You're not fretting over your jewels, are you?" Daphne asked, knowing the answer but anxious to divert her mother's line of thought.

A sad smile touched Elizabeth's lips. "Hardly. You know how little rings and brooches mean to me. The workhouses need food more than I need adornments. Although God help me if Harwick were to hear me say that."

"He won't. But think, Mama. Think how many people our gems are going to help." Daphne's eyes glowed. "I only wish I'd had more to give him. As it is, I had naught but my pearls and my cameo, so—"

"Give him?" Elizabeth cut in.

Daphne's mouth snapped shut.

"Daphne." Her mother's expression had turned incredulous. "Did you *see* the bandit last night?"

Feeling like a fly caught in a web, Daphne sought escape and found none. "Yes, I saw him," she admitted reluctantly. "I gave him whatever aid I could. Then I sent him away so he wouldn't be caught."

"Dear Lord." Elizabeth's thin hands were shaking. "If Harwick had an inkling—even the slightest hint—Daphne, have you any idea what he'd—"

"Yes." Daphne raised her chin proudly. "But it was worth the risk. I'd do it again."

For a fleeting instant, a hundred questions danced in Elizabeth's eyes, and Daphne had a glimpse of the sparkling young woman who was no longer. Then, just as quickly, shutters of fear descended, blanketing the curiosity with years of instilled submission. "I don't want to hear any more." Nervously, Elizabeth glanced at the closed door. "Let's pretend we never had this conversation."

"But, Mama—"

"Daphne, please." The terrified plea lay naked in Elizabeth's eyes, tearing at Daphne's heart.

"Of course, Mama. As you wish."

"As it must be," Elizabeth murmured. She rose to her feet, pausing almost against her will. "You're dreadfully pale. Some fresh air would do you a world of good. A walk perhaps? To the village?"

Slowly, Daphne raised her head, meeting her mother's gaze. "The village?"

"Yes. I think a brisk stroll would put some color back in your cheeks. I would suggest taking Emily along, but the magistrate does need to question all the servants. So, given the circumstances, you'd best go alone. Is that all right, dear?"

A grateful smile touched Daphne's lips. "Yes, Mama, that's fine."

"Good. Then I'll leave you to dress. I'd best see if your father needs me." Elizabeth bent to kiss Daphne's forehead. "Send my warmest regards to the vicar," she added in a breath of a whisper, "and tell him our stableboys will be requiring new boots this winter. They should be arriving at about the same time as the shipment of wool."

Daphne's whole face lit up. "Oh, Mama."

With an adamant shake of her head, Elizabeth silenced Daphne by pressing a forefinger to her lips. "Have a lovely walk, darling." She straightened. "I shan't expect you home for several hours."

"God bless you, Mama," Daphne said softly to her mother's retreating back.

Elizabeth paused, her head bowed. "May He protect us all."

The door closed behind her.

Daphne was dressed and ready in a quarter hour.

Running a comb through her hair, she rehearsed what she would say if she encountered her father on the way out, although most likely her mother had already paved the way.

A walk. About the grounds. Through the thick woods surrounding Tragmore.

That could take hours.

Descending to the first level, Daphne walked gingerly by her father's study and straight into the oncoming inferno that was her father.

"That arrogant bastard! I refuse to allow him to provoke me again!" Harwick exploded, waving a sheet of paper in the air. "I'm going to bring him down if it's the last thing I do."

Daphne's first thought was that her father had unearthed the bandit, and stark fear for her hero's safety eclipsed the customary dread her father's outbursts evoked.

"Father?" she blurted out. "What's happened? Have you discovered something about the robbery?"

"What?" Harwick blinked, focusing on Daphne as if he were seeing her for the first time. A vein throbbed in his temple. "No. As if last night's theft weren't enough, I'm being forced to meet with the lowlife I'm compelled to do business with, and at my own home, no less."

"Oh." Daphne was totally at sea, and terrified to question her father further. Convinced that his current rampage wasn't connected with the bandit, common sense re-surfaced, urging her to flee before the marquis turned his anger on her.

Slowly, she inched toward the door.

Harwick whirled about, shaking his fist in Daphne's direction. "He's insisting on a meeting now. Today. At Tragmore."

Daphne's terrified gaze was riveted to her father's tightly clenched fist. Frantically, she sought the words to appease him. "Today? But surely if you told him about last night's theft—"

"It would change nothing. That gutter rat cares for nothing but his own pocket."

The irony of her father's scathing description struck Daphne even through her fear. Greed was something Harwick knew much about, and usually admired. Evidently not in this case. "Who are you speaking of, Father? Who is this dreadful man?"

"That bloody Pierce Thornton, that's who."

"Pierce Thornton?" Daphne blinked in amazement. "The gentleman I met at Newmarket?"

"He's no gentleman, daughter. He's a parasite, a predatory bloodsucker who drains men of their dignity and their money."

"But I thought you were business associates?"

"I don't willingly associate with worthless, nameless gamblers."

"I don't understand." Daphne's head was reeling.

"Nor do you need to," the marquis roared, advancing toward her. "Why are you wandering about the manor? Your mother said you were out walking."

All the color drained from Daphne's face and, inadvertently, she backed away. "I am—I mean, I'm about to. I'm leaving now."

"Then go!"

"Yes, Father. Forgive me for disturbing you." Spinning about, she bolted out the door and through the woods.

She didn't stop until the manor was swallowed up by the towering oaks that surrounded it. Then, she slowed, dragging air into her lungs, trying to still her trembling.

Lord, how she loathed this feeling of helplessness. Perhaps if she were more like her mother, accepting, malleable, her plight would be bearable.

The fact was, Daphne was neither accepting nor malleable. She tolerated her incessant, oppressive fear because her choices were nil. But somewhere inside her a voice cried out that living conditions such as hers were unjust, cruel, unfair. That the same crushing tyranny perpetuating the English workhouses pervaded Tragmore as well, and always had, spawned by the blatant prejudice and hostility of its master.

The sight of the vicar chatting with a messenger in the church garden made Daphne's sagging spirits lift instantly.

"Vicar!" She waved, picking up her pace until she was half running toward him.

Chambers turned, his face breaking into a broad smile. "Daphne! What a delightful surprise." He pressed a few shillings into the message boy's hand as he unfolded the note he'd just been given. "Thank you for your trouble, lad."

"Thank you, sir." Clutching the coins, the boy dashed off, mounted his horse, and was gone.

"Who was that?" Daphne asked, breathlessly reaching the vicar's side.

"Hmmm?" Her friend was already immersed in his reading.

"That messenger. What news did he deliver?"

Quirking a brow, the vicar replied, "Evidently, you know the answer to that better than I."

"'Tis about last night's robbery, isn't it?" Daphne gripped his forearm. "Isn't it?"

"Indeed."

"Oh, tell me, Vicar. How much did he leave them?"

A dry chuckle. "You are a constant source of amazement to me, Snowdrop. No fear, no disquiet, only your usual loving curiosity. One would never suspect it was your home the bandit had invaded."

"How much?"

"Ten thousand pounds."

Daphne gasped. "The jewelry and silver he took weren't worth half that amount."

"Nevertheless, that is the sum the headmaster discovered in the tin cup on his desk. Oddly, though, there was also a written threat."

"A threat? What kind of threat?"

The vicar glanced down, rereading the note. "According

to the headmaster, the bandit demanded the money be used for the benefit of the workhouse or he'd return to ensure that it was."

"What a heroic gesture!" Daphne's eyes sparkled. "And perfectly understandable, given the large sum involved. Vicar—" Anxiety clouded Daphne's face. "Are you well acquainted with the Leicester headmaster? He isn't the type to squander funds, is he?"

"Certainly not. He's a decent, honorable—" Abruptly, the vicar broke off. "If you already knew where the funds went, why are you questioning me?"

"I knew where they went, yes. But that's all I know. No details have reached Tragmore yet."

"If no details have reached Tragmore, how did you know the bandit donated your family's funds to the Leicester workhouse?"

Daphne met her friend's puzzled gaze. "Because he promised me he would."

Mr. Chambers's eyes widened with disbelief. "He? The bandit?"

"Yes."

A sharp intake of breath. "I think we'd best go inside the church and talk."

"I was hoping you'd say that."

Seated in a pew beside her friend, Daphne poured out the whole story, leaving out only her very private, very unsettling physical reaction to the apparition who'd stood in her bedchamber the night before, stirring her in ways she didn't fully understand, but very much wanted to.

"Daphne." Chambers leaned forward. "You're telling me you helped the man rob your house, and that you yourself placed the tin cup containing the ruby on Harwick's pillow?"

"I couldn't risk Father discovering the bandit in his bedchamber. You of all people understand that. Father would not only have turned him over to the authorities, but beaten him senseless as well. Please Vicar," Daphne's gaze was pleading, "don't condemn me for doing what I must."

"I'm not condemning you, Snowdrop." The vicar took

her hands in his. "But do you understand the risk you took? Had your father awakened, that fierce beating would have been yours."

"I would have withstood it. I've withstood others."

Lines of pain tightened the vicar's mouth. "How well I know that." A pause. "Your mother—is she all right?"

"Yes. Father is so obsessed with apprehending the bandit, he has little time to vent his rage on others." Daphne's expression grew thoughtful. "With the exception of Pierce Thornton."

"Pierce Thornton? The gentleman you met at Newmarket? I don't understand."

"I'm not certain I do either. But, if you recall, I told you that Father's behavior around Mr. Thornton was odd, that I sensed Mr. Thornton has some kind of hold over him."

"I remember."

"Well, as I was leaving the manor today, Father was raving about a meeting Mr. Thornton had demanded. A meeting to take place today. At Tragmore."

"In light of the robbery it does seem odd that Harwick would agree to such a meeting," the vicar admitted. "Still . . ."

"That's just it. Father obviously didn't want to agree to the meeting. I think he was just afraid to refuse Mr. Thornton. He referred to Mr. Thornton in a most scathing manner, and implied that he loathed doing any business with him at all."

"Then why does he continue to do so?"

"Coercion, evidently. Mr. Thornton's."

"Harwick said that?"

"He implied it, yes."

Chambers was quiet for a long moment. "An untitled, uncelebrated colleague whom your father dislikes and distrusts, yet continues to do business with. A man you clearly found likable and trustworthy."

"Not only likable and trustworthy, but compassionate. I shan't forget the way he rescued me from Father's biting tongue." Daphne shook her head emphatically. "It makes no sense. Father describes Mr. Thornton as greedy and selfish. The man I met at Newmarket was anything but. Still, even if my assessments were wrong, greed and selfishness are qualities Father generally applauds in his colleagues. Why not now?"

"I don't know, Snowdrop. Does it matter?"

A faraway look came into Daphne's eyes. "Yes, Vicar, it matters. My instincts tell me it matters a lot."

5

THE FRONT DOOR AT TRAGMORE—AN INTERESTING ALTERNATIVE to the parlor window.

Pierce stifled a sardonic grin, glancing about Tragmore's polished hallway—the same hallway he'd crept through mere hours before, valuables tucked in his coat.

"The marquis will see you in his study," announced the poker-faced butler.

"Will he? Very gracious of him," Pierce replied, the essence of polished congeniality. "Lead the way."

Moments later, he was ushered into a dimly lit, unoccupied room and abruptly left to his own devices.

I'm being shown my place, Pierce determined with wry amusement. *Not only am I an undesirable, I'm an unwanted undesirable.*

So be it.

Pondering that thought, he helped himself to a brandy, chose his chair, and waited.

"All right, Thornton, I'm here." Tragmore strode into the study three quarters of an hour later. "I'm also harried and busy." He broke off, gaping. "What is the meaning of this?" he exploded, when he'd found his voice. "What the hell do you think you're doing?"

"Hmm?" Pierce lowered the newspaper he'd been reading, peering at the marquis over his long legs, which were propped on the desk and casually crossed at the ankles. "Oh, hello Tragmore. Your timing is perfect. I've just finished my brandy. Would you pour me another?" He extended his empty glass.

"Why are you drinking my brandy? Sitting in my chair? At my desk. With your bloody feet up, no less." The marquis advanced furiously toward Pierce.

Like a tiger whose claim had been challenged, Pierce shot to his feet, his eyes blazing with rage. *"Your* desk? *Your* chair? *Your* brandy? Listen to me, Tragmore, and listen well. Nothing in this house is yours. I own it all: your possessions, your businesses, *you.* But for my good nature, you'd be living in the gutter, the very place you accuse me of coming from. Bear that in mind and don't antagonize me further. Should you or your servants—" a lethal pause, *"my* servants—ever treat me in so shabby a manner again, I might be forced to lose my temper. And my compassion. Is that clear?"

Throughout Pierce's tirade, Tragmore's color had gone from pink to red to green. Now, he merely nodded, gritting his teeth as he snatched Pierce's empty glass and crossed the room to refill it. "You've made your point, Thornton." He thrust the drink at his adversary, obviously struggling to check his escalating anger. "You'll have to excuse my ill humor. I'm out of sorts today. During the night I was robbed by that contemptible Tin Cup Bandit."

"Were you?" Pierce's brows rose. "How intriguing. What did he take?"

"All Elizabeth's jewelry, my silver, my cash box and notes, everything of value he could put his hands on. Why, he even took that lovely necklace of Daphne's you and I spoke of at Newmarket."

"The one you claimed was an inexpensive copy?"

Silence.

"Your family, are they all right?" Pierce continued after a brief pause.

"Naturally, they're very upset. Elizabeth spent most of

the day in her chambers and Daphne left hers scant hours ago to go walking."

"Walking? Alone?"

"Only on the grounds of the estate," Tragmore replied with a dismissive wave. "She does it often. Lord alone knows what nonsensical notions fill her head. In any case, it's best for her not to be underfoot today. The authorities need as few distractions as possible. They are meticulously interviewing the servants, searching for clues."

"And have they found any?"

"None. The bastard left nothing behind. Except, of course, for one ruby, which I found in a tin cup on my pillow. A ruby I'm certain he removed from the Viscountess Druige's necklace."

"Was Druige the bandit's most recent victim prior to you?"

"He was." Tragmore took out a handkerchief and mopped at his face. "As I'm sure you've read in the lurid newspaper accounts, the bandit's trademark is to leave a jewel from his previous robbery at the scene of his current one. Unfortunately, that is the only clue he ever leaves. Thus far neither the constable nor the magistrate has a hint as to the scoundrel's identity."

"I see. Peculiar, to say the least." Pierce shrugged, perching comfortably on the edge of the desk. "Still, that doesn't change the fact that you and I have things to discuss."

"What things?"

"Your debts."

The marquis stiffened. "I was under the impression your solicitor was going to contact me to arrange a meeting away from Tragmore and at a mutually convenient time."

"I changed my mind." Pierce sipped appreciatively at his brandy. "I can do that, you know. I'm the one holding your notes and your future in my hands. So, let's get right to the point, shall we?"

"What point?"

"When can I expect to be paid or when shall I toss you from your home and subject you to the public ridicule of bankruptcy?"

Tragmore's eyes narrowed. "You heartless bastard."

A muscle worked in Pierce's jaw. "A bastard, yes. But heartless? Coming from you, that's laughable."

"What is it you want?" the marquis demanded.

"Payment."

"No, this involves more than money, Thornton. What is it you really want from me?"

A glint of hatred darkened Pierce's eyes to near black. "More than you could possibly offer." He came to his feet. "Every iota of which I intend to collect in due time. For now, I'll expect my first payment by week's end."

"But that's impossible."

"Find a way. Should I not receive your money by Friday evening, I'll have no choice but to contact the *London Gazette* and have your name published for all to see. Then, I'll arrange for everything in this manor to be confiscated and everyone living here to be tossed into the cold. Is that understood?"

"You filthy bast—"

"Bastard," Pierce finished, his voice eerily devoid of emotion. "And I believe we've already established the accuracy of that term. Now, as I was saying, you have until Friday. Or the actions I take will make your traumatic little robbery last night seem like a minor incursion."

"Before you carry out your sordid threat, let me issue one of my own," Tragmore shot back, triumph blazing in his eyes. "I gathered a bit of personal data on you, just in case your strategy for buying my notes included blackmail. Should you even attempt to publicly ruin me, I will tell all the world that the wealthy, polished Pierce Thornton sprang from the womb of a workhouse whore."

Pierce went ominously still. "I would suggest you never breathe my mother's name, Tragmore. Not if you want to live. As for the information your pathetically transparent investigators uncovered about my past, you can publish the details on the front page of the bloody *London Times* for all I care." Pierce cocked a brow, enjoying the look of shock on Tragmore's face. "Did you think I didn't know of your men's recent inquiries? I assure you, Tragmore, I know every arrangement you make, everything you do. As I said, I own you." Pierce's lips curved into a mocking smile. "You wasted your money, what little of it remains. I would have told you anything you wished to know, free of charge. I've never made a secret of my past—not my place of birth, nor my unknown parentage. You had only to ask."

"Then I'll keep searching until I find something else," Tragmore roared, words of enraged impotence. "A lowlife such as yourself must have scores of reprehensible secrets. I won't rest until I find—"

"Then you'll expire from exhaustion and have nothing to show for it." Pierce took a subtle, menacing step in Tragmore's direction. "Drop your investigations. You're squandering what is now *my* money. That angers me. Continue and I'll be forced to call in my debts that much sooner."

"Why are you doing this?" Tragmore exploded in frustration. "Why are you single-handedly purchasing all my notes? And why do you hate me so?"

"You'll have your answers when I'm ready to supply them. Not one moment sooner. And Tragmore," Pierce added with icy reserve, "if you ever attempt to blackmail me again, I'll ruin you without a backward glance."

The marquis drew a slow inward breath. "You're obviously far more cunning than I realized."

"One of the benefits of growing up on the streets." With bitter finesse, Pierce set his glass on the desk and rose. "Good day, Tragmore. I'll expect my first payment Friday."

With deadly calm, he crossed the room and left.

Outside the manor, Pierce unclenched his fists and inhaled sharply, trying to dispel his tightly coiled enmity. There was no record of what the marquis sought, just as there was no measure for Pierce's hatred. Tragmore didn't even recall the skinny urchin of eighteen years before. But then, why should he? To him, all workhouse children looked alike, *were* alike, fit for naught but abuse. Pierce was just one of them; a nameless, faceless lowlife, common filth in the sea of riffraff that defined the House of Perpetual Hope. And, as the only witness to the marquis's corrupt exchanges with Barrings, Pierce accepted that role gratefully, blending in, biding his time, anonymously plotting his vengeance.

At long last, Tragmore's undoing loomed near.

Heading for his waiting carriage, Pierce wondered for the hundredth time if killing the son of a bitch would prove more satisfactory and infinitely quicker than draining his funds and driving him to his knees. But, no. For all Tragmore's crimes; the blood money he'd stolen, the indignities he'd rendered, he deserved a prolonged agony far more heinous than death.

An unconscionable thought sprang from that reality.

How could Pierce destroy Tragmore without subjecting his family to the same devastating end?

Beside his carriage, Pierce came to a grinding halt. Averting his head, he scanned the woods instinctively for a sign of Daphne.

Suddenly, obsessively, he needed to see her.

"Ride to the main road," he advised his driver, already walking away. "I shall meet you there shortly."

"Yes, sir." The driver urged the horses into a trot, and disappeared around the curved drive.

Cautiously, Pierce made his way through the trees, along the leaf-strewn paths, searching for the enigma who'd haunted his memories since Newmarket.

He was just about to try a different direction when he heard the muted sound of a stick snap.

Shading his eyes from the late-afternoon sun, Pierce assessed the area until he saw a moving spot of color by a small pond. Noiselessly, he followed it, then stopped in rapt fascination to watch.

Across the pond, Daphne was creeping along, silent and careful, her attention riveted on a snake that was slithering forward, preparing to prey on an unsuspecting chipmunk. Slowly, Daphne approached, sidestepping sticks and leaves that might emit telltale sounds and reveal her presence.

Twenty feet away, she stopped.

Whipping a blade from beneath her skirts, she sent it sailing on ahead, watching as it landed directly between the predator and his prey. Startled, the chipmunk dropped the crumb of food it had been eating and darted off into the woods, leaving the snake and its threat far behind.

Satisfied with her work, Daphne rearranged her skirts and

walked over to reclaim her blade. "That was beneath you," she informed the snake. "In the future, please choose targets that can adequately defend themselves. Else you'll answer to me."

"I don't know about the snake, but I'm certainly convinced."

Daphne started, dropping her knife and spinning about as Pierce approached her.

"Mr. Thornton!" She flushed, regaining her composure with great difficulty. "You startled me."

Pierce grinned, gazing down into her beautiful, flustered face. "I could say the same. That was the most admirable display of skill, execution, and approach I've seen in ages."

She gave him a tentative smile. "Thank you."

"Where on earth did you learn to throw a knife so adeptly?"

"I wasn't taught, if that's what you're asking," Daphne replied warily.

"An innate skill." Pierce nodded his understanding. "I'm impressed. Am I to assume you exercise this ability frequently?"

Her smile faded. "You're mocking me."

"Never. I'm just curious why a well-bred young lady would need to carry a weapon when strolling the grounds of her estate."

"I—" She averted her gaze, obviously uncomfortable with the question. "I walked a bit beyond Tragmore. I generally do."

"Really? To where?"

"To the village." Impulsively, she leaned forward, clutching Pierce's coat as she went on in a rush. "No one but Mama knows of my visits there. Please, sir, I ask that you—"

"I won't mention a word to anyone, especially your father." Pierce covered her hands with his, strangely moved by her trust. "Why do you go to the village? To shop?"

"No. I visit a friend."

"A friend," Pierce repeated, his eyes narrowing. "Can't this friend come to Tragmore?"

"Unfortunately not. Father detests him."

"Him?" A surge of jealousy coursed through Pierce's blood. "Your friend is a man?"

"A vicar. Mr. Chambers. He's known Mama since she was a girl, and he's been my dearest friend for as long as I can remember."

"I see." Jealousy vanished, supplanted by keen interest. "Why does your father hate the vicar?"

Sadness clouded Daphne's lovely face. "Many reasons. Too many to enumerate."

"So you travel to the church to see him. Alone."

"Not entirely alone," Daphne corrected. "I have my blade. Not that I've ever had occasion to use it. But the vicar worries incessantly about me. So I carry it to ease his mind."

"Your vicar sounds like a fine man." Pierce caressed Daphne's fingers gently. "Should you ever decide you need an escort to the village, I'd be happy to stand in for your knife."

Clearly moved, Daphne swallowed, staring at their joined hands. "Thank you, Mr. Thornton. I shan't forget your kind offer."

Lord, she was beautiful. More so each time he saw her.

Clad in a simple beige day dress, her tawny hair was adorably disheveled, insistently falling free of its pins. Like Daphne herself, it appeared unwilling to be bound by either ribbons or convention, and Pierce wondered if she knew how enchanting she looked, how badly he wanted to haul her into his arms.

He seriously doubted she suspected either.

"Are you on your way to meet with my father?" Daphne inquired, turning those mesmerizing eyes up to his.

"Actually, the marquis and I have concluded our business. I was on my way home."

"You walked to Tragmore?"

"No. But I asked my driver to await me by the main road."

"Why?"

"Your father mentioned you were strolling the grounds. I wanted to find you."

"Oh. I see." Her eyes twinkled. "Your forthrightness again, Mr. Thornton?"

"Definitely." Pierce hooked a finger beneath her chin, caressing her lower lip with his thumb. "Your naiveté again, Daphne?"

She smiled, her lips curving against his thumb. "Evidently, yes."

"Do you know you have the most radiant smile I've ever seen?" Pierce's voice grew husky, his gaze fixed on her mouth. "And lips that are even softer than I imagined?"

That faint pulse began beating in her neck.

"You're not afraid of me, are you?"

"Should I be?"

Pierce shook his head slowly. "No." He smoothed his knuckles across her cheek. "Your skin feels like silk."

"Mr. Thornton—"

"Hmm?"

"What business do you have with my father?" Daphne blurted out.

"Various dealings." Pierce freed his other hand, looping his arm about her waist and urging her against him. "Do you know how badly I want to kiss you, Daphne?"

Her eyes grew wide with an intoxicating combination of fascination and uncertainty. "I—I don't—"

"Very badly. So badly it's unendurable." He brushed her lips lightly with his. "I need to taste you. Will you let me?"

"You're asking me?" Her breath was tantalizingly warm against his lips, but Pierce could feel her tremble as she balanced on this new yet exhilarating threshold.

"Yes, I'm asking you. I'd never take what you didn't willingly offer."

Wonder and something painfully akin to relief flashed in her eyes, softening Pierce's hunger into something achingly tender as it melded with a wave of blind protectiveness. He wanted to enfold her in his arms, shield her from anything or anyone who tried to harm her.

"Kiss me, Daphne," he whispered. "Let me show you how safe you can be."

A soft moan escaped her, and she nodded, lifting her mouth to offer him what he sought.

She had no idea how much he sought and how much he found in that kiss.

Rich, deep, more profound than the mere act itself, the kiss ignited slowly, exquisitely, like the growing embers of a fire newly kindled, radiantly aglow.

A hard shudder racked Pierce's body, and he wrapped Daphne closer, opening his mouth over hers in a poignant conveyance of desire, possessiveness, pain, and tenderness.

She was heaven.

That was his first coherent thought as the fire caught, spread, causing Daphne to lean into him, shyly pressing her palms to his chest, and kissing him back with an enticing blend of innocence and ardor more seductive than the intimate acts of the most practiced courtesans.

Pierce heard himself groan, capturing Daphne's hands to bring them around his neck, deepening the kiss until she opened her mouth to his seeking tongue, whimpering as it stroked hers.

"Daphne." He said her name reverently, lifting her small, delicate frame up and into him until there was nothing between them but the hindering layers of their clothes.

Even those could not hide the hardening contours of Pierce's body.

Daphne tensed, tearing her mouth away and staring bewilderedly at Pierce.

He relaxed his grip, but didn't release her. "Don't be afraid," he murmured. "I told you, you're safe. I just—" He swallowed convulsively, his vulnerability as unique and frightening as it was unsurprising.

As if sensing his raw emotions, Daphne lay her hand tenderly on his jaw. "I'm not afraid. Not really. I've just never felt such—done such—"

"There's a powerful pull between us," Pierce replied soberly. "I feel it. And so do you."

"I don't deny it." She lowered her eyes to his coat.

"Have you ever been kissed, Daphne?"

Her cheeks turned pink, and she hesitated for so long that Pierce began to seethe, planning the demise of any other man who'd tasted her lips.

"No," she admitted at last, her voice tiny. "Not kissed."

She was remembering last night with the Tin Cup Bandit. Pierce knew it, just as surely as he knew he wanted to wipe that memory from her mind, replace it with burning memories of him. Only him.

"Not kissed? What does that mean? What intimacies *have* you shared with a man?"

"None." Daphne started at the fervor of his tone. Misunderstanding its cause, she gave him a look of heartbreaking apology. "I suppose I'm even more naive than you imagined."

"You're perfect," Pierce informed her fiercely, livid at himself for inciting her self-doubt. He lowered her feet to the ground, his hands tightly gripping her waist. "What you're hearing is not disapproval. It's jealousy."

"Jealousy?" She gave him a quizzical look. "Why?"

"I don't want anyone's arms around you but mine."

Daphne blinked. "Surely you're joking."

"Why would I be joking?"

"Because you're handsome, wealthy, charming, and very accomplished—er, experienced." Her cheeks flamed. "You must have dozens of women eager for your attentions."

Pierce's chuckle vibrated through her. "Only dozens?"

"Are there more?"

"Daphne." He caressed the soft material of her gown. "I really don't give a damn about other women. As for your description of my assets—" His smile grew wicked. "Thank you. I think. Now let me return the compliment, with the exception of the last item you mentioned. You're enchanting and sensitive and beautiful in every way, some of which are more important than the mere physical."

"So are you," she blurted out. "I'll never forget the way you rescued me at Newmarket. I was so absorbed in watching those desperate, hungry people, the bitter futility I could see on their faces, that I never heard Father's introduction. Thank you."

So that was what had preoccupied her at Newmarket. Compassion for the poor.

Tenderness unfurled inside Pierce like warm wisps of smoke. "I don't want thanks, Daphne. I want you." He saw panic invade her eyes, and read her thoughts easily. "I'm not afraid of your father."

"I know you're not. My guess is he's afraid of you."

79

Pierce's brows lifted in surprised admiration. "Add astute to your list of attributes."

"Why, Pierce? Why is he afraid of you?"

"Say that again."

She shook her head in confusion. "Say what again?"

"My name. I like the sound of it on your lips."

A soft smile. "Pierce."

"Now let me taste it." He lowered his head, brushing his mouth back and forth across hers. "Say it now, when I can feel it, savor it, breathe it."

"Pierce."

It was an exquisite whisper of sound, and Pierce drank it in, deepening and lengthening the kiss until Daphne pulled away, breathless.

"You're impossible," she informed him.

"And you're intoxicating."

Their gazes locked.

"Ask," he murmured.

"Your interest in me, is it because of your dealings with my father?"

Pierce's expression hardened. "No. It's despite my dealings with your father."

"You hate him. I saw it in your eyes during the race, and I see it again now. Why?"

"Many reasons. None of which I'm prepared to discuss yet."

"Is his title one of those reasons?"

A muscle worked in Pierce's jaw. "I have little use for the noble class."

"I was born of that class," Daphne reminded him.

"Born of it, yes. A part of it, no."

"Pierce," she said softly, her delicate brows knit with concern. "Father despises you. I can feel it when he speaks of you."

"I don't doubt it. Tell me, what does the marquis say about me?"

Chewing her lip, Daphne hesitated.

"He calls me a gutter rat, a lowlife, and a bastard," Pierce supplied.

"I don't believe—"

"You should. Every word of it is true. I grew up in the streets and I haven't the faintest idea who sired me."

To Pierce's amazement, Daphne stood on tiptoe, clasping his forearms and brushing her lips to his chin. "The loss is your father's then. He has no idea what a fine son he's produced." A shadow crossed her face. "Moreover, your sire, whoever he is, could be no less admirable than mine. Trust me, don't underestimate the consequences of Father's rage. Be careful."

Pierce could scarcely speak past the constriction in his chest. Not only was Daphne accepting him without question or censure, but she was trying to shield him from harm. When was the last time anyone had worried for his safety?

"Your father can't hurt me, sweetheart," Pierce managed in a raw tone, threading his fingers through Daphne's hair. "But thank you for warning me. And for caring."

"You don't understand. Father can be violent when provoked."

Pierce went deathly still, his hands tightening in her hair. "Has he ever been violent with you?"

Silence.

"Daphne, does that son of a bitch strike you?"

"He's my father, Pierce."

A vicious oath exploded from Pierce's lips. "I'll kill him."

"I can take care of myself. Besides, this discussion is not about Father's behavior toward me. It's about his behavior toward you."

"You still defend him, regardless of the fact that he abuses you?"

"It isn't defense, for there is none. It's—I'm not certain —loyalty, perhaps. Or duty."

"To a man who beats you?" Pierce shot back, incredulous. "Simply because he sired you?" He shook his head in furious incomprehension. "If being born in wedlock breeds such blind devotion to an unworthy scoundrel, then I'm delighted to be a bastard."

"I can't fault you for your sentiments," Daphne replied softly, lowering her eyes. "Nor can I alter mine. Worthy or not, the scoundrel you describe is my father, and I have no choice but to answer to him." She turned away. "I'd best return to the manor now, before darkness falls."

"Wait." Pierce came up behind her, caught her arms with gentle hands. "Forgive me. I had no right."

"I have the strangest feeling you have every right."

This was the moment he'd dreaded. "Suppose I were to tell you you're right, that I have a score to settle with your father that is older than you, deeper than you can fathom. Would you refuse to see me again?"

No answer.

"Daphne." He buried his lips in her hair. "I want you, but I won't lie to you. Not about my roots, nor about my hatred for your father. However, I also give you my word that I will never intentionally cause you pain. Are those declarations enough, or is what you feel for your father stronger than what you feel when you're in my arms? You'll have to tell me, for a lowly bastard such as I would have no knowledge—"

"Stop it!" She spun about to face him, her exquisite eyes the green-gray of a stormy sea. "Don't ever call yourself that again. I don't care how shrouded your lineage is, you're not a bastard."

All Pierce's tension drained away, and he caught Daphne's face between his palms. "Your defense is almost as beautiful as you are," he murmured with a tender smile. "Thank you."

"You have nothing to thank me for. Your actions speak for themselves. Whatever your history, you're every bit a gentleman."

"Not every bit." Pierce's eyes twinkled as he lowered his mouth to hers. "For instance, a proper gentleman would never demand so scandalous a good-bye before allowing you to return to Tragmore. *I* would."

"I see," Daphne acknowledged breathlessly. "Well then, an improper gentleman."

A husky chuckle rumbled from Pierce's chest. "What exactly is an improper gentleman?"

"The most fascinating sort—inherently decent, excitingly unconventional."

"Ah." He nibbled lightly at her lower lip. "And could such a gentleman entice you to see him again?"

"Indeed he could."

Reflexively, Pierce's hand tightened about her nape. "Is that your answer then?"

"No." Daphne reached up and twined her arms around Pierce's neck, tugging his mouth down to hers. "This is."

Stifling a groan, Pierce gave Daphne what she sought, forcing himself to relinquish control of the kiss. He sensed how important this moment was, her first tentative emergence from the tightly woven cocoon she'd spun about herself. He gave only as much as she took, moving with her, tasting the trembling sweetness of her lips, fighting the urge to crush her in his arms and ravish her mouth with his own.

At last he could take no more. "Go," he murmured. "It's nearly dusk."

Daphne nodded, her eyes aglow, her cheeks as triumphantly flushed as they'd been at Newmarket when she'd selected the winning horse. "You'll be back?"

"Without question." Stooping, Pierce retrieved Daphne's forgotten blade, placing it in her palm only after he'd kissed each of her fingers, the delicate veins at her wrist. "Nothing could keep me away," he promised, his gaze as unwavering as his purpose. "Nothing, and no one."

6

THE MESSENGER SHOT TO HIS FEET THE MOMENT PIERCE'S CAR-
riage turned into the drive. Brushing his uniform free of the
hour's worth of dust he'd acquired sitting on the stoop, he
stood at attention, waiting for Pierce to alight.

With a puzzled frown, Pierce descended, mounting the
front steps to his home.

"Mr. Thornton?" the lad inquired.

"Yes. What can I do for you?"

"I'm to give you this, sir." Efficiently, he extended a
sealed note. "And to wait," he added.

"I see." Pierce glanced down at the unmarked missive.
Tucking it in his pocket, he extracted a key and opened the
entranceway door. "Come in."

The boy shifted uncomfortably, hovering in the hall as
Pierce went into the sitting room to pour himself a drink. "I
believe it's a matter of some urgency, sir," he called out at
last. "At least that's what I've been told."

"Really?" Pierce emerged, sipping at his brandy. "And
who told you this?"

"Mr. Hollingsby, sir. The gentleman who sent me."

"Hollingsby?" Pierce cocked a surprised brow. George

84

Hollingsby was a well known and prominent solicitor, who handled much of the *ton*'s legal dealings. Had Tragmore put him up to something?

His curiosity aroused, Pierce set his glass aside and removed the missive from his pocket. "You said that Mr. Hollingsby asked you to wait while I read this?"

"Yes, Mr. Thornton. He did."

"Very well. You've piqued my interest." Pierce tore open the sealed flap and unfolded a tersely worded message.

Mr. Thornton: it read. *I earnestly request that you travel to my London office as soon as possible. I do not make this request lightly and, were it not a matter of grave urgency, I would not presume upon your time. Please advise my messenger when I can expect you. Cordially, George Hollingsby*

After reading the note through twice, Pierce calmly refolded it. "How long have you been waiting for me to return home?"

"About an hour, sir."

Nodding, Pierce extracted a one-pound note and handed it to the lad. "Thank you for your efficiency and your patience. Tell Mr. Hollingsby he can expect me first thing in the morning."

"Oh, yes, sir." The boy beamed. "Thank you, sir. I'll tell him directly, sir." Bowing profusely, he fairly flew from the house, almost as if he were afraid Pierce would come to his senses and reclaim the outrageous sum.

Chuckling, Pierce returned to the sitting room, dropping to the sofa and tucking the missive back in his pocket. The day had turned out to be anything but dull. First, his ugly meeting with Tragmore, then his remarkable moments with Daphne, and now this intriguing message from Hollingsby.

Again, Pierce wondered if Hollingsby were acting as Tragmore's agent and if the solicitor's urgently requested meeting had anything to do with the marquis's threats. If Hollingsby planned to flourish a damning report of Pierce's workhouse history, he was going to be terribly disappointed with the reaction he received. And, Pierce reflected, he himself would have made a long trip for nothing.

Tomorrow would tell.

Closing his eyes, Pierce dismissed the forthcoming inconvenience from his mind, instantly replacing it with the image of a far more appealing subject: Daphne.

A satisfied smile curved his lips as he relived their encounter in the woods. Physically, emotionally, they'd reached a new level of involvement today, both of them tacitly accepting the pull between them as a tangible force that neither denial nor escape could negate. Pierce's instincts told him that Daphne was as unaccustomed as he to baring her heart, yet she'd opened up to him, shared thoughts, feelings, and intimacies he was certain she'd never shared with another.

And he?

He'd plunged one step deeper into a commitment he'd never conceived of making.

She felt so bloody right in his arms, so natural and responsive. Like a newly opened flower, she'd unfurled to his touch, reaching trustingly for the promise of sustenance and warmth he offered.

He'd be damned if he'd burn her.

Pierce slammed his fist into the cushion. Where was this leading? Where *could* it lead?

Most frightening for him, where did he want it to lead?

Were it only to bed, he wouldn't feel this acute sense of alarm. Lust could be—would be—tempered. His compulsion to shelter Daphne was more powerful than his craving to possess her. He'd protect her from everyone, even himself.

But he wanted so much more than her body, and he knew it. He wanted the rare and precious quality that was Daphne herself, the beauty she submerged, the fire she restrained, the compassion she stifled.

The spirit of adventure he knew he could induce.

It was there. He'd seen sparks of it. And so had the Tin Cup Bandit.

A wave of arrogance surged through Pierce as he evaluated the dilemma of his dual identity. True, Daphne was doubtless still enamored with her mysterious champion of the poor. But after today Pierce harbored not the slightest doubt that she was also captivated by Pierce Thornton.

That bloody bandit didn't stand a chance.

George Hollingsby rose when Pierce entered, gesturing for his clerk to close the door and leave them alone.

"Mr. Thornton." He extended his hand. "Thank you for traveling to London on such short notice."

Warily, Pierce shook the solicitor's proffered hand. "Your message sounded quite urgent. And quite mysterious, I might add."

"I apologize for that. In a moment, you'll understand why the matter is both urgent and somewhat delicate. Please, have a seat. May I offer you some refreshment?"

"No, thank you." Pierce lowered himself into a chair. "Only an explanation."

"Very well." Adjusting his spectacles, Hollingsby glanced down at the document on his desk. "Does the name Francis Ashford mean anything to you?"

"Ashford?" Pierce repeated woodenly, instantly accosted by waves of hateful memories.

"Perhaps by his titled name then," Hollingsby clarified, mistaking Pierce's silence for non-comprehension. "The Duke of Markham."

"Yes, I've heard of him."

Everything inside Pierce had gone cold. Heard of him? Markham was the one sketchy link to his puzzle, the one aspect of Tragmore's visits to the workhouse that Pierce had never quite understood.

Markham had accompanied Tragmore on almost every occasion, shared the covert meetings with Barrings that Pierce continued to observe. But rather than actively participating in the division of illegal funds, Markham usually remained silent, aloof, as if he didn't give a damn about the money Tragmore was procuring for him. And when Tragmore went on a rampage, shouting his hatred to the children, Markham would detach himself, strolling idly in the garden or wandering aimlessly about the building, surveying the occupants with dark, brooding eyes.

What was he seeking? Why was he there?

Pierce had tortured himself with those questions for years, both during his workhouse days and long after he'd left the hated walls behind. A decade before, when he'd begun actively plotting Tragmore's demise, he'd made some discreet inquiries into Markham's life. He'd learned nothing of what the duke's motives might have been for his work-house visits, but he did learn that Markham's duchess had since died and that he'd recently lost his only child, his beloved son, to a riding mishap, after which the aged duke had become a recluse. Armed with that knowledge, ven-geance had suddenly seemed unduly cruel, especially since, in Pierce's mind, Markham had been no more than Tragmore's passive companion. It was Tragmore Pierce despised, Tragmore he intended to destroy.

But the unresolved questions persisted.

"Mr. Thornton?"

Pierce blinked, returning to the present, meeting Hollingsby's quizzical gaze. "Hmm?"

"Are you well? You look a bit green."

"I'm fine." Pierce's jaw tightened fractionally. "You were saying about the Duke of Markham?"

"Yes, well, the poor soul passed away several days ago. No one has been notified because, quite frankly, he hadn't any friends or known living relatives. In truth, he hadn't even ventured from his estate in more than ten years."

"I'm sorry to hear that. But what has it to do with me?"

The solicitor shifted uncomfortably. "More than you could ever imagine." He cleared his throat. "Any way I phrase this, it's going to come as a shock."

"Then I suggest you merely state what you must."

"Very well." Hollingsby gripped the edge of his desk. "As of two days past, you are the Duke of Markham."

A ponderous silence.

"Is this some kind of a jest?" Pierce managed at last. "Because I'm decidedly unamused."

"I assure you, Mr. Thorn—er, Your Grace, this is no jest. If you'll allow me to—"

"I'll allow you to nothing." Pierce was on his feet, striding toward the door. "You've obviously received some gravely erroneous information. I didn't even know the Duke of Mark—"

"Did you know Cara Thornton?" Hollingsby asked quietly.

Pierce came to an abrupt halt. Turning, he stared at the solicitor through furiously narrowed eyes. "You'd best have a damned good reason for speaking my mother's name. She's dead. If you've been paid to sully her character—"

"Cruelty is not my forte, sir. Nor am I so badly in need of funds that I would compromise my integrity. I assure you, no one has paid me to ruin your deceased mother. Quite the contrary, in fact. Now, will you sit and listen to what I have to say?"

Like a prowling tiger, Pierce crossed the room and perched, whip taut, on the edge of the chair.

"Thank you," Hollingsby said, resettling himself and pointing to the pages in his hand. "I have here a letter and a legally binding codicil to the Duke of Markham's will. Several months ago he summoned me to his manor, where he asked me to draw up the papers. I complied. It is my opinion that he meant to send for you in order to reveal the contents himself. Unfortunately, he took sick shortly after the papers were executed, with an illness from which he never recovered. Therefore, you are hearing this information today for the first time."

"What information?"

"The late Duke of Markham was your father."

Father.

The word hit him like an avalanche, its odious shock waves crashing through Pierce in harsh, physical blows.

"The letter is written in the duke's own hand," Hollingsby was continuing. "I can attest to that. Of course, you're welcome to read it yourself, and the codicil as well, after I've had the opportunity to explain its terms and conditions. First, however, I'd like to clarify your true origins by recounting the details of the duke's letter." When he was greeted with nothing but silence, Hollingsby looked up, taking in Pierce's rigid jaw. "Are you all right, sir?"

"Go on," Pierce ordered through clenched teeth.

Hollingsby nodded, skimming the first page he held. "The duke met your mother some two and thirty years ago in a London pub. It was a dismal time of his life. He was estranged from his duchess, embittered by the knowledge that she seemed unable to give him a child. Your mother was a young and beautiful tavern maid, filled with vitality, hope, and passion. Markham fell in love with her on the spot.

"Over the next six months he returned to the tavern, and Cara, as often as he could, casting protocol and consequence to the wind, heeding only the dictates of his heart."

"But consequence caught up with him," Pierce interrupted, the heinous pieces falling rapidly into place. "He filled my mother's belly with his child, then cast her aside and returned to his rightful title, his rightful position, and his rightful wife."

Hollingsby nodded again, scanning that section of the letter. "Yes. Markham says himself that he was weak. Much as he loved Cara, he couldn't bring himself to sacrifice everything and endure ostracism and scandal. So he turned her, and their unborn child, away.

"But, try though he would, he couldn't forget them, nor would his conscience allow him to rest. After months of internal struggle, he went in search of Cara, only to find she'd lost her job and vanished. He panicked, and began an investigation of her whereabouts. It took months before he discovered her and the son she'd borne him living at the House of Perpetual Hope in Leicester. His intentions were to forsake everything and come forward to claim them.

"It was at that time his duchess announced she was with child. Needless to say, that altered everything."

"Needless to say," Pierce bit out, venom burning his throat.

"Markham had no choice but to commit himself to his wife and unborn heir. However, that didn't prevent him from worrying over Cara and their son. He sent money as often as he could—anonymously, of course—and prayed that it reached them."

"It didn't."

Hollingsby flinched at the hatred in Pierce's tone. "Then

the duke received a report of Cara's death. At that point he knew he had to do more."

"More than what? More than allow her to waste away and die in a workhouse? More than condemn his son to hell?"

"He began making personal visits to the workhouse," Hollingsby responded. "The letter is vague about what explanation he gave the headmaster, but clearly no one knew his true reason for being there."

"Which was?"

"To check on his son—Cara's son." The solicitor lifted his gaze, blanching beneath Pierce's frigid stare. "You."

"How touching." Abruptly, Pierce rose, turning his back to Hollingsby. "And, having seen me, was he deeply moved? Did he make any attempt to free me from the prison I was living in?"

"He couldn't. If he had—"

"If he had, everyone of importance would have known he'd fathered a bastard," Pierce supplied with brutal accuracy. "And that might have angered his duchess and compromised the position of his legitimate heir. Right, Hollingsby? Isn't that what you're saying?"

"Yes. That's what I'm saying."

Slowly, Pierce pivoted, his jaw working convulsively. "Had the duke's son not perished in a riding accident, we wouldn't be having this conversation, would we?"

"Yes, I believe we would. Markham made it clear to me that, even had you not been his sole heir, he was determined for you to know your true parentage."

"What a fine man. I feel infinitely better knowing I carry his blood in my veins." Pierce swallowed. "What else are you responsible for relaying to me before I walk out and dismiss everything you've said?"

"Sir," Hollingsby walked to the front of his desk, the document clutched in his hands. "I understand your shock, even your anger. But I don't think you understand what I'm telling you. You are the duke's only surviving child. Were it not for you, the Ashford name would die along with your father. It is imperative that you assume his title."

"Imperative? I think not. No, Hollingsby, I decline the honor."

The solicitor gaped. "Have you any idea what you're refusing? The size of the estate you stand to inherit? How vast were the duke's wealth, his land, his influence?"

"I don't give a damn."

"But His Grace wished—"

"His Grace wished?" Pierce exploded, advancing toward the disconcerted solicitor. "His Grace wished? What about my mother's wishes? What about my wishes? He condemned us to rot in a filthy, diseased workhouse without so much as a second thought. And now, with my mother cold in her grave, he wants to welcome me to his coveted world? To acknowledge me as his son? Now that he himself is dead and gone, and the ensuing scandal can no longer hurt him? Now I'm to step forward and proudly assume the role of the Duke of Markham—because *he* wishes it?" Eyes ablaze, Pierce kicked a chair from his path, then veered toward the door. *"My* wish is for the filthy blackguard to burn in hell. And, if there is any justice at all, he already has. Good day, Hollingsby."

"There's more," the solicitor said quietly.

Pierce swung around. "Find another victim."

"Please, Mr. Thornton. I have yet to enumerate the terms and conditions I spoke of."

A harsh laugh erupted from Pierce's chest. "Terms and conditions? Don't bother. I've denounced the title."

"Please, sir. I beseech you. My job is to relay the specifics of the codicil. What you choose to do about them is your concern."

Pierce sucked in his breath, struck by the truth of Hollingsby's plea. Markham's coldhearted negligence was not the solicitor's doing. "Very well, Hollingsby. Come to the conclusion of this nightmare."

"Thank you." Turning the page, Hollingsby shoved his spectacles back up on his nose. "The codicil states the following: In order to retain your newly acquired title and to permanently reap the benefits and privileges thereof, you must fulfill two stipulations. First, you must not only accept the title of the Duke of Markham, but you must assume all related responsibilities for a minimum of two years. That means living at Markham, overseeing the estate and the servants, supervising the businesses—"

"You've made your point. And the other stipulation?"

"Second, you must marry and produce a legitimate heir to the dukedom."

"A legitimate heir. In other words, not a bastard like me," Pierce clarified, bitterly precise.

"Correct."

"Tell me, Hollingsby, what if my duchess turns out to be as uncooperative a vessel as Markham's was? How many years did you say it took her to conceive? Or perhaps my duchess will be totally barren? Or, heaven forbid, she might bear me a daughter rather than a son. Have you considered that?" Pierce demanded mockingly. "What if I myself am incapable of fathering a child? It does happen, you know. Then what? All Markham's provisions will have been for naught."

"The duke considered that. During my final visit to Markham he presented me with a sealed envelope, instructing me to lock it in my office strongbox, to be removed precisely two years from the day you accept your rightful position as his heir. At that point, should any of the circumstances you just described exist, I am to send for you and reveal the contents of the letter, assuming, that is, you've fulfilled all your other ducal obligations during the prescribed time."

"And if, over the two-year period, I do produce the necessary heir?"

"Then the provisos contained therein will be declared null and void, and I shall give the envelope to you, unopened, to do with as you wish."

"The son of a bitch thought of everything, didn't he?"

Hollingsby wet his lips. "To resume the codicil's terms," he pushed on. "During the two-year probation period you'll be furnished with a generous weekly allowance of ten thousand pounds."

"Ten thousand pounds?" One brow rose. "How charitable."

"Finally, once the two years have elapsed and presuming

you've fulfilled both conditions, you are free to recommence your old life or continue your new one. In either case, you will have full access, within reason, of course, to the Markham funds, heirlooms, property, etcetera, for the rest of your life, and your son will be groomed as the future Duke of Markham."

"Lucky lad."

"Indeed," Hollingsby agreed, tactfully ignoring Pierce's cutting sarcasm. "No expense will be spared—"

"How much do all these assets amount to?" Pierce interrupted suddenly.

"Pardon me?"

"I want to know exactly how much my poor mother was being denied."

A pause. "If you're asking what the total worth of the duke's estate is, it's in excess of twenty million pounds."

"Hell." Pierce raked furious fingers through his hair. "Bloody, bloody hell. If the spineless coward weren't already dead, I'd kill him myself."

"Nevertheless, now that you've heard all the facts, I'm certain you've amended your earlier decision."

"I've amended nothing." Pierce yanked open the door. "Tear up that bloody codicil, Hollingsby. I don't need or want one shilling from the scum who sired me."

"Think about—"

"It's too late." Pierce stalked out without a backward glance. "Thirty years too late."

7

Pierce had no idea how many trips his carriage had made around Town, nor how much time had passed since he'd stormed from Hollingsby's office. Pausing only to purchase a bottle of whiskey, he'd climbed into his carriage and ordered his driver to circle the congested London streets until otherwise advised. Sliding to the far corner of the seat, Pierce then proceeded to toss off half the contents of the bottle while staring moodily out the window, his thoughts slamming against his brain like a hammer.

He? A duke?

Never. *Never.*

To hell with Markham. To hell with his title, his money, his name. To hell with—

His father.

Fortifying himself with another deep swallow of whiskey, Pierce forced himself to confront the situation and its consequences.

The Duke of Markham was his father.

All the pieces fit: his mother's talk of her nobleman lover, Markham's consistent but inexplicable workhouse visits, the background details Hollingsby had just revealed.

The story was true. Pierce's instincts confirmed that without question. Much of it was also unsurprising. After all, he had always known of his noble lineage, just as he'd long ago discerned his sire's reasons for denouncing him and abandoning Cara. Having a name to put to the anonymous blackguard who'd sired him was unexpected, but inconsequential at this point in his life.

But having a face to accompany the name, especially Markham's face, now *that* was disconcerting. How vividly he recalled those brooding eyes, that air of reserve. God help him, he could even see the resemblance. Yes, now that he knew the truth, Pierce realized the likeness between him and Markham was startling.

But even that was endurable.

What was unendurable, unconscionable, untenable, was what the arrogant bastard demanded of him now.

After a lifetime of rejection, to become a son.

Abhorring the highborn, to become a duke.

A shout from ahead brought Pierce up short. As he watched, a dirty lad of perhaps twelve darted down Regent Street, weaving his way among the pedestrians and carriages, a wallet clutched in his hand. In his wake, a distinguished gray-haired gentleman waved his fist furiously, bellowing for the authorities, urging a small group of sympathetic onlookers to apprehend the culprit.

They'll never catch him, Pierce thought, mentally gauging the distance between the boy and the oncoming mob. *At least not if he's any good. If he knows what he's doing, in precisely twelve paces, he'll veer down Conduit Street and duck down that tiny alley just shy of the corner. It's so narrow no well-fed person can fit. By the time the crowd gives up trying, he'll have scaled the low wall at the alley's end and be long gone.*

No sooner had Pierce assessed the situation than the urchin came to a halt, and swerved down Conduit Street. Five steps in he flattened his skinny frame against a brick wall and slithered down the nearly invisible alleyway.

Moments later, as Pierce's carriage rumbled by the cross street, the raging masses were still gathered at the alley opening, commanding the lad to emerge with the stolen wallet.

The boy was safe—this time.

Pierce leaned his head back against the cushion. How many this times had there been for him? How many escapes had he made down that very alley, his heart pounding so furiously he feared it might burst? How many almosts, when he'd nearly been caught?

For the two years following his flight from the workhouse, he'd survived on the streets, picking pockets, making his bed on piles of rags, stealing crusts of bread from Covent Garden in the pre-dawn hours. How many nights had he lain awake, weak to the point of delirium, shaking so violently with cold and loneliness and dread that death actually would have been welcome?

But life had prevailed. At least for him. He'd always been one hell of a gambler, steered by infallible instinct as he bet on everything from when a particular winter's first snow would fall to who would receive the next whipping from Barrings. At the workhouse, his stakes had been food. In the streets, they became money. No longer mere sustenance, but survival.

And survive he had, doubling and tripling his stolen pound notes with each successful wager, earning the respect of London's notorious thieves as he relieved them of their spoils, hoisting himself from the hopelessness of his plight.

Never forgetting that others hadn't been so fortunate.

How many children had died, were still dying, on London's thriving streets?

Lord, if he could only spare them that fate.

But even The Tin Cup Bandit's stolen jewels together with Pierce's acquired affluence weren't enough. Hundreds of thousands of pounds were needed to reach the vast number of starving people. It was so bloody frustrating. If only he had greater influence, greater wealth, greater access—

Reality exploded like gunfire.

He did. Or rather, he would as the Duke of Markham.

Suddenly all vows of "never" faded as the monumental truth struck home. For years he'd sought ways to help. Now the ultimate opportunity was being handed to him with but a few annoying stipulations to impede his path. And he was turning his back on it? Was he mad?

Squelching the bitter protests still clamoring inside him, Pierce forced himself to weigh the facts with unemotional objectivity.

He was being offered a dukedom and all its privileges.

His refusal was based primarily in pride and deep-seated anger. That, and the repudiation of a way of life he abhorred.

The way of life—where was it written he had to emulate it?

If he'd learned anything from his years of poverty, he'd learned that titled wealth bred its own set of rules. Therefore, if the new Duke of Markham chose to mingle with riffraff, scandalously refuse the "right" invitations, and disburse his money in an unorthodox manner, who would dare challenge his eccentricity?

As for pride and anger, wouldn't accepting the terms of the codicil appease both? After all, as the Duke of Markham he'd be accepted in the very houses he robbed, privy to the details of the aristocracy's latest acquisitions, their most valuable jewels. He'd hear firsthand who'd won at Newmarket, played the highest stakes at White's, invested wisely and well.

Consequently, the Tin Cup Bandit could escalate his number of burglaries, taking the *ton* by storm and utterly annihilating their fortunes. By combining the bandit's spoils and his own allocated ten thousand pounds a week, Pierce could ensure that England's workhouses thrived.

Not to mention the sheer joy of flaunting his newly acquired blue-blood status in Tragmore's face and reminding the blackguard that a duke most emphatically outranked a marquis.

Yes, the final victory would indeed be Pierce's.

Conversely, what exactly would he be relinquishing?

Two years of his life. Two years to live at Markham's wretched estate, run his businesses, direct his staff of servants. Two years to make his assets prosper.

Pierce lowered the bottle of whiskey thoughtfully. That

task posed no foreseeable difficulty. After all, business ventures were his forte. He'd honed his investment skills over long, hungry years, ultimately earning a sizeable sum of his own. He'd make Markham's bloody fortune flourish. In fact, he'd leave it healthier than ever. Two years hence, Markham's assets would reach new heights, and his own commitment would be satisfied.

Not quite, Pierce reminded himself. In order to retain permanent access to the Markham fortune, he had also to produce an heir. A legitimate heir.

Which meant taking a wife.

Pierce frowned. The thought was distinctly unappealing. Given his double identity and his illegal missions, he needed his freedom. Hell, the Tin Cup Bandit notwithstanding, Pierce *wanted* his freedom. So whomever he selected as his duchess would have to tolerate his independence, at least for two years.

Two years? Pierce sat up with a start. Marriage couldn't be negated as easily as business ventures. Even if his wife were willing to go her own way once she'd completed her task, she would be bound to him forever, bearing not only his name, but his child.

Daphne.

Her image came as naturally as the vision of her by his side, and Pierce felt his heart lift for the first time since the day's madness had begun. Daphne—his wife, his duchess, the mother of his child.

An intrigued smile curved Pierce's lips. Perhaps the notion of marriage was not so unattractive after all, he mused, digesting this new and fascinating possibility. If he had to be permanently tied to one woman, who but Daphne could fill that role?

Would Daphne want to fill that role? Even with the powerful pull that drew them together, it was far too soon for her to have considered anything as significant as marriage. And while Pierce was worldly enough to discern the rarity of what hovered between them, Daphne was young, inexperienced. So how could he expect her to comprehend the magnitude of what occurred when they met, spoke, touched?

He did know that she trusted him, reached out to him for a complexity of reasons too vast to put into words. She'd even taken a few tentative steps closer to the fire that blazed to life when she was in his arms.

But it still wasn't enough.

So, how would she react to the thought of becoming his wife? Now. Immediately. She'd be stunned. That was a certainty. But when the shock had subsided, when she'd had time to think, then what? Would she flatly refuse his proposal, or would she entertain the idea of becoming Mrs. Pierce Thornton?

Tragmore. What would he do?

Pierce's smile vanished. The son of a bitch would be furious. More than furious. His rage would be boundless; vented—how? By striking out at Pierce, or at Daphne?

Just the thought of Tragmore laying one of his contemptible hands on Daphne made Pierce's skin crawl. Clenching his fists, he cursed aloud.

By wedding Daphne he could wrest her from her father's brutality. He'd do it in a minute, with or without Tragmore's consent, if he were certain it was what Daphne wanted. But was it?

I'll never take what you don't willingly offer. Pierce had spoken that vow just yesterday as he'd drawn Daphne into his arms for the first time. He wouldn't break it. Not now, not ever. She had to freely choose to become his wife.

But was the fragile thread of feeling that had grown between them strong enough? Was Daphne strong enough to defy her father, knowing how much he loathed Pierce?

No. Not yet. There hadn't been enough opportunity.

But, dammit, there would be.

Abruptly, Pierce leaned forward. "Rakins!" he called to his driver. "Head back to Hollingsby's office at once."

"Mr. Thornton. You can't just walk in there! Mr. Hollingsby is a busy man." The scrawny clerk made one final attempt to block Pierce's path.

Sidestepping the man's flailing arms, Pierce flung open the solicitor's door and stalked in.

"Don't blame your clerk, Hollingsby," Pierce announced,

dropping into a chair. "I intended to see you immediately. And nothing and no one was going to stop me."

"I see." Hollingsby had jolted to his feet, and now began furiously polishing his spectacles. "You may leave us, Carter," he told the clerk.

"Yes, sir." Carter mopped at his brow, sent an aggravated look in Pierce's direction, and walked out.

"I didn't expect to see you again, Mr. Thornton." Hollingsby shoved his spectacles back into place. "And certainly not so soon."

"I'm sure you didn't." Pierce folded his hands behind his head and began without preliminaries. "I have a few questions. First, how did Markham know I was capable of managing his funds?"

Hollingsby's eyes widened in surprise, but he answered without hesitation. "The late duke knew a great deal about you. He followed your life, at a discreet distance, of course, quite closely. Therefore, he was aware of your brilliant business investments and your equally brilliant mind. When he had me draw up the codicil, he was fully confident that his estate would be entrusted to the very best of hands."

"How flattering. Next question. You mentioned that once my responsibilities had been fulfilled I would have complete access, within reason, to the Markham funds. Define within reason."

Now Hollingsby's jaw dropped. "Does this mean you've reconsidered and intend to—"

"Just answer the question."

"Very well. The only reason your father—er, the late duke, added that phrase was to ensure that his family name and fortune remained essentially intact for his grandson."

"His grandson. You mean, my son?"

"Yes."

"In other words, Markham was afraid I would intentionally tarnish his name and squander his money?"

"The possibility occurred to him, yes."

"Which, in turn, would leave my son destitute, much the way Markham left me, correct, Hollingsby?"

Averting his gaze, the solicitor shifted from one foot to the other.

"He needn't have worried," Pierce continued icily. "Lowly bastard that I am, I possess far higher principles than His Grace ever had. I will assure my son every shred of security, both financial and emotional, that my sire denied me. The Markham estate, and the Ashford name, will remain unimpugned."

"So you are reversing your earlier decision."

"I am."

"May I ask why?"

"For many reasons, few of which you would understand. Suffice it to say my conscience refused to permit retreat."

"You understand the stipulations I described?"

"I do. I also accept them. And to make your job slightly less untenable, I invite you to openly scrutinize my investments as I effect them. You'll find each to be completely acceptable." A glimmer of a smile. "In this case, Markham was right. I'm damned good at what I do."

"I don't doubt it." Hollingsby's obvious relief was mixed with a touch of admiration. "And my scrutiny won't be necessary, although I thank you for your generous offer. Since I'll be meeting with you weekly to issue your ten thousand pounds, we can discuss the status of your assets at those times."

"As you wish." Pierce rose. "I have one request."

"Which is?"

"That I be given the right to announce my newfound status on my own."

"You're asking me to say nothing?"

"Precisely. Only for a day or two, until I can find the proper setting for my coming out."

Hollingsby stifled a chuckle. "Very well, Mr.—forgive me—Your Grace. Although I must say I'd hate to miss your grand proclamation."

"Then don't. In fact, as I'm new to all this, I could use a suggestion. Where is the next large, pretentious house party scheduled to take place?"

"The Earl of Gantry is hosting an enormous gathering, complete with fox hunt and ball. It begins the day after tomorrow and continues for Lord knows how many days."

"Pity I don't have an invitation." Pierce cocked a pointed brow in Hollingsby's direction.

This time the solicitor laughed aloud. "I admire your spunk, sir. As it happens, I *do* have an invitation. And I'd be delighted to have you accompany me as my guest. Would that interest you?"

"The earl won't object, I presume?"

"Certainly not. At least, not once he learns who you are."

"That goes without saying." Pierce seized a quill from the desk. "I accept your kind invitation. Now, I presume there are documents I must sign?"

"Indeed."

"Then let's hurry the process along." Pierce's lips curved in amusement. "I have a legacy to see to."

8

"WE SHALL REMAIN AT GANTRY'S BALL FOR TWO HOURS, NOT A minute longer," Tragmore instructed Daphne and her mother as their carriage rounded the drive to Gantry's estate. "I'm in no mood for festivities. Unfortunately, I must endure the fox hunt tomorrow, as well as the dinner that follows it. But I shan't stay a day beyond that. As for tonight's party, we'll take our leave the moment it is plausible for us to do so. Is that clear?"

"Perfectly clear, Harwick," Elizabeth concurred instantly.

"We could have sent our regrets, Father," Daphne pointed out. "Given our recent burglary, I'm sure the earl would have understood."

"The earl would *not* have understood." Tragmore snapped. "He himself was a victim of that bloody bandit less than a fortnight ago. The difference is, he has no noose hanging around his neck."

Daphne inclined her head quizzically. "What do you mean, Father?"

"Nothing! Just mingle, ingratiate yourself with the right people, and hope that a never-before-met, wealthy nobleman becomes smitten with you."

"That's hardly likely, given that we are already acquainted with all the guests," Daphne replied, trying to fathom her father's uncharacteristic mood. He was neither volatile nor disdainful. Rather, he seemed nervous, uncommonly off balance, almost desperate. "Are you seeking a husband for me?" she tried.

"What?" Tragmore gave her a disoriented look.

"You mentioned my snaring a man's affections. I assumed—"

"I don't give a damn if you wed or not, Daphne," he cut in impatiently. "Unless of course your betrothed arrives with a fortune he is eager to share."

So it was money. For whatever reason her father was worried about funds. Why? He would be amply compensated for their stolen jewels. Had some other business loss occurred? One she knew nothing about?

She glanced at her mother, who shrugged and averted her head. Daphne sighed. She should know better. Elizabeth stayed as far from the flame as possible.

"We're here," the marquis muttered. "Now remember what I said. Two hours. No more."

"Of course, Harwick." Elizabeth lay a soothing hand on his arm. "We'll retire early so you can be rested for the hunt."

Alighting from the carriage, they were ushered to the ballroom door and announced.

"Tragmore, welcome." The Earl of Gantry made his way toward them. "And to your lovely wife and daughter, as well."

"Thank you, Gantry," Tragmore responded, instantly assuming his composed public veneer. "We've looked forward to your party for weeks."

"I'm delighted to hear that." Gantry smoothed the ends of his mustache and bowed to the ladies. "Lady Tragmore, Lady Daphne, my home is at your disposal. Your rooms have been prepared and your bags taken there by my servants. Now, you have nothing to concern yourselves with but laughter and merriment."

"You are a most gracious host, sir," Elizabeth smiled.

Gently, she took Daphne's arm. "Come, dear, let's find the ladies."

"Oh, Tragmore?" Gantry stayed him with his hand. "Before you join the party, I have news I believe you should hear."

Tragmore's brows rose. "Have you received further word on that lowlife who invaded our homes?"

"Hmm? Oh, the bandit. No, unfortunately, I know as little now as I did a fortnight ago. Perhaps later in the evening we can compare our sordid stories and together deduce the scoundrel's strategy. But, no, the news I refer to does not concern the bandit: It concerns Markham."

"Markham?" Tragmore had expected anything but this. "Has he finally emerged from his estate? I haven't seen or heard from him in years." Tragmore glanced beyond Gantry, into the crowded ballroom. "Is he here tonight?"

"Hardly. He's dead."

"Dead?" Tragmore started. "When?"

"Nearly a week ago, from what I understand. No one seems able to supply many details. As you'd suspect, he'd died alone."

"I'm sorry to hear that. Not only because of Markham's passing, but because, as his son is also gone, the Markham line has reached its end."

"True." Gantry shook his head. "'Tis a pity. One's name means so much." He cleared his throat. "Which reminds me, I had occasion to ride into the village two days past, and I happened to see your daughter."

"Daphne?" A warning spark ignited Tragmore's blood.

"Yes. I must admit, I was surprised. I distinctly recall your mentioning that you'd forbidden her from visiting that peculiar vicar who so generously disperses our funds to the poor."

"You saw her conversing with the vicar?"

"I did. They were taking tea in his garden." Gantry averted his head, his attention captured by a group of men gesturing for him to join them. "You'll have to excuse me, Tragmore. I'm being summoned. We'll continue our talk a bit later." He leaned forward conspiratorially. "As for your daughter, may I suggest you use a heavier hand? It might ensure her obedience."

Tragmore didn't reply. He waited only until Gantry had moved off. Then he acted.

Elizabeth and Daphne were but twenty feet away. He reached them in three strides.

"Come with me." His fingers bit into Daphne's arm. "Now."

Daphne flinched, her eyes widening with fear as she saw the rage on her father's face.

"Harwick, what is it?" Elizabeth asked in a quivering voice.

"Stay out of this, Elizabeth," he commanded. "I intend to have a private talk with our daughter. Immediately. And I suggest"—he turned blazing eyes on Daphne—"that she not make a scene."

"Very well, Father." Daphne's mind was already racing, desperately trying to envision what damning information her father had just gleaned. Her hands shook violently as she gathered up her skirts and followed him to a deserted sitting room down the hall.

"You were with that bloody vicar again," Tragmore ground out the moment he'd closed the door. "How many times have I forbidden you to go there? How many times have you disobeyed me?" He began to advance toward Daphne, his rage terrifying in its intensity.

Daphne's heart began slamming against her ribs.

"'Twas only for a few minutes, Father," she began.

"Liar!" His palm struck her face, and she cried out, instinctively pressing her fingers to her cheek.

"I'm not lying," she whispered, backing away. "I was at the church for a mere quarter hour."

"That's a quarter hour more than you're permitted." The marquis lunged forward again, slapping Daphne so hard she lost her balance and toppled to the couch. "Damn you! I'd beat you within an inch of your life were we at Tragmore."

"Please, Father." Daphne crept to the far corner of the sofa, frantically trying to think of words to appease him.

An insistent pounding at the door rescued her.

"Tragmore? Tragmore are you in there?" The Earl of Gantry's voice accompanied his determined knock.

Glowering at Daphne, Tragmore crossed the room and yanked open the door. "I'm in the midst of a discussion with my daughter, Gantry."

The earl nodded his understanding. "I apologize for intruding. But a most intriguing situation is in the process of unfolding. Hollingsby just arrived, bringing an uninvited guest, who, according to our solicitor, has an important announcement to make. He's requested that everyone converge in the ballroom."

"Very well," Tragmore agreed with a reluctant glance over his shoulder. "I'll be there directly." Closing the door, he waited until Gantry's footsteps had faded. Then, he whirled about. "We are not finished, Daphne. Your defiance will be dealt with—*severely* dealt with—when we arrive home. Until then, make yourself scarce." Eyes narrowed, he scrutinized the red welts on her cheek, which had already begun to swell. "The marks of my discipline are unfortunately quite visible this time. You will not embarrass me further. Go to your room. And remain there until tomorrow when we take our leave. I shall tell the countess you're not feeling well and are in bed." He reached for the door handle once more. "We'll resume your punishment at Tragmore."

The slam reverberated behind him.

Long moments passed before Daphne rose, drawing a few steadying breaths to compose herself. Fate had granted her a temporary reprieve, and she was profoundly grateful for it. The thought of staying in her assigned chamber, far away from her father's rage, was pure bliss. Oh, she'd bear the brunt of his beating once they returned home, but perhaps by then the edge would be off his anger, and her back would not be as badly whipped.

She'd face that ordeal when she had to. For now, all she wanted was the sanctuary of a quiet room, a soft bed, and her private thoughts.

Creeping into the hall, Daphne assured herself that it was empty. Evidently, all the guests had gathered in the ballroom for the grand announcement Lord Gantry had spoken of.

Weak with relief, Daphne was about to veer toward the guest quarters when she spied Mr. Hollingsby in the ball-room entranceway, leading a tall, starkly handsome man into the ballroom.

Pierce Thornton.

For an instant, Daphne was convinced her eyes deceived her. What on earth would Pierce Thornton be doing at the Earl of Gantry's ball? He who detested the nobility and all they represented. He couldn't be the bearer of the mysterious proclamation. 'Twas impossible.

But there was no mistaking that bold, assessing stare, that confident walk, those meltingly hard good looks.

It was most emphatically he.

Curiosity overshadowing pain, Daphne tiptoed down the deserted hallway, straining to hear the grand announcement Pierce was apparently about to make.

"Well, hello, Tragmore," Pierce's deep voice reached her ears. "I'm delighted to see you here tonight."

"Thornton!" Her father's muffled response sounded stunned—and frightened. *You're* Hollingsby's guest?"

"Indeed I am. For tonight only. After which, invitations can be forwarded directly to my estate."

"Your estate? What the hell are you talking about?"

"You're about to find out." Pierce's tone was mocking.

Daphne peeked around the corner and into the ballroom in time to see Pierce walk away from Hollingsby and her father, toward the crowd of questioning faces. "Mr. Hollingsby was kind enough to invite me here tonight so that I might share my extraordinary news with all of you at once."

A hum of speculation arose among the guests.

"As most of you know, the Duke of Markham passed on recently, alone and presumably without an heir." Pierce's arresting gaze swept the room. "I'm here tonight as the duke's sole living heir—the newly named Duke of Markham."

Stunned silence prevailed, hovering for a full minute before exploding into loud exclamations of astonishment and wonder.

"It's all quite true," Hollingsby interjected. "I myself

drew up the codicil to the late duke's will. Mr. Thornton—" he broke off, coughed discreetly, "His Grace—is Markham's sole surviving son."

Hundreds of people seemed to swarm around Pierce at once, but Daphne was aware of only two things: her own anguished surprise, and the look of sheer terror on her father's face.

The strings resumed playing, the guests broke into small, gossiping groups, and suddenly Daphne realized how vulnerable her position was. How long did she expect to remain undetected? Any moment someone was bound to stroll into the hallway and see her.

Reversing her steps, she slipped back toward the guest chambers.

For what purpose? To sleep?

That question brought her up short. After this latest shocking revelation, sleep would be an impossibility.

Acting on impulse, Daphne slipped into the morning room, then out the door leading to Gantry's fragrant gardens.

Here, she could be alone with her thoughts.

Pierce, the Duke of Markham.

She pressed her fingers to her temples, trying to sort it all out. What would this mean? How long had he known? Would this change him, his priorities? Why hadn't he told her at Tragmore? What did he want of her? Was the announcement of his title related to the mysterious hold he had over her father?

"Here you are. I thought I'd have to tear down the manor in order to find you."

Daphne whipped about to see Pierce leaning against a tree, watching her intently.

"I had no idea you were looking for me, Mr. Thornton—pardon me, Your Grace."

"So, you did hear my announcement. I thought I caught a glimpse of you in the hall." Slowly, Pierce strolled toward her.

"Yes. I heard." Daphne bowed her head and turned away.

"You must have many questions."

Silence.

"Ask them."

To Daphne's dismay, hot tears filled her eyes. "I—I don't know where to begin."

"You can begin by looking at me." Gently, Pierce turned her around, framing her face between his palms.

Daphne flinched.

"Daphne?" Questioningly, Pierce raised her chin with his thumb and took in her swollen cheek. Thunder erupted on his face. "That filthy son of a bitch. I'm going in there and kill him."

"Pierce—don't. Please." Daphne grabbed his arm. "I can't bear any more violence tonight. I just can't." Her defenses crumbling, she relented, letting the scalding tears course down her cheeks. "I can't bear any more."

"You don't have to." Instantly, Pierce enfolded her in his arms, pressing her wet face to his waistcoat. "I'm here, sweetheart. I'm right here. You don't have to endure it alone anymore."

Daphne melted into his strength, unable to refuse these few moments of comfort, the joy of feeling Pierce's arms around her. "How could you be a duke?" she wept.

Pierce kissed her hair. "That sounds more like an accusation than a celebration," he noted dryly.

"But you loathe the nobility."

"I do, don't I?"

Pulling back, Daphne stared up into his eyes. "Yes. You do. Still. Even now. Then why are you joining its ranks? And why did you lie to me about who you are?"

"I never lied to you. Everything I told you was true. I grew up in the streets. I *am* a bastard. Until the day before yesterday, I had no idea who my father was."

Daphne's damp eyes widened. "He didn't tell you himself?"

"No. Evidently, the late duke never felt the need to impart that tidbit of information to me. He let Hollingsby do it. In fact, my esteemed sire had no use for either my mother or me while he lived. But now that he's dead, he needs someone to accept his precious title, a title that would otherwise be extinct. Thus, his bastard must be validated."

"I told you never to refer to yourself that way." Daphne

lay her palm on Pierce's jaw, wanting somehow to ease his pain.

Pierce turned his lips into her hand. "I've missed you," he murmured. "And I still want to kill your father."

"You wanted to kill him long before you discovered he struck me. Why?"

"We have quite a history together, the marquis and I."

"Did he know you were Markham's son prior to tonight?"

"Judging from his pallor after I made my announcement, I would say no."

Daphne lightly stroked Pierce's mouth. "You're telling me the truth, aren't you?"

"What do you think?"

A small smile. "I think you're exceedingly good at stopping a lady's tears."

Pierce's expression grew tender, his eyes hauntingly vulnerable. "Daphne, I need to hold you, to reaffirm all I feel when you're in my arms."

"I need that, too," she whispered.

They acted at the same time, fitting together as perfectly as two interlocking pieces of a puzzle. Pierce's mouth closed over Daphne's with poignant desperation, seeking something too profound to express, offering something too long denied. This time Daphne didn't hesitate, but twined her arms about his neck, giving him all he needed, reaching for the wondrous blend of passion and comfort she found only with Pierce.

For long, exquisite moments they kissed, deep, hungry kisses that satisfied one craving, created another.

"Open your mouth to me," he commanded softly, threading his fingers through her hair. "Give me more of you."

Daphne complied at once, parting her lips, shivering as Pierce's tongue invaded her mouth, stroked hers with bone-melting possessiveness.

"Am I frightening you?" he murmured.

"No."

"Shall I stop?"

"No." Daphne shook her head, pressing closer, wishing she knew how to convey all she was feeling.

Pierce seemed to know.

He lifted her against him, kissing her until she was breathless, melding their tongues, their breath, the fire in their souls. Then, in a whisper of motion, he gentled the caress, lightly brushing his lips across the angry welts on her cheek, showing her without words that he shared her pain.

"Oh, Pierce." Daphne's eyes slid closed, emotion clogging her throat.

"Trust me, Daphne," he breathed into her hair. "Let the magic between us happen."

"I do trust you. Lord knows why. I don't know a thing about you. Nonetheless, I trust you."

His lips feathered across her forehead, the bridge of her nose. "You know many things."

"What do I know?" she countered. "Only of your questionable roots, which matter nothing, at least not to me. What I care about is the man you are today. Who are you, Pierce Thornton?"

"Other than a duke, you mean?"

"Don't mock me."

"Never." He gathered up handfuls of her tawny tresses. "Your hair glistens in the moonlight."

"And you're avoiding my question."

He chuckled. "So very astute. You, my beautiful Daphne, are a constant source of wonder."

"And you are a constant source of mystery. I've given you my trust. Can you not give me yours in return?"

Pierce's smile faded. "You have no idea how difficult it is for me to contemplate the idea of trust."

Slowly, Daphne nodded, seeing years of suffering reflected in Pierce's forest green eyes. "Yes, I believe I do." Unconsciously, she caressed his nape. "You say you grew up in the streets. How did you survive?"

"By my wits and my will to live." His arms tightened about her, as if he feared his answer might drive her away. "Are you certain you want to hear this?"

"I'm certain."

He held her gaze. "I grew up in a workhouse. I ran away when I was twelve, confident that even the gutter would be better than the hell from which I'd escaped. I was wrong. For two years I slept in deserted alleyways, picking pockets and

113

stealing fragments of food to eat. After that, I took to the road. I've wandered ever since."

A hollow ache pervaded Daphne's heart. "You must have been so frightened—and so very strong. Dear God, Pierce, what devastating obstacles you've overcome."

"Don't dub me a hero. I was a thief."

"You were a child," she replied softly. "A lonely, terrified boy. You stole only to live."

Pierce's jaw tightened, a private spark lighting his eyes. "I enjoyed every minute of pilfering noblemen's riches. I still do."

"What did you say?"

Instantly, Pierce stiffened, pausing for a heartbeat to search Daphne's face. "I'm a gambler," he resumed smoothly. "Which, in the opinion of many, is no better than a thief."

Daphne ingested his reply, carefully weighing her own. "I thought you made your fortune investing in profitable business ventures?"

"Is that not the definition of a gambler?"

Her lips curved. "I suppose it is."

"I've gambled since I could walk, and discovered almost as quickly that I was damned good at it."

"Was that the instinct you spoke of at Newmarket?"

"Precisely." Pierce steeled himself. "Have I frightened you off?"

"On the contrary. I'm awed by your self-assurance and your strength of character. I wish I possessed them."

Pierce's fingertips drifted up and down Daphne's waist. "I don't think you have any idea how precious you are."

She shivered. "I like when you show me."

"Ah, Daphne, if you only knew how much I want to show you," he murmured, capturing her mouth under his.

The kiss went on and on until, weak with reaction, Daphne pulled away.

"You're like fire," she confessed breathlessly when she was able to speak. "You seep into my blood, lure me close to the flames, but at the same time I'm terrified of being burned."

"I'll never burn you, love. You have my word."

"Pierce." She pressed her forehead to his shirt, wishing the security she felt could last forever. "This can't happen."

"It already has."

"Then it can't continue. There are too many obstacles."

"Damn the obstacles. They're all meaningless. All but one." He raised her chin, carefully avoiding her bruised cheek. "Do you want this to happen? Do you want it as much as I do?"

"You must know I do," she whispered.

"Then it *will* happen. I'll make it happen. All I needed were those words."

"But my father."

"I'll handle your father."

Daphne inclined her head. "Will you tell me what's between you?"

"Hatred."

"Why?"

A pause. "Daphne, you said you trusted me, did you not?"

She nodded.

"Then trust me to tell you when the time is right."

"Very well, Pierce. I'll try." Another pause as Daphne grappled with her questions. "There's a reason you want this title, isn't there?" she blurted out.

"Yes."

"Is that reason my father, or is it something more?"

Pierce frowned. "Both."

Again, Daphne studied his face. "Whatever you plan to do, it requires the late duke's money and influence, doesn't it?"

"Yes."

"And you're not going to tell me what that plan is, I presume?"

"Daphne, I've already told you far more than I've ever told another."

"Another woman?"

"Another person." Despite the magnitude of their exchange, Pierce shot her a wicked grin. "You're jealous. I like that."

Laughter erupted inside her. "And you're incorrigible."

Even as the retort left her lips, amazement registered on her face.

"Don't look so surprised," Pierce said softly, tracing the curve of her shoulder with gentle fingers. "There's a whole other Daphne inside you, one who's bold and daring and impulsive. I intend to coax that Daphne from her protective shell, to call forth her pride, her courage, but most of all, her smile."

Daphne's eyes grew damp. "How do you know me so well?" she whispered. "And after so brief a time?"

"The same way you know me. Here." Pierce pressed her palm to his shirtfront, let her feel the beating of his heart.

"I'd best go in," Daphne managed, wanting only to melt back into his arms. "My father thinks I'm in bed, where he'll expect me to stay until we leave for Tragmore the morning after next."

All the gentleness in Pierce's eyes vanished. "Why did that blackguard hit you tonight?"

She lowered her gaze.

"Daphne, tell me."

"Evidently he discovered I'd visited Mr. Chambers this week."

"He beat you because you visited the vicar?" Pierce asked in revulsion.

"Father detests the vicar, spurns all his beliefs," Daphne explained. Sighing, she added, "I, on the other hand, share them. I can't stop trying to help, to ease the pain of those who have nothing. Not even for Father." She shuddered. "Not even to avert his beatings."

"Surely your vicar must know of your father's brutality?"

"He does, only too well. But I won't let him interfere. It would endanger his position in the parish, and resolve nothing. By law, I am under my father's rule."

Pierce's lips thinned into a grim line. "Tell me, what does Mr. Chambers say when you arrive at his church with bruises such as these?" He cupped her chin between his palms.

Fondly, Daphne smiled. "He says, 'Don't come here any longer, Snowdrop. The Lord knows how much you care. But neither He nor I can bear to see you hurt.'"

"Snowdrop?"

"Yes. He's called me that since I was small. He thinks I'm as durable and tenacious as a snowdrop, despite my fragile veneer."

"Does he?" Pierce threaded his fingers through her hair, bent to kiss her cheeks, her lips, the sensitive pulse in her neck. "Well, your vicar is right. But only in part." Nibbling at her ear, Pierce murmured, "Snowdrop? Perhaps, but so much more. Snow flame. Now that's a better choice. Delicate and untouched as snow, burning with an inner fire only I can elicit. Yes. Snow flame. With all the spirit and determination of a snowdrop and all the passion, the multifaceted beauty of a flame." He sought her mouth. "My extraordinary snow flame."

"Pierce." She melted against him, an unfamiliar heat coursing through her in wide rivers of sensation.

"And you said *I* was fire," he breathed, burying his lips in hers.

This time it was he who ended the kiss, gasping as he fought for control.

"Did I do something wrong?" Daphne asked in a ragged whisper.

"Never. If you were any more right I'd lower you to the grass here and now and make love to you."

Daphne blushed.

"Do you find that notion upsetting?"

Her chin came up, her eyes wide with disbelief. "Do I find what notion upsetting?"

"The notion of my making love to you."

"Is it proper for you to ask me such questions?"

"No." Pierce's smile was devilish. "But I'd like an answer nonetheless."

Her own lips twitched. "Very well. No, I don't find the notion of your making love to me upsetting. In fact, although I'm not certain of all the nuances involved, I find the notion terribly appealing."

Something tender and profound flashed in Pierce's eyes. "So do I, my beautiful snow flame. So do I."

Muffled laughter drifted from the manor, and far away the strings struck up another waltz.

"It suddenly occurs to me," Pierce noted, his arms still around Daphne's waist, "that I have yet to enjoy my first dance as a duke."

"Oh." She shook her head, disoriented. "I suppose that's true."

"I'd hate to waste skills I so painstakingly learned once I became a law-abiding businessman. Wouldn't you agree?"

"I suppose so."

He pressed his lips to her forehead. "Then, may I have the honor?"

"Pierce, I can't return to the ball. My father ordered me—"

"Who said anything about the ball?" Pierce released her, stepping back to execute a formal bow. "I'd prefer my first dance to take place privately, with the glow of the moon above me, the fragrance of the garden surrounding me, and the feeling of you in my arms." He held out his hand. "May I have this dance, my lady?"

Her heart pounding wildly, Daphne sank into a curtsy. "I'd be delighted, Your Grace." She placed her fingers in his.

Had she ever danced before?

Daphne thought not.

Certainly she'd gone through the motions. But nothing could match the sheer wonder of floating about the garden with no impeding crowds, no harsh lights, nothing but pleasure and freedom—and Pierce.

"Are you happy, Daphne?" he asked, whirling her toward him.

Wordlessly, she nodded. "You're a splendid dancer, Your Grace," she managed, praying Pierce would understand the magnitude of what she couldn't put into words.

He did. "And you're a breathtaking partner, my lady." Coming to a halt, he pressed her palm to his lips.

"I wish we could stay here all night," she blurted.

"As do I. But I don't want the marquis to discover you're not abed. Then he'd be forced to lash out and I'd be forced to kill him."

"Pierce."

"Go, love. Before I forget I'm reputedly now a gentleman." His tone was mocking.

"Will you be all right?"

"I? You're the one who's been hurt."

"There are many different kinds of wounds," Daphne replied quietly. "Some are worn on the surface. Others are not."

"True." He didn't pretend to misunderstand. "And, to answer your question, yes, I'll be fine. I always am."

She stood on tiptoe and kissed him. "I'll pray for you."

Pierce's muscles tightened beneath her fingers. "What did you say?"

"Only that I'll pray for you."

"And if I were to tell you I don't believe in prayers?"

Daphne smiled, resting her hand over Pierce's heart. "Then I'd say, fortunately for you, I do."

9

"WELCOME, YOUR GRACE."

The uniformed gatekeeper bowed, then moved to swing Markham's iron gates wide, admitting the carriage of the new duke.

"Thank you," Pierce returned. Leveling his gaze straight ahead, he coolly assessed the hundreds of acres of land that now belonged to him.

"Impressive, wouldn't you say?" Hollingsby inquired, watching Pierce's unchanged expression.

"The land itself? Or the fact that I control it?"

"Both."

"Then my answer is yes and no. Yes, the land is impressive. Only a fool would remain unawed by its splendor. As for my controlling it, that I owe to an accident of fate. I neither earned it myself, nor came upon it through cleverness or cunning. Therefore, I feel little pride in the knowledge that it is mine."

Hollingsby shook his head in amazement. "You constantly astonish me, Thornton—er, Markham."

That declaration elicited the satisfied gleam Hollingsby had expected when Pierce first beheld his land. "Do I?" Pierce flashed him a broad grin. "Now *that* is a tribute to my skill. Rendering people off balance is a particular talent of mine, one of which I am quite proud." He leaned back in his seat. "As for your uncertain form of address, let me ease your quandary. I've been Pierce Thornton for thirty years. I intend to remain Pierce Thornton."

"Your family name is Ashford," Hollingsby protested.

"My father's name was Ashford. Mine is not. However, that is irrelevant for, if my paltry education serves me correctly, I can henceforth expect to be addressed as either Markham or Your Grace. Isn't that right?"

"It is."

"Then you call me Thornton. Or Pierce, my given name."

"But as you just pointed out—"

"Why not dare to be different?" Pierce cocked a challenging brow in Hollingsby's direction. "Or are you too steeped in the *ton*'s rules to risk it?"

"What does that mean?"

"I like you, Hollingsby. I think you're a decent, honorable man. I also think you're so dull it tires even you."

"Well, I—" The solicitor looked totally flabbergasted.

"Tell me the truth." Pierce leaned forward. "Don't you ever contemplate what it would feel like to break all those rigid rules within which you live? To do precisely what you want to do, say what you wish to say?"

"And lose the business of every noted gentleman in England."

"A few, perhaps. But most would stay. And do you know why? Because the highborn would be forced to give you something more than just their business, something that would ensure you their patronage for life."

"Which is?"

"Their respect."

An instant of silence, broken by Hollingsby's shout of laughter. "You're teaching me to be a gambler."

"No. I'm teaching you to be your own person." Pierce's lips twitched. "And to be a *good* gambler."

Growing sober, Hollingsby studied Pierce for a long, thoughtful moment. "I serve the wealthiest, most renowned noblemen of the *ton*," he mused aloud. "They pay me a great deal of money, rely heavily upon my legal skills, include me in their social gatherings. Yet, for the life of me, I cannot think of a single one of them I'd choose to call friend." He shook his head and grinned. "You are by far the most irreverent, unconventional rebel I have yet to meet, the utter antithesis of those whose company I customarily keep." His grin widened. "But, hell and damnation, I like you, Thornton. You might be just the fire needed to thaw a stuffy old man like me."

Fire? Pierce smiled. That was what Daphne had called him last night in the garden. Well, if he were the fire, she was the spark that ignited it.

"Thornton? Have I offended you?"

"Hmm? No, of course not." Pierce temporarily relinquished last night's memories. "If anything you've cheered me by proving I was right about you. Think of what we can teach each other: you can keep me on the proper ducal course and I can teach you to take risks, to venture from your narrow world on occasion."

"The manor is straight ahead," Hollingsby interrupted, pointing. "Have a look."

Quietly, Pierce scrutinized the imposing Gothic structure, thinking it was much as he'd expected it to be: palatial in size, devoid of warmth, a series of gray turrets and spires amid colorful, carefully manicured gardens.

"Magnificent, isn't it?"

"Actually, I prefer my own residence."

"Thornton, your lodgings in Wellingborough could fit into Markham's morning room."

"True. But the warmth and comfort of that modest abode is worth more than all of Markham's grandeur. Trust me, Hollingsby. To a man who's spent most of his life on the streets, home is a gift to be treasured."

Hollingsby cleared his throat awkwardly. "Forgive me. I didn't mean—"

"No forgiveness is necessary," Pierce assured him in a matter-of-fact tone. "I was merely pointing out that magnificence is a relative term."

"Agreed." Hollingsby adjusted his waistcoat as the carriage rounded the curved drive and stopped before the entranceway doors.

Barely had the horses come to a halt, when the manor doors were flung wide and a bevy of footmen scurried out to transport the duke's luggage to his new quarters. One tall, dignified man in uniform remained at rapt attention in the doorway, presumably awaiting his master's entrance.

"That is your butler, Langley," Hollingsby muttered as they alit. "He was with your father for thirty years."

"I see." Pierce nodded, strolling forward to meet the man of whom Hollingsby spoke.

"Your Grace." Langley bowed deeply. "Welcome to your new home. I shall be proud to serve you as I did your father."

"Thank you, Langley." Pierce extended his hand. "I shall rely heavily upon your knowledge of the estate and the staff as I learn my way about."

Langley stared at Pierce's hand in utter stupefaction.

"Go ahead. Grasp it. I'm told dukes's hands closely resemble those of mortals in both shape and texture."

"I couldn't, sir."

Pierce grinned. "Try."

Slowly, as if he were reaching into a blazing furnace, Langley extended his hand.

Pierce clasped it. "Excellent. You've just passed two very important tests of mine."

"Tests, sir?" Retracting his fingers, Langley mopped his forehead with a handkerchief.

"Yes. You've proven yourself to be both diligent and inventive. I will not work alongside a man who can't carry out his tasks, nor one who does so without imagination. I'm now confident you and I will get on famously."

"Thank you, Your Grace." The butler looked uncertain as to what he had done, but delighted to have done it. "Would you care to rest after your journey, or would you prefer to meet the staff now?"

Pierce almost laughed aloud. Journey? It was ten miles from Wellingborough to Northampton. He traveled ten times that distance the nights the bandit struck. "As luck would have it, I'm not at all fatigued. I'd enjoy meeting Markham's other residents."

"Very good, Your Grace." Langley bowed again, this time

with his hands firmly clasped behind his back. "I'll summon them at once."

"I think you can safely dismiss the idea of suggesting to Langley that he call you by your given name," Hollingsby noted dryly as the butler scurried off. "I don't think he'd be receptive."

"Evidently not." Pierce chuckled, wandering about the grand hallway, taking in the marble columns and priceless statues. "The trinkets in this room alone could feed a half dozen starving families for years."

"As I indicated, your father was an enormously wealthy man."

"So I see."

"The staff awaits you in the library, Your Grace," Langley announced.

Staff?

Pierce would more aptly describe the hundred-some-odd uniformed servants who stood, straight backed, against the library wall as an army.

"First, your valet, Bedrick."

"Welcome, Your Grace." The lean, square-jawed man bowed. "I look forward to serving you."

"Bedrick. A pleasure," Pierce acknowledged.

"Mrs. Gates, your housekeeper," Langley continued, designating the buxom, gray-haired woman who reigned over the unending row of female servants.

"Mrs. Gates."

"Your Grace." She dropped a curtsy.

Next came the coachmen and the head gardener, followed by an assembly of footmen, pages, grooms, gardeners, and gamekeepers, and a horde of housemaids, parlormaids, chambermaids, and scullery maids.

"What the hell did my father do with all these people?" Pierce whispered to Hollingsby in between nods and smiles. "He was alone, without even a wife, for God's sake."

"They represent status, Thornton." The solicitor waited to reply until Pierce had greeted and dismissed his sizable staff. "The number of servants one has speaks clearly of one's social and financial position."

"Markham was a bloody recluse!" Pierce exclaimed.

Veering about, he stared after the staff as they hastened back to their respective tasks. "Why would a man who'd committed himself to self-imposed exile give a damn about his social position?" Even as he spoke, Pierce held up a silencing hand, checking whatever Hollingsby was about to answer. "Don't bother. The unwritten rules of the nobility."

"If retaining so many servants troubles you, you could dismiss some of them," Hollingsby pointed out.

Pierce's expression turned fierce. "And toss them into the gutter? Force them to beg for work where none exists? See them perish in the streets? Never. Langley!" he called after the retreating butler.

"Your Grace?"

"I'd like a complete written list of my staff, including their names and duties. This past half hour has confused me so thoroughly that I can scarcely recall my own name, let alone scores of others. I realize what I'm asking is a cumbersome task, but perhaps if you and Mrs. Gates do it jointly, you can have it to me in several days."

"Of course, sir. Will there be anything else?"

"Not at the moment. Except perhaps some refreshment for my guest?" Pierce arched a quizzical brow in Hollingsby's direction.

"Nothing for me," the solicitor demurred. "I'd best be getting back to Gantry in time for supper. As it is, the earl will be incensed that I missed his hunt." Hollingsby's teeth gleamed. "But he'll recover. What I gained here today is far more important than anything I could acquire racing with a pack of hounds. I'm pleased you invited me to accompany you, Thornton."

Pierce's eyes twinkled. "I understand, and I thank you for your assistance. Now, Langley will arrange for my carriage to return you to the ongoing festivities."

"Only until dawn. 'Tis all the time I can spare away from my practice. After which, I'll return to London and be in touch."

"I look forward to it."

Left alone, Pierce gazed restlessly up and down the marble halls, wondering where one could find a warm and peaceful spot to think in this mausoleum.

ANDREA KANE

"Would *you* like some refreshment, Your Grace?" Langley reappeared to inquire.

"Actually, yes, Langley. I'd also like a comfortable place to enjoy it. Any suggestions?"

"The green room is quite pleasant, sir. It's rather small and tends to catch a good deal of afternoon sunlight. Would that be suitable?"

"It sounds ideal. I'll take my brandy in the green room." Pierce frowned. "How does one locate the green room?"

"Down the hall, sixth door on your right," Langley replied.

The green room, as it turned out, was the closest thing to a sitting room Pierce had seen at Markham thus far. Sinking into the tufted sofa, he leaned his head back, raising it only for an occasional sip of brandy.

He had much to do, and a relatively short time in which to do it.

Gantry's house party would continue for days, but according to Daphne, her father intended to pack up his family and take his leave tomorrow. It wasn't difficult to surmise what would happen next. Tragmore would return to his estate and beat Daphne senseless.

Pierce had known from the moment Daphne described her father's reasons for hitting her that Tragmore was far from finished. Pierce knew the man, had seen him in action for years. If the son of a bitch were angry enough to strike his daughter in the midst of a public event, to risk a scandal, he was more than furious. And there was no telling what he would do once he had Daphne in the prison of their home.

Damn it! Pierce struck a velvet pillow with his fist. How could he prevent Tragmore's brutality without further endangering Daphne? If he stepped forward and openly confronted the marquis, the scoundrel would viciously retaliate —not against Pierce, who dwarfed him in both size and power, but against Daphne. And, as Daphne had pointed out, the law was on her father's side. The only way she'd be free of the marquis's cruelty was to leave Tragmore.

And the only way to leave Tragmore was to marry.

Maybe he ought to have proposed the night before, when

she was warm and soft in his arms, when her defenses were down, her body awakening. Maybe he'd made a mistake to wait.

But it was too soon. She'd only just learned to trust him, to begin relinquishing her long-sustained inhibitions. If he frightened her off now, he might not have another opportunity to regain her faith. And he was far too good a gambler to take so stupid a risk.

There was one thing more.

Pierce was arrogant enough to want Daphne to wed him out of desire, not escape.

He had to woo her slowly, tenderly. Yet there was no time for either, for there was no deferring Tragmore's aggression. Further, the marquis would never willingly tolerate Pierce as a suitor for Daphne's hand. He could be coerced, of course. Lord knew, Pierce had enough ammunition to do that. But that would eliminate Daphne's freedom of choice, something Pierce refused to do.

So how could he protect her? What ruse could he use?

Tragmore's first payment.

Sitting bolt upright, Pierce seized the notion, wondering why he hadn't thought of it earlier. He'd informed Tragmore he'd return at week's end to demand a portion of the money he was owed. Very well, return he would. Tomorrow. And somehow, during that visit, he would accomplish the impossible. He would see Daphne alone, push her gently but inexorably toward the altar, and divert Tragmore enough, without compromising Daphne's dignity, to buy himself time and, in the process, to keep Daphne safe.

How he was going to do this he had no idea.

By morning, he would.

"The Duke of Markham to see you, sir."

Tragmore scowled at his butler. "The Duke of—" Sharply, he inhaled. "Send him in to my study."

"Very good, my lord."

Pierce stalked into the study and stopped, carefully scrutinizing the marquis. From the looks of things, he'd come in time. Tragmore's expression was moody, not belligerent; pale, not ruddy, which assured Pierce that the bastard had not undergone a recent physical confrontation. That, combined with the fact that luggage was still being unloaded from the marquis's carriage and carried through the manor, was enough to put Pierce's mind at ease. Since returning from Gantry, Tragmore hadn't had the opportunity to abuse his daughter.

"I've scarcely entered my home, Thornton. What do you want?" Tragmore snapped.

"I believe the proper form of address is Your Grace."

Daggers flashed in Tragmore's eyes. "Markham is bad enough. Don't expect anything more."

"I take it you're not pleased with my announcement," Pierce noted, propping himself irreverently on the edge of Tragmore's desk. "Given the circumstances, I don't blame you."

"I knew your father. Well. How he could have—" The marquis bit off his own words.

"How he could have what? Bestowed his title, name, and fortune on me? I really don't think he had a choice."

"He could have let his title die."

Pierce smiled bitterly. "Rather than entrust it to a worthless street urchin."

"Precisely."

"You're quite outspoken for a man who has everything to lose."

Tragmore's eyes narrowed. "Haven't you acquired enough money? Markham was one of the wealthiest men in England. Surely you don't need my meager holdings as well."

"Ah, so you're hoping I'll abandon my plan to own you?" Pierce's fist sliced through the air, striking the desk with an impact so savage Tragmore flinched. "Think again, you son of a bitch. If anything, I'm more determined than ever to collect. In fact, that's why I'm here today. The first payment on your notes is due." Slowly, Pierce held out his palm. "Now."

"You know damned well I don't have it."

"Don't you? How unfortunate."

"What are you going to do?" The hatred in Tragmore's

eyes was eclipsed by fear. "Ruin me? Publicly declare me bankrupt?"

"That sounds splendid, but premature. I have yet to finish toying with you." Pierce averted his head, openly surveying the room. "I'm sure, given a proper tour of your home, I can find one bauble or another to satisfy this week's payment." Coming to his feet, Pierce strolled about, lifting an occasional statue, running his fingers appraisingly along the carved trim of the walnut furniture.

"Thorn—Markham, you can't be serious! Surely you wouldn't—"

A knock sounded at the door.

"Who is it?" Tragmore snapped.

"Forgive me, my lord," replied his butler, holding out a sealed missive. "But this message just arrived. It's marked urgent."

"Fine. Give it to me." Tragmore snatched the letter, tore it open and scanned its contents. Scowling, he stuffed the note into his pocket. "I have to go to London at once."

"A problem?" Pierce inquired smoothly.

"None that concerns you."

"Perhaps I should be the judge of that."

"You hold my assets," Tragmore hissed. "That does not entitle you to invade my privacy. My missives are for my eyes and my eyes only."

"I could argue that point, but it's not worth the effort. Should the matter involve your finances, I shall learn about it directly." Coldly, Pierce regarded his adversary. "I hope for your sake this is not merely an attempt to avoid settling your debt. Because, if it is, rest assured it will prove unsuccessful. I shall return to collect my payment the morning after next. Doubtless you'll have returned from London by then. And I'll be waiting. Do I make myself clear, Tragmore?"

The marquis turned three shades of red before storming by Pierce. "Show the duke out," he paused to fire at his butler.

"Yes, sir."

"I can show myself out." Calmly, Pierce crossed the room and sidestepped the incensed marquis. "Good day,

Tragmore," he continued, never breaking stride. "Have coffee prepared by sunrise. I detest beginning my day without it."

Hearing the muffled expletives echoing in his wake, Pierce had all he could do to keep from laughing aloud. His plan was working perfectly.

Outside the manor, Pierce climbed into his phaeton and swiftly departed, steering his horses around the drive and through the gates until they'd reached the main road. Abruptly, he urged them to the roadside, maneuvering the phaeton until it was totally concealed by the row of trees he had carefully chosen before entering Tragmore's grounds. There he waited.

Not five minutes later, the marquis's carriage rounded the bend, swept by, and disappeared.

Pierce waited a quarter hour to be certain. Then he swerved his phaeton about, and headed back toward the manor.

Grinning, he recalled the dire contents of the note. Wouldn't the marquis be surprised to learn that the urgency it conveyed was greatly exaggerated? In fact, not only did Hollingsby not truly require Tragmore's immediate presence, the solicitor had no notion the marquis was en route to London.

He would shortly, of course. Pierce's other missive would arrive at Hollingsby's office simultaneously with Hollingsby himself, putting an unaccustomed burden on the solicitor and giving him the first real challenge he'd ever known.

At the same time, giving Pierce time alone with Daphne.

Just outside Tragmore's gates, Pierce abandoned his phaeton, taking the remaining distance by foot. His reasons were twofold: he was determined to remain undetected by any of Tragmore's residents, and he instinctively knew that the place in which he was most likely to find Daphne was far more accessible by foot than by vehicle.

The woods.

Treading lightly, Pierce made his way among the thick brush, keeping his head up, his ears tuned to any noise that might reveal Daphne's presence.

She was easier to find than he'd expected.

The soft inflection of her voice drifted to him in brief, indistinguishable phrases. She was talking to someone, he mused, although thus far there had been no reply.

He soon found out why.

"Russet, what is it? What do you see?"

A flash of copper and a rustle of fabric accompanied Daphne's questions, and Pierce emerged from the trees to see a bushy tail disappear from view and Daphne struggling to her feet.

"I'm afraid I'm the cause of your friend's flight," he chuckled.

"Pierce!"

Breathless, with a smudge of dirt on her nose and tawny hair tousled about her shoulders, Daphne looked as innocent as a child and as captivating as a wood nymph.

And delectably happy to see him.

"I startled you. Forgive me." Pierce drew nearer, halting only when he could gaze into those mesmerizing hazel eyes. "And forgive me for frightening off your friend."

Daphne glanced back over her shoulder at the now-deserted foxhole entry. "Russet is wary of all people, since most have treated him with abysmal cruelty."

"I caught a glimpse of orange. Russet, I presume, is a fox?"

She nodded. "And a very loyal friend."

"I see." Pierce's fingers brushed lightly over the fading welts on Daphne's cheek. "And, when I arrived, what were you confiding in your very loyal friend? Were you telling him of the ugly bout with your father? Or were you speaking of the ball's more exhilarating encounter?"

Pierce could actually feel the tiny shiver his words elicited.

"Both." She wet her lips with the tip of her tongue. "Pierce, if my father finds you here—"

"He's gone."

Her eyes widened. "Gone? Gone where?"

A cocky grin. "Let's just say I'm extremely resourceful when I choose to be."

"You summoned him from Tragmore?"

"I lured him."

"Is there a difference?"

"A vast one. If I'd summoned him, I'd have to receive him. Since I lured him, I used bait other than myself, and as a result can remain detached and anonymous. Consequently, he's on his way to London and I'm here."

"But—"

"I needed to be alone with you," Pierce murmured, threading his fingers through Daphne's hair. "Moreover, I had no intention of allowing the blackguard time to finish the beating he began at Gantry. I am in time, aren't I?"

Quietly, Daphne nodded, ingesting Pierce's words. "So you came here to rescue me?"

"You sound surprised."

"No, not surprised. It's only that I hadn't expected to see you again so soon after—" She blushed.

"So soon?" Pierce shook his head in amazement. "Since those moments in the garden, I've thought of nothing but the feel of you in my arms. Had I not gone home that same night, I would have sought you out at dawn. As it was, I left immediately after the ball. I had to arrange for my move to Markham."

"You've moved already?"

"Yesterday."

"Are you settled in then?"

Pierce frowned, absently rubbing a sunlit tress. "My belongings have been transferred. Settled in? I don't think I'll ever be that." He blinked, startled by the natural candor of his own response.

Evidently, Daphne wasn't. "You're wrong, Pierce. Just give yourself time. And remember, there are all varieties of dukes. You will merely enhance that number by one."

Acting on gut emotion, Pierce pulled Daphne into his arms. "Must I ask permission?"

"No," she whispered, twining her arms about his neck. "You know what my answer would be."

This time the magic was abrupt, shattering, exploding the instant it began. Pierce took Daphne's mouth fiercely, kissing her with bone-melting thoroughness and heart-rending need. His tongue swept inside to mate with hers, his hands trembled as they dragged her closer, fitted her more totally against him.

Daphne's response nearly brought him to his knees. As urgent as he, she met his tongue, stroke for stroke, leaning into him until he could feel the very pounding of her heart.

"Daphne."

Whose raw, aching voice was that? Pierce wondered dazedly. Who was this unknown stranger whose control was as diaphanous as the finest silk?

Evidently it was he.

As if from afar, Pierce watched himself ease Daphne to the grass. Never breaking the kiss, he lay on his side, clasping her to him with all the desperation of a drowning man seeking shelter. With a will of their own, his fingers unfastened the tiny row of buttons down the back of her gown, tugging at the sleeves until he'd bared the upper slope of her breasts.

Tearing his mouth from hers, Pierce kissed her neck, her throat, moving slowly down to the warm skin he'd exposed. He felt Daphne shiver, heard the small, inarticulate sound of pleasure she made as his lips caressed her.

"Do you like that?" he rasped.

"Yes. Oh, yes." Daphne's arms slid up to cradle his head, her breath breaking as he kissed the hollow between her breasts.

"Tell me you want more." His fingertips grazed her nipples, felt them tighten beneath the confines of her gown and chemise.

"Pierce." Her reverently whispered word was all the reply he needed.

In one sharp tug, her bodice and chemise slid lower, freeing her breasts to his greedy gaze.

"Christ, you're beautiful." Pierce was shuddering so violently he could scarcely speak. Moreover, there were no words vivid enough to describe what he was feeling. He had to show her.

Arching Daphne closer, Pierce captured her nipple between his lips, surrounding it in liquid heat. She cried out, and he deepened the contact, alternately tugging the hardened peak, then soothing it with gentle sweeps of his tongue.

"Pierce. Stop," she gasped, shaking her head from side to side.

Instantly, Pierce raised his head, met Daphne's smoky gaze. "Am I hurting you?"

"No."

"Frightening you?"

"No."

A muscle worked in his jaw as he combatted desire, attempted comprehension. "Tell me it's not shame. Tell me you know how right this is between us."

"What?" Daphne's eyes were heavy lidded with passion.

"Is this a matter of honor? Of virtue?"

With a breathy sigh, she sifted her fingers through his hair. "Neither. It's a matter of torment."

Now it was Pierce's turn to look baffled. "Torment?"

"When you—" she blushed, "caressed me like that, it was unbearable. Not painful, just unbearable." She inclined her head in quizzical apology. "What I really wanted was to beg you to stop—and, at the same time, never to stop. Does that make any sense?"

Pierce wanted her so much at that moment he thought he'd die. Closing his eyes, he fought for the iron control that disintegrated more with each heartbeat.

"Please," she murmured, "don't be angry. I've just never—"

The rest of Daphne's apology was swallowed by Pierce's kiss. Fervently, he devoured her, his mouth ravaging hers, his hands molding her breasts in shuddering, relentless possession.

"Do you have any idea what you do to me?" he demanded, rolling her to her back. "Do you, my innocent snow flame?"

"I know what you do to me," she answered with that artless naiveté that tore at his heart. "Is it the same?"

Pierce stared down at her, taking in the soft flush of her cheeks, the perfect contour of her naked breasts bared for his eyes alone. "Somewhat," he managed, tangling his fingers in her disheveled tawny mane. "Only I know where this can lead. You don't."

Her smile was wise and thoroughly female. "I know exactly where this can lead."

Despite the painful throbbing in his loins, Pierce had to grin at the conviction of her tone. "Really? Where?"

"That depends on who you ask. Mama would say 'to a woman's performance of her duty in the marriage bed.' Given the circumstances, the vicar would say 'to sin.'"

Pierce chuckled. "And what would you say?"

The trust in Daphne's eyes was the most potent aphrodisiac Pierce had ever known. "With you? To heaven."

Sucking in his breath, Pierce went rigid, fighting to calm the screaming urgency of his need. "Keep talking like that, looking at me like that, and we'll experience heaven far sooner than I'd planned."

"What's just happened is already a miracle to me," Daphne said, her tone laced with wonder. "It's the first time I've been touched with gentleness and joy, rather than with brutality."

"Marry me, Daphne."

The words were out before Pierce realized he'd uttered them, yet he wouldn't have called them back if he could.

"What did you say?" Her eyes were as wide as saucers.

"I asked you to marry me." Tenderly, he eased her bodice back into place, stating without words that his proposal was not spawned by the ardor of the past few moments.

"Marry you," she repeated softly, tasting each word as she voiced it. Myriad emotions flashed across her face in rapid succession: surprise, quizzical uncertainty, veiled speculation, a touch of confusion, a flicker of hope. "Why?" she whispered at last.

"Many reasons."

"But are they the right ones?" Daphne struggled to sit up, simultaneously brushing leaves from her hair. "We've know each other less than a fortnight."

"We've *known* each other from the instant we met," Pierce countered. "As for the rightness of my reasons, is it right that I want to keep you safe? To see you smile? To give you things you can never have at Tragmore, wrench you from things you can otherwise never escape?"

"And what will I give you in return?"

Pierce leaned forward, reaching around to fasten her buttons. "You," he said huskily, brushing her lips with his. "Your magnificent spirit, which I have yet to free."

Daphne's breath broke on a shiver. "Only my spirit?"

His fingers paused, feathered over her bare shoulder. "No. Not only your spirit. All of you. Your fire, your innocence, your passion."

A soft moan escaped Daphne's lips. "I shouldn't have asked."

"Why not?"

"Because I can't think clearly when you say such things."

"You don't have to think. You have only to say yes."

"Pierce, my father—"

"Damn your father."

She stiffened. "Will that be hastened by my marrying you?"

"Will what be hastened?"

"Damning my father." She drew back, her gaze delving deep into Pierce's. "Does your sudden urge to make me your wife factor into whatever plans you have for him?"

A muscle flexed in Pierce's jaw. "The urge isn't sudden. I've been combatting it for days. I want you, Daphne. By my side. In my life. In my bed."

"That's not an answer."

"Then perhaps this is. Your father's damning is a fait accompli whether or not we wed. So, no, my proposal is not linked to his downfall. It is, however, partially spawned by my firsthand knowledge of his cruelty, which makes me eager to wrest you from his contemptible presence. The marquis and I go back many years, more years than even he recalls." Pierce drew a harsh breath, instantly realizing he'd revealed more than he intended. "I'd prefer you didn't jog his memory by mentioning our early acquaintanceship. I'll tell him myself, when I'm ready." Pausing, Pierce waited, half expecting Daphne to refuse his unsubstantiated request, and unable to blame her if she did. He was asking her to betray her father with silence, while giving her no justification for doing so.

He was prepared for any reaction other than the one he got.

"Thank you," Daphne murmured, caressing the taut line of his jaw. That simple phrase, together with the consummate faith shining in her eyes, humbled Pierce as nothing else could. And her next words shattered his reserve into fragments of nothingness. "You've just offered me the most wondrous gift: the first sign of your trust. I don't pretend to understand the basis for your request. But in my heart I know your motives are sound. You have my word, Pierce. I'll guard your secret. When Father hears the truth, whatever that may be, he shall hear it entirely from you."

With a low groan, Pierce tugged Daphne to his chest, threading his fingers through her hair. "Be patient with me, Snow flame," he said in a raw tone. "It's not only trusting I find difficult. It's more. My past. There are portions of it I buried long ago, portions too painful to discuss."

Daphne rubbed her cheek against his waistcoat. "I know how difficult it is to share pain," she whispered. "Especially pain that's been submerged in your soul for years. You'll tell me when you're ready. I can wait."

Too moved to speak, Pierce lightly caressed Daphne's nape, focusing his attention on the refastening of her top two buttons. "It is I who thank you," he said simply, when he'd regained a measure of self-control. "For now, just understand that I need to take you away from Tragmore, out of that bastard's house, away from his brutality."

"You mentioned before that you'd summoned—" Daphne broke off, correcting herself with a conspiratorial grin, *"lured* Father to London?"

"Indeed I did. He'll be there for two days."

That made Daphne's chin come up, and she stared at Pierce with those exquisite hazel eyes. "Two days! How on earth did you manage that? Father loathes racing from one excursion to the next, and we only returned from Gantry an hour ago."

Chuckling, Pierce kissed the inquisitive pucker between her brows. "I told you, I'm resourceful. I merely asked an associate to summon the marquis on a matter of great financial urgency."

"Would that matter be the insurance money on our stolen jewelry?"

"Excellent," Pierce commended with a twinkle. "Your intuition constantly astounds me."

"Coming from so cunning a strategist, I'll consider that the most splendid of compliments," Daphne teased, her cheeks flushed with pleasure.

Pierce wondered if she had any idea how beautiful the real Daphne was.

"Pierce?" Lost in a new thought, Daphne caught her lower lip between her teeth. "How much money will Father recover?"

"That depends upon the value of what was taken."

"I see. Was my pearl necklace worth a great deal?"

A practiced warning chord sounded in Pierce's head, a self-developed signal he'd perfected over the years, triggered whenever the topic commanded he protect his secret life.

And, despite the fact that Daphne was anything but the enemy, Pierce mentally segregated his one-time glimpse of her pearls from the more extensive examinations made by the Tin Cup Bandit. "Your pearl necklace?"

"Yes, you remember, the one you admired at Newmarket. Was it valuable?"

Without realizing it, she'd provided him with the perfect course of evasion.

He seized it. "Did I? I don't recall. I was too busy looking at you."

Daphne quirked a brow. "You said it was my necklace you were admiring."

"I lied."

Her spontaneous burst of laughter obliterated Pierce's tension, brought his mind back to the subject at hand—making Daphne his bride.

"Have I gifted my trust to a scoundrel then?" Daphne's eyes danced with amusement.

"I fear you have, my lady." Tenderly, Pierce stroked loose strands of hair from her forehead. "But bear in mind that this scoundrel has honorable intentions."

"I shan't forget." She was suddenly utterly solemn.

"Take these two days," Pierce murmured huskily, nudging her lips apart and circling them with his own. "Your father is away, so you're safe. Stroll through the village, visit your vicar, do whatever makes you happy. But at night, alone in your bed, think of me, of us, of what happens when we're together. Think of all I can give you, all we can give each other. Think of the real Daphne, the one who shows herself only to me. Think of what happens when she's in my arms, when she lets the fire inside her rage free. Think of exploring every exhilarating nuance of passion life has to offer—and I don't mean only those we'll experience in bed. Although, God knows, I can't wait much longer to have you under me. Ponder all that, my breathtaking snow flame. Then say you'll be my wife." Pierce kissed her deeply, hungrily, with all the possessiveness of a man who knew the woman he held belonged to him. "I'll be back in two days for your answer. *Then* I shall deal with your father."

10

DAPHNE DOUBTED SHE'D EVER SLEEP AGAIN.

Rolling onto her back, she stared at the thin stream of light filtering through her bedroom window, wondering whether it was daylight's first rays or moonlight's final vestiges she was witnessing. She prayed for the former, as it seemed an eternity since she'd extinguished her candle and begun her unsuccessful attempt at slumber.

Tonight's sleeplessness was totally unexpected, though not inexplicable.

Normally her fitful nights were rooted in the relentless dread that any moment her father would burst in, and begin another painful session of "teaching Daphne compliance."

But there was no threat of a beating tonight. Her father was away from Tragmore, which customarily assured Daphne of a tranquil and undisturbed rest.

Neither of which was forthcoming.

In fact, rather than reveling in her temporary reprieve, Daphne's emotions were encased in turmoil.

Pierce.

He dominated her so thoroughly it was overwhelming. Her mind was consumed with the mystery of his secrets, her heart was haunted by the torment of his pain, her spirit clamored for the freedom he'd promised.

And her body burned for something only he could provide.

How could one man have such extraordinary control over her?

Contemplating the particular man involved, Daphne dismissed the question.

Her next question, however, was not so easy to dismiss.

Why did Pierce want to marry her?

Not some of his reasons, but all.

Oh, she didn't doubt that what he'd told her had been the truth, or, to be more precise, a part thereof. He did want to protect her, did, somehow, know her father well enough to deduce his propensity for violence. And yes, there was that emotional pull between them, one that had been there from the start. Not to mention the physical pull. Daphne had never dreamt that one man could make her feel thus, as if everything inside her were pooling into a white-hot liquid knot of need.

But there was more. She knew it, just as surely as she knew there were dark caches of Pierce's past that would test her, again and again, until he could put them to rest.

What had motivated the timing of his proposal? He was too practiced in self-control to blurt out such a life-altering question without forethought, too hardened by life to allow sympathy and desire to propel him.

He was enacting some plan, a plan that would destroy not only her father but, based upon Pierce's hatred for the *ton,* countless other noblemen as well.

He was a nobleman himself now, a duke. That provided him with assets until now unheld, assets and obligations. Did the acquisition of a title impel him to seek a wife?

No. Not Pierce. He was too irreverent. He wouldn't give a damn what was proper. Duke or not, if he chose to remain unmarried—why, if he chose to transport a half dozen courtesans to Markham to pleasure him on the front lawn for all to see—he would.

Then what piece of the puzzle was missing?

Daphne glanced at the clock on her mantle. Six A.M. That did it.

She flung back the covers and climbed out of bed. Unlike her father, Pierce was continually urging her to be herself, to be an active participant, not a victim. Very well. It was time she sought answers, not the ones Pierce was yet unwilling to supply, but those that were within her grasp, those that would determine her future. She would go to the one person who'd never failed to help her, who, in his infinite wisdom, had comforted and guided her all her life.

Slices of morning sunlight illuminated the church when Daphne entered its modest walls. "Vicar? Are you here?"

"Good morning, Snowdrop. What a delightful surprise." Chambers came to greet her, hands extended.

His smile vanished the moment he saw the fading welts on her cheek. "Why has Harwick struck you?"

"It doesn't matter."

"It most certainly does!" Instinctively, the vicar gripped her shoulders, as if to steady her with his support. "Are you all right? Are you suffering any ill effects from Harwick's assault?"

Daphne shook her head. "None. Truly. The reason for my visit has nothing to do with Father. In fact, he's in London until tomorrow, so I'm free to spend as much time with you as I like. I tried to collect Russet so he might join us in a jaunt to the school, but he wanted no part of me once he realized my plans involved abandoning the woods. Perhaps tomorrow I'll try again. I so want to return to the children. I promised them another visit, this time with my fox cub. I'm hoping Mother will receive a delivery while Father is away, so I can bring the boots and woolen shawls at the same time, and—"

"Daphne," the vicar interrupted quietly. "Why did your father strike you? Is it because of your visits to the church? Did he learn of them and retaliate?"

A pause.

Then, "Yes."

Chambers inhaled sharply. "I want you to go home. Now."

"Didn't you hear what I said?" Daphne asked, clutching his arms. "Father is away until tomorrow."

"But not all his associates are with him. If one of Harwick's colleagues should see you here, he will doubtless report back to your father. I shudder to think how Harwick will react to your committing *another* offense, especially in light of this recent beating."

"I've withstood Father's wrath for twenty years," Daphne replied. Touching her fingers to her cheek, she wondered for the umpteenth time how the vicar would react if he knew the true extent of her father's brutality, the lashing wounds he purposely confined to places none could see. "I'll continue to withstand what I must. I cannot stop seeing my friends, or helping those in need." A soft smile touched her lips. "Then again, this whole discussion might be unnecessary."

"Unnecessary? Why?"

"That's the reason for my visit. I have something very important to share with you. In truth, I've wanted to tell you since it first began. Please. I know you're busy, but may we talk for a few moments?"

"You have my ear for as long as you need it. You know that, Snowdrop." Chambers gestured for Daphne to sit.

"Thank you." Daphne lowered herself to the pew, turning brilliant eyes toward the vicar. "I don't know where to begin. So much has happened. So much has changed. *I've* changed."

He studied her intently. "Does this involve the gentleman we discussed last week? Pierce Thornton?"

She started. "Yes. How did you know?"

"One needn't be a prophet to discern human emotion," the vicar chuckled. "Your eyes glowed when you spoke of Mr. Thornton and your day at Newmarket. They're glowing the same way now." He sat beside her, took her hand between both of his. "Do you care for him, child?"

"Oh, yes," Daphne breathed. "I care for him. He's kind and gentle and—" She broke off, blushing.

"I think I understand." The vicar cleared his throat. "Tell me, Daphne, what is your father's reaction? I recall your mentioning there was some discomfort between Mr. Thornton and the marquis."

"They despise each other."

"Then . . . ?"

"Father has no notion I've been seeing Pierce. If he did, he'd kill me. Especially now." She took a deep breath. "Vicar, Pierce attended the Gantry ball three nights past. He had a rather extraordinary announcement to make. He's just discovered he's now the Duke of Markham."

Chambers blinked. "Goodness! That's quite a discovery."

"Evidently, the late duke was Pierce's father."

"And he never contacted his son to tell him so?"

Daphne hesitated. "No. Pierce was illegitimate. He grew up in a workhouse, then made his own way in the world."

"He sounds like a remarkable man. But I'm a bit confused, Snowdrop. If your Pierce has now ascertained he's a member of the peerage, your father's objections should be silenced."

"Not in this case. Do you recall my mentioning my belief that Pierce has some kind of hold over Father?" She waited for the vicar's nod, cautioning herself not to reveal too much. She'd promised Pierce not to divulge the far-reaching history he had with her father, and she would honor that pledge. "Well, apparently, Pierce's exalted position has increased Father's fear, and thereby his enmity, immeasurably. I saw the hatred and dread on his face when he heard Pierce's announcement."

"Daphne," the vicar said with a frown, "if what you suspect is true, is it possible the duke's interest in you is somehow linked to the cause of your Father's hostility?"

"No," she returned with an adamant shake of her head. "Although I must admit I asked Pierce that question directly. But I needn't have. I already knew my answer. What's between us is very real, an entity unto itself."

Gently, the vicar lifted Daphne's chin. "Are you falling in love with him, child?"

Daphne's answer struck her in a joyous flash of insight. "I don't think Pierce would have it any other way." She smiled, dazed and jubilant all at once. "Yes, Vicar, I'm falling in love with him."

"And he?"

"He's asked me to marry him."

"Marriage!" Chambers came to his feet in a rush. "Isn't that a rather drastic step? After all, you've known this man a very short time."

"I know he cares for me, and he wants to take me away from Tragmore—from Father," Daphne explained carefully, wishing she could blurt out everything, equally determined not to. She would protect Pierce as she had vowed, to him, and to herself. "That's what I meant when I said your concern was unnecessary. If Pierce has his way, I'll be safe—with him."

"I see." The vicar gazed thoughtfully down at her. "Is your decision made then?"

Silence.

"Snowdrop." He drew her to her feet. "If you're certain of your feelings, and the duke's, then what is distressing you? Are you worried about Harwick's censure?"

Tears filled Daphne's eyes. "No. God forgive me, but I don't care what Father thinks of Pierce. I don't even care if he condemns the marriage and me. Lord knows it wouldn't be the first time. No, Vicar, it's something else, something that's rather difficult to explain."

"Try."

She nodded, dashing the tears from her cheeks. "Pierce's life is a complex lock that has been secured for thirty years. My heart tells me I must be patient, for Pierce alone possesses the lock's key, a key he will hand me when he's ready, and not before. I understand that, and I accept it. You would, too, if you knew him. He has the most astonishing degree of discipline and self-control I've ever seen. I feel it every time we're together. It's as if he gives himself up in small, measured doses, while at the same time rendering me completely helpless and emotionally exposed."

"To me, it sounds as if he's erected walls to avoid being hurt. Given his painful childhood, that's not surprising."

"No. It isn't. But tell me, Vicar, what am I to think when, out of nowhere, this rigidly disciplined and controlled man blurts out something as significant as a marriage proposal?"

145

Daphne shook her head. "The contradiction is staggering. *Too* staggering."

"I understand your bafflement," Chambers concurred. "My next question is, did you express your concern to the duke?"

Again, Daphne nodded. "He insists the proposal was not impulsive, but long thought out."

"And you don't believe him?"

"No. Yes. Somewhat." Daphne made a choked sound. "I do believe he wishes to wed me. I just have the nagging feeling there's more to his reasoning than he's admitted." Pleadingly, she searched the vicar's face. "Help me. You always do."

Her friend's smile was tinged with regret. "Your belief in me far exceeds my abilities, Snowdrop. There are some answers we must seek within ourselves."

"But I can't."

"Can't you? Look inside your heart, Daphne. Haven't you already found what you're seeking?"

Her lips trembled as she absorbed the clergyman's words. "Yes," she whispered at last.

"Good." He removed his spectacles, rubbing his eyes to dislodge whatever unseen particles were causing them to tear. "It appears your future has been chosen by the one whose rightful job it is to do so. You." He shoved the spectacles back into place. "However, I do request the opportunity to meet this lucky gentleman on whom you've bestowed your heart."

"Oh, would you?" Daphne's whole face lit up. "Your blessing would mean so much to me." Impulsively, she hugged him. "Thank you, Vicar. Pierce will be returning to Tragmore tomorrow for my answer. I'll arrange a meeting then."

"Does the duke realize how badly Harwick is going to take the news of your betrothal? How violent your father can get?"

"Yes, I believe he does."

The vicar inclined his head quizzically. "You never did specify the basis for their hatred. How did your father's and the duke's paths first cross?"

"Pierce refuses to discuss it," Daphne replied candidly, grateful that the vicar had asked *how* and not *when*. "So I'm not certain precisely what is between them. But I suspect it involves Father's monetary assets."

"What makes you think that?"

"Because there is little ammunition one could use against my father. He fears nothing save financial and social embarrassment. And I do have cause to believe he is worried over a lack of funds."

Her friend's brows rose. "Harwick? In financial difficulty?"

Daphne nodded. "Evidently, that's the reason he raced off to London directly after returning from Gantry. He wanted to secure the insurance money on our stolen jewels as quickly as possible."

"Possessions mean a great deal to your father, Snowdrop. Just because he wants to regain what he considers rightfully his doesn't mean he's in a precarious monetary position."

"True. And that act alone wouldn't give me pause. But his behavior on our journey to Gantry was most unusual. Rather than being tyrannical, he was nervous and distracted, muttering that I should marry a wealthy nobleman who could remove the noose that is hanging about his neck."

"And you think your duke might be that noose?"

"Or involved in whatever has created that noose. Yes, I believe it's possible. But that's only speculation on my part. I've pressed Pierce but, thus far, he has evaded the subject entirely."

"Hmm. Well, I must say, I'm looking forward to meeting this enigmatic champion of yours."

The vicar's particular choice of words made Daphne smile. "Yes, Vicar, I, too, look forward to your meeting my enigmatic champion."

Pierce was feeling anything but a champion.

Tossing down his second cup of black coffee, he ignored the sun's early morning rays, instead pacing the length of his bedchamber and wondering for the hundredth time since midnight, when he'd abandoned all attempts at sleep, why the hell he hadn't carried Daphne off when he'd had the chance. Instead, he'd gambled stupidly, giving her two days to think, hoping that her heart would subsequently convince her to accept his proposal.

And, in the process, leaving her in her father's domain.

The risk suddenly seemed too precarious, more so as his confidence in Hollingsby began to falter. What if he'd overestimated the solicitor's potential? What if Hollingsby were unable, or unwilling, to keep Tragmore in London?

Pierce slammed his cup onto the night stand, raked his fingers through his hair.

Hollingsby's answering missive, delivered late last night, had done nothing to appease his worry. Oh, the older man had accepted the unexpected challenge he'd been handed, agreed to do his best to keep Tragmore occupied for a day or two. But, in closing, he warned Pierce that Tragmore was not stupid nor easily manipulated, and he, therefore, could make no promises.

Damn.

Dropping into a chair, Pierce stared, unseeing, at the bedchamber window, illuminated now by a full patch of morning sunlight. With great effort, he tamped down his emotions, forcing himself to think rationally.

In truth, Hollingsby's abilities were, in this case, not pivotal. Even if the solicitor were an unconvincing accomplice, Tragmore was in no hurry to return home, not with the knowledge that Pierce's visit was imminent, his determination to collect his debt unyielding. No, the marquis would stay away as long as possible—at least until mid-day tomorrow, in the hopes of dodging his nemesis. But he wouldn't succeed. For Pierce would be lying in wait, savoring his own impending announcement.

After which, Daphne would be his.

Pierce's conscience reared its head, reminding him that Daphne knew but a portion of the truth. Granted, it was the most significant part, the part that involved the feelings unfurling between them. But that didn't change the fact that she deserved to know everything, including the terms of Markham's will.

But the risk of driving her away had silenced him. Her

trust in him was new, fragile. He'd finally convinced her she played no part in his battle with Tragmore. The last thing he wanted was to reignite her self-doubt by implying she was a mere vessel for his requisite heir. Were that to happen, he'd lose her—spirit, faith and hand. As it was, he could only pray that her feelings for him outweighed her fear and her commitment to her father.

Daphne's commitment to Tragmore.

That spawned an interesting line of thought which diverted Pierce from his musings.

Daphne had been decidedly curious over the details of her father's monetary recovery from the burglary. Not surprising. Given Daphne's fine instincts, Pierce assumed she'd arrived at the accurate conclusion that Tragmore was undergoing financial hardship. Moreover, it was likely she'd further deduced that Pierce was somehow connected to those difficulties. What she didn't know, but was doubtless racking her brain to discern, was his motive.

He wondered if she would understand if he told her, if he delved into the heinous history he shared with the marquis. Were she anyone but Daphne, he wouldn't even consider doing so. But his spirited snow flame, with her generous heart and limitless compassion—perhaps she could fathom the helpless degradation he'd endured, the hatred that burned within him.

But the man he planned to destroy was her father.

Would that same compassion cause her to sympathize with the marquis? Would dutiful feelings for her father intercede on his behalf?

Based upon past actions, the answer was no. After all, hadn't she helped Pierce rob her house? Hadn't she protected him from Tragmore's wrath?

No. She hadn't. The man she'd aided was the Tin Cup Bandit.

Irrational jealousy surged through Pierce, and he clenched his fists to stem its flow. This was insanity. The man he resented didn't exist, was but a fictitious hero Pierce himself had created.

That reality did nothing to appease him. For the first time Pierce found himself wishing his disguise weren't quite so flawless, that he hadn't been hooded, masked, swathed in black from head to toe when Daphne had awakened. He wished the hushed darkness of night hadn't cast her bed-chamber in shadows, that he'd employed more than the light of a single taper to illuminate himself. Perhaps if he'd touched her, held her, spoken to her in his own voice rather than a practiced rasp, she would have known.

Known? Pierce drew himself up short. Known what? An undisclosed truth he'd sworn never to reveal? A truth that would jeopardize everything he stood for, not to mention endangering the person who discovered it?

Christ, he really was losing his mind. If Daphne were infatuated with the bandit, there wasn't a damned thing he could do about it—yet. Once she was his wife, once he had her in his bed—Pierce swallowed, feeling everything inside him go hard with desire. Once that happened, he'd make her forget all about her bloody champion of the poor.

Reflexively, Pierce stood, crossing the room to open his desk drawer. Reaching beneath the hidden panel, he ex-tracted the small, perfect pearl he had pried from Daphne's necklace—his souvenir from the Tragmore burglary, and his intended token for the next.

It began, that familiar restlessness churning inside him, this time magnified threefold by the emotional turmoil over Daphne. Whip taut with tension, Pierce rolled the pearl between his fingers, watching it catch the morning light in an incandescent glow. There was only one remedy for his fervor: to channel his energy into something useful, some-thing to keep his mind off Daphne until he could go to Tragmore and claim her.

A burglary. The ideal distraction.

Now the question was who.

A slow smile curved Pierce's lips as he contemplated the gem in his hand, recalled the vast assortment of jewelry he'd spied on every noblewoman attending the Gantry ball. Doubtless the jewels they wore were only a small sample of what remained behind in their respective manors. He distinctly remembered Hollingsby telling him that the party at Gantry's would drag on for days, despite the fact that

Tragmore's foul humor had evidently compelled him to depart early. But the rest of the *ton* would be carrying on with the festivities.

Leaving their homes blissfully short of occupants—

And providing endless possibilities for the Tin Cup Bandit.

11

THE EARL OF SELBERT'S MANSFIELD ESTATE WAS EVERY BIT AS lavish as his countess's dazzling jewels had suggested.

The bandit smiled, a self-satisfied smile, surveying the library's costly sculpture and paintings by the light of his single taper. It had been worth the long ride from Markham, as well as the special provisions he'd been forced to make deferring his visit to Thompson's store until tomorrow.

Under normal circumstances, an all-night journey wouldn't trouble him in the least. His customary procedure right after each theft was to hasten to Thompson's shop at Covent Garden, make his exchange, then, just before dawn, leave his tin cup in the night's chosen workhouse and travel home in the morning.

But not this time. This time he needed to be home by dawn to reach Tragmore—and Daphne—by the first light of day.

Checking his timepiece, the bandit frowned. Seven after two. It had taken him ten minutes longer than usual to gain access to the manor. Clearly, the *ton* was taking extra precautions to prevent his intrusion, as was evidenced by the solid, newly installed catch boasted by Selbert's drawing-room window. The catch would require a quarter hour to force back, even with his expertise. Accordingly, he'd improvised, cutting a pane of glass just large enough to accommodate him.

He'd have to make up the time.

On that thought, the bandit swiftly and methodically began to strip Selbert of his assets, helping himself to the generous stack of notes that filled the strongbox, the opulent silver lining the pantry shelves.

Making his way upstairs, he entered Lady Selbert's empty bedchamber. It took mere minutes to discover that her gem collection, though horribly garish, was even more extensive than he'd hoped. Quickly, he pocketed the gaudy rings and flamboyant necklaces, pausing occasionally to grimace with distaste over a particularly ostentatious piece. A sudden image flashed through his mind of Daphne's face were she to see these horrid jewels, and his lips twitched with amusement. His snow flame would shudder with revulsion if she stood beside him right now. Why, these trinkets made the Viscount Druige's necklace appear refined.

He was still grinning when he made his way into the master bedchamber, placed Daphne's delicate pearl into a tin cup, and left both on the earl's pillow. Keenly aware of the time, he retraced his steps, careful to remain utterly silent, and eased through the hall, down the steps, and back to the drawing room.

A heartbeat later, he hoisted himself through the window, sliding the shutters into place so no one glancing at the manor could discern the missing pane of glass.

The first portion of tonight's job was done.

Riding at breakneck speed, the bandit mentally added the fifteen hundred pounds he'd removed from Selbert's strongbox to the two thousand pounds of his own money he'd brought. Three thousand five hundred pounds—a respectable sum for the shoddy workhouse he'd selected on the outskirts of Mansfield.

He was in and out of the workhouse in a quarter hour, the gleaming tin cup filled with notes just beside the headmaster's door.

It was fifty miles back to Northamptonshire and less than three hours until dawn. There wasn't time to stop in

Wellingborough and secrete the jewels. He'd have to go directly to Markham and somehow evade the bevy of servants long enough to hide his clothes and his spoils, then prepare for the all-important excursion to Tragmore.

Where Daphne would give him her answer.

"Good morning, Mrs. Frame."

With a warm smile, Daphne sailed into the kitchen, bright and perky as if it were not still dark outside.

Unsurprised, the plump cook returned her smile wanly, gesturing for the kitchen maids to continue their pre-dawn preparations. "I'm glad you're up and about early, Miss Daphne. I need to speak with you."

"Oh, can't it wait?" Daphne appealed, glancing about at the array of fruits and biscuits being readied for the morning meal. "I have very little time before Father returns from London. I'd like to gather up whatever food you've saved for me and ride to the village and back before he arrives."

"Unfortunately, no, it can't wait." Uncomfortably, Mrs. Frame wiped her hands on the front of her starched apron.

This time her unhappy tone penetrated Daphne's absorbed train of thought. "What is it, Mrs. Frame? Is something wrong?"

"I'm afraid it is." The older woman led Daphne into a corner where they could remain unheard. "I didn't want to have to tell you this, but it can't be avoided any longer."

"Goodness! What is it?"

Mrs. Frame inhaled sharply, as if to steel herself. "It's the marquis. He's threatened to discharge me."

"What?" Daphne turned sheet-white.

"'Twas the night before you left for Gantry. He came to the kitchen in a rage, sought me out to condemn me for wasting food. He was very specific in his accusation, and his ultimatum. Unless I do a better, more frugal job of rationing the meals, he'll hire another cook and cast me into the street." Mrs. Frame's eyes grew damp. "I'm sorry, Miss Daphne. But I need my job."

"Oh, God." Daphne seized the cook's trembling hands. "This is all my fault. I asked you to set aside portions of our food so I could take them to the vicar."

"I know. And I didn't say a word to your Father, I swear it. But I just can't do it anymore, Miss Daphne. I spent the last few days trying to think of another way to help you, but I—"

"No." Daphne interrupted. "Don't even consider trying to outwit Father. 'Tis impossible. He'll deduce what you're up to and vent his fury full force. I couldn't live with that. Please, Mrs. Frame, don't endanger your job." Or yourself, she added silently.

"I'm so sorry, my lady." The cook wrung her hands. "How are you going to help those poor children now?"

"I'll find another way." Impulsively, Daphne hugged her. "I'm glad you came to me. I don't know what I'd do if we lost you. Now don't you worry. I'll think of something."

Back in the privacy of her room, Daphne perched dejectedly on the edge of the bed, wishing she felt as confident as she'd sounded. Without her weekly donations of food, what could she offer the children? How would they get enough to eat? Who would aid the vicar in his mission to care for them?

Pierce would.

Immediately, Daphne squelched that notion. Oh, she knew without a doubt Pierce would help her if she asked. She also knew, however, that she had no right to ask. She wasn't his wife—at least not yet.

No, for the time being she was on her own.

Unless . . .

Torn by indecision, Daphne contemplated her last resort, her mother.

Like Pierce, Elizabeth would not hesitate to offer whatever aid she could. But at what cost? Daphne shuddered to think what her father would do if he discovered his wife had crossed that long-established forbidden line.

If he discovered.

Daphne bolted to her feet. Her father was still in London. Perhaps if she acted quickly she could elicit her mother's help. Together, they could make a difference without the marquis ever finding out.

Bursting into the hallway, Daphne sprinted down the hall to her mother's room.

"Yes?" the marchioness's sleepy voice greeted her knock.

"Mother?" Daphne eased the door open. "I apologize for awakening you before dawn. But I must speak with you."

Elizabeth sat up, alarmed. "Are you all right?"

"Yes, I'm fine." Daphne crossed the room, lit the nightstand lamp, and sat down beside her mother. "But I need your help."

"Of course." Elizabeth gave her a quizzical look. Rarely did Daphne seek her out to share confidences, and certainly never before daylight was upon them. "What is it, dear?"

Taking a deep breath, Daphne poured out her situation.

"I had nowhere else to turn," she concluded, watching her mother's features soften with compassion. "Nor did I know when Father was returning, else I wouldn't have disturbed you so early. But I was afraid that if I waited, I'd run the risk of his overhearing us. Mama," Daphne's voice quavered, "I must do something."

Slowly, Elizabeth nodded, her chin set in a rare expression of determination. "Yes, you must. As must I."

Daphne started. "But what if Father—"

"The missive I received from your father said he wouldn't arrive home until late this afternoon." As she spoke, Elizabeth leaned over and slid open her nightstand drawer, reaching in to grope around. "Therefore, if we act quickly, we shan't have to take him on." A triumphant glint lit her eyes, and she pulled out a small velvet jewelcase. "This should do nicely." Unfastening it, she extracted a grotesquely large ruby-and-sapphire brooch. "It will bring you a handsome sum, more than enough to feed the parish children."

A soft gasp escaped Daphne's lips. "I don't recall ever seeing that particular piece."

"I rarely wear it." Elizabeth grinned wryly. "It's gruesome, isn't it?"

"But, I don't understand. Why didn't the bandit take it the night of the burglary?"

"I had loaned it to Aunt Edith toward the end of this past Season. She thinks it a rare prize, but then, it's much more her taste than mine. In any event, she only just returned it." Turning the heavy brooch over in her hands, Elizabeth sighed. "In truth, I'd hoped she'd forget to do so. Heirloom or not, I hate it. So does Harwick. He never even noticed its absence." Elizabeth's eyes twinkled as she extended her hand to Daphne. "As things turned out, however, I'm glad the monstrosity is back in my possession. It can provide food and clothing to those who need them."

"Mama."

"Take it, Daphne. You know as well as I that I was once as dedicated as you to the poor. We also know why I ceased my attempts to help them. My only way now is through you. So take the brooch. Find a jeweler who will pay dearly for it. Then take the money to the vicar. Do it today, before Harwick returns."

Tears of gratitude clogged Daphne's throat. "Thank you, Mama," she whispered.

Elizabeth held out her arms. "I'm so very proud of you, Daphne. I don't dare say it unless we're alone. But I am."

With a choked sound, Daphne leaned into her mother's embrace. "It will all turn out well, Mama," she vowed. "You'll see."

After a long, silent moment, Elizabeth cleared her throat. "When you asked to speak with me, I thought at first it might have something to do with Mr. Thorn—the Duke of Markham," she amended.

Daphne drew back, startled. "You know?"

"Know what? That you're drawn to him? That there's something between the two of you—probably more than even I suspect? I've lost my youth, Daphne, not my intuition. I'm still a woman, and I remember what it's like to fall in love." A faraway look came into her eyes, a memory of a woman who was no longer, a love not destined to be.

Studying her mother's face, Daphne was struck by a sudden realization, one she was amazed she'd never before considered. "The way you say that—there was someone else in your life, wasn't there, Mama? Someone before Father?"

Elizabeth lowered her gaze. "That was many years ago, and ill fated from the start. There's little point in dredging it up now. Besides," she took Daphne's hand between both of hers. "I'd rather hear about you and the duke."

"You're not shocked?"

"Why would I be? He's handsome, charming, and, from what I witnessed at Newmarket, both clever and charismatic. Not to mention that he couldn't take his eyes off you."

"Mama." Daphne moistened her lips. "Pierce and Father—"

"Do business together," Elizabeth supplied. "I've noticed the duke arrive at Tragmore several times for meetings with Harwick. I've also glimpsed him leaving the manor—but not the grounds. I presume he was seeking you out."

"Yes, he was. Mama," Daphne tried again, "I know Father conducts business with Pierce. But that doesn't mean he'd accept him as my suitor."

Elizabeth nodded resignedly. "I don't pretend to concur with your father's ideas on class distinction. But, in this case, the point is a moot one. True, last week your Pierce was a commoner. But all that's changed now. He's a duke. And even Harwick can find no objection to your association with such a high-ranking nobleman."

Daphne bit her tongue, wishing she could blurt out the truth: that her mother was wrong, that the enmity existing between Pierce and her father went far deeper than the difference in their social standing.

"You care for him a great deal, don't you?" Elizabeth pressed softly.

"You sound like Mr. Chambers."

A faint smile. "Do I?"

"Yes. He asked me the same question."

"And what was your answer?"

"My answer was, yes, I care for Pierce. So much that it leaves me breathless. He makes me feel safe and protected and, in some unknown but extraordinary way, treasured. I'm not certain how else to describe it."

"You've described it perfectly. Now, tell me what you're going to do about these wondrous feelings of yours."

Daphne took a deep breath. "Pierce has asked me to marry him, Mama."

Two tears slid down Elizabeth's cheeks, and, impatiently, she dashed them away. "Pay no attention to my foolish, motherly tears. I'm thrilled for you, darling. Truly I am."

"I don't think Father will share your joy," Daphne cautioned, choosing her words with the utmost care. "Pierce might be a duke, but he grew up in the streets, which is hardly the type of background Father would consider appropriate for my husband."

"The duke proposed to *you*, not Harwick," Elizabeth surprised her by replying. "Your feelings—and Pierce's—are all that's important. Don't let anything else deter you."

Quizzically, Daphne studied her mother, wondering at the unprecedented fervor in Elizabeth's tone and the ill-fated love that inspired it. With great difficulty, she restrained herself from asking, sensing that her mother was not yet ready to share that chapter of her life. "I haven't given Pierce my answer yet."

"Why not?"

"Everything happened so quickly. I needed time to think."

Elizabeth stroked her daughter's hair. "Daphne, listen to your heart. If you don't, you'll regret it for the rest of your life. Believe me, I speak from experience." That faraway look reappeared, then vanished. "Now, when will your duke return for his answer?"

"Today."

In response, Elizabeth pressed the brooch into Daphne's palm. "Then I suggest you hurry off and dispose of this repulsive bauble. Give the money to the vicar, then fly home to greet Pierce."

Daphne kissed her mother's cheek. "Thank you, Mama. Thank you for everything."

"It's barely dawn, Your Grace. And, I repeat, I can't help you."

The Tragmore butler addressed Pierce with haughty censure, simultaneously blocking his entry into the manor. "I've specified, three times, in fact, that Lord Tragmore is in London."

"And *I've* specified, three times, in fact, that if such is the case I insist on seeing Lady Daphne." Pierce was fast losing his patience. He'd scarcely had time to bathe and change his clothing before riding to Tragmore. He was in no mood to argue with an ornery servant who was hell-bent on thwarting his attempts to see Daphne.

"It appears that Lady Daphne has gone out."

"Out?" Pierce stifled the urge to choke him. "At dawn? Where?"

"I really couldn't say, Your Grace."

"Perhaps I can be of some assistance." Elizabeth's tentative voice drifted from the hallway. "I'll speak to the duke."

The butler started, then swerved to face the marchioness. "Very good, Madam," he agreed with a bow. Casting one last distasteful look at Pierce, he stalked off.

"Good morning, Your Grace." Elizabeth smiled as she approached him.

"Lady Tragmore, thank you for seeing me. I apologize for arriving at this ungodly hour. I hope I didn't disturb your sleep."

"Not at all. As you can see, I'm up and dressed." Elizabeth hovered in the doorway. "Forgive me for not inviting you in. To be candid, I'm simply too much of a coward."

"I understand." Pierce nodded gravely, besieged, once again, by a wave of compassion for this gentle, broken woman, and the indignities she must suffer. "I assume the marquis is not at home?"

"No, or I wouldn't be taking this chance. He's not due home until late this afternoon."

"I see."

"But then, you're not here to call on Harwick, are you? You're here for Daphne."

Pierce started, carefully scrutinizing Elizabeth's face. How much had Daphne told her?

"She said she was expecting you today," Elizabeth eased his way by supplying. "But I don't think she expected you quite this early. Otherwise I know she'd be home to receive you."

"So she really is out?"

"Yes. She left Tragmore about an hour ago."

"Before dawn? Why?"

Elizabeth studied the intricate pattern of the marble floor.

"I'm not free to discuss Daphne's activities with you, sir. I can tell you that her intentions are sound."

"She is well, though?"

At that, Elizabeth's head came up. "Yes." Her gaze locked with Pierce's. "Safe and well. You can see for yourself later today."

"All right, I shall." Pierce nodded, convinced Daphne's mother spoke the truth. "Would you give her a message for me, please? Tell her I'll be back for tea and a reply."

"Very well."

"And one thing more."

"Yes?"

"If your husband returns, tell him of my impending visit. I want him to expect me."

A shadow of fear crossed Elizabeth's face. "I'll see that Harwick receives word of your forthcoming call, Your Grace." Nervously, she glanced about the deserted hallway. "Now I have a message for you." She leaned toward Pierce. "Keep Daphne safe," she whispered. "And make her happy. Please."

A current of communication ran between them.

"I shall, Madam," Pierce replied solemnly. "You have my word."

The noon hour was approaching, and Covent Garden bustled with activity.

Daphne shifted from one aching foot to the other, wishing she had some idea where to find the highest-paying buyer for her mother's brooch. In the several hours since she'd arrived in London, she'd cautiously wandered the streets, ducking whenever she saw a man who even remotely resembled her father. She was taking an enormous risk, and she knew it. But the high price she intended to procure for the brooch could not be found in her little village. Hence, she'd appealed to the vicar, using the only avenue of persuasion she knew would succeed: the children, and how much this money would mean to them. Muttering a fervent prayer for her safety, the vicar had arranged for a carriage, and Daphne had been off to London.

Her goal had been to conduct her business and be gone

within the hour. What a childishly naive idea that proved to be.

The eminent West End jewelers were acquainted with her father, which made dealing with them akin to suicide. Should they breathe a word of her actions to him—Daphne shuddered at the thought. So, she'd limited herself to the lesser-known, more modest proprietors elsewhere in London, very few of whom, she soon discovered, could be trusted.

Covent Garden was her last resort.

The innkeeper she'd approached two blocks from here had mumbled something about a man named Thompson, a jeweler who reputedly paid well and asked no questions.

Now all she needed to do was find him.

"You did well, my friend."

Frowning in concentration, Thompson pried a single emerald from the last garish necklace, studying each of the stone's glittering facets. "Every one of these trinkets you brought me is worth a pretty penny. Now I see why you made that long trip to Mansfield to pilfer them."

Pierce nodded, stretching his booted legs out in front of him. "I thought you might come to that conclusion once you'd seen the spoils from last night's venture. Now, tell me, how much are they worth?"

"I'll need a few minutes to figure that out." Thompson set down the stone, his eyes alight with curiosity. "What I can't figure out is why you couldn't get here last night. You know I hate doing this type of business during the day."

"I have my reasons. As for your concerns, that's why we meet in your back room. If you're suddenly swarmed with avid patrons," Pierce's sarcasm clearly indicated he didn't see that as a likelihood, "you can sprint right up front and sell them your wares. No one need ever know I hover in wait."

As if to challenge Pierce's skepticism, a bell tinkled, indicating that someone had entered the shop.

"You were saying?" Thompson asked triumphantly, smoothing his worn coat. "It appears I have a customer."

"It appears so. You'd best hurry, before he discovers your

seedy reputation and races back whence he came." Chuckling at Thompson's poisonous look, he folded his arms behind his head. "I shall patiently await your return. Don't bleed the chap too badly."

Thompson swore under his breath, then pasted a smile on his face as he exited for the front room.

"May I help you—ma'am?"

Whoever his female patron was, Pierce mused, Thompson sounded totally taken aback. She was either rife with gaudy jewels or blatantly available. Pierce grinned, listening.

"I hope so," a feminine voice replied. "I was told you purchase fine jewelry. What can you offer me for this elaborate brooch?"

Pierce's grin vanished, and he came to his feet like a bullet. That voice belonged to Daphne.

He took two strides forward, then checked himself. What the hell was she doing here? Before he charged out and dragged her from Thompson's disreputable clutches, he had to know.

"Hmm," Thompson was saying. "The brooch is well made, the pattern ornate. Did you have a specific price in mind?"

"I was hoping you would tell me."

"I see." Pierce could almost hear Thompson's slimy little wheels turning. "Well, let's have a closer look. Ah, I didn't notice this at first."

"Notice what?"

"The stones are a bit cloudy. And the quality of the engraved gold?" A deep sigh. "Passable at best." A pause. "I'll be as generous as I can, my good lady. I'll give you one thousand pounds."

Daphne gasped. "A thousand pounds? Why, the brooch is worth more than three times that amount."

"Really? Have you actually been offered that lavish sum?" Silence.

"You appear to be a sensible young woman. Also one who is eager, for reasons that are none of my concern, to sell your jewels here, rather than in a more appropriate, fashionable establishment in the West End. Therefore, I shall disregard my better judgment and raise my initial offer. I'll give you fifteen hundred pounds for the brooch." He sighed dramatically. "I'll take a large loss, no doubt, but I always was a fool for a beautiful lady in distress."

"You're robbing me. I'm well aware of that. But I haven't any—"

That did it.

Pierce lifted his chair and banged it loudly against the wall, not once, but twice.

"Shouldn't you check to see what that commotion is?" Daphne asked, her voice fraught with the anguish of her decision.

"No. I'm sure it's nothing."

Pierce took an empty ale bottle and let it crash to the floor.

"Perhaps someone has broken into your shop!" Daphne exclaimed.

Thompson couldn't wave away that possibility without arousing Daphne's suspicions. "It's probably some stray cats who wandered in searching for food," he muttered. "But I'll check. Wait here."

A moment later he plunged into the back room.

"What the hell are you doing?" he whispered angrily at Pierce.

"Summoning you." Pierce's eyes were blazing. "Now the question is, what the hell are *you* doing?"

"Business!"

"You're stealing that young woman's money."

Thompson blinked in disbelief. "Coming from you, that's almost funny."

"I don't find it the least bit amusing. My targets are greedy noblemen, not helpless women." A muscle worked in Pierce's jaw. "Offer her five thousand pounds."

"What?"

"You heard me. Get out there and offer her five thousand pounds for that bloody brooch."

"Are you insane? I can't sell that thing for—"

"I'll buy it."

A long pause.

"You'll buy it?" Thompson stared. "Why?"

"That's my concern."

"You haven't even seen it."

"Nor do I care to. Just do as I say. Now."

Thompson shook his head in amazement. "You're a bloody lunatic, you know that, Thornton? A bloody lunatic. What am I supposed to tell her? That I abruptly changed my mind and realized the brooch was worth a fortune?"

"You'll think of something. You're good at that."

With a disgusted grunt, Thompson turned on his heel and stalked out.

"Is everything all right?" Pierce heard Daphne ask.

"Hmm? Oh, yes, everything is fine. Some boxes just fell over and knocked a bottle to the floor. A bit of a mess, but nothing serious."

"I'm glad." Daphne inhaled sharply. "Mr. Thompson—"

"While I was cleaning up the shattered glass, I suddenly remembered a particular customer of mine, an eccentric old lady whose particular tastes run to sapphires and rubies. As I recall, she's willing to pay a fortune for a piece made entirely of those two stones combined. She'll be ecstatic when she sees your brooch. Doubtless she will buy it on the spot, no matter what the cost." He paused for effect. "So, since I won't have to take that loss after all, I'm going to be a gentleman and offer you five thousand pounds."

"Five thousand pounds!" she managed. "But you said the brooch wasn't worth anywhere near that amount."

"Worth is a relative term. I'm a fair man. If I make a profit, you make a profit. So, how about it? Is five thousand pounds more like what you had in mind?"

"You're certain this woman will pay enough to compensate you? I wouldn't want—"

"I'm sure."

Daphne made no attempt to hide her relief. "That's wonderful. Consider the brooch yours. And I thank you very, very much."

There was a rustle of activity as the exchange was made.

Then, the jingling bell indicating Daphne's departure sounded. Simultaneously, Thompson re-entered the rear chamber.

"Christ!" the jeweler exclaimed. "Instead of snatching

that ludicrous sum and bolting before I came to my senses, she's worried about my profit? She's as daft as you! Doesn't she know a gift when she's handed one?"

"Perhaps she has a conscience."

Thompson shot Pierce a suspicious look. "And you? You just paid five thousand pounds for this." He tossed Pierce the brooch. "Now are you going to tell me why?"

"No." Pierce leaned forward, snatching up the single emerald Thompson had removed from the stolen necklace and shoving it into his pocket along with the brooch. "These are mine. And these," he extracted ten five hundred pound notes and thrust them at Thompson, "are yours."

The jeweler shook his head as he accepted the proffered money. "I still say you're crazy. But that's your problem. In any case, we're even except for what I owe you for the impressive spoils you brought in today."

"Keep the jewels—and the money you make on them."

"Why?"

Pierce grinned, already halfway out the door. "Don't you know a gift when you're handed one?"

He was gone before Thompson could reply.

12

TRAGMORE WAS IN THE FOULEST OF TEMPERS WHEN HE STORMED into the manor in the mid afternoon, still irked by having been dragged into an unproductive two-day excursion to London. Hollingsby's missive had led him to believe that the insurance claim on his stolen jewels was finalized, when all the solicitor really needed were more signatures on yet more documents.

If he weren't so eager to avoid another meeting with Thornton, he would have discharged Hollingsby on the spot and taken his leave. As it was, however, he'd stayed and signed the bloody papers—whatever purpose they served—and lingered in Town, hoping against hope that his remuneration would be expedited.

It wasn't.

"Where are the marchioness and Lady Daphne?" he barked now, spying his butler.

"The marchioness wasn't expecting you for several hours, my lord," the servant replied. "But I believe she is in her chambers. Lady Daphne has yet to return to Tragmore."

"Return? Return from where?"

"I don't know, sir. As I advised the duke, she didn't tell

167

me her destination, nor did I see her leave. It was quite early."

"The duke?" A vein throbbed in Tragmore's temple.

"The Duke of Markham, my lord. He was here at dawn, asking for both you and Lady Daphne."

"Why the hell would he want to see my daughter?" Tragmore didn't wait for an answer. He was already heading down the hall toward the staircase.

Taking the steps two at a time, he rounded the second-floor landing and, an instant later, flung open the door to his wife's bedchamber.

"Harwick!" Elizabeth rose from her needlepoint, surprise and fear mixing on her face. "You've arrived home earlier than expected."

"Evidently." He shut the door behind him. "Where is Daphne?"

Elizabeth wet her lips with the tip of her tongue. "I told her you wouldn't be home until late. Otherwise, I'm sure she'd be—"

"I didn't ask you why she wasn't here!" he snapped. "I asked you where she was."

Silence.

"Has she gone to visit that miserable vicar again?"

"I'm not certain precisely where she is," Elizabeth replied truthfully.

"Really? Then suppose I ride to the village. I'm confident I can locate her."

"He's her only friend, Harwick." Elizabeth's eyes beseeched him. "There can be no harm if she spends a few hours at the church."

Rage ignited and spread swiftly through the marquis's being. "She's been away from the manor since dawn. By now, knowing Daphne's pathetically soft heart, Chambers has doubtless convinced her to join him in yet another of his blasphemous crusades for the poor. Well, I've warned her one time too many." He turned on his heel. "This time is the last."

"Harwick, wait!" Elizabeth grabbed his arm. "Please don't."

He flung her aside. "Get out of my way!"

"For God's sake, let her be," she pleaded, recovering her balance. "Give her a chance to be happy."

Something about Elizabeth's tone gave Harwick pause. He turned, eyes narrowed on his wife's face.

"Happy? What does that mean?"

Instantly, she recognized her faux pas. "Only that Daphne has done everything you've demanded for twenty years. It's time she was allowed to pursue her own life."

"Her own life?" Suspicion tempered outrage. "She's been sneaking off to visit that weak-minded vicar since she was a child. Why would those visits suddenly alter her life?" He bore down on his wife in a flash, one hand closing around her throat. "Tell me, Elizabeth. What are Daphne and the vicar planning?"

"I didn't mean the vicar," Elizabeth denied, her eyes wide with terror. "I meant—" She broke off.

"Who?" His grip tightened. "Who else could Daphne be consorting with." A new thought struck. "Thornton?" His affirmation came in the acceleration of Elizabeth's pulse. "It is Thornton, isn't it? Is that why he asked for Daphne earlier today when he invaded my home?"

Elizabeth sucked in air. "The duke came to see you. He plans to return to Tragmore later this afternoon. He asked me to tell you so."

"Did he? And whom will he be visiting, Daphne or me?" Again, silence.

"Why did he want to see our daughter?" A muscle flexed in Tragmore's cheek. "Is that bastard involving Daphne in his attempt to bleed me? Is he?" His fingers dug into Elizabeth's throat.

"Harwick, please. You're choking me." She caught at his hand, fought to free herself.

In one violent motion, he hurled her against the wall, watching with callous brutality as she crumpled to the floor. "I'll do worse than that if you've encouraged her to deceive me." He veered toward the door. "You'd best pray my suspicions prove false, Elizabeth. Else your life won't be worth a damn."

"Where are you going?" she whispered in a tiny, broken voice.

He turned, his features distorted by rage. "To teach our daughter the lesson of a lifetime."

"She's as beautiful as she looked in the shop window," Daphne declared, holding up the flaxen-haired doll for the vicar's inspection. "Don't you think so?"

"I think you're going to make little Prudence happier than she ever dreamed possible," he replied, continuing their walk toward the schoolhouse.

"I know what one special doll can mean to a little girl," Daphne murmured, reliving, once again, that long-ago moment at the House of Perpetual Hope—the child's unforgettable stare as vivid now as it had been twelve years past. "I couldn't bear for Prudence to be deprived of that joy."

"I understand." They trudged on in silence. "I was worried to death about you, Snowdrop," the vicar admitted at last. "You were gone for hours."

"I'm sorry. I expected to be back much earlier. But it proved more difficult than I'd imagined to find a buyer for Mama's brooch."

The vicar's brows rose in surprise. "I would have thought the piece would be snatched right up. To me, it appeared quite lavish, a source of profit for any jeweler."

"It was. The merchants were unanimously enthusiastic. Unfortunately, their ethics fell short of their enthusiasm. I had quite a time finding a jeweler who was even moderately honest."

"I see."

"In any case, I did finally locate one who, for reasons of his own, chose not to rob me."

Abruptly, the vicar recalled something Daphne didn't know. "Speaking of robbing, it seems your bandit struck again last night."

She stopped in her tracks. "He did? Where? What happened?"

"From what I've heard thus far, he invaded the Earl of

Selbert's Mansfield estate, making off with a vast assortment of jewelry, silver, and notes. Coincidentally," the vicar's lips curved, "hours later the Mansfield workhouse was the happy recipient of thirty-five hundred pounds."

"No one saw him?"

"No. Except for you, Snowdrop, no one has ever seen him."

"Then he's safe." Daphne raised her eyes to the heavens, more grateful now than ever before. "Thank God." She resumed walking.

"I see you're still captivated by this altruistic hero of yours," the vicar commented with a sideways glance. "I thought perhaps that would change in light of your feelings for Pierce Thornton."

"One has nothing to do with the other. Pierce is a wonderful, compelling man. The bandit is . . ." Her voice trailed off.

"Yes?"

"I was going to say the bandit is a savior. But in his own way, so is Pierce. The difference is the bandit rescues many; Pierce has only to rescue me."

"Both roles are indispensable."

Daphne smiled. "Thank you." Absently, she studied the doll she'd cautiously removed from her wardrobe and transported to the church at dawn, stroking the pink satin gown. "Let's hurry, Vicar," she urged suddenly, picking up her pace as they neared the schoolhouse. "As it is, we'll miss the older children. They've doubtless gone home to do their chores. But I so want to see the little ones."

Miss Redmund opened the door moments later, a surprised expression on her face. "Vicar, Lady Daphne. I didn't expect you today." She cast a quick look over her shoulder, her brow furrowed. "Our lessons are over. Half the children have already taken their leave."

"Are the younger ones still about?" Daphne asked eagerly. "Timmy? William? Prudence? I apologize for arriving so late and without any notice but there truly wasn't a choice, and I so want to see them. We won't stay but a few minutes, I promise."

"You'd be wise to agree, Miss Redmund," the vicar added with pointed authority. "Lady Daphne has a miraculous gift to share with all of you."

"Gift?" The schoolmistress's speculative gaze fell on the doll in Daphne's hands. "Very well." She shrugged, evidently unimpressed by what she saw. "Come in."

"Daphne!" Timmy fairly flew to the door, his eyes wide with delight. "See, William? I told ye she'd be back."

"Of course I'm back." Daphne ruffled Timmy's hair. "Did you doubt it?"

"Well, ye said ye'd be back sooner, and William thought maybe ye didn't like us much."

"I apologize for my tardiness," Daphne said solemnly, her gaze meeting William's. "But I was needed at home and couldn't get away. Then I wasted a great deal of time trying to coax Russet into joining me."

"Did ye bring him?" Timmy interrupted, looking expectantly about.

"No, I'm afraid not." Daphne sighed. "As I'm sure you've discovered with your lizard, animals often have minds of their own."

"Yeah." Timmy's nod was sympathetic. "'enry won't stay in the bed I made 'im, even though I put lots of grass 'n bugs 'n stuff in there. 'e keeps crawlin' out at night. The other day 'e was in my mum's basin when she went to wash. Boy, was she mad."

Daphne fought her smile. "Thank you for understanding. I promise to keep trying to soften Russet's attitude."

"Is it true ye was robbed? That the Tin Cup Bandit was at yer 'ouse?" Timmy demanded.

Daphne exchanged glances with the vicar.

"Yes, it's true."

"Tell us," William urged, his reticence vanishing in a heartbeat.

"There isn't much to tell. 'Twas the night after my last visit here. He took all our valuables and, evidently, donated the money to a Leicester workhouse."

"Wow! Did ye see 'im? Did ye talk to 'im? Did ye—"

"I believe Lady Daphne has something for us," Miss

Redmund broke in, unknowingly sparing Daphne the strain of evading Timmy's inflammatory questions.

"Yes, I do. The first part is for Prudence." Smiling, Daphne gestured toward the child, who was hiding behind William, her eyes glued to the doll in Daphne's hands. "I see you're wearing your lovely new dress," Daphne encouraged, as Prudence took a tentative step in her direction. "Did you guess I'd be visiting today?"

"No." Prudence's reply was a barely audible whisper. "I just wear it all the time—hoping."

Emotion constricted Daphne's throat. "Well, your hoping must be magic. Because it helped bring me here today. And what's more, I've brought along a new friend." She held out her arms. "Here is that lonely doll I mentioned to you. She was ecstatic when I told her she would be getting a home and someone to love her."

"Dolls don't talk," Timmy protested. "Ow!" He glared at William, rubbing his ribs where the other boy had poked him.

"They only talk to those who listen," Daphne amended with a conspiratorial wink at Prudence. "Right?"

Mesmerized, Prudence nodded, walking over and touching the hem of the doll's gown. "She's so beautiful," she whispered. Her eyes were huge, filled with hope. "Is she really mine?"

"She is indeed." Daphne placed her in Prudence's arms. "Now it's up to you to cherish her. And, of course, to name her. Have you thought of a name?"

Prudence shook her head.

"Well, take your time in doing so. Her name must fit her perfectly."

"Like Snowdrop fits you?" the child asked with a shy smile.

"Like Snowdrop fits me," Daphne agreed, feeling a warm tug at her heart. "Now, for the rest of you. I had hoped to bring you baskets of food and clothing for the winter. Unfortunately, that appears to be impossible at this time. However," she removed the stack of notes from her pocket, "I want you each to take a portion of this money and bring it home to your parents. I'll leave enough with Miss Redmund to distribute to the other students tomorrow. The rest will be spent on a sturdy new roof for the school and new books and slates for everyone. How would that be?"

Miss Redmund's eyes bulged at the sight of the enormous sum. "My goodness! There must be—"

"Five thousand pounds," the vicar supplied. "Every pence of which Lady Daphne is contributing to our school and its children."

"I see." The schoolmistress's eyes narrowed. "Why?" she blurted.

Daphne flinched, silencing the vicar's oncoming protest with a gentle touch of his arm. "Because you're my friends," she replied simply. "And friends help each other." Lowering her gaze, she began counting out bills.

"That's an awful lot of money, Daphne," Timmy said, his freckled face delighted and amazed all at once. "Where'd ye get it?"

"That's my little secret."

"Like the Tin Cup Bandit!"

A private smile played about Daphne's lips. "A bit, yes. Only not nearly as exciting and mysterious." She moved from child to child, carefully placing several hundred pound notes in each of their hands. "Guard these carefully, and make certain to deliver them to your parents, all right?"

A series of heads bobbed up and down.

"That's quite a generous sum Lady Daphne is donating," Miss Redmund muttered to the vicar.

"Yes, it is."

"What does the marquis have to say about it?"

The vicar turned to regard her soberly. "I think you know the answer to that question. Lord Tragmore has no knowledge of Daphne's contribution. You also know that, should he learn of it, he'd swoop down upon us in an instant and seize every last shilling—not to mention what he'd do to his daughter. Daphne is taking quite a risk, bless her tender heart, and asking for nothing in return. Therefore, I strongly urge you to forget the source of your endowment. Permanently. Am I making myself clear, Miss Redmund?"

"Perfectly, Vicar." The schoolmistress flushed in embarrassment. "I didn't mean to appear ungrateful."

"Perhaps not. But it would serve you well to open your heart, at least enough to recognize true goodness when it stares you in the face." With that, he walked off, coming to stand behind Daphne. "It's getting late, Snowdrop. We should be on our way."

"I know." Reluctantly, Daphne nodded.

"Already?" Timmy protested. "But ye just got 'ere."

"The sun is beginning to set, Timmy," Miss Redmund intervened. "We want Lady Daphne to have a safe and uneventful walk home. That way she'll be more inclined to continue indulging us with her visits."

Daphne looked up in surprise, seeing the schoolmistress's pudgy cheeks lift in a semblance of a smile.

"Well, all right." Timmy chewed his lip. "Daphne, do ye think Russet will come with ye next time?"

"I hope so," Daphne grinned. "But remember, foxes can be as difficult as lizards. You understand."

"I sure do." He stood up tall.

Prudence tugged at Daphne's skirt, clutching the flaxen-haired doll to her chest. "Thank you," she said in a breath of a whisper.

Daphne hugged her. "Now remember, Prudence, you have to love her with all your heart, and choose just the right name for her. All right?"

A wide-eyed nod.

"Good. Then you can properly introduce us on my next visit." The school clock chimed and Daphne's smile vanished. "I must be getting home."

"Yes, indeed you must." Chambers urged her toward the door. "Good day, children, Miss Redmund."

"Good day." Miss Redmund followed them outside, looking as if she wanted to say more. "God bless you, Lady Daphne," she barked suddenly. "God bless you both." Red faced, she disappeared into the school.

The vicar and Daphne looked at each other and dissolved into laughter.

"I think you've even managed to thaw Miss Redmund,"

he chuckled, guiding Daphne toward the road. "And to think there are those who claim miracles don't exist."

They'd just begun their walk when a speeding carriage rounded the bend, bearing down on them and screeching to a halt.

Daphne went sheet-white as her father leapt from the carriage.

"Why am I not surprised to find you here."

"Father. I—I—"

"You were visiting those filthy urchins again, weren't you? Even though I expressly forbade it."

"Harwick—" the vicar began.

"Shut up!" Tragmore's head snapped around, his eyes blazing with rage. "How dare you encourage my daughter to disobey me? You, who presume to call yourself a man of the cloth? If I have my way you'll lose your parish, your home, *and* your reputation."

"Father, no!" Daphne shook her head emphatically. "The vicar has done nothing. 'Twas my idea to visit the children, not his."

"Get in the carriage," Tragmore bit out through clenched teeth. "I'll deal with your vicar later."

Daphne's whole body began to tremble.

"Did you hear me? Get in that carriage!" He grabbed her arm, twisting it violently as he dragged her with him.

A cry of pain escaped Daphne's lips.

"Let her go, Tragmore."

Pierce's voice sliced the air like a bullet.

"Pierce?" Daphne's head whipped around, and she stared at him, stunned.

"Well, Your Grace, why am I not surprised to find you here as well?" The marquis made no move to relinquish his punishing grip.

"I don't think you heard me." Pierce advanced toward him, predatory hatred glinting in his eyes. "I said take your filthy hands off Daphne."

Tragmore's lip curled in a snarl. "You audacious bastard. How dare you interfere. This," he jerked Daphne's arm, eliciting another muted cry of pain, "is my daughter. I'll deal with her in whatever manner I choose."

Liked a coiled viper, Pierce struck, lunging forward, his fist cracking into Tragmore's jaw. "Not any more, you won't."

"Pierce, don't!" Falling free of her father's hold, Daphne regained her balance in time to see Harwick retaliate. Charging at Pierce, he swung violently, his fist aimed at Pierce's jaw.

The blow never found its mark.

Pierce caught Tragmore's arm, simultaneously slamming his own fist into the marquis's gut—once, twice, three times. Dragging air into his lungs, he watched Tragmore fold at his feet. "Get up, you son of a bitch. Get up and find out what a gutter rat does best."

"Pierce!" Daphne blocked Pierce's path, beseeching him in the instant before the marquis rose. "Don't do this."

Ignoring Daphne entirely, Pierce stood rigid, staring down at Tragmore and awaiting his next onslaught. The venom darkening his gaze from forest green to nearly black was blistering in its intensity, but somehow Daphne was not afraid. Instinctively she knew Pierce was somewhere else, somewhere far away, and it was up to her to bring him back.

"Pierce!" She gripped his lapels, shaking him. "Please," she added in a wrenching whisper.

Slowly, he glanced down, seeming to see her for the first time. "Daphne." He reached out, touched her arm. "Are you all right?"

That brief contact seemed to infuse the marquis with renewed ire. Gasping, he shoved himself to his feet. "Don't lay one lowlife finger on my daughter." He thrust Daphne aside, unsteadily preparing to deliver his next punch.

"Stop it, Father." Daphne stepped between them.

"Stand aside, Daphne," he shot back.

"No."

Tragmore's eyes bulged. "You dare defy me?" he thundered.

"Yes." Her chin came up. "I dare defy you."

"Why you insolent—"

"Strike her and you're a dead man, Tragmore." Pierce's voice was lethally quiet. "Not just now, but ever. As of today, Daphne is no longer your concern or your victim."

"I'm her father, you odious bastard."

"And I'm her husband."

The proclamation erupted like thunder, a deadly silence hovering in its wake.

"You're lying," Harwick spat at last.

"No, Harwick, he's not. I married them today. In my church."

The vicar's false declaration jolted through Daphne, and she jerked about, staring at him in amazement.

Utterly composed, he continued addressing the marquis. "Now cease this violence at once. It will accomplish nothing."

"You married—" Tragmore was still reeling. "Who else was present at this farce of a wedding?"

Another silence.

"Elizabeth." Harwick abruptly answered his own question. "So that's what my faithless wife was desperate to keep from me, damn her. Well, I'll deal with her first. Then I'll have this bloody marriage annulled."

"No, Father, you won't," Daphne heard herself say. "The decision was mine, and I've made it. Neither threats nor violence can alter that fact."

Tragmore's fists clenched and unclenched. "We'll see about that," he ground out through gritted teeth. Abruptly, he turned, climbed into his carriage, and disappeared in a cloud of dust.

"Mama," Daphne murmured, gripping Pierce's sleeve in alarm.

"I'll have her out of the manor before Tragmore arrives home."

"But he's already on his way."

"I'm faster. Trust me."

Daphne looked up at him through bewildered eyes. "I have no idea what just happened."

The lines of fury on Pierce's face eased, a corner of his mouth lifting slightly. "I believe you just accepted my marriage proposal."

"Evidently, I did." She turned to the vicar. "You lied. Blatantly. You've never done that before."

"Nor have I done so now. I merely told Harwick I married

you and the duke today in my church. Which I fully intend to do, just as soon as the duke returns from Tragmore with your mother." Chambers frowned. "If Harwick should reach Elizabeth first—"

"He won't." Pierce was in motion again. "My mount is just beyond those trees. I'll ride through the woods, bypassing the village and traveling as the crow flies. I'll beat Tragmore by a good quarter hour. I'll meet you at the church with the marchioness. Now go." He vanished into the cluster of trees.

A moment later, the sound of galloping hooves and snapping twigs reached Daphne's ears. Then, silence.

"Your savior, I believe you said. A most accurate description." The vicar nodded with satisfaction. "He's a fine man, Snowdrop. You've chosen well."

"My husband." Daphne shook her head dazedly. "Is this really happening?"

"Indeed it is. And I suggest we hasten to the church in order to make what limited arrangements we can. Although," tenderly, he patted her cheek, "regardless of what we do, you will be the most beautiful of brides." He cast a worried glance toward the woods. "I only pray your Pierce reaches Elizabeth before it's too late."

"He will." A smile of infinite wonder played about Daphne's lips. "Pierce always answers prayers."

13

~~~

THE LAST RAYS OF DAYLIGHT HAD JUST DISAPPEARED FROM VIEW
when the church door burst open.

"Daphne." Hastening forward, Elizabeth embraced her
daughter, who was alone and pacing in the empty church.

"Mama, are you all right?"

"Yes, now that I've seen you." The marchioness anxiously
searched Daphne's face. "I was so worried."

Daphne's gaze met Pierce's as he entered the room.
"Thank you."

He nodded soberly. "My pleasure."

"Tell me what happened," Elizabeth demanded. "Your
father was wild with rage when he went looking for you. Mr.
Thornton—pardon me—His Grace said they came to
blows. He also said you wanted me with you; that the two of
you are about to be married."

"Are you shocked?"

"By the marriage? No. Only by the urgency." Despite her
emotional turmoil, Elizabeth smiled. "As you recall, I
already knew what your decision would be."

Hearing that, Pierce's brows rose, a self-satisfied grin
curving his lips. "I'm delighted to learn you'd decided in my
favor."

"Did you doubt it?" Daphne asked softly.

"At moments, yes."

Glancing from her daughter to Pierce, Elizabeth asked, "Where did Harwick find you and what happened?"

"You'd better sit down, Mama," Daphne replied. She drew her mother to a pew, lowering herself beside her. "Father thinks Pierce and I are already wed."

Elizabeth started. "Why would he think that?"

"Possibly because I told him so," Pierce supplied.

"But why?" Elizabeth's eyes grew wide with fear. "Did he find you and Daphne together?"

"It was worse than that," Daphne murmured. "He found me at the schoolhouse. I'd just returned from completing the errand you and I had discussed." She gave her mother a meaningful look. "I stopped in the village, first to visit the vicar, then the children. I was on my way to Tragmore when Father appeared, enraged. Pierce interceded. One thing led to another, and—" She broke off, inclining her head quizzically in Pierce's direction. "How did you arrive on the scene when you did?"

"I followed you."

"From the church?"

"From London."

"From London?" Daphne gasped. "How did you know?"

"I traveled to Tragmore at dawn, as promised. Your mother said you were out. I went to Town to conduct some business, intending to return to your father's estate later today. I happened to spy you as your carriage left London for Northampton. As you know, I was eager for your answer to my marriage proposal. So I followed you. I arrived at the church in time to see you and the vicar depart. Knowing how you feel about the village children, it wasn't difficult to determine your destination. So, I acted on instinct and rode to the school. Fortunately, my instinct was right."

A warm glow lit Daphne's eyes. "Isn't it always?"

"Most times, yes."

"Daphne," Elizabeth interjected, "what incited the duke to lie to your father? What did Harwick do to you?"

Daphne shuddered. "It isn't what he did to me, it's what he intended to do. I've never seen him so angry. Then, when

Pierce informed him we were already wed, he went berserk. He seemed to believe we were all part of some conspiracy. He took off for Tragmore—to thrash you and to have my marriage annulled."

"So that's why you dragged me away so swiftly," Elizabeth realized aloud, looking at Pierce with a mixture of gratitude and fear. "I thank you, sir. But it won't help. Eventually, I have to return to Tragmore and Harwick's wrath."

"No. You don't." Pierce shook his head. "Along with my title, I've acquired five enormous, currently unoccupied estates. Take your choice. You have only to move in. I'll arrange the rest."

A twinge of hope flickered, then died. "Harwick will find me."

"I'm certain he will. But he'll never get past the men I have guarding the property." Pierce's lips quirked. "There are distinct advantages to growing up in the streets. One meets the most resourceful people."

"But the law says—"

"One also learns to ignore the law, if need be."

Elizabeth's mouth snapped shut. "I—Thank you, Your Grace."

"Pierce," he amended. "After all, within the hour we'll be family. I believe a touch of informality would be in order."

The door at the head of the church opened. "Snowdrop, the license is now in order. I've also managed to amass an ample supply of wildflowers for your bouquet and enough candles to bathe the church in a suitably reverent glow." The vicar came to a halt. "Elizabeth." He came forward in a rush. "Are you all right?"

She smiled a smile that, for once, reached her eyes. "It's wonderful to see you, Alfred. And yes, I'm quite well. Thanks to the duke—Pierce."

"And to God," the vicar murmured, scrutinizing Elizabeth as if to ensure himself of her safety. At last, he drew a slow, inward breath and glanced past her to Daphne and Pierce. "Let's proceed with the wedding then, shall we?"

182

With a flourish, he opened his book. "Dearly beloved . . ."

Ageless words, timeless in duration, poignant in significance.

Daphne felt her hands tremble, heard the quiver in her voice as she recited her vows. A gamut of emotions engulfed her all at once: awe, disbelief, excitement, wonder.

But never doubt. And never fear.

Not with Pierce.

The vicar paused, having reached that portion of the ceremony involving the ring. "I nearly forgot," he murmured to himself. Digging into his pocket, he extracted a dainty silver band, two narrow circles endlessly entwined. "Given the unplanned urgency of this ceremony, I assume you hadn't time to shop," he began, the tremor in his voice belying the frivolity of his words. His gaze fell on the delicate scrap of silver in his hands, and he abandoned all pretense. "This ring means a great deal to me." He cleared his throat roughly. "I've kept it safe for years, somehow knowing it would one day be needed for just the right purpose. That day has arrived." He extended the ring to Pierce. "Please. It would be my pleasure, no, my privilege, if you would seal your vows by placing this band on Daphne's finger."

Visibly moved, Pierce accepted the clergyman's gift.

"Thank you, Vicar," Daphne whispered, wiping tears from her cheeks, vaguely aware of her mother's quiet weeping. "Not only is the ring lovely and symbolic but, as it comes from you, it's value is immeasurable." She turned to Pierce and placed her hand in his, watching as he slid the band onto her fourth finger. Slowly, she raised her gaze to meet her new husband's.

"I now pronounce you man and wife," she heard the vicar proclaim.

A profound silence permeated the room.

Tenderly, Pierce cupped Daphne's face, and she was stunned to feel his hands tremble as he bent to brush her lips with his. "You're mine now, Snow flame," he said in a breath of a whisper. "No one will ever hurt you again."

Straightening, he extended his hand to the vicar. "Thank you. You're all Daphne claimed and more."

"I return the compliment." The vicar clasped Pierce's hand warmly. "I wish you a lifetime of joy." He kissed Daphne atop her head. "Be happy, Snowdrop."

Daphne hugged him, then her mother, feeling utterly light-headed and disoriented.

"Go," Chambers said, seeing the dazed look in her eyes. "You and your new husband need time together."

"Mama?" Daphne turned to her mother.

"We'll take your mother to Markham," Pierce answered. "Until I can make other arrangements, she'll be safest there."

"Oh, no." Elizabeth shook her head, still dabbing at her eyes. "I won't impose. Not tonight. It's your wedding night."

Pierce grinned. "You won't be imposing. I'll leave you in my staff's capable hands, giving them strict instructions to advise all visitors that no one is home and no guests are permitted. Then, Daphne and I will travel on to my house in Wellingborough."

"In that case, I accept."

"Excellent. Then let's be on our way before the marquis begins tearing up Northamptonshire looking for you." Pierce frowned. "I hesitate to travel the main road, lest we run into him."

"I was quite a good rider in my youth," Elizabeth put in. "And, though my practice over the years has been limited, I'm certain I can still take the woods at a breakneck pace—astride, incidentally, not sidesaddle." She gave Pierce a mischievous grin. "Does that ease our dilemma?"

"I begin to see whom Daphne takes after," Pierce chuckled. "Indeed, I ask only that you don't leave Daphne and me behind in the dust."

"I'll bear that in mind." Elizabeth turned to the vicar and her smile faded. "Thank you, Alfred," she said softly. "I think you know what your love and protection of Daphne mean to me."

"Perhaps Daphne isn't the only one who can now begin anew," he replied. "Perhaps your time has arrived, as well."

"Perhaps." She squeezed his hands. "God bless you," she whispered.

"Thank you, Vicar," Pierce repeated solemnly. "The doors at Markham and at Wellingborough are always open to you."

"Visit us," Daphne urged the vicar with a final hug. "Please."

"You couldn't keep me away." Glancing at the clock, he urged them toward the door. "Now go."

Two hours later, Pierce and Daphne rode up to the door of Pierce's Wellingborough residence. Dismounting, Pierce lifted Daphne from the saddle and lowered her feet to the ground.

"We're home," he said simply.

Daphne smiled, surveying the modest structure with a contented glow. "I'm glad. 'Home' is something new to me. I've never truly lived in one. Only a house."

Pierce's eyes darkened with emotion. "Let's go in."

Strolling about the sitting room, Daphne drank in the understated furnishings with infinite pleasure. "Lovely. Also very much you: solid, unpretentious, and overwhelmingly masculine."

"And that's only the sitting room," Pierce teased huskily, coming up behind her.

Daphne closed her eyes, leaned back against his reassuring strength. "I'm nervous. Isn't that ridiculous? I've withstood years with a violent and unpredictable father, taken stupid risks that yielded painful results, and married a man I've known but a fortnight all without succumbing to nerves. And now, when I'm on the verge of a night I've dreamed of, yearned for, my heart is pounding frantically and my stomach is churning. Absurd, wouldn't you say?"

"No." Pierce wrapped his arms about her waist, kissed the side of her neck. "Understandable, I would say. Understandable, and beautiful, and honest." He turned her into his arms. "I won't hurt you, Snow flame," he murmured, feathering his lips over hers.

"I know." She sighed blissfully. "I just keep wondering if

185

I'm going to wake up and find this is all a dream, that the last few hours never occurred."

"You're not dreaming," he assured her, lifting her arms about his neck. "I promise you. This is very real and very right."

She gazed up at him, the trust in her eyes so absolute it made his chest tighten. "I know it's right," she whispered. "Somehow I always have. I just don't want to disappoint you."

"You never could." Pierce met her honesty with his own. "Would it help if you knew I was equally apprehensive?"

Startled, Daphne blinked. "You? Why?"

"Because it's never mattered so much. Because a woman has never mattered so much." He paused, forcing out the next words as if they were a death sentence. "Because there are things I need to tell you before I take you to bed. Things that could change your feelings about tonight."

Thoughtfully, Daphne searched his face. "You're going to fill in the missing pieces, tell me the real reasons for our hasty wedding."

"No," he amended, shaking his head vehemently. "I'm going to fill in the missing *piece*. But it has nothing to do with my wanting you for my wife, or with our hasty ceremony. I didn't intend to dash you down the aisle. That was strictly your father's doing. As for my wanting you," he caressed the delicate curve of her waist, "I think you know how much I want you under my roof, under my protection," his eyes darkened, "under me."

A tiny shiver went through her. "But there is more. I sensed it from the moment you proposed."

"The late Duke of Markham—" he faltered. "My father left several conditions in the codicil to his will. Specifically, there are two stipulations to my retaining possession of his coveted title and fortune. First, I must assume not only the role of the Duke of Markham, but all its pertinent responsibilities for a period of two years. And second, during that time, I must produce a legitimate heir to the dukedom. Once I've fulfilled those provisos I am free to resume my previous life as a commoner, retaining all access to the Markham estate."

"And if you fail?"

"I lose it all."

"I see." Daphne lowered her gaze, her long lashes brushing her cheeks.

"I don't want the bloody title. I think you know that. But I need it—for reasons I can't fully explain." Staring at her bowed head, his jaw clenched in frustration. "I can imagine what you're thinking. Here I've given you indisputable cause for doubt, perfect grounds to disbelieve all I've professed to feel. There's no earthly reason for you to trust me, and yet, that's just what I'm asking you to do. Do you see now why I was reluctant to tell all this to you?"

Daphne's lashes lifted, and Pierce was stunned to see tears of wonder shimmering in her eyes. "Yes." She lay her hand on his jaw, soothing away the tension with her fingertips. "You were reluctant to tell me because you were afraid you'd lose me. Yet you did tell me—and before our union was complete—despite your qualms about my reaction." A tremulous smile hovered about her lips. "You took an unfavorable risk—a forbiddance for a good gambler. And why? Because of your feelings for me. Caring and respect. I've never been offered such precious gifts before. Thank you, Pierce."

A harsh groan erupted from his chest. "Daphne." He enfolded her against him, his lips in her hair. "God, I need you."

"I need you, too," she whispered, shy and eager all at once. "Just tell me what to do."

His muscles tightened as he struggled with his next offer. "Snow flame. What's about to happen between us—there are ways to alter its outcome."

She leaned back, regarded him quizzically. "What do you mean?"

"You're a rare and priceless jewel, one that has been cruelly mistreated, and is only now on the brink of being treasured as it was meant to be. If you need time, there are ways—"

"Are you saying you don't plan to make love to me?"

Pierce started. "Am I saying—No. That is definitely *not* what I'm saying." His restless gaze swept over her, his features hardening with desire. "I'm afraid that measure of nobility is beyond me."

"Then what are you saying?"

"I'm saying you're more than a vessel for my seed. If you're not ready to conceive a child, there are ways to prevent it."

Quizzically, Daphne inclined her head. "How?"

"I can refrain from spilling my seed inside you."

"Just like that?" Daphne looked puzzled rather than embarrassed. "Wouldn't that diminish your pleasure?"

"I'll survive. I've done so for years."

"I don't understand."

His smile was bitter. "I'm a bastard, Daphne. I grew up on the streets, never knowing who my father was or when my next meal would be. I swore to myself I'd never be responsible for doing that to another human being."

"You wouldn't be," she countered softly. "We're legally wed. Were I to conceive, our child would not be a bastard."

"The reason for my self-discipline would be different in our case, but no less valid. If and when we have a child, I want it to be a decision we both make, not one I make alone, and certainly not one incited by the codicil of my late sire's will."

"I see." Daphne nodded, reaching up to unfasten the top button of Pierce's shirt. "Well, then, if this discussion is finally at an end," she struggled with the next button, giving her husband a heart-melting smile, "I believe we've done enough talking on our wedding night." She slid her fingers inside to touch the warmth of Pierce's skin. "Will you please make love to me now?"

Her innocent question, her tentative explorations, blasted through his loins like cannon fire, obliterating every vestige of his staunch discipline. "Christ." He dragged her mouth to his, delving inside to taste her sweetness with all the urgency of a drowning man. He tore open his remaining buttons, covering her hand with his and guiding it along the hard, hair-roughened planes of his chest. "I want you so much I'm going to explode."

"Teach me how to please you," she urged, caressing his hot skin with feather-light strokes.

That did it. "Later." He swept her into his arms, crossed the sitting room in four long strides. "Much later. Right now, I can't even make it to a bed."

He paused at the sofa, bending to seize the row of brocade cushions, which he tossed, one by one, to the floor. Lowering Daphne to the makeshift bed, he followed her down, covering her with himself. "I'm going to make love to you until neither of us can breathe," he vowed against her parted lips. Lifting her head, he spread her tawny tresses out like a golden fan beneath them, tracing his fingers down the sides of her neck, her shoulders, absorbing each delicate shiver with a fierce sense of satisfaction as new to him as the frenzy pounding through his veins. His mouth left hers, blazing a trail of hot, open-mouthed kisses down her throat, the upper slope of her breasts. He slid his arm beneath her, lifting her into his kisses and simultaneously tearing each hook of her gown from its casing until only her chemise stood between him and the treasure he craved.

He made quick work of that, tugging down both gown and undergarment, freeing first one arm then the other, lifting them to clasp about his neck. "You're beautiful," he breathed, baring her breasts to his gaze, his touch. "So bloody, incomparably beautiful." He watched her breath come faster, her nipples tightening beneath his heated gaze. Slowly, slowly, he lowered his head, surrounding one peak with his mouth, teasing it with his tongue.

Daphne cried out, arching reflexively, her fingers gliding through the rough silk of his hair.

Pierce deepened his caress, tugging and releasing until he was nearly wild, consumed by her taste and scent, her harsh pleas for more. He raised his head, panting, watching her flushed face, the look of wonder in her eyes.

"Don't stop." Daphne shifted restlessly, unconsciously beckoning him forward, urging him toward her other breast.

Instantly, he answered her plea, stroking the pad of his thumb over her sensitized nipple once, twice, finally bending to taste this breast as he had the other.

Suddenly, unbearably, it wasn't enough—not for either of them.

Vaulting to his feet, Pierce kicked off his boots, shedding

his coat, open shirt, and waistcoat with the same predatory grace that accompanied all his actions. He dropped to his knees, easing Daphne's gown down and off, taking her chemise, stockings and petticoats with it.

Seconds later, she was naked, lying before him like an exquisite, ethereal goddess.

Nervously, Daphne stirred, watching his burning gaze lick over her, torn between the desire to cover herself and the equally powerful desire to launch herself into his arms.

Pierce met her stare. "You're flawless, Mrs. Thornton," he whispered roughly. Sensing her uncertainty, he reached out, took her hands in his. "See how I'm shaking?" he murmured, letting her feel the tremors of desire quivering through him. "I'm like an untried schoolboy. That's the effect you have on me." He kissed her palms. "Don't pull away, Snow flame. If I don't have you, I'll die."

"Oh, Pierce." She freed her hands, glided them up his chest to his shoulders. "I feel as if I were dying now. I ache so."

"Do you?" He stretched out beside her, gathering her close, intentionally rubbing her sensitized breasts against his chest, reveling in her moan of pleasure, her hard shudder. "God, I love the way you respond to me." He kissed her again, melding their tongues, their breath, beginning an intimate rhythm meant to drive them both out of their minds.

He succeeded.

Feeling Daphne undulate against him, Pierce devoured her with his hands, caressing her hips, her legs, the satiny skin of her inner thighs with strokes of fire, his control dangling precariously by a thread.

Unaware she was doing so, Daphne shredded that thread into tatters, instinctively parting her thighs and offering him the very core of all he craved.

His fingers found her, wet and warm and so breathtakingly ready for him it annihilated all reason from his mind. He entered her with one finger, groaning aloud at the clinging resistance. "So damned tight," he rasped, easing another finger in, stretching her gently to accommodate his penetration. "So excruciatingly tight and hot and—" He broke off, unable to continue.

"Is that bad?" Daphne gasped, inadvertently gripping his fingers inside her. "Because I can't help—"

"Christ." Pierce pulled away only long enough to shed the rest of his clothes. "No, it's not bad. It's perfect. You're perfect." He was already settling himself in the cradle of her thighs. "You need more time, more preparation. I can't give them to you." He braced himself on his forearms, easing into her beckoning warmth. "Daphne, I've got to be inside you. I'm going to—" He threw back his head, groaning as he felt her inner muscles expand, stretch to accommodate him. "I'm going to hurt you, Snow flame. And I swore I wouldn't." He went deeper, his hips moving rhythmically with a will all their own. "Take me—now. God I'm sorry. Daphne—" In one inexorable thrust, he entered her, feeling her maidenhead give beneath the onslaught, burying himself deep, deep inside her.

Daphne cried out, a brief instant of sharp pain vanishing into a sense of fullness, converging with the overwhelming realization that Pierce was inside her.

Emotion, vast and fervent, surged to life, annihilating all traces of discomfort, transforming to wonder as Pierce began to move within her. Hard and fast, his powerful body drove forward, again and again, the taut muscles of his back contracting with each plunging thrust.

"Move with me," he rasped, lifting her legs about his waist. "Christ, Daphne, I can't stop."

Immersed in her husband's passion, impaled by his power, Daphne rose to meet him, clutching him to her, pulling him deeper, deeper each time, physical pleasure coiling so tight inside her she thought she'd die.

"Yes," Pierce growled in her ear, gripping her bottom and hauling her up, hard, until she cried out his name. "Just like that. Again. Yes, like that. Ah, God, Daphne."

A red haze exploded inside his head, toppling all his self-protective walls, stripping away any semblance of control he ever had. Driven by compulsion and yearning, he buried himself in his wife, groaning her name as he drove them closer and closer to the shattering brink of sensation.

ANDREA KANE

"Pierce." Daphne dug her nails in his back, overwhelmed by the unknown pressure escalating inside her, threatening to tear her apart. "I—"

"Yes." Feeling the coiled tension take over Daphne's body, the frantic clenching of her slick passage around him, Pierce knew far better than his wife where she hovered, how close she was to the raging vortex they sought. He moved up higher, intentionally angling his body to stroke her, inside and out, on his next downward thrust. Watching her fevered expression, he drove forward, relentlessly opening her, stretching her, caressing his full length against her most sensitive, throbbing core.

The world came apart.

Daphne screamed, unraveling in a series of pulsing spasms that wrenched at her, tossing her into euphoric sensations too acute to withstand—and gripping Pierce with fingers of fire too lethal to endure.

Withdrawal was unthinkable.

With a feral roar, Pierce erupted, plunging deep, his seed exploding from his body into hers in an endless torrent. Crushing Daphne into him, he surrendered totally, meeting each of her contractions with a scalding burst of fire, pouring his very soul into the mouth of her womb.

Then all was still, their harsh breathing the only audible sound in the room.

Pierce recovered first.

"Damn it," he breathed, stunned by his unprecedented total lack of control. With what little strength he had left, he raised his head. "Snow flame—are you all right?"

Her eyes closed, Daphne smiled. "You tell me. Am I?"

Contentment, as unique as his passion, washed over Pierce in great, wondrous waves, and he rolled over on the cushions, taking Daphne with him. "No," he murmured, cradling her in his arms, "you're not all right. You're magnificent."

"I return the compliment." She nuzzled his throat. "Just as I suspected—heaven."

Tenderness spawned guilt. "I intended to leave you be-fore—"

"I didn't intend to let you," she interrupted, smiling against his damp skin. "It was too beautiful to experience alone. I wanted you with me."

"I've never lost control like that," he murmured, more to himself than to her. "Hell, I couldn't have left you if there had been a gun to my head."

"You can lose control with me, Pierce," she whispered. "I know it's a risk you've never taken. But with me, there's no risk at all. I'll never hurt you."

Pierce didn't answer. The tensing of his muscles was Daphne's only indication that he'd heard her.

"We should get some sleep," he said at last. "Tomorrow we'll go to Tragmore and collect your things."

A tremor of fear shot through her. *"We?"*

"We."

"But Father—"

"I'll deal with your father." He reached over, seizing his coat and draping its woolen warmth around them. "But I won't leave you here as ready prey for his venom. At least at Tragmore, I'll be beside you, should he attack. And trust me, Daphne," Pierce's mouth thinned into a grim line, "the marquis won't overstep his bounds with me."

"He's terrified of you."

"He should be. I own him."

Daphne blinked. "What does that mean?"

"It means that his outstanding notes far exceed his wealth. It means that every asset he owns belongs to the holder of those notes, which, as luck would have it, happens to be me." Pierce's smile didn't reach his eyes. "It means that I'm the spider and he the fly."

"Of course." Daphne nodded, realization illuminating her face. "That would explain everything: Father's monetary worries, his rigidity with the staff, and his utter dread and hatred of you. Do you plan to ruin him?" She sounded more curious than concerned.

"Would you care?"

"That depends on how you do it. And why."

"Witnessing his mistreatment of you today—that in itself would have been reason enough."

That look of wonder returned to Daphne's eyes. "I never imagined I could feel so safe, or that anyone would care enough about me to ensure that I was."

Pierce tangled his hands in her hair, brushing her lips tenderly with his. "As I said, Snow flame, no one will ever hurt you again." He looked away, his laugh self-deprecating. "That's a ludicrous statement, coming from me, isn't it? Considering I myself just hurt you not ten minutes past."

"No, you didn't. You evoked sensations within me too glorious to describe. If a split second of pain was the prelude to that splendor, it was a small price to pay."

The tenderness reappeared on Pierce's face. "Next time, I'll prolong your pleasure, make it better for you. I promise."

"It couldn't be any better." She wrapped her arms about his neck. "But, speaking of promises, I distinctly recall your vowing to teach me how to please you. Also something about making love to me until neither of us could breathe." Her smile was radiant. "Well, so far as I can see, we're both still breathing, are we not?"

With a half laugh, half groan, Pierce pulled her over him, covering her teasing mouth with his. "Not for long, Snow flame. Not for long."

14

Daphne slept like a contented child, curled trustingly in her husband's arms.

Pierce sifted his fingers through her hair, staring at the ceiling, lost in thought.

Today had been a monumental day, a series of events exploding one after the other, leaving no time for assessment.

He'd begun the day determined to make Daphne his betrothed. Instead, he'd made her his wife.

Overall, the outcome was a vast relief. He'd removed her from Tragmore's poisonous hands, legally taken over responsibility for her protection and safety, and ensured that she was his, in body and fact, for the rest of their lives.

The problem was that, in effecting the unplanned immediacy of their wedding, he'd allowed himself no time for preparation in certain critical areas. For example, how was he going to deal with Daphne's questions about his plans for her father? How much was he going to relate of the part Tragmore had played in his past?

And last, but most important, was the delicate matter of his other life. How was he going to incorporate the noctur-

nal activities of the Tin Cup Bandit with marriage to a very
bright, very curious young woman?

Pondering Daphne's heroic view of the bandit, Pierce had
to grin. Doubtless, she'd be thrilled to learn she was wed to
the masked marauder of the rich, that the two men she was
drawn to were, in fact, one and the same. No, Pierce was
quite certain he needn't fear his wife's condemnation,
should she discover the truth. Nor had he any reservations
as to her loyalty. She would keep his secret unconditionally
and proudly, applauding him each time the bandit em-
barked on a nightly excursion.

Nevertheless, he couldn't—wouldn't—tell her. The danger was too great. He, better than anyone, recognized the
risk he took each time he invaded a nobleman's home. But,
for him, it was a risk well worth taking, assumed with the
absolute fearlessness spawned by having lived in hell and
survived. Now he was coldly unthreatened by anything life
might dole out.

No, it was one thing for *him* to defy the law, challenge the
odds, and, someday inevitably lose. But not Daphne. Never
Daphne.

Although his innocent wife had demonstrated herself to
be quite resourceful for an amateur, Pierce reflected. He
stifled a chuckle as he relived the scene in Thompson's store.
Daphne had managed to locate just the right man: a
somewhat shady though reputedly high-paying jeweler.
Then, she'd determinedly held out for the best price she
could get for her brooch.

And all so the parish children could eat.

Pierce's smile vanished, a tidal wave of emotion engulfing
his heart. Until Daphne, he'd never witnessed such selflessness, never even believed it existed. But exist it did. He was
holding the proof of it in his arms.

Christ, these feelings were more than he'd anticipated,
Pierce admitted to himself, gazing down at his sleeping wife.
He'd perceived the wealth of spirit and passion burning
within her from the moment they'd met, but he hadn't
perceived how profoundly their emergence would affect
him, especially in bed.

Bed? That was a laugh. They'd never even made it past the sitting room.

From dusk till dawn he'd made love to her, drowning in the relentless passion that welled up between them when they touched, devouring her, again and again, until exhaustion compelled them to sleep. Even then, he'd drifted off for but an hour, awakening to the scent and feel of her, his body achingly aroused before he'd even opened his eyes.

It was damned disconcerting.

Never in his wildest dreams had Pierce imagined either the staggering intensity of their lovemaking or his own decimated self-control. A control, he reminded himself grimly, that he'd never regained throughout their long, torrid hours together. In truth, he'd abandoned all thought of withdrawal. Pouring himself into Daphne was both celebration and compulsion, as natural and necessary to him as breathing.

He buried his lips in her hair, watching narrow slices of dawn peak through the drapes. In a short while he'd have to awaken her to talk. They had much to accomplish today: moving Daphne to Markham, providing safe living arrangements for her mother, facing Tragmore, and establishing ground rules the bastard wouldn't violate.

Devising those rules and resolving how much of the past to tell Daphne were Pierce's current dilemmas.

Dilemmas he needed to resolve posthaste.

Daphne stirred, frowning at the abrasiveness of her bedcovers. She shifted, seeking a softer spot, and was startled into wakefulness by the fervent protest of her aching muscles.

Memory exploded like fireworks.

Pushing herself up on one elbow, Daphne tossed her hair back and surveyed the room with sleepy disorientation, searching for Pierce.

She spotted him not ten feet away, clad only in his trousers, staring intently out the window.

"Pierce?"

He turned, a tender look in his eyes. "Good morning, Snow flame. I was just about to awaken you."

ANDREA KANE

"How long have you been up?" Daphne asked, attempting to wrap his coat about her.

"A while." Pierce stooped to retrieve his shirt. "I believe you'll find this more comfortable."

"Thank you." Daphne shrugged into it and rose, buttoning the shirt as she came to stand beside her husband. "Are you all right?"

A corner of Pierce's mouth lifted, and he feathered his fingers through her disheveled mane. "I believe that question belongs to me."

Daphne blushed. "I'm fine. A bit tender, but fine." Her smile was shy. "More than that, actually."

"I'm glad." He cupped her face, brushed his mouth gently across hers. "Although I fear our wedding night was as unconventional as our wedding. I apologize. The least I could have done was carried you to my bed."

"I rather liked our makeshift bed—and the urgency that precluded us from leaving it," Daphne confessed.

Pierce's eyes darkened. "I wanted you again. The moment I awoke, in fact."

"Then why didn't you—?"

"You needed your rest. As it is, I overtaxed your poor body beyond its endurance."

"I have no complaints. Neither does my body."

Pierce chuckled, stroking her cheek bones. "There will be other nights, Snow flame. Countless ones. I promise."

"But for today there is reality," Daphne concluded, sobering as she interpreted his unspoken words.

"Yes," he agreed solemnly. "For today there is reality."

"Pierce," Daphne took a deep breath, plunging right in, "we have much to discuss. To begin with, I'm concerned about going to Tragmore. Father is brutally angry. I'm afraid of what he might do."

"I swore to you he'll never hurt you again."

"I wasn't referring to myself. I'm not the only one Father has hurt."

"I'll ensure your mother's safety as well."

"I wasn't referring to Mama either. I was referring to you." She saw her husband go rigid, but pressed on nonethe-

198

less. "What did he do to you, Pierce? Why do you hate him so?"

"This is a complex issue, Daphne, one I've never discussed. To be frank, I'm not sure I'm able to."

"You must." Daphne lay a tentative hand on his chest. "Again and again, you've spoken of the undeniable wonder that draws us together. You've asked for my trust and I've gladly offered it. You asked for my hand in marriage, and, although I hadn't a chance to properly accept your proposal, I intended to, joyfully. I've just become your wife—in every way—and the physical joining we shared was more beautiful than I ever imagined, much less believed, possible. Is all that not powerful enough for you to offer me even a shred of trust in return? Pierce," she caressed his jaw, urging it down so their gazes locked, "I know the coldness that lines my father's heart. Please tell me. What has he done to you?"

"Nearly killed me," Pierce bit out. "Me and hundreds of other pathetic children who had no manner of protection and nowhere to turn."

"How?"

Some unknown emotion compelled him to continue. "I told you I grew up in a workhouse. The headmaster was a contemptible, greedy son of a bitch who got his position by knowing certain influential people, one *nobleman* in particular. The arrangement was simple. Barrings retained his job in exchange for providing the man who ensured it with a healthy portion of the workhouse donations. The rich prospered, the headmaster prevailed, and the children starved, and were beaten mercilessly by men who felt urchins were better off dead."

Daphne paled, but she didn't flinch or look away. "Your story doesn't surprise me. The vicar has warned me such arrangements exist."

"Has he? Has he told you what it's like to be whipped until you bleed? Starved until you faint? Tormented until you're numb? Has he told you what's it like to see your mother die before your eyes, then have her denied a proper burial? And all because of the sick whims of a certain *nobleman?* The same nobleman who stole your money and ensured your suffering by keeping Barrings at the helm?"

Sick at heart, Daphne murmured, "You're telling me that man was my father."

"Yes. That's what I'm telling you."

"How often did he whip you?"

"Whenever I or any of the children had the misfortune to stumble into his path. In between visits, he left strict orders for Barrings to thrash us daily, if he wanted to remain the headmaster."

"Then Father *does* know the connection, the reason for your hatred."

"No."

"No? But certainly he recalls what he did to you when you were a child?"

"He never even knew my name. Oh, he knows Pierce Thornton grew up in a workhouse. He uncovered that fact when he investigated my background. But he never once associated his lowlife business associate with one of the scrawny bastards he beat senseless. Quite simply, he never knew one workhouse child from another. In his eyes, we were all the same, nameless and unnecessary."

"I understand."

"Do you?" Pierce searched her face, his eyes hard with bitterness.

Slowly, resignedly, Daphne pivoted, dropping Pierce's shirt from her shoulders and stepping into the path of the morning sunlight as it peeped through the open drapes. Then she swept up her tousled hair, twisting it into a knot atop her head. "Yes, Pierce, I understand," she repeated simply.

Bile rose in Pierce's throat as he stared at Daphne's bare back, confronting the heinous evidence of Tragmore's brutality—evidence the darkness and his own urgency had eclipsed from view.

Dozens of scars, some faded, some fresh, covered her naked flesh, obscene marks on the delicate satin of her skin.

Never had Pierce felt more capable of murder than at that moment.

"That filthy scum." Beyond fury, he acted on instinct, wrapping his arms around Daphne and enfolding her against him as if to ward off the pain she'd already endured.

"That vile, despicable son of a bitch." With infinite gentleness, he brushed his lips across her nape. "In my gut I knew something like this was happening. An animal like that could never leave such flawless beauty unscathed. I just couldn't allow myself to contemplate that he might— Christ, I'm sorry. I'm so bloody sorry, Snow flame."

"Don't be." She turned in his arms, pressed her fingers to his lips. "You rescued me, and I'll never have to bear his beatings again. I just wanted you to know that I do understand some of what you went through."

"He hurt you, and for that I want to kill him. But Daphne, he could never truly touch your beauty. It's submerged deep inside you, in a place your father could never reach, much less fathom." He kissed her fingertips. "Don't ever forget that."

Tears filled Daphne's eyes. "You're such a wonderful man," she whispered. "And you've endured so much. Watching your mother die—starving in the streets." Daphne bowed her head, two tears trickling down her cheeks. "I hate him, too, Pierce."

Abruptly, her pain was Pierce's.

"Don't." He gathered her against him. "Please sweetheart, don't cry for me."

"I'm not crying for you," she managed, her voice muffled against his chest. "I'm crying for the little boy you were when my father tortured you."

Pierce closed his eyes, buried his face in the fragrant cloud of her hair. "That boy is gone now."

She leaned back. "Is he? I don't think so. I think he's very much here and very much responsible for the man you've become and for his actions. No wonder you do what you do. And that you don't believe in prayers."

Prayers.

Fleetingly, Pierce smiled, remembering the occasions on which they'd discussed his lack of faith in prayers: the evening they'd waltzed in Gantry's garden, and in the privacy of her bedchamber, when the Tin Cup Bandit had robbed her house.

"I've endured nothing in comparison to you." Oblivious to her husband's tender recollections, Daphne rebuttoned her borrowed shirt. "But I have known the pain of my father's beatings since I was small. Moreover, I had to endure the even more unbearable agony of hearing my mother's sobs when he beat her. Lord, how many nights I covered my ears to drown out the sound of her anguished weeping."

"All that's over now."

This time it was Daphne who shook her head sadly. "You, better than anyone, know that certain things can never be over. They're burned in your memory forever, hopefully haunting you less and less as the years go by." She averted her gaze, her eyes veiled. "From the day I was born, my father decided I was far too much like my mother, too good-hearted, too compassionate. By the time I turned eight, he ruled that beatings alone were no longer sufficient; firsthand experience was necessary. With that in mind, he dragged me to a workhouse and forced me inside. God, how I fought him. I knew once I entered those walls, my life would never be the same. And not because I'd experience the revulsion Father anticipated. Quite the contrary. I knew I'd never be able to forget the faces, the hopeless futility of those who truly do without. And I was right. Father thrust me in and I've never been the same. Nor will I ever forget."

"You're astounding," Pierce replied, his voice unsteady. "You've never lived there, and yet, you have."

"I remember it all. The women scrubbing on their knees, coughing until their frail bodies were racked with it; the smells of disease; the children pumping water, especially that one little girl with the hollow eyes and the tattered doll in her arms—everything." Daphne's lips trembled. "And that taunting sign hanging over the building, it's name the antithesis of all I'd witnessed. Perpetual hope? More like eternal hopelessness."

Pierce's head snapped around. "Perpetual hope?"

She nodded. "Yes. That was the name of the workhouse. The House of Perpetual Hope."

"Damn." A muscle worked in Pierce's jaw.

"You've seen it?"

"I grew up in it."

"You grew up—" Daphne's fingers flew to her mouth, all

the color draining from her face. "That's the workhouse you lived in?" she whispered. "That deplorable place in Leicester I just described?"

"And what you described was hardly the worst of it," Pierce confirmed, a tortured look in his eyes. "There was the dead room, where I was frequently punished by being locked amid decaying dead bodies and darkness—longer each time I disobeyed the headmaster's inhuman demands. Alongside the dead room was the foul ward, where women tortured by syphilis screamed in agony on the beds and floors, together with those women distorted by unnameable skin diseases caused by living in filth. There was no ventilation, the smell was everywhere—" Pierce broke off, his breathing harsh.

Wordlessly, Daphne went to him, fighting back tears of revulsion and pain. Pierce needed her now—needed her strength, not her pity. She wrapped her arms securely about his waist, lay her head on his chest. "There is purpose to everything, even if we ourselves cannot discern it. You were subjected to such a life for a reason, perhaps the same reason you survived it. My God, you're strong." Daphne turned her face, brushing her lips against his skin.

Slowly, Pierce averted his head, staring down at her as she shared his remembered pain. "I'm sorry, Snow flame," he said gruffly, his arms closing around her. "I never should have exposed you to such horrors."

"I'm proud you trusted me enough to confide in me," Daphne demurred. She leaned back to meet his gaze. "Tell me about your mother."

"My mother." A resigned sadness settled over Pierce. "She was beautiful—or perhaps she only seemed so to me." He shrugged. "It doesn't matter. After long years of workhouse life her beauty faded, her health deteriorated, and I lost her."

"She gave birth to you in the workhouse?"

"Yes. She had been a tavern maid at a London pub. That's where she met Markham. Evidently, their affair was torrid, but, at least from his perspective, temporary. You see, the duke had a very proper, very legal duchess at home. Ironic how he conveniently dismissed that reality when he bedded my mother, just as he unfeelingly dismissed my mother when she went to him with the knowledge that she carried his child."

"He offered her nothing?"

"Initially, no. According to the letter he left with his solicitor, he had a change of heart some months later and went back to the tavern to see for himself that my mother was well. By that time it was too late. Mother was long gone, dismissed the instant the tavern keeper discovered she was with child."

"Did your father abandon his search at that point?" Daphne asked softly.

"Seemingly not. I've been told he hired investigators who traced my mother and me to the workhouse in Leicester, and that he intended to forsake his glittering life and claim us." Pierce gave a harsh laugh. "That never came to pass. The duke's wife chose that moment to do what she'd been unable to for years. She conceived his child. Needless to say, a legitimate heir has priority over a bastard. So the duke remained at Markham, and we remained in hell. Mother held on as long as she could. But she was never very strong. She died when I was seven."

"You were so young. How devastated you must have been."

"She was the only stability in my life. I never knew my father, and I hated him for what he'd done. When my mother died, it was the first time I felt truly abandoned."

Instinctively, Daphne ran caressing fingers along Pierce's spine. "Your father paid dearly for his selfishness." Her eyes misted with emotion. "He never had the joy of knowing you."

"Clearly, he considered that no great loss."

"You can't be certain of that," she protested.

"Can't I? If he were so distressed, why didn't he damn protocol and claim me? No, Daphne. I don't think Markham agonized over my absence from his life."

"Then the misfortune was his. Moreover, from what I've heard, you weren't his only loss. His other son was killed in a riding accident, which drove the duke into seclusion."

"I presume Tragmore told you that."

"He did, yes." Daphne nodded. "I believe he was fairly well acquainted with the late duke."

Another harsh laugh. "*Very* well acquainted." Pierce's hands clenched in Daphne's hair as he answered her questioning look. "In order to collect the funds Barrings owed him, Tragmore visited the headmaster frequently. I eavesdropped on every one of their meetings."

"I see." Daphne blinked at the rapid change of subject. "I assume my father never discovered your presence?"

"Never." Pierce shook his head. "To this day he has no idea I witnessed his illegal dealings, nor that I observed him and his companion each time they arrived."

"His companion?"

"Tragmore didn't visit Barrings alone. He was accompanied by none other than the Duke of Markham."

Daphne inhaled sharply as Pierce's point struck home. "The duke was involved with Father's scheme?"

"Yes and no."

"What does that mean? Did he accept money from Barrings or didn't he?"

"None that I witnessed. Whether or not he took his share when he and Tragmore were alone, I don't know. In truth, he was removed and disinterested during the actual meetings, more restless than avid. Actually, his entire presence at the workhouse always struck me as rather odd. The moment the meetings ended, he would wander about, saying nothing, doing nothing, merely looking. It's only now that I understand what his purpose was."

Realization dawned in Daphne's eyes. "To see you."

"Evidently. It was his pathetic way of keeping an eye on his bastard son. He'd received word of my mother's death and was, supposedly, distraught. Not distraught enough to compromise his legitimate heir by acknowledging me; just enough to pay an occasional visit to the workhouse to verify that I lived."

"He was weak, Pierce. But it's obvious that, in his own way, he cared."

"Cared?" Pierce's expression was incredulous. "If he cared he wouldn't have cast my mother out when she told him she was carrying his child. Nor would he have relegated us to the atrocity of a workhouse existence. No, Daphne, he didn't care."

Daphne considered arguing the point, then thought better of it. Later, when her husband was ready, she would confront the pain of his abandonment and, hopefully, help him find peace of mind. But instinct cautioned her that now was not the time. "You said my father didn't know you by name," she clarified instead. "Then that means he never made the connection between you and the duke's workhouse visits."

"Not then. By now I'm sure he's figured it out. Between his investigation of my background and his realization that Markham sired me, I'm certain he's put it all together."

"I wonder what excuse the duke gave Father for accompanying him to his meetings with Barrings."

"I assume Markham must have, at the very least, feigned interest in receiving financial compensation. Money is the only incentive your father understands."

"I'm so sorry." Daphne's voice broke as she pressed her forehead to Pierce's chest. "I know I'm not responsible for my father's actions, but that doesn't prevent me from wishing I could undo them. Because of him you endured hell."

"And I intend to see him there in my stead."

Daphne raised her chin, tears glistening on her lashes. "Will you tell me what you have planned?" she asked softly, uncertain if Pierce would comply. "Why have you accepted a title you despise and how will it help bring my father down?"

"Very well." Determined to offer his wife as vast a measure of honesty as possible, Pierce squelched his qualms that she wouldn't—couldn't—condone tactics spawned solely by hate. "I accepted the title because it offers me two things I lacked as a commoner: great wealth and great power. And you're right. For myself, I give a damn for neither. But it's not myself I'm considering." Earnestly, he gripped her shoulders. "Daphne, each week of my two years as the Duke of Markham I receive an allowance of ten thousand pounds. If I fulfill Markham's two stipulations, I leave a free man, with access to an estate worth over twenty million pounds. Do you have any idea what that money could buy?"

She studied him, comprehension dawning. "Yes, I do. You want to help the workhouses, don't you?"

He nodded. "I'm far from a poor man. But the sum of my own funds is but a fraction of Markham's fortune. I could do so much. Not just token donations, but rampant reformation—providing more sanitary conditions, higher quality food, less crowded space. The possibilities are endless. Plus I'd have influence with the magistrates, the kind of influence only wealth and a title can provide."

"And my father? Where does he factor into all this?"

Pierce drew a deep breath. "As I told you, I own each and every one of your father's outstanding notes. He lives in perpetual fear of when I'll choose to call them in. His sole comfort has been that, unless I went ahead and scandalized him with enforced bankruptcy, my nonexistent social status precluded me from penetrating his coveted social circles and slandering his name. Now even that peace of mind is gone. Overnight I've become a lofty nobleman, respected by all the *ton*. Why, I can stroll into White's, attend grand country house parties—the options are limitless. I'll be a constant, taunting thorn in Tragmore's side. I doubt he'll ever sleep again." Jaw clenched, Pierce steeled himself for Daphne's response.

It was anything but the one he'd expected.

With uncanny insight rather than shock, Daphne replied, "I know the kind of man you are, Pierce, despite the depth of your hatred. You don't plan to call in those notes at all. You don't want to bankrupt Father, any more than you want his money."

"You're right. I don't. But not because I'm so fine a man. Because I want to see Tragmore squirm, to render him as helpless as all the people he's victimized over the years."

"Yes. But now complete that line of reasoning. You want to render him helpless, not merely to gloat, but so he can never again brutalize anyone as he did you, me, and Mama."

Silently, Pierce ingested his wife's words. Then he nodded. "I can't dispute your point. Nevertheless, Tragmore will never know that holding those notes is the only victory I seek. So far as he's concerned I could call them in at any time. He's vulnerable and he's terrified, and I glory in both. So don't paint me a hero, Daphne. Given that blackmail is the only weapon capable of striking down a black-hearted bastard like your father, I use it without guilt or regret."

"I agree."

Pierce started. "You agree?"

"Absolutely. Father must be stopped. And threatening his wealth and social position is the only way to do it." Daphne punctuated her declaration with an emphatic nod. "Now, tell me how I can help. What do you intend to accomplish today when we go to Tragmore and in what ways can I assist you?"

A mixture of pride and relief swept over Pierce's face, and he shook his head in wondrous disbelief. "What an extraordinary combination of contradictions you are, Snow flame. So delicate, so strong."

"Spirit and fire, I believe you said. Rife with untapped passion and exceptional instincts."

He chuckled. "So I did." Tenderly, he framed her face between his palms. "Let's get dressed. During our carriage ride, I'll explain my plan. Then we can put your exceptional instincts to work."

Daphne's smile was both jubilant and mischievous. "Wonderful! And, upon our return, may we do the same for my untapped passion?"

Stepping away, Pierce executed a formal bow, bringing Daphne's fingers to his lips. "My pleasure, Your Grace."

She brought her hand around to caress his jaw. "No, Your Grace. The pleasure will belong to us both."

It wasn't until after Daphne had walked off to gather her discarded gown that two staggering realizations struck Pierce.

He had just unflinchingly acted the part of a duke and he had actually taken the first tentative steps toward trust.

Perhaps prayers could, after all, be answered.

15

Daphne climbed down from the carriage and paused, scanning the woods surrounding her father's estate.

"Pierce, when we've finished with Father . . ." She hesitated, uncertain whether Pierce would honor or laugh at her request.

"We'll peruse the woods before heading to Markham," Pierce finished for her, his lips curving with tenderness rather than amusement. "I'm sure we can convince your friend—what was his name, Russet?—to join us. Markham has three times the acreage of Tragmore, resulting in thrice as many cozy foxholes in which to build one's home."

"Thank you." Daphne's smile was radiant, reminding Pierce yet again how seldom his wife had been indulged, how little it took to bring her joy.

He intended to drown her in it.

"Are you sure you want to do this?" he asked quietly. "It isn't necessary. You can go right upstairs and pack your things, leaving your father to me."

"I'm sure." Daphne gathered up her skirts. "Consider it another victory for my newly freed spirit." So saying, she marched up to the front door and knocked.

The Tragmore butler paled when he saw them there. "Lady Daphne. I wasn't told to expect you."

"I'm here to collect my things. But first, the duke and I would like to see my father."

"Your f-father?" A fine sheen of perspiration broke out on his forehead. "He's—That is, I—"

"Well, well." Tragmore stalked into the hallway, the dark circles under his eyes the only overt sign he'd lost sleep over yesterday's events. "If it isn't my wayward daughter and her hastily acquired husband."

"We want to speak with you, Tragmore," Pierce commanded. "Alone. Now."

"By all means." Enmity glittered in the marquis's eyes. "Come into my study." He dismissed the harried butler with a wave of his hand, then turned on his heel and strode down the hall. "You know the way."

Cupping Daphne's elbow, Pierce guided her to Tragmore's study, closing the door behind them.

"Your gown looks rather the worse for wear, daughter." Tragmore's disdainful gaze swept Daphne head to toe. "Ah, I forgot your husband's odiously crude upbringing. Did he demand his marital rights posthaste, tossing up your skirts in the carriage?"

Pierce acted before Daphne's gasp had died on her lips. He stepped in front of his wife, clearly stating his intention to shield her from her father's abuse. "Let me begin with rule number one, Tragmore. You will address my wife with all the respect due a duchess. If you raise your voice to her or insult her in any way, I'll finish the thrashing I began yesterday. And, if you so much as raise a hand to strike her, I'll kill you where you stand. Is that clear?"

Tragmore's eyes narrowed. "You contemptible gutter rat. My assets weren't enough, Markham's title wasn't enough. You didn't rest until you'd seduced my daughter into joining your sick cat-and-mouse game."

"Pierce didn't seduce me, Father." Shoulders back, Daphne walked out from behind her husband, coming to stand beside him. "He asked me to marry him while you were in London. I accepted. I consider myself a very lucky woman.

Pierce gave me the strength to escape your brutality while I still held a small measure of self-respect."

"Are you aware that your esteemed husband is blackmailing me?"

"I am." Daphne smiled proudly. "And I commend his efforts. In fact, I've offered to help him in any way I can. So far as I'm concerned, you deserve to suffer poverty and public ridicule. For what you did to me and to Mama I hope Pierce calls in each and every one of your notes."

The marquis's shock at Daphne's brazenness was instantly eclipsed by the implication of her final words. "Your mother? Is she involved, too? Damn you to hell, Thornton, have you stashed my wife at Markham?"

"Why?" Pierce's brows rose in sardonic amusement. "Have you misplaced her?"

"You son of a—"

"Careful, Tragmore. That sounds suspiciously like an insult."

Tragmore clenched his fists, which were white and trembling with rage. "So that's why my messenger was turned away from Markham last night. I thought it stemmed from your spiteful determination to keep me from my daughter. In reality, it sprang from something far more ominous. You've not only abducted Daphne, you've seized Elizabeth as well."

"Daphne is my wife."

"Elizabeth is mine."

"Is she, Father?" Daphne asked. "Then why don't you treat her as such, with some care and respect? Instead, she is naught but your prey, the object of your violence. 'Tis no wonder she's so desperate to escape you." A flash of anger ignited Daphne's eyes. "Pierce didn't abduct Mama. She chose to go."

"Chose?" Tragmore roared. "She has no right to choose. She relinquished that right and all her others the day she married me." He shoved past Pierce. "I'll drag her out of there myself."

"No, you won't." Pierce clamped a hand on Tragmore's forearm, staying his departure.

The marquis made several ineffective attempts to free himself. "Your threats mean nothing, Thornton. Not this time. This time the law is on *my* side. If you block my entry to Markham, I'll contact my solicitor and—"

"I repeat, no you won't. Because if you do I'll call in your notes so fast, your head will spin."

"You'll do that anyway."

"Perhaps not."

Tragmore ceased his struggles. Slowly, he turned his head, his eyes narrowed on Pierce's face. "What does that mean?"

"It means I have a proposition for you."

"I'm listening."

"I thought you might." Pierce released his grip, thrusting Tragmore away like a hideous insect. "I'm willing to have Hollingsby draw up a paper, which we both will sign, attesting to the fact that I won't call in a single one of your notes."

"And in return?"

"In return, the agreement will contain a stipulation clause."

"Which is?"

"That you make no attempt to see, speak with, or in any other way contact Daphne or the marchioness."

"What?"

"You heard me."

"For how long?"

"As long as the ladies wish it."

"Thorn—Markham," the marquis amended, obviously striving with great difficulty to temper his fury, "I'm willing to compromise. But you're not being reasonable. Daphne is one issue, Elizabeth quite another. I'll agree to relinquish Daphne to you. Whether or not I approve, the two of you are wed. But Elizabeth—For heaven's sake, Markham, surely you see the ramifications of what you're demanding."

"Frankly, no."

"No?" Tragmore wiped his brow. "How would you suggest I explain my wife's disappearance to the world?"

"The world? Ah, you mean the *ton.*"

"Well, of course I mean the *ton*. Whom else would I mean?"

"If that's your only concern, the problem is easily resolved," Daphne intervened, unable to bear another moment of her father's unfeeling tirade. "Tell the *ton* Mama is staying with me, helping me to oversee a staff, to adjust to my new role as a duchess, to adapt to married life in general. That should stifle the gossips."

Tragmore hesitated.

"The final decision, of course, is yours." Pierce shrugged, turning to his wife. "Do you need help collecting your things?"

"No. I'll be just a few moments." Taking Pierce's cue, Daphne eased open the door.

"Good. By that time, your father will have made a decision. At which point I'll know what to advise Hollingsby—whether he'll be drawing up an agreement or arranging for a bankruptcy notice to be placed in the London *Gazette*."

"You vile—"

Daphne closed the door behind her, cutting off her father's expletive. Pierce could more than handle things from here. Now all she needed was to collect her few treasured possessions, locate Russet, and leave Tragmore forever.

She hastened up the stairs and to her bedchamber, leaning back against the closed door and taking deep, calming breaths. Looking down at her hands, she was stunned to see they were shaking. Evidently, the confrontation with her father had affected her more profoundly than she'd realized.

Soberly, Daphne forced herself to look about her bedchamber, to remind herself that she was leaving her sadness and fear behind, that the foundation for her dread was no more. It was over at last, and the only thing that remained was to gather her things and bid her past good bye.

Crossing over to the dressing table, Daphne scooped up her brush and comb, suddenly struck by how very little else she truly cared to take. Her clothing consisted of but a few modest day and evening gowns, her personal items only an ongoing needlepoint that made her sleepless nights easier to bear and a few favorite books.

And her two prized possessions.

Having packed all she intended to, Daphne hastened to the bed, sliding her hand beneath the mattress to retrieve her scrapbook: a collection of articles describing the thefts of the Tin Cup Bandit. With a fond smile, she slipped the scrapbook into one of her bags, then turned to her nightstand and her final remaining treasure.

Juliet.

Daphne's gaze softened as she picked up the elegant doll who, so far as she was concerned, was as beautiful as she'd been a dozen Christmases before, when her mother had flourished her before Daphne's enchanted eyes. It mattered not that her dress was worn in spots, nor that her golden hair had lost some of its luster. She was Juliet, the precious doll who had absorbed Daphne's childhood tears, listened patiently to her loneliness and fear, and offered her the constancy and comfort denied to her by fate.

For the umpteenth time, an image of the little girl at the workhouse flashed before Daphne's eyes, evoking the same aching sadness as always. Unexpectedly, the blanket of hopelessness that customarily followed in its wake never occurred. Instead came a startling and miraculous realization, one that spawned the wonders of faith and hope, rather than futility and despair.

She was no longer her father's daughter, but Pierce's wife.

Exhilaration surged through Daphne's blood as she envisioned all she could finally do, how many people she could aid. Why, with Pierce's influence and their mutual resolve, the possibilities were limitless.

Infused with newly born hope, Daphne tucked Juliet beside the scrapbook and took up her bags, casting a final look about the bedchamber. Devoid of her personal touches, it looked coldly austere, like Tragmore's other rooms and like the man who owned them. The similarity wasn't surprising. Neither her father nor his manor had a soul.

Without a backward glance, Daphne abandoned her childhood.

"Hollingsby will notify us when the agreement is ready to be signed," she heard Pierce saying as she descended the stairs.

Her husband glanced up and saw her, instantly making his way to her side, relieving her of her luggage with a smoothly possessive motion that told the world and the marquis that she was his.

"That concludes our business, Tragmore." Pierce guided Daphne to the entranceway. "I expect we won't be seeing you anytime soon, except in Hollingsby's office." He tossed Tragmore a mocking grin. "And, of course, at the procession of Christmas houseparties next month."

Daphne was still glowing with newfound optimism when, after a thirty-minute cajoling session in the woods, their carriage sprinted off toward Markham.

"Your fox is exhausting, Snow flame," Pierce muttered, settling himself across from his wife. "I thought he'd never agree to abandon his den."

"He is a bit stubborn," Daphne agreed, stroking Russet's fur with a reassuring hand. "Not to mention skeptical. But surely you can relate to those qualities."

"Am I being likened to a fox?"

"In some ways, yes. You're both fiercely independent and loyal." She smiled, reveling in the unfamiliar sense of well-being. "I'm a lucky woman."

A corner of Pierce's mouth lifted. "I won't argue, since I applaud your conclusion."

The carriage swerved onto the main road, and Daphne glanced back at the rapidly receding mansion. "From what I overheard, I presume Father agreed with your stipulation that he sever ties with Mama."

Pierce's amusement vanished. "Did you doubt it? After all, I offered him the finest of incentives, the use of his bloody money without my noose around his neck."

Daphne nodded. "I know. No, I assumed he'd prefer financial security even to castigating his wayward wife." She paused, lowering her gaze. "I spent my entire life in that house and I felt nothing upon leaving it, Pierce, not even a pang."

"Does that surprise you?"

"No. Nor does it matter. Once we managed to retrieve

215

Russet, the last of my bonds with Tragmore was severed. I don't intend to return."

At the sound of his name, Russet raised his head from Daphne's lap, his sharp eyes darting about the carriage. Evidently content with what he saw, he wrapped his tail around him, curled closer in the folds of his mistress's gown, and went to sleep.

"Your fox cub appears to be taking his transition rather well," Pierce observed dryly. "Granted, he was leery at first, but he certainly seems at peace now."

"He's accustomed to upheaval. He was abandoned young —at birth I fear—and had to make his own way."

"He and I have a great deal in common."

A sad smile touched Daphne's lips. "So you do. Well, like you, Russet is a survivor. He'll resettle himself in no time, so long as I'm nearby."

"A great deal in common," Pierce repeated huskily, reaching across to take Daphne's hand in his.

Their gazes locked, their fingers touched, and Daphne's heart skipped a beat at the unconcealed longing burning in her husband's forest green eyes.

"I wonder if I'll always feel this way when you look at me like that," she whispered.

"Like what?" Pierce kissed her fingertips, one by one, his breath a heated caress on her sensitized skin.

"Like you are now. Like you did last night."

"Ah, last night." Pierce eased across to sit beside her, his palms gliding up her arms to her shoulders, tugging her to him. "I can still feel you, taste you, hear your cries of pleasure as you shuddered under me." His fingers slid beneath her hair, stroking her nape as his mouth found hers. "Ah, Daphne, I want to drown in you again."

She gripped his coat, moaning softly as his words brought back all the excitement, the wonder of their wedding night. Her mouth opened to his, welcoming his tongue, melding it with her own. Had Russet not been occupying her lap, she would have flung herself into Pierce's embrace, given herself up to his magic then and there.

Pierce sensed and shared her frustration. "When we arrive at Markham, I'll introduce you to the staff—at least

the first wave of them," he murmured against her lips.
"Then, I'll arrange for a hot bath to be drawn for you. While
you're bathing, I'll be making final provisions for your
mother." He circled his lips against hers. "Moreover, I
suggest you concentrate on soaking the ache from your
muscles. Because Daphne," he nipped lightly, "I fully
intend to tax each and every one of those beautiful muscles,
plus some new ones that have yet to be exhausted, again
tonight." He absorbed her tiny shiver. "Are you amenable to
that?"

"Y-yes. But Pierce?"

"Hmm?"

"I think my muscles will be renewed long before night-
fall."

"Prophetic as well as insightful and passionate." Pierce
traced her lower lip with his tongue. "Very well, then. Dusk,
shall we say?"

"Late afternoon would be better."

This time it was Pierce who shuddered. "Continue baiting
me like that and I'll make love to you in the carriage, fox or
not."

"That sounds intriguing." Daphne gazed up at him, her
cheeks flushed, her eyes sparkling with mischief.

Pierce went rigid, then abruptly checked himself. "No,
Mrs. Thornton. When I have you next, it's going to be in a
bed. *My* bed. Where we can enjoy each other with total and
utter abandon. With no carriage seats nor sofa cushions to
inhibit our movements or our pleasure. All right?"

"All right." Daphne was barely able to speak.

"Good." He glanced impatiently out the carriage window. "I am suddenly very eager to reach Markham."

The bath water did indeed feel wonderful, Daphne
thought gratefully, sinking deeper into the tub. She'd insisted on bathing herself, much to the chagrin of her new
lady's maid, Lily, whom she'd selected from the profusion
of female servants she'd met earlier. Lily was of middle
years, kind faced and experienced, having served the late
Duchess of Markham for a dozen years.

Markham itself was not nearly so stark and intimidating

as Daphne had anticipated. Oh, the manor was enormous, with hundreds of rooms on thousands of acres. But there was a seed of potential floating about, almost as if the estate were sleeping and needed the right touch to awaken it.

Daphne smiled at her fanciful notion. Perhaps it was the hot water making her silly, or perhaps it was the lingering elation over the hope she'd spied in her mother's eyes when Pierce had described his various properties to her, as well as his various contacts, who would ensure her safety day and night. At this moment, Elizabeth was readying herself for her morning trip to Rutland, where Pierce owned a small, picturesque estate of modest acreage and beautiful scenery, an estate Elizabeth was most eager to make her home.

Once again, Pierce had answered a prayer.

"Sleeping, Snow flame?"

Pierce's deep, resonant voice jarred Daphne from her reverie. She started, her eyes flying open to see her husband crouched down beside her, clad only in trousers and an open shirt.

"Pierce. I thought you were gathering men to safeguard your estate in Rutland."

"The arrangements have been completed. Missives are in the process of being delivered. Rutland will be well guarded by the time of your mother's arrival."

"You're wonderful."

He smiled, lowering himself to his knees and rolling up his sleeves. "And you're beautiful." He brushed her damp hair aside to kiss her nape. "Did I waken you?"

"I wasn't asleep. I was daydreaming."

"About what?" His hands dipped into the water, then glided up and down her bare arms with slow, lazy motions, breaking the surface to caress her shoulders.

"About you," she managed.

"I'm flattered." Submerging again, his fingers found her waist, curved about her tingling skin, stroking up and down, pausing on each upward journey, always stopping just shy of her breasts.

Daphne began to tremble violently, everything inside her going liquid. With each whisper-soft caress, her stomach

knotted, her nipples tightened into hard buds of need.
"Pierce—"

He kissed her nape again, shifting a bit to feather teasing
kisses down her neck.

"Pierce." His name was a plea. She was going to die from
the tension.

He claimed her breasts in one fluid motion, cupping their
weight in his palms, lazing his thumbs over her nipples.

A muted whimper escaped Daphne's lips.

"It's late afternoon, my exquisite wife," he murmured.
"Are you ready for me?"

Wordlessly, she nodded.

"Are you certain?" His hands left her breasts, drifted over
her rib cage and hips, then slipped between her thighs.

She bit her lip to silence the harsh cry threatening to
erupt.

"Are you, sweetheart?" He touched her, parting her with
his fingers, circling with his thumb. "Are you certain?"

"Yes," she sobbed, nearly unraveling from his first intimate caress. "Pierce!"

He was on his feet, taking her with him, sloshing water
everywhere and not giving a damn. Their rooms were
adjoining. Pierce carried Daphne through her bedchamber
and into his, lowering them both to his bed.

"I'm drenching your sheets." She uttered a token protest,
simultaneously tugging at his shirt.

"You are, aren't you?" Live flames blazed in Pierce's eyes.
"Let's remedy that." Lowering his head, he began licking
droplets from her throat, the hollow between her breasts.
"Better?" he breathed raggedly, brushing her hands away to
tear off his shirt, fling it to the floor.

"God." Daphne's eyes drifted closed. "Better. And
worse."

"Ah. More droplets of water." Pierce's tongue flicked
over her nipple once, twice, then, together with his lips,
surrounded the velvet peak, drawing it deep into his mouth.

"I'm going to die," she gasped.

"Only of pleasure."

"Pierce."

"I love the sound of my name on your lips." He moved up to kiss her, opening his mouth hungrily over hers. "You taste like scented rain." He lowered his torso over hers, crushing her sensitized breasts beneath the hard wall of his chest. "Christ," he rasped, rubbing his skin against hers. "You feel like heaven."

Helplessly, Daphne arched against him, feeling the hard ridge of his erection pulse against her tender flesh, impeded only by his trousers. "Now, Pierce. Please, now." She tugged at the hindering material.

He rose to his knees, his gaze hot and restless, his face hard with desire, and Daphne caught her breath as she waited for him to shed his clothing and come to her.

In one swift motion, he raised her legs over his shoulders, opening her totally to his possession. Before Daphne could protest, he bent his head, sinking his tongue deep, deep into her moist sweetness.

From somewhere in the distance, Daphne heard her own muffled shriek, and then the world spun away until she knew only Pierce's mouth, Pierce's tongue, and the forbidden ecstasy he was lavishing on her senses. She couldn't bear it, struggling for him to stop at the same time as she begged him to continue. Pinpoints of unendurable need melded into one, spiraling endlessly, converging until they exploded into a shattering starburst of sensation that convulsed throughout her body, leaving her limp and barely conscious.

Vaguely, she heard Pierce make a sound of inarticulate wonder, felt the bed give as he vaulted to his feet, dragged his trousers from his body.

"Daphne." Her name was an endearment, and Daphne's lashes lifted as her husband came down over her. He nudged her legs apart, then paused, whip-taut, in the cradle of her thighs. "I have to have you."

She welcomed him, body and soul, reaching up to caress the taut muscles of his forearms, wrapping her legs around his as she gave him the answer he sought. "You do have me, Pierce. You always will."

With a ragged groan, Pierce thrust into her, one long, inexorable stroke, stretching the tender skin that still reeled from his earlier assault.

Oblivious to the minor twinge of discomfort, Daphne sobbed her pleasure, utterly engulfed in renewed sensation. She arched to meet him, opening herself to take him as totally as her body would allow.

Pierce stiffened as he sensed her body's resistance. "Snow flame." He could scarcely breathe, much less speak. "Am I hurting you?"

Fiercely, Daphne shook her head, winding her arms and legs about him. "No. Don't stop."

Bracing himself on his forearms, Pierce withdrew slowly, shuddering as he searched his wife's flushed face. "God help me, I don't think I can." Even as he spoke, he was pushing into her again, groaning aloud as her muscles clasped him tightly, lured him deeper into her velvety wetness. "Christ, you strip away all my control." His hips were moving of their own volition, the friction of her tight passage around his rigid shaft more than he could bear. "Daphne, I can't go slowly. I've got to—"

"Yes," she whispered.

He swore softly, hooking his arms beneath her knees to bring her up harder, open her more fully to the dark craving that clawed at his soul. "If I hurt you—"

"You won't." She threaded her fingers through the damp hair at his nape, as unafraid as she was certain of Pierce's need and her own. "I love you, Pierce."

The world exploded at her vow.

His restraint splintering into nothingness, Pierce surrendered to the wildness, his urgency beating inside him like a relentless wave pounding at the shore, to be assuaged only when its power was spent. His thrusts became savage, incessant, demanding every ounce of passion Daphne could give.

She gave it all.

With a fervor she never knew she possessed, Daphne met her husband's body thrust for thrust, immersed in his frenzied drive for fulfillment. Drowning in sensation, she dug her nails in his back, whimpering his name with each downward stroke, moaning uninhibited pleas for more that at any other time would make her blush.

"Daphne." Pierce's powerful muscles went rigid, his body

drenched in sweat. He threw back his head, the tendons in his neck standing out as his body reached a pinnacle of sensation too sharp to withstand, too miraculous to define. "Take me, Snow flame," he ground out, crushing her loins to his. "Meld your fire with mine."

His words ended on a groan, and he shuddered, once, twice, his hips moving convulsively, his fingers biting into the tender skin of her thighs.

Daphne felt his first burst of wet heat inside her—a sensation so profoundly beautiful, so excruciatingly erotic that it pushed her over the edge. Absorbing the enormity of his climax, she surrendered to her own, dissolving around him in hard, gripping contractions that made him shudder anew, pour into her with a second climax more powerful than the first.

He collapsed on top of her, the intimacy of his weight as wondrous as the passion that preceded it.

Joyously content, Daphne trailed her fingers along the hard, damp planes of Pierce's back, feeling the muscles flex against her fingertips, the tremors of reaction still rippling through him.

"Snow flame," he managed, his lips in her hair. "It's never been—"

"I know." She brushed her open mouth against his shoulder, repeating the declaration she'd given him at the height of their passion. "I love you, Pierce."

She felt, rather than saw, his reaction; a slight tensing of his body against hers.

"Christ, I need you," he choked out, reluctant and incredulous all at once. "It scares the hell out of me how much."

"I know both those things as well," Daphne acknowledged, rubbing her cheek against his skin. "But Pierce?"

He raised his head, gazed down at her.

"Your fear will subside. My love won't." A tremulous smile hovered about her lips. "Snow flames bloom forever."

16

Pierce leaned against the door frame of the dining room
entranceway, smiling tenderly as his beautiful wife, a whirl-
wind in lilac, dashed about, first to the sideboard to make
certain the brandy decanter was full, next to the table to
realign the silverware, then on to the draperies to readjust
the amount of moonlight infusing the room. Intermittently,
she would snatch a tray from a passing servant, chiding him
for carrying too heavy a load, and call out to Mrs. Gates that
she was working herself and her staff far too hard.

So this was what it meant to have a home.

Overwhelmed by contentment, Pierce reveled in a new
sense of belonging, one he'd been denied for thirty years.
Now, after only six weeks of marriage to Daphne, he could
actually feel the empty spaces of his heart begin to fill,
pervaded by the rare, unspoiled wonder that was his wife.

He was one hell of a lucky gambler.

Slowly, he strolled into the room, coming up behind
Daphne and, indifferent to their lack of privacy, wrapping
his arms about her waist. "Unfurrow that beautiful brow.
Everything looks perfect."

Daphne started. "Pierce. I didn't hear you come in."

He kissed her hair. "Obviously not. You were too busy organizing this grand banquet."

She disengaged herself with a murmur of protest. "Don't be irreverent. This is our first official dinner party."

His grin was indulgent. "Sweetheart, it's only the vicar, not a swarm of strangers."

"I know." Unappeased, Daphne looked worriedly about the room. "Nevertheless, he is our first guest since I became your wife. I want everything to be flawless."

Pierce felt strangely touched by the sentimentality behind his wife's apprehension. "It will be, Snow flame. With you at the table, how could it be anything less?"

He was rewarded with a brilliant smile.

"Your Grace?" Mrs. Gates appeared at Daphne's elbow. "Forgive me for interrupting, but, as your dinner guest is due any moment, may I please be allowed to resume my duties? I've idled about as you insisted for a quarter hour. I assure you, I am quite renewed. And I'd like to make certain Cook has things well in hand."

"Of course." Daphne nodded cheerfully, wondering why her housekeeper seemed so flustered by a simple suggestion that she rest. "But call me if you or Cook need any help in the kitchen."

Mrs. Gates's mouth opened and closed several times. "Yes, Your Grace." Still gaping, she returned to her domain.

Laughter rumbled from Pierce's chest.

"Why are you laughing?" Daphne questioned. "And why is Mrs. Gates behaving so oddly?"

"I imagine she's wondering much the same about you," Pierce replied, desperately trying to straighten his face.

"I? What did I do that was odd? I merely offered my assistance—an offer she evidently found less than appealing. Am I really *that* dreadful a housekeeper?"

"I don't believe your skills are the issue, sweet. Tell me, who runs the house, or for that matter, the kitchen at Tragmore?"

"Mrs. Frame runs both." Daphne smiled fondly as she explained. "She's been at Tragmore since I was a child, and she's quite indispensable. Why, the entire female staff reports to her for their duties. And with good reason. Oh

Pierce, she's so wonderful. Not only is she an incomparable cook and housekeeper, she's also a fine, compassionate woman. Why, without her help—" Abruptly, Daphne halted.

As always, Pierce's gaze probed deep inside his wife, touching a place only he could reach. "Without her, you couldn't have brought food to the village children," he finished, noting the flicker of surprise that crossed his wife's face. "I watched you at the schoolhouse that day. I saw you share yourself with the children. It wasn't difficult to put the pieces together and guess what you've been doing. Besides, I know you, Snow flame. Not only your beautiful body, but your even more beautiful soul. I thought by now you understood that." Tenderly, he cupped Daphne's face, his thumbs stroking her cheeks. "Mrs. Frame sounds like a remarkable person. Almost as remarkable as the enchanting young woman she aided." His fingers paused. "Never be afraid to tell me anything, least of all about your gifts to others. The days of being punished for your kindness are over. I'm so bloody proud of you. Your selflessness, especially with those children, means more to me than I can explain."

"You needn't explain," Daphne whispered, reaching up to kiss her husband's chin. "Because, you see, just as you know me, I know you, as well."

"So you do."

An instant of silence hung between them.

"Why did you ask about Mrs. Frame?" Daphne inquired, studying her husband's veiled expression as if trying to assess its cause. "And what has she to do with Mrs. Gates's strange behavior?"

Pierce's brooding look vanished; his grin returned. "I suspect the late Duke and Duchess of Markham conducted themselves in a most conventional manner. Therefore, Mrs. Gates is as unaccustomed as the rest of the servants to our, shall we say informal, overseeing of the staff."

"Oh." Daphne ingested that possibility. "You're saying my offer to help out in the kitchen was improper?"

"I'm saying that the offer was totally improper and equally wonderful. Never change, Daphne. Your decency and lack of arrogance are humbling. Even to me." Pierce's eyes twinkled. "Moreover, if Mrs. Gates is unsettled by *your* actions, imagine what Langley and Bedrick are saying about mine. Why, poor Langley still clasps his gloved hands behind his back the instant he sees me approaching, terrified that I might repeat my original attempt to shake his hand in greeting. And Bedrick continues to appear dutifully in my bedchamber each morning, desperately hoping I'll reconsider and allow him to dress and shave me, although I repeatedly tell him to give it up. I doubt if either of them will ever be quite the same again."

Daphne laughed, smoothing the ends of Pierce's cravat. "We are a bit disconcerting, now that you call it to my attention."

Seeing the glow in his wife's eyes, feeling her small, delicate hands on his chest, Pierce was seized by a surge of lust, coupled with another, more complex emotion so powerful it nearly brought him to his knees.

"What is it?" Daphne reacted to the tensing of her husband's muscles.

Pierce stared down at her, feeling off balance in a way he'd never experienced and vulnerable in his inability to conquer it. Fiercely, he caught Daphne's fingers in his, brought her palms to his mouth, searching for words to explain what he himself couldn't fathom. "Your touch," he said hoarsely, responding to the only uncomplicated part of this madness —his lust. "The moment you put your hands on me, I'm on fire. It's as simple as that." He kissed the fluttering pulse at her wrist, traced the delicate veins with his tongue. "If the vicar weren't due here this minute, I'd lock that damned door, lower you to the carpet, and make love to you until you begged me to stop."

Daphne made a soft sound of pleasure, rising up on tiptoes to brush Pierce's lips with her own. "If my begging you to stop is the prerequisite to our receiving visitors, then I fear Markham will be sadly lacking in guests."

With a rough sound, Pierce dragged her into his arms. "You tempt me beyond reason."

"That's not temptation," Daphne demurred, her expression as heated as his. "'Tis merely gambling where I'm certain I'll win."

"Damn." Pierce's hands slid down to her bottom, lifting her purposefully against the rigid contours of his lower body. "Is the vicar ever late?"

"Never." Daphne pressed closer, her face flushed. "He'll be here any second."

"The way I feel now, I won't require much more than that." Hungrily, Pierce covered her mouth with his.

"Mr. Chambers."

Langley's proper announcement rang out, a deluge of ice water on Daphne and Pierce's intensifying embrace. Hastily, they broke apart, snapping about to face their mortified butler and distinguished dinner guest.

"F-forgive me, Your Grace," Langley attempted. "You told me to escort the vicar directly into the dining room."

"It's all right, Langley." As always, Pierce recovered his composure posthaste. "Thank you for showing the vicar in. You may leave us now."

Daphne was as shaken as the rapidly retreating butler. Blushing furiously, she went forward to greet her friend. "Vicar, I don't know what to say. I can imagine what you're thinking. I must have looked a total wanton."

"Shall I tell you how you looked, Snowdrop?" The clergyman smiled, reaching out to draw Daphne to him. With a gentle forefinger he raised her chin, beholding the miraculous transformation six weeks had wrought. "You looked happy. Happy and unconstrained by the past. And I was thinking how wonderful it is, at last, to feel your joy and to see your eyes alight with love."

Misty eyed, Daphne hugged her lifelong friend. "I'm so glad you're here."

"As am I."

"Let me pour you a brandy before I make a total fool of myself." Dashing away her tears, Daphne crossed the room to the sideboard.

With an expression of profound satisfaction, the vicar turned to Pierce. "Thank you for inviting me."

Pierce shook his head. "You nurtured my wife for twenty

years, offered her solace when she had none, and wed us without question or censure, despite the upheaval that precipitated our less-than-traditional ceremony. It is I who should be thanking you."

"You love Daphne," the vicar replied quietly, with uncanny insight. "'Tis all the thanks I need."

With that simple proclamation he went to get his brandy, leaving Pierce feeling as if he'd been punched. He was still reeling from his earlier emotional onslaught with Daphne, unnerved by the intensity of his feelings. That, combined with the vicar's declaration, was too much.

Inhaling slowly, Pierce fought for control and comprehension. It wasn't that the vicar's conclusion was erroneous, nor that it was so extraordinary a revelation. Pierce had known he cared deeply about his wife for weeks, maybe months. But to hear those irrevocable words spoken aloud, not by Daphne, when she shuddered in his arms or curled close to his side, but by a stranger—a stranger who referred, not to Daphne's feelings for him, but to his for her. Lord, the impact was staggering.

"Pierce? Would you like a brandy?"

Daphne's quizzical tone indicated that this was not the first time she'd asked.

"Yes, brandy would be excellent right about now." Veering toward the sideboard, Pierce took the proffered glass, drained it, then poured himself another.

"Are you all right?" Daphne asked.

"Never better." He tossed off the second drink, refilling the glass yet again.

"I think your husband is just nervous," Chambers put in, visibly amused. "Perhaps my visit is proving to be more taxing than he expected."

"Indeed." Pierce stared broodingly into his drink.

"What on earth are the two of you talking about?" Daphne demanded. "Nothing unnerves Pierce, so why should a dinner gathering?"

"Perhaps that was true once, but no longer." The vicar sipped at his drink. "Not since you became his wife, Snowdrop. Now, anything that affects you affects your husband. Which is as it should be. You'll be cared for and safe."

Pierce's head came up, like a wolf scenting danger. "Safe? Has Tragmore—?"

"No, nothing like that." Chambers negated Pierce's fears with an emphatic shake of his head. "I was just speaking generally. I haven't seen Harwick since the two of you signed your agreement. I didn't mean to alarm you."

"You're certain you haven't seen him? Not even at Rutland?"

"Not either of the times I visited, no."

Daphne stared from one man to the other. "You've been at Rutland?" she asked the vicar at last.

"I wanted to verify that your mother was well." He smiled. "Which, as you know, she is."

"We visited Mama last week." Daphne inclined her head in Pierce's direction. "You knew of the vicar's visits?"

"My guards advised me, yes."

"You said nothing." Daphne's brows drew together. "Neither, for that matter, did Mama."

A corner of Pierce's mouth lifted. "Despite my unorthodox upbringing, I do believe it is the mother who oversees her children, not the other way around."

"I suppose so. Still, I would think she'd say something."

"Not to mention how abbreviated our visit was." Pierce's eyes twinkled wickedly. "The two of you had scarcely begun chatting when our carriage was on its way back to Markham. There was hardly time for tea, much less conversation. It appears you and I have become surprisingly attached to this estate. One venture from its grounds and we can scarcely wait to return. An interesting twist of fate."

"Let me refill your drink, Vicar," Daphne urged hastily, her charming blush telling Pierce she'd grasped the implication of his words.

"I haven't finished this one." The vicar looked suspiciously close to laughter. "But I am quite famished," he added, graciously providing Daphne with the diversion she sought. "And whatever your cook has prepared smells superb."

"Wonderful!" Daphne gestured toward the table. "Please, sit. I'll check with Cook to see if our first course is ready."

Her departure was nearly as rapid as Langley's.

Chuckling, Pierce watched Daphne bolt, thinking how damned arousing her innocence was, how intoxicating he found each one of her facets. So shy in public, so passionate in bed. His beautiful, dazzling snow flame.

"There's no shame in loving your wife," the vicar murmured, studying Pierce with far-reaching wisdom.

"No, there isn't." Stiffening, Pierce made his way to the table and lowered himself into his chair. "Shame is not an issue. Risk is."

"Risk?" The vicar frowned, settling himself beside Pierce and immediately concentrating on the task of unfolding his napkin. "Funny, I seem to recall Daphne mentioning you were an exceptional gambler. According to her, the Markham investments have soared since you assumed your title."

"She's right. I am an exceptional gambler. And part of being an exceptional gambler is recognizing what you're willing to wager and what you're not. Sometimes the risk is simply too great."

"And sometimes the risk is nonexistent."

A muscle worked in Pierce's jaw.

"Daphne is deeply in love with you. You're a lucky man, one who has everything to gain and nothing to lose."

"Nothing to lose? I beg to differ with you, Vicar. I'm submerged in unchartered waters, wagering something I never knew I possessed and can't fathom losing. In short, I'm terrified." Pierce averted his head. "You say I'm lucky. Well, I've never relied upon luck, nor has it ever been my ally. All my life I fought for what I needed: food, money, survival. I battled for each victory with my blood, my sweat, or both. Now I'm being offered this rare and priceless gift, one I need far more than all the others combined." He drew a sharp breath. "And I keep waiting for it to be snatched away."

"You're a fine, compassionate man, Pierce. Did it ever occur to you that this blessing won't be snatched away? That perhaps, after the life you've just described, you truly deserve some happiness?" The clergyman cleared his throat. "I'm not privy to all the details of your past. But I am witnessing your present and, hopefully, your future. And yes, as I said, you are indeed lucky. Daphne's love belongs to you and that is a gift more precious than money can buy. But Daphne is equally lucky. Because, whether you perceive it or not, your love belongs to her as well."

As if to accentuate the fact, Daphne's laughter drifted in from the butler's pantry, permeating Pierce's heart like a warm summer breeze.

Warily, he nodded. "I can't argue with what I know to be true. Nevertheless, the reality is overwhelming. I've relied only upon myself for thirty years. I'm going to need some time to adjust."

"As I recall, you have until death do you part."

"So we do." For a long moment Pierce was silent. Then he met the vicar's gaze. "I understand now why Daphne cares so much about you. You're an extraordinary man."

"I return the compliment."

Again, silence.

"You've something else on your mind," Chambers stated quietly. "Feel free to speak it."

"Very well. You've known Daphne's father a long time. Do you think he'll honor our agreement?"

"You're worried."

"I have reason to be."

"Evidently, you know Harwick as well as I do."

"Too well," was the bitter reply. "And his lack of retaliation is making me very nervous."

"Perhaps having unencumbered access to his funds is enough vengeance for him."

Pierce gave a harsh laugh. "Hardly. Tragmore's vengeance would be to see me in hell."

"Then he's destined to be disappointed. Your hell is in the past. You won't see another."

A slight smile, followed by a measured look. "Vicar, I presume you've known the marchioness for many years, as well."

"Elizabeth? Yes. Many years."

"Then perhaps you can shed light on another concern of mine. Do you think Daphne's mother has the strength to pursue a divorce?"

Chambers looked sad rather than startled. "Perhaps once

my answer might have been yes. But now? After one and twenty years of torment? I seriously doubt it." He stared at the tablecloth. "Am I to presume you've given thought to aiding Elizabeth in severing her ties with Harwick?"

"I have. Great thought."

"And your grounds? Extreme cruelty?"

"Given the physical violence she's endured, yes, without question. But I wouldn't stop with the Church. I'd demand an Act of Parliament, granting the marchioness a legal divorce."

Now the vicar did start. "I assumed you meant divorce *a mensa et a thoro,* a Church-granted separation to protect Elizabeth from Harwick's cruelty. But a legal divorce? That is unheard of."

"Unusual, Vicar, but not unheard of." Pierce's jaw set in staunch determination. "The separation you've just described has ramifications I refuse to abide. Elizabeth would be safe, yes, but she'd also be permanently alone, unable to remarry. Worse than that, Daphne would be rendered illegitimate."

"You'd have to take your suit to the House of Lords."

"To a Court of the Common Law *and* the House of Lords," Pierce corrected. "I'm prepared to do both. Surely you can understand why. I've endured thirty years as a bastard, Vicar. I'd sell my soul before allowing Daphne to bear the brand of illegitimacy. The only way I have of protecting her is to secure, not only a religious, but a legal divorce for her mother."

The vicar drew a slow, inward breath. "I, of all people, yearn for Elizabeth's happiness. But a Parliamentary grant is rare enough for a man to obtain. Elizabeth is a woman. That makes your goal next to impossible, even with unlimited wealth and influence."

"As I told you earlier, I'm an exceptional gambler, one who has taken on far more insurmountable odds than these and won. As for wealth and influence, I have more than enough of both. I can make this divorce happen, I assure you. But not unless Daphne's mother truly wants it, wants it badly enough to let me fight for her freedom."

"She'd be ostracized by nearly everyone she knows."

"Perhaps. But do you truly believe that would be a great enough deterrent to stop her?"

"No," the vicar replied, his tone rich with memory's keen recall. "Deep inside Elizabeth lies the same strong and independent girl I knew in my youth."

"I agree. I've seen traces of that girl myself."

The two men's gazes locked.

Roughly, Chambers cleared his throat. "What can I do to help?"

"Talk to her. I think we both know she'll listen to you."

"Very well, Pierce. I'll try."

"Cook is hovering over our first course, ensuring its perfection," Daphne announced as she re-entered the room. "Having tasted it myself, I can assure you it is heavenly. She, however, is dubious. Hence, the entire staff, footmen and serving girls alike, are cajoling her into relinquishing it into their capable hands. Whoever is successful will be along straightaway with our food." Instantly, Daphne's alert gaze flickered from her husband to her old friend. "What are you two discussing so heatedly?"

"You," Pierce replied, coming to his feet. "The vicar was just reminding me of my great fortune and excellent taste in wives."

"And your husband was just concurring with my assessment," Chambers added.

Daphne flushed. "You're both inordinately biased. Besides, it is I who am fortunate. Not many women can boast of dining with two such heroic men at one time." She smiled up at Pierce, settling herself at the table. "Speaking of heroics," she turned to the vicar, "did Pierce tell you he plans to donate all the profits he reaped from his latest business investment—nearly twenty thousand pounds—to the parish schoolhouse? Why, with that vast sum we can provide, not only a new roof, but a whole new structure—a sturdier, warmer one, perhaps even of brick, plus new slates, books," Daphne's eyes twinkled, "even higher wages for Miss Redmund. Why, our subdued schoolmistress might just break down and smile; even laugh outright."

"No, he didn't mention it." A myriad of emotions crossed

the vicar's face. "God bless you, Pierce. Such generosity defies words."

"None are necessary." Determination hardened Pierce's features. "Children need both love and hope in order to survive, much less flourish. I have the funds to provide them with hope, and Daphne has the fullness of heart to provide them with love. If my wife and I have our way, those children will never know the onus of futility."

Joy and pride shone in Daphne's eyes, followed by a spark of illumination. "Vicar, what would you think about the children and us helping to rebuild their schoolhouse? I know we're not trained," she added hastily, seeing the vicar's surprised expression, "and perhaps all we can do is hand tools to the workmen. But think of the sense of fellowship it would give the children, the wondrous feeling of working side by side to accomplish something important to us all. Why, we'd be like a family, a unit. Wouldn't that teach them one of life's most important lessons: that respect, cooperation, and hard work yield success? Wouldn't it give them a tremendous sense of accomplishment? Of sharing? Of pride?"

"Enough!" the vicar laughed. "I can't dispute your point, Snowdrop. Nor can I think of any reason why we can't participate in the school's restoration."

"Pierce?" Daphne waited for her husband's response.

A corner of Pierce's mouth lifted. "It's December, sweetheart. Hardly the time to begin so massive an undertaking."

"But the roof is old and rotted. It can't last until spring." Daphne sat up straighter as another idea dawned. "How would it be if we replaced the roof immediately, and waited to rebuild the schoolhouse until spring? That would give us time to hire an architect who could, in turn, have three months to devise the most beneficial plans possible for a new school. We'd begin building on the site just after the first thaw. Why, we'd have months to erect the new structure."

Laughter erupted from Pierce's chest. "How can I argue with such unbridled enthusiasm? Your plan is excellent. I'll begin contacting workmen tomorrow. The new roof is as good as on."

"Oh, thank you, Pierce." Daphne leaned forward, impulsively hugging her husband. "When may we tell the children? I've missed visiting them, and I so want you to meet them, and they you. Perhaps we can convince Russet to finally join us."

"Vicar?" Pierce turned to their guest. "When is your next scheduled visit to the schoolhouse? My wife, her fox, and I would like to join you."

"I have business to attend to over the next few days," Chambers said, giving Pierce a meaningful look. "How would next week be?"

"Excellent," Pierce concurred at once.

"No, it isn't." Daphne looked positively crestfallen. "We accepted our first holiday invitation for next week. Viscount Benchley is hosting a lavish Christmas party at his country estate. We agreed to attend weeks ago."

"We could send our regrets," Pierce suggested.

"Don't tempt her," the vicar said affectionately. "Given a choice between an elegant ball and an afternoon at the schoolhouse, Daphne will undoubtedly opt for the latter." Growing sober, he took Daphne's hand. "I want you to go, Snowdrop. The merriment will do you good. Besides, the joy you share with your new husband is contagious. Perhaps you can infect others with it."

"But the children—"

"When does the party commence?"

"We leave for Benchley on Wednesday."

"Excellent. Then we shall visit the school on Monday. How would that be?"

"That would be wonderful." Daphne squeezed his hand. "Thank you, Vicar." She glanced up as a slender serving girl entered the room carrying a tray with three steaming bowls of artichoke soup. "At last! Our first course has arrived. Congratulations, Jane. I feared Cook might never be persuaded to relinquish her soup. Now hurry along and have a bowl yourself, you and the rest of the staff. Cook made enough for an army."

"Yes, ma'am, she did." The girl's head bobbed up and down, a genuine smile alighting her face. "Thank ye, ma'am." She scurried off.

"Wait until you sample this," Daphne told the vicar proudly. "You may decide never to leave."

Two hours later, full of roast pheasant, stewed mushrooms, Yorkshire pudding, and lemon pie, the vicar wholeheartedly agreed.

Pushing back his plate, he groaned. "You were right, Snowdrop. Not only do I not wish to leave such a splendid feast, I fear I might never be able to. With the massive amounts of food I've just consumed, I doubt I can stand, much less walk."

Daphne laughed, rising from the table. "Why don't we adjourn to the sitting room? I'm sure some conversation and an exceptional glass of claret will do wonders for—" She broke off, swaying on her feet, groping for a nonexistent object upon which to brace herself.

Pierce caught her just before she fell.

"She's fainted," the vicar said, his features tight with concern.

"She's white as a sheet," Pierce managed, looking as pale as his wife. Swiftly, he carried Daphne into the sitting room where he placed her gently on the sofa. "Snow flame?" Lightly, he stroked her face, brushing tendrils of hair from her forehead. When she didn't respond, he turned paralyzed eyes to the vicar. "What do I do?"

Instantly, the vicar appraised the situation. Pierce was bordering on panic. In that state, he could do naught but get in the way. "Go to Daphne's bedchamber. I'm certain you'll find a vial of smelling salts there."

Pierce's eyes narrowed. "This has happened before?"

"On occasion, yes."

Comprehension dawned. "When that bloody bastard beat her."

"Get the smelling salts, Pierce," the vicar instructed quietly. "Daphne will be fine."

This time Pierce complied, taking the steps two at a time, bursting into Daphne's bedchamber like a man possessed. "Lily!" he bellowed. Not waiting for a reply, he began flinging items from Daphne's dressing table, frantically searching for the vial he sought.

Nothing.

236

Her nightstand.

Veering around, Pierce crossed the room, yanking open Daphne's nightstand drawer. The vial was right in front, the first thing he spied. Seizing it, he raced back to the sitting room where the vicar, surrounded by over a dozen worried servants, was pressing cold compresses to Daphne's forehead.

"Let me through," Pierce ordered. Instantly, the servants complied, hastily making a path for the duke to pass. He knelt at Daphne's side, waving the vial beneath her nose. "Please, sweetheart. Open your eyes. Damn it, Vicar, she's been unconscious for at least a quarter hour!"

"It's been a scant two minutes, Pierce. See? There, she's coming around."

Daphne shook her head and blinked, slowly opening her eyes. "Pierce?" She pushed the smelling salts away, her fingers going to the cold cloth against her forehead. "What happened? Why are you all staring at me?"

"You fainted, Snow flame. You scared the hell out of me. Are you all right?"

"Yes, I'm fine. That's odd. I normally never faint unless Father—" She saw the murderous glint in Pierce's eyes and checked herself.

"Is the duchess well, Your Grace?" Langley demanded.

"Apparently, yes. Nevertheless, she is going straight to bed." So saying, Pierce scooped Daphne into his arms and rose. "Vicar, you'll forgive us. I want Daphne to rest."

"Of course."

"I don't need rest," Daphne protested.

"You're going to get it anyway." Pierce was already halfway across the room.

"Vicar, don't forget our visit to the schoolhouse Monday," Daphne called over her husband's retreating shoulder.

"I won't. In the interim, you take care of yourself."

"Really, Pierce, this is ridiculous," Daphne demurred.

Her husband's taut jaw told her she was wasting her time.

"Where the hell is Lily?" Pierce demanded, depositing Daphne on her bed.

"I gave her the evening off."

"Fine. Then I'll stand in as your lady's maid."

Daphne couldn't suppress a smile. With his towering height, powerful build, and smoldering expression, Pierce looked about as much like a lady's maid as an avenging Greek god. "Are you adept at braiding hair?"

"Very amusing." He began unbuttoning the back of her gown.

"Pierce, I really am fine," she said softly, stroking his arm.

"And you'll be finer still once you've rested." Systematically, he undressed her down to her chemise, then tucked her beneath the bedcovers. "Mr. Chambers seemed unsurprised by your fainting spell. In fact, he was even aware that you kept smelling salts. Why is that?"

With a resigned sigh, Daphne replied, "Because this has happened two or three times in the past, when I was particularly overwrought by an encounter with Father."

"An encounter," Pierce echoed bitterly. "You mean a thrashing. I take it that means you've shared the full extent of your father's brutality with the vicar."

"No." Daphne shook her head, a troubled frown forming on her face. "The vicar knows only that Father strikes me when his temper overcomes his reason. But constant beatings? The scars on my back? Only you know of those, Pierce." She gripped her husband's forearms tightly. "If the vicar were privy to the whole truth, it would kill him. Not only for me, but for Mama."

Privately, Pierce disagreed with Daphne's assessment of the vicar's insights. Perhaps the clergyman had never viewed Daphne's or Elizabeth's scars firsthand, but the anguish on his face when he'd spoken of Elizabeth's torment, the resignation in his voice—no, Pierce was certain Chambers perceived only too well what transpired under Tragmore's roof. And that perception, together with his own helpless inability to set things right, was tearing him apart.

"Pierce?" Daphne probed anxiously. "You won't tell him, will you?"

"No, Snow flame," Pierce assured his wife. "I won't burden the vicar with any more than he already knows. What you've shared with me, showed me, will remain between us. However, I'm now thoroughly confused. You just said your previous fainting spells were caused by episodes with your father. Yet, in order to keep the truth from Mr. Chambers I have to assume you didn't flee directly to the church after your father's assaults; that you waited long enough to compose yourself. Therefore, how could the vicar have been with you when you fainted?"

Daphne plucked at the bedcovers, attempting to explain something she wasn't sure could be conveyed. "I didn't compose myself. I was quite hysterical when I reached the church."

"I don't understand."

"I know. But I believe you of all people can. For my most terrifying moments, like yours, were caused not by physical but emotional pain. The salvation I craved and that which the vicar provided, the times when circumstances seemed most unbearable, came not after Father had beaten me, but rather after days had passed when he hadn't." She shuddered. "I can't begin to describe my mounting dread, lying awake, night after night, never knowing when my bedchamber door would burst open and Father would charge in, eyes ablaze, stick clenched violently in his fist."

"You don't have to describe that feeling," Pierce broke in, assailed by dark childhood memories.

Daphne nodded and drew a slow, trembling breath. "I thought not. In any case, there were times the apprehension became unendurable. I dared not go to Mama. The consequences would be dire. So I raced to the church, and the vicar. He was all I had until you. And, in answer to your question, he demanded no explanation nor did I provide one. I wept, and he took my hands in his, offered me his prayers and his friendship. Several times that wasn't enough. The combination of my nerves, which were long since frayed, and the frantic run to the village sapped my strength to the point where my body simply gave out."

"And you fainted."

"Yes."

With painstaking tenderness, Pierce gathered Daphne to him, pressing her head against his shoulder. "Never again," he said, his voice hoarse with emotion. "Never again will you be without the strength you need. When your own subsides, mine will replace it." Softly, he kissed her hair.

"But why tonight, Snow flame?" he murmured. "You were so happy. And you're far away from Tragmore, unthreatened by your father's rage. What caused you to faint?"

With a self-deprecating smile, Daphne leaned back in his arms. "Stupidity. Mingled with excitement. I was so caught up with the arrangements for tonight, and the arrival of our first dinner guest, that I skipped breakfast and didn't eat all day. That wine I drank at dinner must have gone straight to my head."

"You're right," Pierce retorted, nearly weak with relief. "It was stupid. Now go to sleep. And don't scare me like that again."

Daphne laughed, unfooled by her husband's show of bravado. "You become more heroic by the day. Reluctant, perhaps, unconventional, for certain, but heroic." She yawned, settling back against the pillows. "I'm not the least bit tired." Her lashes drifted to her cheeks.

Seconds later, she was asleep.

For long moments Pierce remained where he was, drinking in his wife's incredible, untainted beauty, not only that which was visible to the eye, but that which was not. How fiercely she protected those she loved, even at the risk of her own safety. And her values—as unsullied and precious as the innocence she'd gifted only to him. A one-guest dinner party and the concept of restoring a battered roof exhilarated her more than a deluge of elegant balls and a strongbox of jewels. Her heart was full—with love, with compassion, with the wonder of discovery. And, by some miracle, that incomparable heart belonged to him.

As his did to her.

Pierce rose, walking inanely about the room. He'd never uttered the words *I love you* aloud, never even dreamed he was capable of feeling them. But all that was once dead inside him had been reborn that fateful day at Newmarket when Daphne came into his life. And whether he uttered the words or not, they were there.

Reveling in this strange, new emotion, Pierce glanced back at the bed, smiling when he saw how deeply asleep his "untired" wife was. He strolled over to the nightstand, intending to extinguish the lamp. Noting the chaos he'd created in her open drawer, he paused to rearrange the items he'd flung about in his earlier search for smelling salts. He was about to slide the drawer shut when the corner of a sheet of paper caught his eye. The headline, "Tin Cup Bandit Eludes Authorities Again," immediately captured his attention. Without thinking, he reached in to extract the paper, only to find that it was part of a bound volume of some sort. His curiosity thoroughly aroused, Pierce eased the book from its home, opening the volume to scan its contents.

"Bandit Succeeds—Workhouse Prospers!," was the first headline Pierce turned to. He recognized the article at once. It was one of the first reported by the London *Times* when the bandit had made his debut amid the beau monde.

Brows drawn in bafflement, Pierce turned the page once, twice, three times. Each page was the same: an article recounting the bandit's latest crime, right up to his most recent theft at the Earl of Selbert's Mansfield estate, together with the authorities' frustration at not being able to thwart the mysterious phantom who preyed on the rich and gave to the needy.

What Pierce was holding was a damned testimonial to the Tin Cup Bandit.

Slamming the book onto the nightstand, Pierce was seized by unreasonable, irrational jealousy that blasted through him like gunfire. At the same time, he was appalled at the ludicrousness of his own reaction. What the hell was he jealous of? *He* was the bandit, for God's sake. Not to mention the fact that the bandit wasn't actually a man, but a legend, a valiant figment of Daphne's fanciful mind.

But he wasn't only a legend, damn it. He was flesh and blood, a man Daphne had met in the intimacy of her own bedchamber. They'd stood tantalizingly close, heat blazing between them, and her response to his touch had *not* been his imagination. He was a man, all right, one who had wanted Daphne Wyndham with every fiber of his being.

What was more, the blossoming woman within Daphne had wanted him, too.

She hadn't—couldn't—have recognized that, he argued with himself for the umpteenth time. She was too damned naive.

Still, she'd gazed up at him, adoration lighting those mesmerizing kaleidoscope eyes, and her breath had quickened when he'd come near. Consciously or not, she'd responded to him. And all this time he'd excused it away with the fact that she'd never been this close to a man and was therefore too inexperienced to recognize what was happening or to dismiss it in lieu of something real—the something she experienced in Pierce's arms.

But she was a married woman now. And she bloody well understood what passion was about. Hell, not mere passion. Explosive, consuming passion that was intensified all the more by the fact that it was rooted in love. She belonged to him, body and soul. So why the hell had she brought that bloody journal with her to her new life as his wife?

No. Any way he contemplated it, the result was the same. His wife, in love with him or not, was at the same time completely enthralled with another man.

Even as he flinched at the thought, Pierce shook his head in self-censuring disbelief. For the love of heaven, he was behaving as if Daphne had been unfaithful to him.

Well, hadn't she?

No. Yes. In a matter of speaking.

Pierce uttered a muffled curse. His deduction was utter lunacy, and he knew it, and that only served to heighten his rage. Daphne's betrayal, if one could call it that, was only in thought, not fact. Yet it was still thoroughly untenable. Especially tonight, when he'd finally admitted to himself that he loved her, when the vulnerability spawned by his newly acknowledged emotions demanded that she belong wholly and forever to him.

Determinedly, Pierce lowered himself to the edge of a chair, gripping his knees as he began his evening vigil. He'd wait for Daphne to waken.

At which time she had a great deal of explaining to do.

The heavyset man arrived at Tragmore precisely on schedule. Ushered to the marquis's study, he extracted a folded sheet of paper from his coat pocket and shifted uncomfortably from one foot to the other.

"You have a report for me?" Tragmore demanded, sipping at his brandy.

"Yes, sir. However, my findings are rather disappointing."

"I'll be the judge of that."

"Very well." The man cleared his throat. "Lady Tragmore has received a mere three visitors at Rutland."

"Really? Who?"

"Your daughter, for one. Accompanied by her new husband."

Tragmore waved that information away. "And the third guest?"

Pudgy cheeks drooped lower still. "Your church vicar."

The marquis's glass came down with a thud. "Chambers?" His eyes glinted. "You're certain?"

A nod. "I'm certain. Is that significant?"

"I don't pay you to ask questions, Larson. I pay you to answer them." Tragmore walked around to the front of his desk. "How many times did the vicar call on my wife?"

"Twice."

"And how long did he stay?"

Larson glanced at his notes. "A quarter hour the first time, a bit longer the second."

"Let me see that." Tragmore snatched the paper from Larson, scanning it with the greatest of interest.

"That copy is yours, my lord."

"Excellent." With a grand sweep, Tragmore placed the page on his desk. "Precisely what I'd hoped to see." Reaching into his pocket, he extracted a hundred-pound note. "Here's something for your diligence, Larson. Now keep up the fine work."

The investigator blinked, accepting the note with as much bewilderment as pleasure. "Keep up . . . ? I thought you'd no longer require my services. I mean, given that your wife hasn't done anything indiscreet."

"I beg to differ with you." An ugly smile curved Tragmore's lips. "I need your services now more than ever. So return to your post. I'll expect your next report in a week."

Larson shrugged. "Whatever you say, sir."

"Good. We understand each other. Good night, Larson."

"Good night, my lord." Larson took his leave, greedily fingering the hundred-pound note before shoving it into his pocket.

Harsh laughter exploded from Tragmore's chest. Let the fool have his hundred pounds. If things continued as planned, the rewards would render that sum insignificant.

Yes, in a very short time the Marquis of Tragmore would have money to burn.

17

IT WAS JUST AFTER MIDNIGHT WHEN DAPHNE OPENED HER EYES.

She was greeted by Pierce's brooding stare.

"Pierce?" She pushed herself to a sitting position, wondering with sleepy disorientation why her husband looked so angry. "What time is it?"

"Five after twelve. You've been asleep for nearly three hours."

"Three hours? I must have been more exhausted than I realized." She inclined her head quizzically. "Is something wrong?"

"Wrong? Yes." Pierce bolted to his feet, snatching the journal from her nightstand and thrusting it at her. "This is wrong."

Briefly, Daphne glanced at the journal. Then, her gaze lifted back to her husband. "It's a collection of articles reporting the triumphs of the Tin Cup Bandit."

"I *know* what it is," he snapped. "What I *don't* know is why you have it."

Daphne gave him a baffled look. "I collected it."

"Obviously. But why?"

She blinked. "Because I admire him more than I can say.

245

Because he's a hero. In my opinion, one of the greatest heroes of our time, despite his unorthodox methods."

"How touching." Pierce tossed the journal aside, struggling with a blistering resurgence of jealousy.

"I don't understand why this angers you so." Daphne rose from the bed, staring at Pierce with a thoroughly perplexed expression. "Surely you don't condemn me for applauding someone who takes from the rich and greedy and bestows upon those in need?"

"For applauding him, no. But that," Pierce gestured toward the journal, "is not acclaim, it's preoccupation."

Daphne looked torn between annoyance and laughter. "This conversation is ridiculous."

"Why? Because it troubles me that my wife keeps an ever growing testimonial to another man?"

"Another man? My only link to the bandit is through these articles, Pierce. I would hardly describe that as a scandalous relationship. Why, I've scarcely even spoken to—" She broke off, blushing furiously.

"You've scarcely even spoken to him?" Pierce jumped on her words. "So you've met this incomparable bandit."

"Only once." Daphne averted her head. "The night he robbed Tragmore. I awakened during the theft. We exchanged a few words, nothing more."

"And where did you come upon him? The library? The sitting room?"

"No." Her voice was barely audible. "My bedchamber."

"Your bedchamber," Pierce repeated.

"Yes. He came to take my jewelry. I arose and assisted him." With a deep breath, Daphne raised her head, her chin set proudly. "I asked that he give the night's booty to the House of Perpetual Hope. He agreed. I then placed his jewel and tin cup on my father's pillow, thus allowing him to make his escape."

A muscle worked in Pierce's jaw. "Have you any idea what your father would have done to you if he'd discovered your actions?"

"Of course. It didn't dissuade me then. It wouldn't now. I'd do the same thing all over again, given the chance. And so would you."

Pierce couldn't dispute that logic. Neither, however, could he dispel his aching sense of betrayal, ludicrous or not. "Tell me about him."

"The bandit? There's nothing to tell. As I said, we scarcely spoke. If it's his appearance you're curious about, I could make out very little. He was swathed in black, from boots to hood. Completely concealed. As was his voice, which he kept to a rasp." Daphne shrugged. "That's the entirety of it."

"Did he touch you?" Pierce was appalled to hear himself blurt.

"Touch me?" The color was back on her cheeks. "I believe he touched my hair."

"You *believe?*"

"All right, yes, he touched my hair. It was clearly an expression of appreciation. He made no improper advances, if that's what you're attempting to discern."

"Would you recognize it if he had?"

Her eyes widened. "Pardon me?"

"You were so bloody innocent. How would you know if a man were making an advance?"

Daphne's lips twitched. "I recall identifying your advances, despite my lack of experience." She wrapped her arms about Pierce's waist. "You're behaving irrationally, you know."

"Don't you think I know that?" he bit out, enfolding her against him, tangling his fingers in her hair. "I've been wild ever since I discovered that journal, smoldering while I waited for you to awaken and explain it away. And, yes, I hear every senseless word I'm raving. I sound like a crazed lunatic, and yet I can't seem to stop myself. I, the consummate gambler, the unruffleable, level-headed essence of reason. I'm jealous of a bloody phantom? A marauder of the night who exists more in people's minds than in fact? Damn it!" He shook his head in self-deprecating amazement, struck by the full irony of the situation. What would his wife say if she knew that the man he resented was none other than himself? "I must be losing my mind."

"No," Daphne whispered, rubbing her cheek against Pierce's shirt. "Your heart, perhaps, but not your mind. As for sounding like a crazed lunatic, I disagree. What you sound is possessive and perhaps a bit vulnerable. Given the circumstances, both are understandable." She lay her hand over his heart. "The vulnerability will subside once you accept the truth: that the risk you fear is unfounded and nonexistent."

"Daphne." Pierce's gaze bore into hers, her name an agonized rumble from deep within his chest.

"I love you," she breathed back, a healing balm to his tortured senses. "Only you. Always you."

The inescapable prison he carried inside him shattered, capitulating at last beneath his wife's gentle attempts to breach its unyielding walls. The senseless envy that had dominated his heart until moments ago receded beneath the intensity of something far more powerful, and the knowledge that, once he gave voice to the words, the circle would be complete and no one, bandit or otherwise, could sever the bond that forged between them.

Pierce brought Daphne's palms to his lips, determined, now more than ever, to say aloud what he knew to be true, thus relinquishing the emotional isolation that had defined his past. "I want to give you the words," he began.

Daphne silenced him with a gentle forefinger to his lips. "You already have. It isn't necessary for you to speak them."

"Yes, it is. Moreover, I *want* to speak them." Pierce kissed the delicate veins at her wrists, the scented skin of her forearms, her shoulders. Slowly, his fingers traced the lacy edge of her chemise where it dipped down at her breasts. "But I want to speak them my way."

Daphne's gaze was fixed on his roving hand, her breath already unsteady. "Your way?"

"Um hum." Pierce watched as soft color suffused her skin, his own body quickening in response. "I've waited thirty years to say these words, precious words I never expected to feel, much less say. So forgive me for being a bit selfish about the circumstances under which they are said."

"How do you wish—"

Daphne's question caught in her throat as Pierce reached down, catching the hem of her chemise and tugging it up and over her head. "In bed," he answered, drinking in her flawless nudity with a hotly intimate look that made her tremble. "When I'm deep inside you. When I can watch your face, your every expression, when I can see, taste, savor your reaction as I tell you, show you, how I feel. Is that all right?"

Dazedly, Daphne nodded, her husband's vows shivering through her. "Can it be now?" she asked in a hushed, heated whisper. "I don't think I can wait."

"And I've waited too long already." Pierce yanked his clothes from his body, flinging them haphazardly about the room, pressing Daphne back into the bedcovers and following her down. "No barriers, my beautiful wife," he murmured, taking her mouth under his. "Nothing but us—and this."

Daphne whimpered, opening instantly to the demand of Pierce's lips. Passion exploded at the first glide of his tongue against hers, their kisses turning frantic, hungry, filled with poignant discovery and aching wonder.

Casting all past demons aside, Pierce gave himself to his wife as he never had before, showing her, not only that she belonged to him, but that he belonged to her as well.

"Touch me," he commanded, capturing her hand and bringing it to his chest. "Touch me everywhere, and feel what you do to me, how much I need you."

Daphne instantly understood what her husband's request implied, eagerly embraced the gift she was being offered. Without hesitation, her fingers glided through the soft mat of hair that curled on his chest, the hard muscles that defined the powerful width of his shoulders and arms. Lovingly, she caressed his back, tracing a line to its base, absorbing Pierce's shudder as she stroked his buttocks, the solid columns of his thighs. With a breathy sigh, she moved around to his abdomen, and Pierce gritted his teeth as her fingers drifted lower, lower still.

He was totally unprepared for the impact of her touch. When Daphne's feather-light fingers brushed his rigid shaft, then curled around to explore its pulsing length, a hoarse groan erupted from his chest and he squeezed his eyes shut, struggling to curtail the hot release already clamoring at his loins.

Instantly, Daphne paused. "Am I hurting you?" she whispered.

Despite the nearly unbearable passion surging through him, Pierce smiled. "Not hurting me. Killing me. Christ." He moved against her hand, another groan shuddering from his chest.

"Shall I stop?"

"Never. Never, Snow flame."

"But—"

Pierce opened his eyes, forcing himself under control at least long enough to erase the concern from Daphne's face. "When you cry out my name, beg me to stop, do you really want me to?"

A spark of understanding lit her hazel gaze. "No."

"Then don't even consider ending your torture. It's heaven—and hell."

Tentatively, Daphne caressed him again, lingering at the velvety tip when Pierce growled harshly, caught her wrist in a vise grip. "Is that good?"

He couldn't speak.

She repeated the caress, fascinated by the warm droplets of fluid that greeted her touch, awed by the very essence that was Pierce.

"Men and women are more alike than I realized," she murmured, more to herself than to him. "I wonder—what pleases me, would it please you as well?"

He might have nodded. He didn't know, or care. For at that moment Daphne bent her head, her silky hair sweeping across his thighs as she took him into her mouth, learning his taste as he had hers.

And the world ceased to exist.

Pierce unraveled at her first exquisite contact, the first brush of her tongue against his throbbing flesh. He heard his irrepressible shout, felt his body and his mind reel out of control. Nothing existed but Daphne's touch, the unendurable ecstasy of being possessed by her hands, her mouth, her breath as it rippled over his painfully sensitive shaft. He tangled his hands in her hair, urging her closer, begging her to take more and more of him, a dark haze dominating his senses as every fiber of his being screamed for release.

In an instant it would be too late.

Abruptly, he shook his head, pushing her away with his last remaining shred of sanity. "No," he gasped. "Not this time. Not this way." He rolled her beneath him before she could finish her initial protest. "Daphne." Every muscle in his body was taut to breaking as he fought back his raging climax.

She responded to the urgency of his tone, her lashes lifting to meet the smoldering frenzy of his gaze.

"Do you feel it?" he demanded, dragging air into his lungs in great gulps. "Do you, Snow flame?"

"Yes," she whispered, opening herself to him as she caressed his trembling forearms. "Oh, yes."

Pierce captured her hands in his, lifting both arms over her head and interlacing their fingers, all the while refusing to relinquish her stare. "I love you." His words coincided with his body's initial penetration. Parting the delicate folds of her skin, he pressed into her welcome wetness, tightening his grasp on her fingers as he battled for a final vestige of control. "I love you," he repeated hoarsely, pushing forward until they were one.

Two tears slid down Daphne's cheeks.

Instantly, Pierce stilled. "Am I hurting you?"

Daphne smiled through her tears, reiterating the very words he had used mere moments ago. "Not hurting me. Killing me. But don't even consider ending your torture."

Pierce laughed, a husky, primitive sound of pure male satisfaction. "Never, my beautiful wife. Never." His words ended on an agonized groan as Daphne raised her hips, drew him deeper inside her. And everything inside him snapped.

Throwing his head back, Pierce began to move in hard, frantic strokes. "I can't." Sweat drenched his back. "Daphne, I can't wait."

From far away he heard her high, feverish cry. Dimly, he felt her legs clamp around his waist, her fingers tighten in his as she met his wildness, thrust for thrust. Already delayed beyond endurance, his climax erupted in a heartbeat, tearing through his loins, setting fire to his every nerve ending as it exploded from his body into Daphne's in an endless, scalding torrent. He shouted her name, unable to still the driving motion of his hips, lunging forward again and again as he poured his being into hers.

He felt Daphne tense, her body arching like a bowstring as the fire ignited, spread as wildly through his wife as it had through him. She cried out, once, twice, then tossed her head on the pillow as the spiraling began, spasms of completion that escalated higher and harder than ever before.

Pierce shuddered, dropped his head into the curve of her shoulder as he reveled in her climax, surrendered himself to the hard contractions that gripped his shaft, made him shudder anew. Amazingly, another wrenching spasm was torn from his loins, liquid heat merging with his wife's final, glorious tremors.

Weak, utterly spent, they collapsed in each other's arms, both loathe to move, unable to speak.

Pierce felt his wife's tears, the gentle quaking of her body as she wept.

"Don't cry, Snow flame," he murmured into her disheveled cloud of hair. "Please, don't cry."

"I never knew such joy existed," Daphne whispered. "Thank you, Pierce. You've just given me the most wondrous gift."

A hard lump formed in Pierce's throat, a constriction too vast to overcome with words, even those he'd just uttered for the first time. Daphne believed his love to be a gift, and so it was. But it was she, not he, who had bestowed it, offering him unconditional love and faith and, the greatest miracle of all, teaching him to do the same.

Reflexively, Pierce's arms tightened around his wife, overwhelmed by the miracle that was his. More fervently than ever he reiterated his silent vow that nothing, no one, would ever hurt Daphne again.

Not her father's hatred.

Nor the exploits of the Tin Cup Bandit.

"Does Pierce seem well to you?" Daphne asked the vicar anxiously.

Her friend blinked in surprise, glancing across the schoolroom to where Pierce stood amid the squealing children, watching Russet chase his tail in wide, vigorous circles.

"Why, yes, he seems fine. The children are enthralled, your reticent little fox cub has unconditionally befriended him. Why, even our difficult-to-please Miss Redmund is smiling. I'd say your new husband's coming out has been an unequivocal success." The clergyman studied Daphne's furrowed brow. "What is disturbing you, Snowdrop?"

Daphne gave a tentative shrug. "I'm not certain. Pierce has been so preoccupied lately, as if something is troubling him, something he chooses not to discuss."

"I noticed no sign of that when I visited Markham last week."

"It's worsened since then."

"Have you questioned him?"

"Of course. He never quite answers. Nor does he deny being troubled. He only changes the subject as rapidly as possible." She inclined her head quizzically. "Would you speak with him, Vicar?"

"What exactly is it you'd like me to say?"

"Convince him that he needn't keep his emotional quandaries to himself. Remind him that love involves more than tenderness and passion. It involves friendship and trust. He respects you, Vicar. If anyone can convince him to share himself, that someone is you."

A flash of insight flickered in the vicar's eyes. "You know precisely what's bothering your husband, don't you?"

"I have my suspicions, yes. But that matters not. In this case it is Pierce who must come to me, not I to him. Please, will you talk to him?"

"Very well, Snowdrop. As it happens, I have another matter I must discuss with Pierce today. I'll bring your concerns up immediately thereafter."

"Thank you." Daphne squeezed his arm. "I feel better already."

"Daphne?" Pierce called. "Would you like to tell the children of our proposed group project?"

She smiled, walking over to join her husband, pausing to scoop her exhausted pet from the floor. "I'd be delighted to."

"What project?" Timmy demanded.

"How would you all like to help us put a new roof on the school?"

"Us?" William's eyes nearly bugged out of his head. "But we don't know nothin' about buildin'."

"Nor do we." Daphne grinned. "But we've hired workmen who do. Tolerant, accommodating workmen who won't mind having us underfoot as they hammer and nail."

"Wow!"

"And that's not all." Daphne inclined her head proudly at her husband. "It appears we've amassed enough funds to arrange for a whole new schoolhouse to be built this spring. Isn't that wonderful, Miss Redmund?"

"Hmm?" The schoolmistress was gazing at Pierce with a foolish expression on her face. "Yes, lovely."

"Did ye 'ear what Daphne said, Miss Redmund?" Timmy demanded, staring at his teacher. "We're gonna 'ave a new school soon. We 'ave lots of money."

Miss Redmund blinked, her attention finally captured. "A new school? How on earth . . . ?"

"I bet the duke is payin' for it," William guessed shrewdly.

"Are you *really* a duke?" one of the older boys asked.

A corner of Pierce's mouth lifted. "It would seem so, yes."

"'ey, Daphne. That makes ye a duchess," Timmy informed her.

"So it does," she agreed.

"Can we pat Russet now?" Evidently, Timmy's awe over Daphne's newly acquired title paled in comparison to his excitement over her pet.

"Only if you do so one at a time and only if I hold him. Russet is a bit wary around strangers. But the fact that he was showing off his tail-chasing skills is a good sign." She stroked the cub's silky head, murmuring softly to him until his ears flattened and he rubbed his chin and nose affectionately against Daphne's hair. "I think he's feeling receptive now," she announced. "Timmy, would you like to be first since it was your idea?"

The children were all enjoying their visit with Russet

when the vicar approached Pierce. "May we talk privately for a few moments?" he murmured.

Nodding, Pierce detached himself from the group, confident that the children were too engrossed to notice his absence. "What's on your mind, Vicar?"

"As I'm sure your guards have advised you, I visited Rutland the day after I dined with you and Daphne."

"You spoke with Elizabeth?"

"I did." The vicar sighed. "She was quite shocked at first, and more than a little dubious that a Parliamentary divorce was possible. But I explained everything you said, and she's willing to place her future in your hands, Pierce." The clergyman's expression softened, a reminiscent light dawning in his eyes. "Evidently, Elizabeth has managed to retain the peppery spark I recall from her youth. I thank God for that."

"I'll contact my solicitor at once, advise him to engage the finest barrister in all of England—and the boldest." Pierce was already making plans aloud. "Then, directly after the holiday party at Benchley, I'll leave for London and meet with them." A corner of his mouth lifted in wry amusement. "Poor Hollingsby. I've hurled his orderly life into chaos these past weeks. And now he'll have yet another unique legal proceeding to contend with on my behalf. Still, I rather suspect that, in his own way, he'll enjoy challenging the odds and emerging triumphant, which I fully intend he should do. This is one victory I can hardly wait to savor." Pierce met the vicar's gaze. Keen insight blended with gratitude. "Thank you."

"For what?"

"For speaking with Elizabeth. I think we both know how much your encouragement influenced her decision."

A shout of laughter interrupted their conversation.

Turning his head, Pierce chuckled as he watched Daphne trying to unseat Russet from his position of safety atop her head. "Evidently, Russet has had enough human contact for one day."

"Your love for Daphne. You've accepted it, taken her into your heart."

Pierce's brows rose at the vicar's unexpected assessment. "That shouldn't surprise you. Not after our chat last week."

"It doesn't. But perhaps you need to reinforce that acceptance, not for my sake, but for your own."

"Why?"

"Because love has many facets, some naturally and easily explored, others quite difficult. The beauty of the more resistant facets is that, once you've probed their depths, you have a lifetime to enjoy the brilliance you've unearthed."

"To which resistant facets are you referring?"

Chambers cleared his throat. "When two people care for each other it's only natural to want to share, not only your hearts and bodies, but your minds as well. Secrets, well meant or not, can do naught but drive a wedge between you. Remember Pierce, never confuse protection with exclusion. One nurtures, the other destroys."

"You've been talking to Daphne."

"She's worried about you."

"I know." Wearily, Pierce rubbed the back of his neck. "And she needn't be. I merely have an aspect of my past yet to resolve. Somehow I must do it, and soon."

"But must you do it alone? Daphne loves you deeply, and she is far stronger than you might imagine. Let her share your unrest, Pierce."

With a troubled sigh, Pierce replied, "I appreciate your advice, Vicar. I, better than anyone, know just how strong Daphne is. But this is not a matter of strength, 'tis a matter of safety. And Daphne's safety supersedes all else, even the trust that has grown between us." Pierce swallowed, his voice growing rough with emotion. "You see, Vicar, I've come to realize that my wife means more to me than anything: my past, my turmoil, even my own life."

"I understand." The clergyman nodded solemnly. "I also perceive that your current dilemma is not a minor one. Therefore, let me add one additional thought. Despite the short duration of our acquaintanceship, I hold you in the highest regard. I admire you and I respect you. In short, I consider you a friend. If ever you need a ready ear, I'd be pleased to provide one."

"That means a great deal." With a quick glance at

Daphne and the children, Pierce added, "Unfortunately, this is one impasse I must conquer on my own."

"Then may God help you do so."

Soberly, Pierce rejoined his wife, wishing yet again that he could do as the vicar suggested: share his dilemma with Daphne and tell her of the decision he faced. He'd evaded the issue for weeks, buried his conflicting emotions in the sweet haven of Daphne's body. But he could avoid the matter no longer. A determination needed to be made.

Would there be a future for the Tin Cup Bandit?

His fists balling at his sides, Pierce was besieged by the usual clashing sentiments, and the nearly irresistible urge to share his anguish with his wife. Silently, he berated himself, reasserting his original vow not to involve Daphne in the reality of his dual identity. Were he ever unmasked, he would be tried, and possibly hanged, for his crimes. And if Daphne had any knowledge of his actions, she would be implicated as well. No. It was simply too dangerous.

His mind was made up. The intricate crossroads he now confronted were his and his alone to traverse.

"Daphne, do ye think the Tin Cup Bandit can find yer new 'ouse as easily as 'e did yer old one?" Inadvertently, Timmy exploded into the very territory Pierce sought to escape. "Because if 'e can't, ye won't ever see him again."

"'e's not gonna rob 'er again, stupid," William replied in an exasperated tone. "'e never robs the same person twice. Besides, why would 'e rob 'er now? She's married to Pierce. And Pierce uses 'is money on us, not jewels and silver."

Daphne cast a sidelong glance at her husband. "I don't think it matters where the bandit strikes," she concluded hastily. "So long as he continues to benefit those who need it."

"Amen," the vicar agreed.

Pierce felt his guts twist, the enormity of his quandary resurging full force.

What was he going to do?

Evading Daphne's speculative gaze, Pierce stared out the window, reflecting back on the bandit's inception and the motives that had incited it.

First and most impelling had been his thirst for vengeance, his need to rectify all the injustice suffered by the poor and effected by the rich. That obsession had melded with the restlessness in his soul, a desperate need to make a difference, to give his wretched life some meaning, his hollow heart some purpose.

From that restless outrage, the Tin Cup Bandit had been born.

Then he'd thrived, fed by the wild exhilaration of his perilous crusades, the growing certainty that he could challenge the odds and win. Again and again, he'd revel in the incredible thrill of conquest, especially in light of the fact that his opponents were the abhorred nobility.

That had been then.

This was now.

And now there was Daphne.

Daphne, who filled his heart with love, leaving no room for vengeance, obliterating all the restlessness from his soul. Along with her love came a peace far more profound than his reckless exhilaration, planting the seeds for a future he'd never envisioned as possible. Until now there had been nothing at stake. Suddenly there was everything.

Which left only his need for justice.

Well, wasn't that need being assuaged as well, not only extensively, but legally and without compromising his safety, or Daphne's?

After all, as the newly instated Duke of Markham, he had all the money he needed. With every bank draft he wrote, every donation he made, wasn't he effecting the very justice he sought by helping the helpless, ensuring a better life for the poor and hungry?

The answer was an unequivocal yes.

So what was holding him back? Why didn't he just relegate the Tin Cup Bandit to the annals of history?

Because there was one nagging reality that wouldn't be silenced.

I have a message for you. Pierce could still see Daphne's face, hear her words the night she'd faced the bandit in her bedchamber. *The children in the village school asked that, should you and I ever meet, I make certain you know you're their hero. Which, given the vast potential of their loving hearts, is a most glowing tribute.*

Timmy, William, Prudence, and all the other Timmys and Williams believed in him, relied on the valiant forays of the Tin Cup Bandit.

How could he forsake the children? He, who knew firsthand what it was like to have no one to rely upon, nothing to believe in. How could he take away the only person who'd ever offered them constancy and hope?

He couldn't.

Pierce closed his eyes, a muscle working in his jaw.

"Don't be angry," Daphne said softly.

He blinked, stared dazedly at her. "What?"

"Don't be angry. They're only children. In their minds, the bandit is a hero."

Vaguely, Pierce realized Daphne had interpreted his brooding silence as resurrected jealousy. "I'm not angry."

She stroked his jaw. "I love you."

Seizing her wrist, Pierce pressed his lips fiercely to her palm. "I know. And I'm not angry." He glanced about, realizing Miss Redmund had resettled the children for their studies and the vicar was waiting tactfully at the door. "Evidently, I was engrossed in my thoughts."

"So it would seem." Daphne situated Russet in the crook of her arm, thoughtfully surveying her husband's troubled expression. "Shall we go?"

Pierce nodded, staring beyond his wife to where the children were bent over their slates. "Yes," he agreed in a hollow tone. "We've done all we can for today."

"Were I not escorting the most beautiful woman in the room, I would abandon this ridiculous ball in an instant," Pierce muttered in Daphne's ear.

Daphne's lips twitched as her husband whirled her about Benchley's crowded ballroom. "I don't know whether to be flattered or offended."

"Neither. Both statements are true. I loathe these pretentious gatherings, and you are so exquisite I very nearly locked our guest room door and rapidly divested you of the gown you so painstakingly donned."

This time Daphne couldn't suppress her laughter. "You shock me, Your Grace."

"Somehow I doubt that," Pierce retorted dryly. "You know me too well."

"Yes, I do." She smiled up at him. "And I know you came to Benchley for my sake. Thank you." She gazed around at the festive holiday decorations. "I normally dislike these parties as much as you do. But it's almost Christmas. And for the first time in my life I truly know what Christmas spirit means. I'm so happy. Perhaps it sounds foolish, but I somehow wanted to glory in that joy, to share it with the world, just this once."

Pierce brought her gloved hand to his lips. "It doesn't sound foolish. And the glow on your cheeks makes the whole disagreeable event worthwhile."

"All of it? Even the two-hour tour Lord Benchley insisted on conducting to demonstrate his latest renovations?" Daphne teased.

Pierce rolled his eyes. "The pompous ass. As if he's the first man to effectively use a fireplace to heat his bedchamber."

"Also the first to install seven water closets and three bathrooms in the main house, all with gilded washstands, basins, and ewers and all for only himself and Lady Benchley," Daphne added with a sad shake of her head. "Such a waste."

"Try telling that to the viscount. Or his insipid wife, for that matter. Why, the trinkets she's wearing tonight could feed an entire village for a year."

"I didn't notice." Daphne frowned, gazing into the hall where the viscountess was loudly berating an obviously terrified serving girl. "But I can't bear the cruel manner in which she treats her servants. That poor child out there is probably still in her teens. Not to mention that the tray she's carrying weighs more than she does."

Pierce spun Daphne about so he could view the scene firsthand. What he saw was a gaunt, terrified young girl nodding vigorously as she endured the viscountess's tirade.

"Now get to the kitchen and fetch a tray of champagne for

the guests," the noblewoman ordered. "And no dawdling! Or you shan't receive a penny of the added wages you've begged me for."

"Yes, ma'am." Knees trembling, the girl turned on her heel and bolted, juggling piles of soiled dishes as she ran.

"That witch," Daphne murmured. "Has she not a shred of compassion?"

"Evidently not."

"So Markham." The Viscount Benchley chose that moment to approach them. "How are you enjoying your first official ball as a member of the peerage?"

Pierce bit back his candid retort. "I'm enjoying this rare opportunity to dance with my wife," he said instead.

"I don't blame you." Benchley's lecherous gaze swept Daphne from head to toe. "Your bride is breathtaking. 'Tis hard to believe she is Tragmore's young daughter."

"I've grown up, my lord," Daphne said, feeling the impending storm that emanated from her husband. "I'm a married woman now."

"So you are." He stroked the ends of his mustache. "How is your father? Has he recovered from that notorious bandit's invasion?"

"Father is quite resilient. He's very much himself again."

"I'm glad to hear that." Benchley displayed the ballroom with a grand sweep of his arm. "Myself, I have nothing to fear from that bandit scoundrel. My house is impenetrable. I've seen to that. Why every lock has been personally installed by the finest locksmiths in England, the grounds protected by the keenest guards to be found anywhere." He laughed harshly. "I'd like to see that rogue just try to gain entry to Benchley. He would quickly learn the meaning of the word defeat. Why the very thought of him robbing reputable people and turning our money over to worthless urchins and filthy gutter rats who will do naught but squander the funds on liquor and women." Hastily, he broke off. "Forgive me, Daphne. I did not mean to go on so in your presence." He bowed. "Continue to enjoy your evening."

Pierce's jaw was so tightly clenched, Daphne feared it

might snap. She felt him make an inadvertent move in the viscount's direction. "Pierce, don't. He isn't worth it. He's a witless, arrogant fool."

"We're leaving."

Her expression soft with compassion, Daphne nodded. "Very well. I, too, have had enough."

"Coming here was a mistake. I don't belong here. I don't *want* to belong here."

"Neither of us does," Daphne replied, covering Pierce's hand with her own. "We belong to each other." Slowly, she extricated herself from his hold. "I apologize for insisting we attend. It was stupid of me to suppose we could infuse joy into the hearts of the heartless. I'll feign a headache. Then we can pack. We'll be home before dawn."

"Snow flame." Despite his fury, Pierce felt a twinge of remorse. "I never want to shatter your dreams."

Daphne smiled. "You couldn't. You *are* my dreams. I'll merely alter my plans and glory in the Christmas spirit at Markham, which is where I'm happiest anyway, rather than at some vapid party. And rather than display my exuberance in front of the world who, for the most part, are thoroughly unworthy, I'll share my joy with the worthiest man I know, my husband."

Gathering up her skirts, she made her way from the ballroom, warmed by the love she'd seen darken her husband's forest green eyes. She truly was the luckiest woman on earth.

A vicious growl and a loud crash transformed Daphne's golden haze into ugly reality. Halting in her tracks, she saw the same young serving girl, this time poised just outside the pantry, a pile of broken glass swimming in spilled champagne at her feet. Her hands were pressed to her mouth, and, at first, Daphne assumed she was distressed over the accident. An instant later, she realized otherwise, simultaneously identifying the source of the growl she'd just heard.

A black dog with bared teeth was advancing on the maid, crouched low to the ground as if to pounce. Lunging forward, he seized the hem of her gown, tearing it between his teeth until she shrieked with fear.

"You stupid chit!"

The viscountess emerged from an anteroom at that moment, seeing naught but the mess in her hallway and the embarrassment of the accompanying din. "See what you've done, you senseless dolt! I knew I shouldn't have succumbed to your pleas to keep you on. I should have discharged you long ago. You're not only frail and simple, you're clumsy and inept as well."

The dog, hearing his mistress's infuriated tone, wasted no time, but relinquished his jaw-full of material and bolted into the pantry.

"But, ma'am—" The girl made a futile gesture toward the deserted pantry door, realizing even as she did so that it was too late. The culprit was gone. With utter resignation, her arms fell to her sides and she awaited her punishment.

So did Daphne, hovering, unseen, in a small alcove down the hall, holding her breath for the castigation she anticipated.

It was far worse than she feared.

"Pack your things at once. I want you off my estate this instant."

The girl's head came up. "Off the estate? But, my lady—"

"Not another word. My mind is made up." The viscountess stepped distastefully around the servant and the glittering puddle at her feet. "I'm going to summon a footman so he can arrange to have this mess cleaned up. By the time I return, I expect you to be gone."

Daphne could see the girl's fingers nervously rubbing the folds of her gown.

"What about my wages, ma'am?" She seemed to drag the question from some reluctant place deep inside her.

"Your wages?" The viscountess drew herself up. "Not only will I not pay you, I have half a mind to strike you. You're fortunate that I'm a lady and therefore will restrain myself."

"I worked a full week, Lady Benchley."

Courageously, the maid maintained her stance, but her voice quavered, and Daphne ached for her humiliation.

"The meals you were fed were lavish compensation for

your pathetic attempts at work. Now be gone before I have you thrown from my home." Sweeping up her skirts, Lady Benchley marched off.

For a long moment the girl did nothing, merely stood, unmoving, where she was. She was too far off for Daphne to discern her expression, but her trembling shoulders left little doubt she was crying.

An instant later she recovered, dashing tears from her cheeks as she walked toward the servants' quarters.

Without hesitation, Daphne went after her, propelled by a myriad of emotions too vast to contain.

Halfway down the corridor, the girl turned, disappearing into one of the tiny bedchambers.

Unthinking, Daphne followed. "Are you all right?" she blurted.

The maid spun to face her, her eyes wide with shock. "Who are you?"

Daphne didn't answer. She couldn't. All she could do was stare, a chill encasing her heart as she confronted the agonizing specter of her past. Those eyes—dark, fathomless, intense. They had haunted her for twelve years, their hollow futility tearing at her heart.

"Who are you?" the girl repeated, backing away.

Her throat tight with remembered pain, Daphne tried to find the words to say and the voice with which to say them. Perhaps she would have succeeded, had her gaze not chosen that moment to fall upon the unadorned nightstand beside the girl's bed.

After which all attempts at speech were forgotten.

There, its unblinking stare as vivid as it had been twelve years past, was the tattered, indelible memory of Daphne's childhood.

The doll from the House of Perpetual Hope.

18

"MA'AM, PLEASE. WHO ARE YOU? WHY ARE YOU HERE?"

Daphne heard the question through a paralyzed haze. Forcing herself to respond, she dragged her mind back from the fateful day that had forever changed her life.

"My name is Daphne Thornton." Her voice sounded odd, strained to her own ears. "I—" She wet her lips. "I saw the disgraceful way Lady Benchley treated you. Forgive me, but I had to make certain you were all right."

The girl lowered her lashes, turning away to begin gathering her belongings. "I'm accustomed to such treatment. It's only that I need this job badly, now that—" Her mouth snapped shut. "'Twas very kind of you to check on me, ma'am. But I assure you, I'm fine." She folded two worn frocks, then collected her brush and comb. "I'd best take my leave."

"Where will you go?"

That hollow futility flashed in the girl's eyes. "I haven't given it any thought. In truth," she added in a voice so tiny it was barely audible. "I'm not sure it matters."

Daphne blocked her path. "It matters to me." She rushed on, desperate to intercede in a way she'd never before been allowed. "What is your name?"

"Sarah."

"And your surname?"

"Cooke." The maid took up her bag, surveying Daphne with wary candor. "Ma'am, I don't mean to sound rude, but why would you care about my name? Or about me, for that matter?"

Sarah. At last. A name to put to the face. The identity of the girl, until now unknown, had, at last, been revealed.

Perhaps the fates are offering me another chance, Daphne mused, the wondrous prospect infusing her heart with joy and hope. Twelve years before she'd been her father's prisoner, a child herself, unable to reach out to the little girl who'd stared with terrified mistrust, clutched her doll as if it were her very lifeline.

Now, Daphne was free.

With the help of fate—and Pierce—Sarah would be, too.

"'Tis not the first time we've met," Daphne began carefully, praying for the right words, knowing she'd have but this one opportunity to extend her hand.

Sarah inclined her head. "You must be mistaken. You're a lady. I'm a maid. Besides, I've only been at Benchley for two months."

"And before that?"

"Before that I worked in a tavern. I doubt you'd know it by name. The east end of London is hardly an area you'd frequent."

"Sarah," Daphne closed the door, leaning back against it. "We haven't much time, so I'll be blunt. My husband is the Duke of Markham."

An intrigued spark of recognition flashed in Sarah's eyes.

"I see you've heard some of the gossip," Daphne responded. "Residing with Lord and Lady Benchley, I rather assumed you had. So you know Pierce's title is newly acquired."

"I've heard only that he was a wealthy commoner and now he's a wealthier duke," Sarah replied carefully.

"A commoner of questionable parentage," Daphne clarified.

"Yes."

"His childhood was a nightmare, Sarah. A living hell that no one in that ballroom could possibly understand."

"Why are you telling this to me?"

"Because you *would* understand."

"I? Why? Because we both grew up without benefit of title or wealth?"

"No. Because you both grew up in the House of Perpetual Hope."

Silence.

Slowly, Sarah sank down on the bed, pressing her shaking hands to her face. "How did you know that?" she whispered.

"Because that was where you and I met. A dozen years ago." Daphne inhaled sharply. "My father is an unfeeling man who believes all those born without should be cast into the streets, and all who oppose that course of action should be beaten into submission. Sadly for me, I was a dissenter, then and now. When I was eight, he decided to alter my convictions by forcing me to witness the horrors of a workhouse firsthand. The workhouse he selected was the House of Perpetual Hope." A painful pause. "I first saw you pumping water in the garden, then again when I was leaving. I picked up your doll." Daphne gestured toward the nightstand and the only possession Sarah had yet to pack. "Father flung her aside. You rescued her—" Daphne broke off, tears clogging her throat. "I don't expect you to remember. But I never forgot."

Sarah's face was pale, her lips quivering with emotion. "I don't recognize your face. But the incident? *That* I remember. How could I not? I'd never seen anyone quite like you before, except in my dreams. I remember thinking how elegantly you were dressed, how beautiful you were—and how fortunate."

"Fortunate," Daphne repeated with hushed irony. "Then, no. But now? Yes, very. My luck has changed dramatically thanks to Pierce. He's given me joy, hope, a future." She lay a tentative palm on Sarah's shoulder. "And, if you'll allow us, we can do the same for you."

"All because of one episode from your childhood?"

"An episode that's haunted me since I was eight. Not to mention the pleasure it would bring my husband to help provide you with a better life."

"How?" Sarah asked skeptically.

"We were just about to make our excuses and leave Benchley. Come to Markham with us."

"Are you offering me a job?"

"If you'd like one."

"As you just witnessed, I'm not terribly strong. I was discharged from the tavern for the same reason. Especially now that—" Again, she broke off.

"Markham is enormous. I'm certain we can find something less taxing for you than carrying heavy trays." More than anything, Daphne wanted to insist that Sarah come to their home, not as an employee, but as a guest. Yet, instinct warned her that Sarah's pride would never permit her to accept what she would doubtless view as charity.

Frantically, Daphne searched her mind for an answer, a logical, physically undemanding position that Sarah might fill.

"You speak exceptionally well," she blurted.

A slight smile played about Sarah's lips. "For a street urchin, you mean."

"For someone who never had the benefit of proper schooling."

"I taught myself. I read every book I could lay my hands on, philosophy, poetry, novels, everything."

"As did Pierce. Unfortunately, few people possess your aptitude, or your initiative." As Daphne spoke, the idea took hold, erupting full force in her mind. "Sarah, how would you feel about giving lessons?"

"Lessons?"

"Yes. English lessons at Markham. I don't know why I didn't think of it immediately."

"I'm not following you, ma'am."

"Sarah," Daphne seized her hands. "Markham has been asleep for many years. I'm only beginning to awaken it. And I need your help. We have scores of servants and, thanks to Pierce's painstaking arrangements, hundreds of tenants.

Consequently, there are hosts of wonderful children now living at Markham, children who could benefit from your knowledge and experience without ever having to leave the estate."

"Isn't there a village schoolhouse?"

"Yes. But few children are able to attend. Their parents simply cannot spare them from their chores. This way, they wouldn't have to. We could conduct evening classes, or pre-dawn classes, whatever was necessary. And we could vary the studies, so the five-year-olds wouldn't be expected to learn at the same pace as the thirteen-year-olds."

"But I'm not qualified to teach," Sarah broke in to protest.

"I beg to differ with you," Daphne countered. "You're inordinately qualified. You can offer these children not only book learning, but youth and enthusiasm. And most of all, hope—the living proof that they can aspire to more and succeed." Pleasure glowed in Daphne's eyes. "Think about it, Sarah. Think about the difference you can make."

Sarah studied Daphne's face. "You're serious about this, aren't you?"

"Extremely serious. Will you consider my offer?"

Another slight smile. "Hadn't you better discuss it with the duke first? Perhaps he won't share your enthusiasm."

"I have no worry on that score." Daphne inclined her head quizzically. "Your answer?"

"My answer?" Sarah echoed the question in utter amazement. "Forgive my impertinence, ma'am, but you ask as if I had somewhere else to go."

"You have. If you don't feel suited to this position, or if, after seeing Markham, you believe it to be too overwhelming to call your home, then Pierce and I will make certain you find an agreeable living arrangement elsewhere."

"Just like that?"

"Just like that."

Sarah swallowed past the lump in her throat. "I don't know how to thank you."

"I don't want your thanks. I want your company. Will you travel to Markham with us?"

For the briefest of instants, Sarah appeared torn, struggling with some internal conflict. At length, she nodded. "With pleasure, ma'am."

"Wonderful!" Daphne beamed. "I need a few minutes to pack. Then, we can be on our way." Half turning, her gaze fell on the nightstand, and she smiled, tenderly picking up the ragged doll. "I've spent a dozen years wondering—what is her name?"

A wistful look. "Tilda. Actually, Matilda. It was my mother's name."

"Tilda," Daphne repeated softly. "'Tis a lovely name."

"Mama gave her to me the morning she left me on the workhouse steps." Sarah's voice broke. "'Twas the last time I saw her. Her body was found the next day, floating in the Thames."

Daphne hugged Sarah fiercely, vowing then and there to ensure this frail yet courageous girl nothing but happiness from then on. "Come," she managed. "Let's collect my things. We can talk while we pack. I can already envision precisely which of Markham's bedchambers will be yours. It has a lovely view of the gardens and a wide ledge at the window just perfect for Tilda to sit and look out—"

"Wait." Abruptly, Sarah stayed Daphne with her hand. "I can't do this to you, not when you've shown me more kindness than I've ever known in my life." She lowered her lashes to hide the pain her refusal evoked. "I can't go with you, Your Grace. I want to—more than you can ever imagine—but I can't."

"Why?" Daphne was taken aback by the rapid turnabout. "Why can't you go?"

Silence.

"You can trust me, Sarah," Daphne murmured. "Tell me what this is all about."

"I'm with child." It was an admission of fact, not shame or remorse. "That's the reason I've been constantly weak and lightheaded. It's also why I can't accept your offer, no matter how much I might want to. To burden you with my condition, and eventually my child, would be dishonest and unfair to you, to the duke, and to the children I'd be instructing."

"The babe's father?"

"Isn't interested in acquiring a wife or a child," Sarah finished. With proud defiance, she raised her chin. "I'd be lying if I said James hadn't made that fact clear from the start. He did. But it changed nothing. Not my love for him, nor my aching need to have his child. I want this babe, Your Grace, want it more than anything on earth. And not only because of James, but because I long for the chance to give my child what I never had: a mother who loves him enough to never leave him." Sarah lay a protective palm over her still flat abdomen. "Can you understand that?"

"Yes. Far better than you think." Daphne's cheeks were damp with tears. "And I greatly appreciate your candor. Now, are you ready to go?"

Sarah gaped. "You still want me?"

"More than ever," Daphne replied fervently. "Anyone who can speak of children with such tenderness and commitment is the ideal candidate to teach them. Moreover, you'll need proper care for yourself and your babe. We'll see that you get it. So," Daphne swung open the door and scooped up Sarah's bag, "if that's all settled, we're off to Markham."

Pierce was deep in thought as he paced before the waiting carriage. He'd reached his breaking point tonight, thanks to Benchley's disdainful remarks and arrogant boast. No longer could he dismiss the inner voice that urged him to act.

Conflicting emotions or not, the Tin Cup Bandit would strike.

Instinctively, Pierce began plotting out details.

He'd nearly completed his strategy when Daphne emerged from the manor thirty minutes later, accompanied by the serving girl Lady Benchley had been chastising earlier.

"Would you please load this as well?" Daphne paused to ask the footman, handing him the maid's suitcase.

"Of course, Your Grace."

Daphne turned to her husband, her gaze saying far more than her words. "Pierce, this is Sarah Cooke. She's just accepted a position at Markham that will solve all our problems concerning the children. In fact, as luck would have it, she's able to travel home with us right now. Sarah, my husband, Pierce Thornton." A twinkle. "The notorious Duke of Markham."

"Your Grace." Sarah curtsied.

"We're delighted to welcome you, Sarah." Blindly, Pierce followed his wife's lead. "Notorious?" he added with a grin.

"Indeed." Daphne leaned conspiratorially forward. "Evidently, your colorful rise to the ranks of the nobility has become quite a topic of conversation among members of the *ton*."

"I'm flattered." Pierce wasn't fooled by his wife's purposeful banter. Scrutinizing her face, he read her unspoken plea and answered it. "I've made our excuses." He opened the carriage door, beckoning to both ladies. "Shall we go?"

The carriage made its way through Benchley's iron gates. With keen insight, Pierce watched Sarah knotting her hands in the folds of her dress, nervously awaiting Daphne's explanation.

Daphne stalled only until they'd reached the main road. Then, as the estate disappeared from view, she turned to Sarah, frowning as she saw the girl's obvious trepidation.

"There's no reason to be apprehensive. Your old life is over. Let's embrace your new one." Daphne's meaningful glance flickered briefly over Pierce before returning to Sarah. "Tomorrow morning we'll begin planning a schedule of lessons for all of Markham's children. We'll consult their parents, of course, and devise times that won't conflict with their chores. Why, with a modicum of effort, you can begin teaching by next week."

Pierce gave Daphne an almost imperceptible nod of understanding.

Chewing her lip, Sarah addressed Pierce. "Sir, I think you should know I have no prior experience. I'm not qualified for this position."

A twinge of amusement lit his eyes. "Clearly, my wife thinks otherwise. And, since I've discovered her instincts to be flawless, I'll make note of your candid admission, then dismiss it."

"I—Thank you, sir."

"You're quite welcome."

Confident that Daphne would explain the situation more fully once they'd arrived home, Pierce resumed his mental arrangements. Shifting restlessly, he glanced at his timepiece. "I hope you ladies don't object. I've asked our driver to make a brief stop."

"Of course not," Daphne assured him, although her brows rose in surprise. "Where are we stopping?"

"Wellingborough." Pierce knew his wife well enough to know she wasn't fooled by his casual demeanor or light tone. Just as she'd perceived his inner conflict, she sensed his current unrest. And he could do nothing to assuage her worry, especially not in light of the decision he'd just made. "I need to collect some business materials for my meeting in London next week. It shouldn't take more than a few minutes. Wellingborough is on our way."

"By all means." Daphne laced her fingers together. "Sarah and I will use that time to get better acquainted."

Silence fell, lingered until the carriage rolled to a stop before Pierce's Wellingborough home.

"I'll be back straightaway," he assured them, alighting swiftly and striding up the walk.

The house was dark, and Pierce lit a single candle to illuminate the hallway. Strange how coldly unoccupied the place seemed, he mused, glancing up and down the shadowed walls. Not long ago it had been his home. Now it was only a house.

Home was with Daphne.

He acted quickly, squatting to remove the appropriate floor plank, reaching beneath to extract the small object he'd carefully secreted on the morning following his wedding while his bride was still blissfully asleep.

The emerald from the Earl of Selbert's Mansfield estate.

Slipping the stone into his pocket, Pierce reached beneath the floorboard again, extracting the mask he wore on his excursions as the Tin Cup Bandit. Pocketing that as well, he replaced the slat, scanning the floor to make certain he'd left no evidence of his hiding place. Then he stood, pausing only to gather up some unneeded papers to support his fabricated excuse for stopping by. Extinguishing the candle, he left.

Sleep was not forthcoming.

Tossing off his brandy, Pierce stared out the sitting room window, wishing Daphne hadn't rushed off to help Sarah settle in. He needed her tonight, needed the gentle touch of her body, the healing warmth of her love.

Perhaps it was better this way.

He refilled his glass, frowning as he realized how little he could tell Daphne of what was transpiring inside him. He refused to amend his decision to protect her from the criminal portion of his life. And yet, selfishly, he wanted her still, if only to wrap herself around him, whisper that she loved him.

Dawn's first rosy glow embraced the horizon, and Pierce massaged his aching temples, finalizing his strategy. He would send a missive to Hollingsby, arranging a meeting for tomorrow between the two of them and the barrister Hollingsby had selected to handle the marchioness's impending divorce. That would serve as an excuse to go to London. If he committed the burglary tonight, then rode directly to Town, he could stop at Thompson's store and the Faithful Heart workhouse in London's East End, all before dawn.

In which case, he had only today.

Today to advise Daphne of his trip and to get enough rest so his senses would be whip-taut when he broke into that arrogant son of a bitch Benchley's impenetrable estate.

Wearily, Pierce climbed the stairs to bed.

His room was still dark, only a trickle of light finding its way beneath the closed curtains. He tossed his robe aside and turned to climb into bed.

Daphne.

His beautiful wife lay on the rumpled sheets, her pristine nightgown covering her from neck to toe, her hair a tawny waterfall upon his pillow. Evidently when she'd finished settling Sarah in her new chamber, she'd come to his room rather than her own.

Strangely touched, Pierce smiled at the exquisite vision

she made, filled with a fierce sense of pride that she belonged to him.

"Snow flame?" He slid in beside her, gathering her soft, warm body in his arms.

"Pierce?" She sounded sleepy, disoriented, and more erotic than he could bear.

"I'm here." He shrugged her out of her nightgown, smoothing his hands over the satin of her skin.

"We have to talk."

"Later." He covered her mouth with his. "We'll discuss our new employee later."

"Not Sarah," Daphne protested, pushing at his shoulders with insistent hands. "About—"

"Later," Pierce whispered fervently, moving against his wife until her nipples hardened against his chest.

"Pierce." Briefly, Daphne shook her head, fighting the sensual spell he was purposely weaving about her senses. "I—"

"Feel like heaven," he finished for her, his lips burning a path to her breasts. "Taste like heaven," he added huskily, drawing one sensitized peak into his mouth.

Daphne relented in a rush, twining her arms about Pierce's neck and murmuring his name in that hushed, seductive way that made his blood heat and his body harden.

"I need you, Snow flame. I need you so bloody much." Pierce's hands shook as he parted her legs, absorbing the tiny quivers of her inner thighs with his fingertips. "Tell me you love me."

"I love you, Pierce," she said in a breathy whisper.

"Keep saying it." He entered her with his fingers, reveling in her wetness, intensifying it with each fiery caress.

"I love you." She arched against his palm, her hips rising and falling in silent invitation.

"Now say it as I go into you." He moved up and over her, his expression as harsh as his command. "Please, Snow flame, I need to know."

Daphne pressed her fingers to his lips to silence him. Slowly, she slid her hand down the length of his body until it closed around his rigid shaft. "I love you, Pierce," she breathed reverently, lifting her flushed face to meet his gaze, staring deep into his eyes as she guided him into her. "Forever and always, I love you."

He climaxed instantly. Her words, the look on her face, the hot, tight feel of her were more than he could bear. Helplessly, he poured himself into her, shuddering with each pulsing surge of his release.

Something inside him refused to touch heaven alone, desperately wanted Daphne with him. Slipping his hand between their bodies, he found her, stroked the velvety flesh that cried out for his touch, responded instantly to it.

Daphne unraveled at once, sobbing Pierce's name as she dissolved into hard, gripping spasms, clutching him inside and out as if to never let him go.

Pierce never intended to go. "I love you," he rasped, dragging great gulps of air into his lungs. "Christ, how I love you."

He closed his eyes, the reality of his feelings for Daphne prompting talons of doubt to claw at his gut.

Should he tell her the truth?

There had always been honesty between them. Did he *owe* it to her to tell her the truth? Or was it his responsibility to protect her from it?

And most of all, did he owe it to her—to them—to abandon the bandit's cause, children or not?

His hands balled into fists, digging deep into the pillow. For a man who always knew just what to do, he was totally at sea. What the hell was his answer?

Daphne's even breathing told Pierce she'd fallen asleep. He leaned up on his elbows, brushing strands of hair from her face and kissing her lightly before he eased himself from her breathtaking warmth.

He jerked on his robe, prowling the room like a caged tiger seeking escape, knowing all the while this was one impasse that was truly insurmountable.

Crossing over to his nightstand, Pierce slid open the drawer, automatically reaching for the emerald he'd placed there earlier, as if by holding the gem he could find the answers he sought.

It was gone.

For a full minute Pierce stared blankly at the empty niche where the stone had been. Then he acted, yanking out the contents of the drawer one by one, tossing them haphazardly about the room as he groped in every emptied space, every vacant corner. Nothing.

Frantically, he searched his mind for an explanation.

"It's with your cravats."

Pierce pivoted about, staring at his wife.

Daphne sat up, pointing helpfully at Pierce's double chest of drawers. "In there. Oh, I realized your hiding place was only temporary. Still, I remember how easily you found my smelling salts and my journal. The nightstand drawer is far too risky, even for a few hours. So I moved the emerald. You needn't panic. It's quite safe."

"You—" Pierce's mouth opened and closed several times. "How did you find it?" he asked inanely.

"I was on my way in to speak with you. I saw you place the jewel in the nightstand, then go downstairs to brood. I knew I had plenty of time to find a more suitable hiding spot, since I fully intended to wait here for you, even if it took all night." She sighed. "Heaven knows, I've waited too long already; borne your suffering as long as I could. Evidently, you were never going to come to me. My only choice, therefore, was to go to you."

In stunned silence, Pierce crossed the room to his double chest, yanking open the drawer that housed his cravats.

"Beneath the folded pile in the back," Daphne instructed.

An instant later his hand emerged, clasping the Selbert emerald.

He turned the brilliant gem over and over in his palms, watching its facets shoot prisms of light through the semi-darkened room.

"You've known?"

"Yes."

"How long?" he asked, his tone deadly quiet. "Damn it. How long have you known?"

"Since the night you robbed Tragmore."

"Since the—" He turned, his expression utterly incredulous. "I was dressed completely in black, from my boots to my hood, with a mask that covered my entire face. I even disguised my voice."

Daphne smiled. "No one else moves like you, Pierce. You're a panther, carefully restrained yet ready to strike; agile, dangerous, exhilaratingly charismatic. You affect me as no other man ever has or ever will. And your eyes—not only the unique green hue, but their intensity, even when lit by a single taper. 'Tis you who claim my instincts are flawless. How could you imagine I wouldn't know you?"

He shook his head in amazement. "And all this time— When I found that journal, vented my jealousy like a madman, you said nothing, let me go on and on."

"I was waiting for *you* to tell *me*." Daphne propped her chin on her knees, inclining her head quizzically. "When did you finally intend to do that?"

Pierce's fingers clutched the emerald so tightly his knuckles turned white. "Today. Tonight. Never. I don't know." He strode over to the bed, sitting down beside her.

"In light of the numerous opportunities I've given you, the answer is clearly never." Daphne drew a shaky breath, a pained look crossing her face. "Why, Pierce? Why would you choose not to tell me? You love me. Despite your past, I believed you trusted me as well."

"I do trust you." Pierce caught her chin, lifted it to meet his gaze. "Have you any idea how much I wanted to share this with you?"

"Then why didn't you?"

"Daphne, what I do is illegal. I could hang for it and so could you, if the authorities ever suspected you aid me in any way." His thumb stroked her lips. "I swore to keep you safe. I intend to keep that vow."

"What about you?"

"What about me?"

"I want you safe as well." Daphne leaned forward, her expression earnest as she gripped Pierce's shoulders. "I love you. The thought of losing you—" Her lips trembled. "I couldn't bear it."

"Precisely my dilemma." A muscle worked in his jaw. "Until you, Snow flame, I had nothing to lose, nothing to live for. Now I have both. But the children. You told me yourself I was their hero. Who else do they have? Who else can they believe in?"

"There are other ways."

"Don't you think I know that?" Pierce came to his feet, raking his fingers through his hair. "And I'd almost reconciled myself to helping solely through those other ways."

"Almost," Daphne repeated woodenly. "Until Viscount Benchley's offensive behavior altered your decision."

Their gazes locked.

"Yes. Until Benchley spoke of the poor as if they were dirt."

"Was it that? Or was it the challenge he inadvertently issued by boasting his manor was impenetrable."

Pierce didn't look away. "You know me well."

"Extraordinarily well. So which was the deciding factor, the cruelty or the pomposity?"

"The combination."

Daphne swallowed, fear and resignation shadowing her eyes. "When?" she whispered. "When do you plan to invade Benchley?"

"Tonight."

"Tonight? But there is a houseful of guests who have yet to depart from the Christmas party."

"True. Which only serves to heighten the challenge." Pierce ached at the broken look on Daphne's face. "Snow flame, I don't expect you to understand."

"Then make me understand."

Pierce started. "How?"

"I care about those children as much as you do." Daphne raised her chin a notch. "And I loathe everything my father and Lord Benchley represent, just as you do. So I understand your anger, as well as your compassion. What I don't understand is your excitement; the way you thrill to the challenge."

"That's not something I can explain."

"Not in words, but in actions."

"Meaning?"

"Take me with you."

"What?"

A spark kindled Daphne's eyes. "Take me to Benchley. Let me be the Tin Cup Bandit's accomplice."

19

"HAVE YOU LOST YOUR MIND?" PIERCE RAGED.

"Not at all. You've enumerated your reasons. Now let me witness them firsthand."

"Daphne." He strove for a filament of control. "You're not thinking clearly. This is not some romp through the woods. Nor is it like the glorified tributes you collect from the *Times*. It's—"

"Cunning, skill, and instinct," Daphne finished for him. "Both cunning and skill I've learned from you. As for instinct, you yourself have repeatedly hailed mine as incomparable." She shot him a quick, mischievous grin, her cheeks tinged with excitement. "You've also heralded me as having magnificent, though hidden, spirit, fire, and passion. Clearly, that is the case, although I believe those traits have come out of hiding these past weeks."

Pierce sucked in his breath and stared, for the first time seeing the total transformation their marriage had effected on his wife. He'd been so engrossed in his own metamorphosis that he'd failed to realize the full extent of Daphne's.

Somewhere during the past six weeks, his delicate little caterpillar had become a butterfly.

"Pierce?" Daphne rose and went to him, oblivious to her nakedness. "I know I can do this. I *want* to do this. Let me."

Warring emotions tore at Pierce's heart, stunning him by their very existence. The reluctance, the protectiveness were the familiar sentiments, the ones that had spawned his decision to keep Daphne from the truth. But the equally powerful unfamiliar longings? The stirring excitement evoked by envisioning Daphne by his side, the compelling need to share with her the exhilaration of the robbery and its inspiring results—those he'd never anticipated feeling.

But feel them he did.

Instantly, Daphne sensed his indecision. "I'll wear my deep purple gown. The color is so dark it will be indiscernible by night. I'll hide my hair, pull a hooded mask over my head. Only my slight build will enable people to tell us apart."

Her final claim made Pierce chuckle, his gaze raking her very feminine, very naked curves. "You won't win on that argument, sweetheart. I assure you, people would have no trouble differentiating us."

Daphne flushed. "I'll be clothed. And I'll wear a full, black cape. Besides, you'll be less conspicuous with me along. If need be we can remove our masks and appear to be merely two of Benchley's house guests."

A glint of intrigued awareness flared in Pierce's eyes, then dissipated along with his smile. "Snow flame." He gathered her close in his arms. "Have you any idea how precious you are to me?"

"Then do this for me," she urged softly, pressing her lips to his chest. "Take me with you. Let me feel what you do when you best a callous scoundrel like Benchley. Share your joy when workhouse children reap the benefits of your skill. Pierce," she raised her head, gazed up at him, "please."

"I must be insane," he muttered, gathering handfuls of her hair.

Triumph glowed in Daphne's eyes. "Thank you," she whispered.

"Now remember. Once we leave the carriage in that grove of trees outside the gates—"

"I remember," Daphne interrupted, gripping her mask in her lap as the horses commenced their final mile to Benchley. With a shiver of excitement, she wrapped her cape more tightly about her. "We go by foot. We don't speak a word. You have the tools and the pistol concealed in your pocket, and the pouch tucked inside the lining of your coat. We make our way around back, far from the sleeping quarters of the family, guests, and servants. You select the proper window—most likely at the rear of the conservatory—then cut your way inside. After which, you'll pull me through. We remove our shoes and leave them there. We move from the conservatory directly to the pantry, then to the library and the study. Last, we climb the stairs to the bedchambers."

"Not *we*," Pierce amended her final point, his jaw set. "*I*. Don't argue with me, Daphne," he cut her off swiftly. "Just reaching the manor itself will be challenge enough, given the skill of the guards Benchley boasted of. The house is filled with sleeping people. The slightest noise could waken them. We'll do the lower floor together. Then you'll stand guard while I relieve the viscountess of her jewel case and leave the emerald on Benchley's pillow."

"What about the guest quarters? Judging from the array of bracelets and necklaces I saw at the ball, the ladies' jewel cases must be brimming."

A corner of Pierce's mouth lifted. "Daring, aren't you? I fear I've created a monster. Very well, Snow flame. If we accomplish all we've discussed without incident, we'll visit the guest wing. You'll remain at the head of the hall while I appropriate whatever trinkets I can."

"Excellent."

"And to think I worried that you cared for the bandit. In truth, you were living vicariously through him."

"Both," Daphne clarified, caressing Pierce's arm. "I was and I do." An impish grin. "You're very potent in black."

"I'll keep that in mind." Sobering, Pierce transferred the reins to one hand, wrapped the other arm about Daphne's waist. "Do everything precisely as I do. Follow my lead, just in case any details of our plan need to be suddenly altered. And Snow flame, most of all, be careful. Exciting or not, this is no game. It's very real. And very dangerous."

"I realize that. I won't disappoint you. Heaven knows, you've never disappointed me." Her own words sparked a thought. "Speaking of which, though this is hardly the time, I want to thank you for taking Sarah in. It meant a great deal to me."

"I could see that." Pierce cast a brief sidelong glance at his wife. "I have the feeling your commitment to Sarah involves more than just sympathy for her plight."

"It does. It will for you as well." Daphne studied her husband's hard profile. "Sarah and I have met before. I didn't realize it at first, not until I burst into her chamber." Seeing Pierce's brows draw in question, she explained. "When I left you at the ball, I stumbled upon an ugly scene between Sarah and Lady Benchley, a scene that resulted in Sarah's dismissal. My heart went out to her."

"So you followed her to offer comfort," Pierce supplied tenderly.

"Yes. Then when I saw her at close range—those eyes—" Daphne swallowed. "Pierce, she was the girl I described to you, the one I saw clutching the tattered doll when I was eight and my father dragged me to the workhouse."

Pierce's head jerked around, brittle realization erupting in his mind. "You're telling me Sarah grew up in the House of Perpetual Hope?"

"Yes. Her mother abandoned her there, then took her own life. Sarah has never had anyone to rely upon. This was my chance. Yours and my chance."

"Without a doubt. You did the right thing."

"I wanted to invite her as our guest. But she's far too proud to accept charity. So I thought, since she taught herself proper English, she could do the same for the children at Markham. Think of the example she'll set, the hope she'll offer."

Pierce brushed his lips across Daphne's head. "My beautiful, compassionate snow flame."

"I intended to divulge all this to you at dawn, directly after we'd finished planning tonight's robbery, but—" She blushed.

"But we forgot everything except each other," he concluded in a husky tone of remembered intimacy.

"Yes." Daphne fiddled with her mask. "Pierce, I told Sarah about you; about The House of Perpetual Hope. Given the circumstances, it eased her despair. Are you angry?"

He shrugged. "I've never made a secret of my background. The only person I've chosen not to discuss the details with, for reasons you already know, is your father."

With a quick nod, Daphne plunged on. "There's one other thing you should be aware of. Sarah is with child."

A heartbeat of silence.

"I see. Has she told the father?"

"Evidently, he wants no part of either her or their babe."

"Why doesn't that surprise me," Pierce muttered, bitter memories scorching his throat.

"But, as was the case with your mother, Sarah *does* want her child. Very much. She's determined to offer it all the constancy and devotion she herself was denied."

"And so she shall." Pierce urged the horses around the bend leading to Benchley. "We'll do everything we can to help her."

"I knew you'd say that." With a sigh of relief, Daphne lay her head against Pierce's shoulder. She felt the almost imperceptible tensing of his body. "We're here," she realized aloud, a statement not a question.

"Yes." Pierce maneuvered the carriage into a small, concealed grove of trees. That done, he turned to Daphne. "Snow flame, are you absolutely certain you want to do this? You can still change your mind."

"I'm very certain." She brushed her lips across his chin. "Moreover, the Tin Cup Bandit cannot strike without me, not tonight." She patted her pocket. "I have the emerald, remember? So you see, changing my mind is not an option. Not for me or for you. Now, shall we make quick work of Benchley's impenetrable abode?"

Admiration flickered in Pierce's eyes. "Very well, Madam Bandit." Slipping on black gloves, he tugged his masked hood over his head, adjusting it to allow him to see. He took Daphne's mask, waiting only until her gloves were on and she'd twisted her hair atop her head, before he pulled the hood on her, helped her conform it to her face. He then billowed the black cape about her until all her feminine curves were eclipsed from view.

Objectively, Pierce scrutinized her, making certain not a shred of evidence was visible that could identify the dark-clad figure as his wife.

"Will I do?" Daphne murmured, intentionally dropping her voice to an unrecognizable drone.

Beneath his mask, Pierce smiled. "Better than even I expected." Lightly, he jumped to the ground, gripping Daphne's waist and lowering her beside him. "Let's go."

They made their way through the trees, careful not to walk on the path leading to the gates, lest their shoes make even the slightest crunch on the roadway.

Two powerfully built guards leaned against the silver gates. Pierce stopped, gesturing to Daphne to stay behind him. Then, he took up a good-sized rock and flung it with all his might.

It hit the dirt on the far side of the gates.

"What the hell was that?" one guard muttered, reaching into his pocket for a pistol.

"We'd better look."

Pierce called upon his incomparable timing, waiting until just the right moment, when the guards had walked far enough from their posts to be out of viewing range, but not so far that they'd halt, thus eliminating their receding, but revealing, footsteps. Then, he acted, beckoning to Daphne, edging swiftly to the gate.

His fine-tuned hearing told him his wife was right behind him. To be certain he waited, carefully easing her between the iron posts before he followed suit.

The vast grounds of the estate loomed before them, illuminated by a full, glittering moon.

Choosing the most thickly treed areas, Pierce led Daphne toward the house, urging her to the ground when the trees ebbed into gardens. Crouched low, they crept through the paths between flower beds, pausing now and again to listen for the steps of the vigilant sentries.

Experience had taught Pierce to surge forward a scant moment after any guards had passed by, as that was when they were most confident, and most careless of the region they'd so recently perused. Armed with that knowledge, he timed each advance perfectly, inching closer and closer to the sleeping manor.

At last their destination was upon them, dark and silent. Pierce squeezed Daphne's gloved hand and pointed toward the conservatory. Then, he moved stealthily toward it.

Taut with anticipation, Daphne followed.

As Pierce had predicted, the conservatory windows were broad, each fastened by a catch on either side. Pausing only to reassure himself no one was about, Pierce whipped out his knife and, in less than ten seconds, had cut a pane of glass just large enough to admit his hand. He reached around, forced back both catches and, an instant later, leaped lightly to his feet on the conservatory floor.

Turning, he eased Daphne in beside him.

In silent unison they removed their shoes, pausing to listen intently for any sound that would indicate their entry had been detected.

Nothing.

They lit a single taper and made their way to the pantry. Gleaming silver beckoned them, and Pierce nodded with great satisfaction, pointing to those pieces small enough and valuable enough to pilfer.

Next they tiptoed to the library. Daphne slid open the desk drawer, removed the strongbox, and was about to slide it closed again when Pierce gripped her wrist to stop her. In rapt fascination, she watched as he reached behind to unlatch the desk's hidden compartment, removing a thick stack of notes and a bejeweled snuffbox, all of which he shoved into his sack before abandoning the room.

The hallway was eerily quiet, the silence broken only by the chimes of the grandfather clock tolling the hour.

Pierce positioned Daphne in the shadowed alcove at the foot of the stairs. Meaningfully, he gripped her shoulders, reminding her to stay put. Daphne gave a terse nod, reaching into her pocket to extract the emerald.

Clutching the gem, Pierce turned and prowled slowly up the staircase, close to its side to avoid making even the slightest creak. His lithe movements reminded Daphne yet again of a potent, stalking panther.

Five minutes later, he was back. Lightly, he tapped the jewel case in his sack, showing Daphne the job was done.

With a quizzical tilt of her head, Daphne gestured toward the guest wing. Pierce nodded.

Outside each bedchamber, Pierce cocked his head, concentrating on the sounds emanating from within. They invaded only those rooms whose occupants' even breathing assured him that they were deeply asleep, and whose doors were either unlocked or could be made so with one quick flick of his knife.

By the time Daphne and Pierce left the guest quarters, their pouch was bulging with jewel cases, silver pieces, and pound notes.

They were just retracing their steps, when Daphne spied what appeared to be a small drawing room tucked away in a tiny nook alongside the conservatory. She grasped Pierce's arm, indicating, not the room's existence, but the ornate lock enhancing its wooded door.

Pierce drew near, frowning beneath his mask. He'd never seen anything quite like it: the lock was of a heavy plate, covering a wide portion of the doorway. Its entire surface was dominated by the figure of a man, fully clad from boots to hat, a weapon clasped in his hands. Nowhere, either near or on the figure, could Pierce detect evidence of a keyhole.

Leaning up on tiptoes, Daphne spoke for the first time, whispering close to her husband's ear. "Such a complex lock. What could it protect?"

Intrigued and frustrated, Pierce nodded, then leaned closer, peering at the man himself. Somewhere beneath the figure was the only logical place for a keyhole to be hidden. But where? Tentatively, he probed at the plating, searching for an answer.

Daphne watched eagerly, squinting as she contemplated the possibilities. Acting on impulse, she reached past Pierce, pressing first the man's arm, then his weapon, and at last his foot.

She felt something give.

Firmly, she pressed the boot again.

A spring released, and the man's foot thrust upward, revealing the dark recess of a keyhole.

Pierce's head jerked about, and Daphne nearly laughed aloud at the surprise she saw reflected in his eyes.

Recovering himself, he whisked out his knife, inserted it in the keyhole, and clicked open the lock.

Daphne handed Pierce the taper, allowing him to precede her into the dark, musty room. The furnishings were unimpressive—two settees, an armed chair, a tea table, and a sideboard—an average drawing room.

Puzzled, Pierce approached the tea table, running his gloved hands over its surface, feeling about for a hidden catch. He straightened, shaking his head. Bypassing the other furnishings, he went to the sideboard, repeating the same process.

A concealed drawer swung open, and Daphne bit her lip to keep from exclaiming aloud.

Blinking up at them was a bejeweled chest the size of a small tome, set in a myriad of multicolored gemstones, each one larger than the last. Its value was incomprehensible.

Triumphantly, Pierce lifted the treasure from its home, carefully sliding the drawer closed before stashing the chest in his coat and urging Daphne toward the door.

The man's boot eased back, but the lock refused to slip into place.

Thoroughly perplexed, Pierce tried pushing the boot in the opposite direction. Then, when that was unsuccessful, he shoved at the other boot. Still, the door remained unbolted.

A sudden feeling came over Daphne, an ominous premonition of danger. Fearfully, she looked about, seeing nothing but darkness, hearing nothing but silence.

Still, the anxiety persisted.

"Let's go," she breathed, tugging at Pierce.

He nodded, simultaneously feeling his way along the man's hat.

The second spring gave, lowering the hat over the man's eyes and sliding the bolt back into place.

A menacing growl sounded.

"The dog." Even as Daphne said the words, she remembered the venomous beast she'd seen tearing at Sarah's gown the night before.

"Come. Now." Pierce's fingers bit into Daphne's arm as he dragged her toward the conservatory.

Violent barking erupted, the sound of racing paws closing in at a rapid pace.

"Dover? What is it?" Viscount Benchley's sleepy voice emanated from the second-floor landing.

"Hurry," Pierce commanded as they reached their destination.

"Who's there?" Benchley evidently heard their running footsteps, for his own approached at an alarming rate.

"Run," Pierce hissed, scooping up their shoes and boosting Daphne out the window all at once. "Wait for me by the road."

"No." Vehemently, she shook her head, understanding instantly that Pierce meant to sacrifice himself to spare her. "I won't go without you."

"I'll be right behind you. Now go."

A heartbeat later, Daphne felt the cold night air against her skin, the ground beneath her feet.

"Run, damn it," Pierce ordered through clenched teeth, already hoisting himself through the open window.

He was standing beside her when the shot rang out.

Pierce's hand flew to his shoulder, a muffled groan escaping his lips.

"Where are you, you bloody bastard?" Benchley bellowed, leaning out to scan the grounds. "You won't escape. Not this time."

With all her strength, Daphne flattened both Pierce and herself against the manor wall, holding her breath as she waited.

The moment Benchley's head disappeared from view, she reached for her husband's arm. "Are you all right?"

"We've got to get off the grounds," Pierce managed, blood seeping through his fingers. "Before Benchley has time to alert his guards."

"But you're—"

"There isn't time." Even as he spoke, the house came to life, voices and lamplight splitting the peace of night. "Let's go." Fighting the stinging pain in his shoulder, Pierce took Daphne's hand, keeping her flush to the manor as they sidestepped their way to the building's edge.

Acres of sprawling land stretched between them and safety.

"We'll never get past all those men," Daphne panted, her terrified gaze taking in the immense stretch of gardens, utterly exposed by the moon's brilliant glow.

"What you suggested earlier," Pierce muttered unsteadily. "I have an idea." In one motion he yanked off his mask, reaching over to remove Daphne's as well. Swiftly, he shoved them inside his coat, then unbound Daphne's tawny tresses, letting them tumble free to her shoulders.

"Pierce, you've been shot. Are you insane?" Daphne gasped.

"Probably." With a grimace of pain, Pierce unclasped his wife's cape, wrapping it around the two of them in an apparently intimate cocoon. "Are the bloodstains covered?"

"Yes, but—"

"Good. So are my unconventional attire and our evening's spoils. Now put on your shoes." He thrust them at her, donning his own in a few quick, jerky movements. Waiting only until she'd complied, Pierce stepped boldly out of the shadows, tugging Daphne in his wake. "Follow my lead. Walk."

"Pierce—"

"Snow flame," he stared down into her confused hazel eyes, a spasm of pain shuddering through him, "trust me."

With a weak nod, she fell into step beside him, hovering a hairsbreadth from hysteria.

From halfway across the grounds, shouts emerged, and a myriad of guards began racing purposefully over the estate, their plodding steps drawing closer and closer.

"Relax," Pierce murmured into Daphne's hair. He paused, waiting until two sentries were nearly within view. Then, he veered Daphne around, drew her against him and covered her lips with his.

"Uh, pardon me, sir."

Pierce raised his head, an obviously irritated expression on his face. "Yes?"

The guard shifted uncomfortably from one foot to the other. "I'm sorry to interrupt—"

"Indeed." Pierce enfolded Daphne protectively against his jewel-laden coat. "A little discretion would be appropriate, if you don't mind."

"I understand, sir," the other guard inserted, turning three shades of red. "But Lord Benchley's just been robbed."

"Robbed?" Pierce looked shocked. "Good lord. What was taken?"

"I don't know the details yet, sir."

"Well, I'd best go to the guest quarters at once and ensure that my belongings are safe."

"Of course. But first—" the guard cleared his throat self-consciously, "Did you happen to see anything or anyone who looked suspicious?"

"No, I can't say I did. Did you, darling?" Pierce asked Daphne.

From somewhere inside her, Daphne found the strength she needed. "No," she murmured breathlessly. "But then, I was hardly looking about." She paused for effect. "Please, my lord, I'd appreciate your returning me to the manor. If my husband should discover my absence—" Delicately, she broke off.

"Of course, sweet." Pierce gave the guards a meaningful look. "I'm sure you'll forgive us? I'd like to see the lady to her room before any irrevocable damage has been done."

"By all means, sir. We apologize for detaining you."

Backing off, the guards darted onward.

Ten minutes later, Pierce shoved Daphne through the gates and weaved his way onto the road beside her. By this time, he was sheet-white, and nothing could disguise the blood soaking through his coat and running down his arm.

"The sentries who were here earlier," Pierce gazed about, blinking to clear his vision, "by now they're all inside, swarming the grounds." Sharply, he inhaled, leaning against a tree. "We should be—all right."

"Stay here," Daphne commanded.

She didn't wait for a reply. Breaking into a run, she raced toward the grove of trees that concealed their carriage.

Minutes later, she rode up to collect her rapidly fading husband.

"The carriage. You're too—close to the manor," Pierce rasped in protest.

"I don't give a damn." Daphne wrapped her arm about his waist. "The sooner you're in that carriage, the sooner we'll be gone. Now, help me."

Between the two of them, Pierce made it into the front seat.

Daphne climbed in beside him, slapped the reins and sped off into the night.

"What if the servants are awake?" Pierce muttered as Daphne half dragged, half carried him up the stairs at Markham.

"That's a chance we'll have to take." She urged him toward the landing, praying they would reach his bedchamber without incident. The ride home had been a nightmare, with Pierce in a semi-conscious state. Never before had Daphne been so grateful to arrive anywhere as she'd been when they passed through Markham's iron gates.

With a physical strength she never knew she possessed, Daphne maneuvered Pierce down the hall and into his chambers. She locked the door behind them, her insides wrenching with apprehension as her husband collapsed on the bed.

She went to him at once, flinging aside her blood-soaked cape, and gingerly peeling off his coat and shirt. Then she fetched a basin of water and went to work cleansing the wounded area, simultaneously assessing the severity of the injury.

"A flesh wound." Despite Pierce's condition, he recognized the panicked look on Daphne's face and attempted to assuage it. Averting his head, he stared dazedly at his oozing shoulder. "The bullet just grazed me."

"Thank God. Still, you've lost a great deal of blood." Schooling her features, Daphne continued to wash the wound, determined to conceal her distress.

Her hands shook as she rinsed out the cloth, watched the basin water turn a sickly shade of red.

"Daphne," Pierce stayed her with his other hand, "I'm fine. Just weak."

"I'll bind the area," she said in a quavery voice, rising to walk to his double chest. "It will help stop the bleeding." She took out several clean handkerchiefs and returned to the bed. Carefully, she wrapped the injured shoulder, putting as much pressure on it as she dared without causing Pierce undue pain.

Her own head spinning, Daphne fought for composure, crossing the room to pour Pierce a brandy. "This will help the pain," she whispered.

Gratefully, Pierce tossed off the drink, relieved as the spirits did their work, dulling the agony to a dull, tolerable throb.

"Is it easing?" Daphne asked, stroking Pierce's jaw with cold, shaking fingers.

He nodded, turning his lips into her palm. "I've survived worse." His glazed stare fell on his discarded coat. "Thompson. He's expecting me in London."

"Thompson?" A pucker formed between Daphne's brows. "Mr. Thompson? The jeweler?"

Pierce gave her a slight smile. "Um-hum. The one who bought your brooch for so unexpectedly high a price."

"How did you know—?" Daphne broke off, realization dawning on her face. "You were there."

"Not only there, but the proud owner of that hideous pin." A chuckle, despite his muddled senses. "You were remarkable for a novice."

"Thompson." Daphne was thinking aloud. "He's your contact, isn't he? The one who buys the jewels you take."

"Passionate, beautiful, and clever."

"That's how you knew I donated the money to the school." Rapidly, the pieces fell into place. "You followed me from Mr. Thompson's shop. How could you be certain I'd choose his store in which to peddle Mama's brooch?"

"I couldn't." Pierce caressed her fingertips. "'Twas not even a gamble, but a lucky twist of fate."

"When is Mr. Thompson expecting you?"

"Before dawn."

"And which workhouse had you planned to visit?"

Silence.

"Pierce, tell me."

"The Faithful Heart," was the reluctant reply.

"In the East End. I know the place." Daphne inhaled sharply. "I'll wash and change clothes. Then, I'll take our booty, plus a bit extra, ride to London and perform both errands. I'll be back by midday." She tapped her chin thoughtfully. "I'll tell the staff you took ill and need complete privacy and bed rest. That way you won't be disturbed during my absence. Have I omitted anything?"

"Yes." Pierce struggled to a sitting position. "I have no intention of allowing you to go."

Daphne bent forward, brushing Pierce's lips in the softest of kisses, thanking God for sparing him. "My heroic husband." She withdrew Pierce's blade from his pocket, raising her skirts and tucking the knife safely beneath her concealing petticoats. "I'm afraid you haven't a choice."

Pierce was up, pacing unsteadily, when Daphne entered his bedchamber just after noon.

"What are you doing?" she demanded, closing the door behind her. "Your wound—"

"Is fine," he retorted, making his way toward her. "I changed the bandage an hour ago. The bleeding has stopped. I'll mend. What am I doing? Worrying about you." Fiercely, he wrapped his good arm about her and drew her against him. "You've been gone forever. Thank God you're safe."

Daphne wound her arms about his waist. "This from the man who doesn't believe in prayers?" she murmured, laying her cheek against his chest.

"Did Thompson try anything unethical? Did he cheat you? Doubt you? Hurt you in any way?"

"No. Actually, he was quite amused by the whole situation." Daphne extracted the blade, handing it to Pierce with an impish grin. "However, he did offer me a job."

"Very humorous. What about the workhouse? Did you have any trouble?"

"No, no, and no." Tentatively, Daphne touched Pierce's bandages. "Tell me you're all right."

"Now I am." He buried his lips in her hair. "Christ, I was frantic."

"I understand. I'd feel precisely the same way."

A heavy silence hung between them.

"Pierce, you were almost killed."

He squeezed his eyes shut, reliving the moment when he'd believed himself caught, when all he could think of was losing Daphne.

When, for the first time in thirty years, his life mattered more than his cause.

And when he'd suddenly, vividly, known what he stood to lose.

"I heard that gunshot," Daphne was saying in a strangled tone. "I saw you struck, and all I could think of was—" She broke off, fought to regain her composure. "No. I won't do this." She drew a deep, shuddering breath. "I need you, Pierce. But I also love you. I can't—won't ask you to relinquish your quest. I understand the bond you share with the children. Lord knows, I care for their happiness as much as you do. So whatever decision you make, I'll respect, and leave it to God to bring you home safely to me." She stepped back, took Pierce's hand in hers. "Here," she said in an aching whisper.

Pierce opened his eyes in time to see his wife press a large sapphire into his palm.

"You didn't specify which stone you wanted me to save," she managed. "So I had Mr. Thompson pry this from the chest. I hope you approve of my choice."

A wave of emotion engulfed Pierce's heart. For a long moment he stared down at the glistening gem, awed by his wife's selflessness, more awed by the realization that the decision he'd so vehemently sought had, in the end, found him.

"A most impressive gem," he replied, his voice oddly choked. "We'll put it in the drawer with my cravats as a covert symbol of our one unforgettable crime together." His thumb stroked tears from her cheeks. "It's time," he pronounced soberly. "As of now the Tin Cup Bandit will restrict himself solely to the second half of his ritual.

"Once a month I'll leave a tin cup of money in a

workhouse of my choosing. And if I'm caught, well, I'll merely attribute my odd brand of generosity to all the inspiring articles I've read on the Tin Cup Bandit. The *retired* Tin Cup Bandit. The difference, however, will be that, unlike my predecessor, my actions will be totally legal. And I can't be shot or hung for donating my own funds, now can I?"

Wordlessly, Daphne smiled through her tears.

"Am I to assume you approve of my plan?" Seeing the question in his wife's eyes, Pierce shook his head. "I'm not doing this for you, Snow flame." He tossed the sapphire to the bed, extending his now empty hand to her, offering her their future. "I'm doing this for me."

"No, Pierce," Daphne demurred softly, drawing his palm close, placing it against her abdomen to share her newly discovered miracle. "You're doing this for our child."

20

"WHAT INFORMATION HAVE YOU BROUGHT ME, LARSON?"

Tragmore perched on the edge of his desk, his eyes narrowed expectantly on the investigator.

"Very little, sir. The marchioness keeps mostly to herself. If you'll forgive me for saying so, I see no evidence of improper behavior, and certainly no indication that your wife is being unfaithful."

"Does that mean no guests have visited Rutland?"

"Other than your clergyman, no."

"Chambers?" Tragmore sat up straighter. "He called on Elizabeth again? Was he alone?"

"Yes sir, just as he was on the two previous occasions." Larson glanced at his notes and shrugged. "He arrived shortly before four in the afternoon, evidently for tea. The butler ushered him into the drawing room, the maid put the flowers in a vase, and—"

"Flowers?" Tragmore jumped on that revelation. "The vicar brought flowers?"

Larson started, clearly taken aback by the vehemence of Tragmore's tone. "A mere formality, my lord," he hastened to assure him. "Nothing more lavish than any casual caller would offer."

"Nothing lavish. Were they yellow, perchance?"

"As a matter of fact, yes, they were."

"Yellow roses," Tragmore muttered, bitterness and satisfaction lacing his tone. "How charming."

"My lord, if you're suggesting that anything indiscreet transpired between the marchioness and the vicar, I must assure you—"

"I don't pay you to assure me, Larson," Tragmore snapped. "Nor do I pay you for your interpretations of my wife's behavior. To refresh your memory, I pay you to uncover information and to relay it. Bear that in mind."

"Very well, my lord."

"The roses. You saw the vicar present them to the marchioness?"

Larson nodded. "I did. I was, as always, concealed in the hedges just outside the drawing-room window. I don't dare move about during daylight hours. The duke has numerous guards stalking the grounds."

Impatiently, Tragmore waved away Larson's meandering explanation. "What happened after Chambers gave Elizabeth the flowers?"

"She gestured for him to take a seat, which he did. He stayed only long enough to drink one cup of tea, then took his leave."

"Did he sit beside Elizabeth?"

"No, my lord." Larson rustled the paper in his hand. "As I've indicated in my report, the vicar sat in an arm chair, the marchioness on a settee. They made not the slightest attempt at physical contact. They simply chatted."

"Could you hear what they were saying?"

"Not through the closed window, no. But judging from their serene expressions, I would suggest the vicar was offering counsel to Lady Tragmore. A qualified opinion, my lord. Not an interpretation," Larson added.

Tragmore leaned forward, gripping his knees. "I want you to think very carefully, Larson. Were any of the servants present during the vicar's stay?"

Larson shifted his substantial weight. "If you'll forgive my impertinence, sir, I'm quite good at what I do, which is the reason you hired me. I needn't think carefully to recall what transpired. It's all recorded on paper." Again, he indicated his written sheet. "To answer your question, the only person other than the butler who entered the drawing room during the vicar's visit was the maid who brought them refreshments."

"And did she remain throughout his stay?"

"No. She served them tea and scones, then took her leave."

"Then they were alone. Excellent." Tragmore came to his feet with a flourish. "'Tis just the additional proof I require." He shoved some bills in Larson's hand. "Another fortnight should be enough time to fulfill my purpose."

"Does that mean you want me to continue surveying the estate, my lord?"

"It does indeed. And pay special attention to the vicar's comings and goings, innocent though they may seem."

"Very well. It's your money, sir."

"Yes." Tragmore's eyes glinted. "It is, isn't it?"

With a puzzled shrug, Larson stuffed the bills in his pocket. "Shall I report to you next week at the same time?"

"Definitely."

"Very well. Good day, Lord Tragmore."

"*Very* good day, Larson."

Tragmore waited only until the investigator had gone before he crossed the room, poured himself a congratulatory drink. Things were proceeding even better than he'd hoped. Oh, he'd known it was only a matter of time before the sentimental dolt began calling on Elizabeth, presumably to see to her well being. But flowers? Yellow roses, no less, even after all these years. And unchaperoned visits? The witless clergyman was making his own job laughably easy.

Lifting his glass, Tragmore smiled malevolently. A fortnight longer, he thought, tossing off the brandy. And then all he cared about would be his: vengeance, money—

A hesitant knock interrupted his celebration.

"Yes? What is it?"

"Forgive me, my lord," the butler murmured, "but your solicitor is here to see you. He apologizes for not having an appointment, but—"

"Hollingsby?" Tragmore's face lit up. "Perfect timing. Send him right in."

"Yes, sir."

The butler disappeared, only to usher the solicitor directly into the study. "Mr. Hollingsby, sir."

"Hollingsby, what a splendid coincidence. I was just thinking of you," Tragmore began.

The solicitor didn't return his smile. "As I told your butler, I apologize for arriving without an appointment. However, I did need to see you on several important matters. Being in the vicinity, I took the liberty of dropping in unannounced."

Hollingsby's stiff demeanor did not go unnoticed. Quizzically, Tragmore inclined his head. "Very well. May I offer you something?"

"Thank you, no. This is not a social call." Purposefully, Hollingsby remained standing, extracting two formal-looking papers from his portfolio and handing the first to Tragmore. "This document is your official notification that I will no longer be representing your interests."

Tragmore's mouth dropped open. "What?"

"To be blunt, Tragmore, those who engage my services pay their bills. I shudder to think how much you owe me. However, rest assured, I plan to determine the full amount of your debt. And once I have, I'll do whatever is necessary to recoup my losses."

"This is an outrage!" Tragmore sputtered. "We've done business together for years."

"Yes. Uncompensated business. I'm no longer willing to endure your unfulfilled promises of payment."

"You're making a grave mistake, Hollingsby. In less than a month, I expect to—"

"Don't humiliate either of us by boasting of some fictitious fortune you're about to attain," Hollingsby interrupted quietly. "My decision is made."

"Fine." Tragmore's lips thinned as he savored the victory that would soon be his. "You're the fool, not I. And when the very real fortune of which I speak is mine, I shall engage a shrewder and more influential solicitor to manage my funds." He laughed, a caustic sound of gloating triumph. "Yes, I believe I shall begin searching for the ideal candidate posthaste."

Hollingsby shrugged. "That, of course, is your right." He extended the second formally prepared paper to Tragmore. "There's a second reason I can no longer represent you, which this document will clarify."

"What is it?" Tragmore snatched the page.

"It's a statement of intent. I thought it only ethical to advise you that I'm representing your wife's interests now."

"My wife's—" Tragmore stared blankly at the paper, hot color suffusing his face.

"The marchioness intends to sever your marriage. I've engaged a barrister."

"Elizabeth is trying to secure a divorce?"

"She is."

"On what grounds?"

"Extreme cruelty."

Tragmore sank slowly into a chair, still gaping at the document in his hands. "Does she understand the ramifications? To her? To Daphne? Elizabeth will be shunned and Daphne will be bastardized."

"Not if we're granted a parliamentary divorce."

The marquis gave a humorless laugh. "A parliamentary divorce? You're more of a fool than I imagined, Hollingsby. Elizabeth is a woman. She and I are estranged. She is, therefore, without money or credibility, both of which are needed in vast amounts to pursue something as unlikely as a legal divorce."

"And both of which are possessed in vast amounts by the Duke of Markham."

A chilling silence.

"Markham? That lowlife, contemptible—"

"The very same." A corner of Hollingsby's mouth lifted. "My association with him, judging from your reaction, represents another conflict of interests."

"Do you realize who he is? What he is?"

"You must know that I do. I was, after all, the one who notified him of his newly acquired title. I represented his late father for decades."

"And you'll trust his word over mine? A workhouse bastard?"

Hollingsby's gaze was icy. "There are all different types of bastards, Tragmore. I'll take a scrupulous one like Thornton any day. Moreover," a biting smile, "he pays his bills. Good day."

Tragmore stared vacantly after Hollingsby's retreating form, blood pounding through his temples. His numbed gaze lowered to the pages he held—Thornton's ultimate degradation.

With a muttered oath, he crumpled the documents into tight fists of fury, hatred for Thornton coursing through his veins.

The bastard had pushed him to the limit; stripped him of his money, his family, and now his dignity.

But it wasn't over. Far from it.

Let Hollingsby do as he would. Let him and the street scum he worked for think they'd won.

He knew better.

Backed into a corner, he knew there was but one way out. One way to flourish and punish all at once.

Unclenching his fists, Tragmore smoothed out the rumpled papers. Then, with deliberate precision, he tore them once, twice, and crossed his study to toss the shreds into the fire.

"Daphne, don't!"

Pierce took the room in five long strides, catching his wife's waist and hoisting her off the chair where she'd stood on tiptoes, reaching for the window. "What the hell are you doing?" he demanded, setting her feet on the floor.

With a start of surprise, Daphne regained her balance, her dismayed gaze darting at once to Pierce's shoulder. "You shouldn't be lifting me. Your shoulder—"

"Is healed, and has been for a week. Now answer my question. What the hell are you doing?"

"I'm adjusting the curtains." Tucking a loose wisp of hair behind her ear, Daphne gazed about Markham's new, neatly arranged classroom with utter satisfaction. "Once the slates and chalk arrive today, our schoolroom will be ready for use." Quizzically, she regarded Pierce's furious scowl. "Why are you angry?"

"Because you could have fallen, damn it. You don't stand on chairs when you're with child."

Daphne's lips twitched. "Really? And how many times have you been with child?"

"I'm not amused."

"No, but you're terribly heroic." Daphne reached up, laying her palm on her husband's jaw. "Fear not. The babe and I are fine. I'm taking excellent care of us both."

"This from the woman who invaded Benchley, endangered her life and the life of our child, knowing she was pregnant."

Daphne gave a resigned sigh. "You're never going to forgive me for that, are you? Even though I've told you time and again that, in my heart, I knew no harm could befall me or our child. You wouldn't allow it."

Pierce pulled her to him. "Your faith is humbling and frightening. What if—"

"It wouldn't. You wouldn't permit it." Daphne pressed her forehead against the hard wall of Pierce's chest, warm even through the barrier of his shirt. "At Benchley, you were beside me. The babe and I were safe. 'Tis as simple as that."

Reflexively, Pierce's arms tightened about her. "You truly believe that, don't you?"

"I do."

He swallowed, audibly. "Snow flame, don't take any more risks, all right? For my sake."

"Very well." She kissed his throat. "Although I must say, my reckless husband, that impending fatherhood has rendered you quite boring and stodgy."

Pierce smiled against her hair. "I heard no complaints last night."

"True." Daphne tilted her head back, her eyes alight with laughter. "Perhaps your recently abated sense of adventure will show itself in new and innovative ways."

"Say the word," Pierce murmured, his voice husky with sensual promise, "and I'll keep you abed for a week, demonstrating my ever-thriving inventiveness."

"We've scarcely left our chambers all week."

"That was a precautionary step." He brushed her lips with his. "My shoulder needed to heal, so we didn't have to explain the coincidence between my sudden injury and that of the Tin Cup Bandit who, as the newspapers reported, was shot and wounded upon fleeing Benchley."

"The staff thinks you were ill." Daphne shivered as Pierce's lips found the pulse point in her neck.

"Tell them I had a relapse."

"Pierce, I can't."

"Then tell them nothing." Releasing his wife, Pierce crossed the room, turning the key in the lock. "Our new schoolroom needs to be initiated." He pivoted, advancing toward Daphne with a suggestive gleam in his eye. "You choose, Snow flame. The oak desk or the oriental rug."

Daphne's eyes widened as she realized what her husband intended. "Pierce." She flushed. "You can't actually mean to—What if someone should—"

"Abated sense of adventure, you said?" Pierce shrugged out of his coat, tossing it to the floor, followed quickly by his shirt and cravat. "Boring? Stodgy?" His arms enveloped Daphne, reaching around to unfasten her buttons in rapid succession. "Am I being innovative enough, my spirited wife?" he breathed just before his mouth closed over hers.

With a soft sound of pleasure, Daphne twined her arms about Pierce's neck, everything inside her going hot and liquid with longing.

"Choose," he commanded as her gown and petticoats slid to the floor.

"I—" Daphne couldn't think, much less choose.

"The rug is softer." His thumbs caressed her nipples until they strained against her chemise. "But on the desk I can go deeper inside you."

"Oh God." Daphne's knees buckled, and she stepped back, bracing herself against the desk. "Here," she managed, tugging her chemise over her head.

Pierce's gaze raked her hungrily. "I applaud your choice, Snow flame." With undisguised urgency, he dragged off the remainder of his clothing, lifting Daphne onto the edge of the desk. "Let me feel you," he demanded in an uneven whisper. Still standing, he urged himself between her thighs, leaving her totally open to receive him. "Do you want me, sweetheart?" He took her mouth under his, simultaneously gliding his fingers into her welcoming wetness.

Daphne moaned, clutching him more tightly to her.

"Ah, Daphne." His lips burned a trail down her neck, her throat. His fingers began an unbearable rhythm that burned through her like a torch. "Yes," he breathed as her hips undulated in response. "Now lean back on your hands."

Immediately, Daphne complied, her eyes closing with pleasure as she gave Pierce free access to her body.

He welcomed the gift, lowering his head to her breast, drawing the aching tip into his mouth, relinquishing it only when Daphne cried out, and then, only to lavish her other breast with the same attention.

"Christ, you're so beautiful," he muttered, his lips moving restlessly down her body. He paused, laying his palm on her abdomen. "My child is growing inside you. Can you imagine what that knowledge does to me?"

Wetting her lips, Daphne attempted to answer.

Her answer never emerged.

Pierce's tongue sank inside her, his fingers drifting up the sensitive skin of her inner thighs as they pressed them wide apart to allow him greater freedom.

Daphne was unable to stifle her cry, arching until she felt the cool wood against her back, her elbows totally giving out beneath Pierce's relentless onslaught. The pleasure was acute and unendurable, converging instantly into a blinding pinpoint of sensation that exploded in seconds, spasms of excruciating ecstasy radiating out from her very core.

"Pierce!" She sobbed his name, reaching for him even in the throes of her release.

She was still shuddering when he entered her, taking her in one deep, inexorable thrust.

"Wrap your legs around me, Snow flame," he rasped, clamping his hands on her hips, holding her while he withdrew, drove forward again.

Daphne whimpered, her spasms intensifying as she raised her legs, gripping Pierce inside and out, reveling in his groan of pleasure.

"Unbelievable," he ground out. "Christ, I want to prolong

it, but—" He threw his head back, giving in to the inevitable, thrusting into his wife again and again until the world erupted, his seed pouring into her in great, endless bursts.

Still embedded in her clinging softness, Pierce stood, lifting Daphne in his arms and turning until he was seated on the desk, his wife cradled to his chest. "It just keeps getting better," he said in a husky whisper, his hand shaking as he stroked her hair.

A faint sigh was his only reply, sparking a new worry.

"Daphne. The babe—I tried not to give you my full weight."

"Your heir and I both feel wonderful, Your Grace." Daphne kissed his damp throat. "And we retract the undeserved comments we made about your sense of adventure being lacking."

Laughter rumbled from Pierce's chest. "I'm glad I redeemed myself." His grin turned wicked. "We'll soon see who is truly the bold one, you or I. Any second you're going to realize what we just did, and where."

Even as he spoke, reality struck full force. "Lord, Pierce, we just made love on the—in the—"

"On the desk in our new schoolroom," Pierce supplied helpfully. "The question is, will you be able to walk in here when Sarah is seated at this desk instructing the children, and not succumb to blushes?"

"Never. Every time I come in, I'll remember." Daphne tilted her head back, gave Pierce an incredulous look. "You won't be at all embarrassed, will you?"

"Not even a bit." Pierce kissed the furrow between her brows. "But I'll enjoy watching you. You're enchanting when you blush." Gently, he set her on her feet. "Speaking of which, we should get dressed. I distinctly recall your mentioning that the chalk and slates are soon to be delivered, and I don't think even your newfound abandon could withstand being discovered in our current state."

He chuckled as Daphne turned a bright shade of crimson, practically flying about the room in her haste to don her clothes.

Ten minutes later Pierce unlocked the door. "Safe," he teased, glancing up and down the empty hallway. "And undiscovered." Turning back, he met Daphne's sober expression. "Snow flame? What is it?"

"Would you mind closing the door? I'd like to talk."

"Of course." Pierce did as she'd asked, his brows drawn in query.

"We haven't talked, *truly* talked, since the robbery," Daphne began. "The emotions were too raw, the revelations too new. But now, especially after what we just shared, I need to know. Are you still angry with me? Not only for assisting you at Benchley in my current condition, but for keeping from you that I was with child?"

A shadow of emotion crossed Pierce's face. Steeling himself, he forced out the gnawing question that had hovered between them, unasked, all week. "How long have you known?"

"The possibility flitted through my mind the night the vicar came to dinner, when I suffered that uncustomary fainting spell. At first, I gave it no credence. But the next morning, I began feeling queasy, mainly at mealtimes. During our brief stay at Benchley, I kept experiencing that same lightheadedness, and the odd sensation of being out of sorts. As I was dressing for the ball, it suddenly occurred to me I haven't bled since our wedding. That's when I knew." Daphne crossed the room, grasped Pierce's forearms. "'Twas only two days. And my reasons for remaining silent were sound. Please don't be angry."

"I wasn't angry," he responded, shaking his head. "Bewildered. Hurt. Even a bit betrayed, if I'm to be honest." He cupped her face. "Honesty. Where was it, Daphne? We've always had that between us, right from the start."

"To a degree, yes," she clarified. "But, if you recall, there were several things, such as your identity, that you refrained from telling me."

"Only to protect you."

"Precisely." Daphne lay her own hands over his. "That was my motive as well."

Pierce's gaze delved deep inside her. "How would denying me the joy of knowing about our babe protect me? Surely you guessed what a child, our child, would mean to me. The only reason you could possibly have for not telling me is—"

"Is?" she prompted.

"That a small part of you is uncertain about the depth of my commitment. That you wonder if perhaps I'd want you to bear my child only to satisfy the terms of my father's will."

"Oh, Pierce." Daphne wrapped her arms about his waist. "Is that what you assumed? For a brilliant man, you're a bloody fool. I've never doubted your feelings. Lord knows, I perceived them long before you spoke them aloud. Nor have I given that absurd codicil a second thought since you told me of its existence. Doubt had nothing to do with my decision."

"Then why?"

"You were in torment," she said in a broken whisper. "The choice you were contemplating was tearing you apart. If I told you about the babe, you would have abandoned the bandit's cause posthaste, whether or not you truly chose to. I couldn't live with myself if you did that. So I waited, hoping you would share your secret with me, praying you'd make a decision that would grant you peace." A tremulous smile hovered about her lips. "The instant you did, I sang out my news, not only for your sake, but for my own." She leaned up, brushed her lips to his. "I know exactly how much you want this child—and why. I want it just as much." Her voice faltered. "I love you so."

"Without you," he shuddered, enfolding her in his arms, "I have nothing."

"You have me. Always. As I have you." Tears shimmered in Daphne's eyes. "We'll surrender our hearts—and our secrets."

"Have you others I don't know of?"

The wariness of his tone made her laugh. "None." She inclined her head. "Have you?"

Surprisingly, he hesitated. "Not a secret," he replied at length. "A suspicion. And an issue I have yet to discuss with you."

Daphne's teasing vanished. "What is it?"

"First I want you to sit down. Not because the subject will upset you," he added hastily, "but because I want you to rest." He traced the pale contours of her cheeks. "Between the intensity of our talk and, prior to that, our unexpected, exhilarating liaison on the desk," his eyes twinkled when she blushed, "I've overtaxed your strength."

"Very well." Daphne pulled back a chair and sat. "Now tell me what this is about."

He regarded her thoughtfully. "Has your mother ever made reference to her past? Before she married your father, that is."

Whatever Daphne had expected, it wasn't this. "My mother? I don't understand."

"Did she ever mention that there had been another man in her life? Someone she cared for? Someone important?"

Memory struck Daphne with the impact of a blow. "As a matter of fact, yes. Not directly, but in a roundabout manner. 'Twas the morning I told her of your proposal. She urged me to follow my heart. Her implication was that she hadn't, but wished she had. Why do you ask?"

"Because I believe I know to whom her heart belonged— still belongs," Pierce amended. "You would, too, were you not so close to the situation."

"Who?"

"Mr. Chambers." Seeing Daphne's eyes widen, Pierce pressed on. "Think about it, Snow flame. The caring that exists between them; the terribly protective way he looks out for her, hurts for her pain. And the ring." He gestured toward Daphne's hand. "When he wed us, he mentioned how significant that particular ring was to him."

"At which point Mama began to cry," Daphne mused aloud, realization dawning in her eyes. "Yes, it makes sense. He's known Mama since childhood, worries incessantly about my father's inexcusable brutality—toward me, yes, but most especially toward Mama. And the way they looked at each other in the church. I thought at the time it was merely friendship, but it was more." She gazed wonderingly up at Pierce. "What made you guess?"

"As I said, I'm more objective than you. Snatches of

phrases, chance innuendos." A corner of his mouth lifted. "And those infallible instincts of mine."

Daphne didn't return the smile. Lost in thought, she rubbed pleats of her gown between her fingers. "This is dreadful. Not only were they denied their love once, lord only knows why, but they can still never be together, not even now that we've wrested Mama from Father's brutality."

"You're wrong."

"Wrong?" She started. "Mama is Father's chattel, you know that, Pierce. How on earth can she extricate herself from that? Not to mention that she's far too moral to carry on an illicit affair. As is the vicar, who's the most honorable of men."

"That's where the issue I mentioned comes in."

"I'm totally at sea."

Pierce folded his arms across his chest. "I'm working with Hollingsby and a barrister who I'm told is an expert in matters such as these. I intend to help your mother secure a legal divorce."

"A divorce." Daphne repeated the words as if they were foreign. "Does Mama know you're doing this?"

"Of course. I have her full cooperation, and the vicar's as well."

Slowly, Daphne rose to her feet. "You've certainly been busy. A divorce." She turned questioning eyes to her husband. "But won't that prohibit Mama from remarrying?"

"Not if the divorce is issued by Parliament, no. And I mean to ensure that it is."

"How?"

Another grin. "I'm the Duke of Markham, remember? Wealthy beyond our wildest comprehension, influential beyond our grandest imaginings. Combine that with cunning, skill, and instinct, and success is guaranteed."

"Will it take long?"

"Some time, yes. Why?"

"Because I hate the thought of Mama and Mr. Chambers being apart any longer than necessary." Daphne chewed her

ANDREA KANE

lip. "The question is, what can we do to bring them together?" Her face lit up. "I know! I'll send Mama a missive telling her I'm with child, that I'm not feeling well and require her assistance. She'll leave for Markham immediately." Just as quickly, Daphne's face fell. "But how can I summon the vicar? What excuse can I give for needing him at Markham?"

"You need no excuse. We'll simply send him a message informing him that Elizabeth is leaving Rutland for Markham. We'll express our concern for her safety, given that Tragmore obviously knows her whereabouts, and request that the vicar chaperon her here. He'll be on his way just as swiftly as she."

A brilliant smile lit Daphne's face. "Have I told you how wonderful you are?"

"I believe so." Pierce tugged her close. "However, now that we've resolved the plights of the world, and all our secrets are out, I feel we should adjourn to my bedchamber where I can truly show you how wonderful—"

A purposeful knock interrupted Pierce's suggestion.

"The arrival of the chalk, probably," Daphne laughed.

"And the slates," Pierce added mournfully. "Very well. I'll curtail my enthusiasm. But later tonight—"

Another knock, accompanied by a "Your Grace?"

"Yes Langley." Reluctantly, Pierce released Daphne. "Come in."

The door opened, and Langley cast a tentative glance into the room. "Forgive me, sir, but Mr. Hollingsby is here to see you."

"Ah. Thank you, Langley. Show him in."

Hollingsby strode into the schoolroom, hand extended. "Hello, Thornton. I hope I'm not coming at an inopportune time?"

"No, of course not." Pierce kept his expression carefully nondescript, despite Daphne's revealing blush. "Sweetheart, you know Mr. Hollingsby, don't you?"

"Certainly. We've met at Tragmore. How are you, sir?"

"Quite well, thank you." Hollingsby bowed. "Congratulations on your marriage, Your Gra—Mrs—" He broke off, a puzzled expression on his face.

"Proudly, it's Mrs. Thornton," Daphne supplied. "But neither formality is necessary. Daphne will suffice."

Hollingsby cocked a brow. "A woman as irreverent as you, Thornton."

"Proudly, yes." Pierce grinned. "What can I offer you?"

"Nothing. I came here directly from—" Another hesitation.

"Daphne knows about our plans for her mother's divorce," Pierce informed him. "So if your visit relates to that, feel free to speak."

"Very well. I just left Tragmore. The marquis didn't take kindly to what we have planned."

"I didn't expect that he would."

Daphne inhaled sharply. "If you gentlemen will excuse me, I'll see to the missives we just discussed."

Pierce caught her elbow. "Are you all right?"

"Yes. But I need not hear of my father's temper. I've experienced it firsthand. And I am eager to pursue that other matter we spoke of."

"Fine." Pierce nodded his understanding.

"Good day, Mr. Hollingsby." Daphne gathered up her skirts. "'Twas a pleasure to see you again."

"And you, Daphne." Hollingsby watched her go, then turned back to Pierce. "I hope I didn't unnerve her."

"You didn't. But it's just as well that she not be involved. I don't want Daphne upset in any way, especially now."

"Now?"

A tender smile touched Pierce's lips. "Daphne is carrying my child." Abruptly, he cut off Hollingsby's anticipated response. "And if you so much as mention that bloody codicil I'll have you thrown out."

"I didn't plan to." With a flicker of surprise, the solicitor studied Pierce's face. "You love your wife a great deal."

"A great deal."

"It's obvious she feels the same. You're a lucky man, Thornton."

"Very lucky. Daphne's love is the most precious of gifts, one I intend to pass on to our child. He'll be part of a home, with both a mother *and* father who want him. Never will he

313

be forced to struggle for survival, nor will he know the futility of abandonment."

"And if he is a she?"

Pierce grinned. "Then I'll probably spoil her shamelessly, especially if she resembles her mother."

"I'm delighted for you. May the future more than make up for all the past has denied you."

"Up until recently, I would have claimed that to be impossible. But now, since Daphne," Pierce shook his head in wonder, "I'm starting to believe in tomorrow, in happiness, even in prayers."

"Is that why you're working so hard to answer Lady Tragmore's?"

Instantly, Pierce's smile vanished. "No. In Elizabeth's case, I'm determined to free her from a man I know to be a monster."

"Tragmore detests you as much as you do him. Oh, he was irate when I terminated our business association. More so when I brought up the divorce. But he became livid when I mentioned your name, though he did his best to hide it." Hollingsby chuckled. "I truly think he was restraining himself from striking me."

"I expected something of the kind."

"You have quite a history together, I gather."

"You gather correctly." Pierce cleared his throat. "I'm sorry I missed that meeting we'd scheduled for last week. Have you any preliminary information for me regarding the divorce?"

Hollingsby frowned thoughtfully. "When I received your note saying you had left Benchley directly after the ball and were home, ill and too weak to travel to London, I met with Colby, the barrister I engaged, alone. He's now fully apprised of the situation. I've brought you a list of his fees and an outline of the procedure he suggested." Extracting several sheets of paper from his portfolio, Hollingsby offered them to Pierce. "Your illness must have been a brief one," he added casually. "You look in perfect health."

"Hmm?" Pierce was scanning the documents. "Oh, I'm feeling fit as ever. Evidently, something I ate at Benchley severely upset my system. It took several days for me to recover." He raised his head. "Incidentally, did you bring a draft for the past week's allocated allowance?"

"I did." Hollingsby withdrew the requisite check. "Why? Are you short of funds?"

A corner of Pierce's mouth lifted. "Fear not, my friend. As you well know, I've sent my father's assets soaring. I merely intend to transfer the sum to some workmen I've hired. I'm investing in a business undertaking of Daphne's."

"That's quite a vast amount to contribute to workmen. What is this undertaking?"

"My kindhearted wife plans to supervise the installation of a new roof on her village schoolhouse, one that will sustain the winter. Then, come spring, she intends to finance the construction of a whole new schoolhouse. As you can see," Pierce indicated Markham's classroom with a grand sweep of his arm, "education for those who can't afford it means a great deal to Daphne. The reason I need the bank draft now is that my impatient duchess is determined to begin overseeing the new roof's installation within the week."

"How benevolent of her *and* of you." Hollingsby regarded him pensively. "'Tis rare to see such generosity."

Pierce shrugged, wincing a bit at the resulting stab of pain that shot through his shoulder, alerting him to the fact that he had overtaxed the wound after all. "I enjoy helping those who cannot help themselves. It gives purpose to the hell I endured." He returned to his reading.

"Are you in discomfort?"

"Pardon me?"

"I asked if you were in discomfort. Your arm seems to be causing you some trouble." Hollingsby gestured to where Pierce was absently rubbing his shoulder.

"Oh, no, not really. I helped carry in that large desk," Pierce lied swiftly, pointing with his opposite hand. "I must have strained myself."

"I see." Hollingsby waited only until Pierce resumed scanning Colby's documents before he began strolling nonchalantly about the classroom. "As I was saying, your generosity is admirable. Rarely does one see that type of behavior, except, of course, from the Tin Cup Bandit." A pause. "Speaking of which, did you happen to read of that cunning thief's latest escapade? He made off with a fortune of the Viscount Benchley's jewels and silver. And in the midst of the Christmas party you abandoned, no less. Of course, the reckless fellow was nearly apprehended. Something about a bullet grazing his shoulder."

Pierce lowered the page he'd been perusing. "Yes, I recall reading about the incident in the *Times* while I was convalescing."

"Convalescing? Oh, from your illness, you mean."

"Hollingsby." Pierce's eyes narrowed. "What are you getting at?"

"I? Why nothing. Only that I must admit to having felt some degree of relief that the scoundrel escaped. I must be getting soft in my old age."

"Indeed."

Hollingsby fingered one of the drapes, intently studying its intricate pattern. "Were I advising the bandit, I might point out that he is tempting the odds in a most foolish manner. I might suggest that he appraise his assets. And I don't mean his financial ones. I might even recommend that, having realized all that is truly his, he find some other way to accomplish his purpose, without jeopardizing his freedom, perhaps his very life. And, with a modicum of luck, I might just get through to him." Sighing, Hollingsby dropped the drape. "Pity I don't know the fellow."

"Yes, isn't it." At this point, Pierce had abandoned all pretense of reading. "Hollingsby—"

"Do you know, I've just remembered an appointment I have in Town," the solicitor interrupted. He shook his head in apparent disgust, closing his portfolio and heading toward the door. "I don't know what is happening to my memory these days. Why, I seem to forget things in the blink of an eye." He halted, turning to regard Pierce quizzically. "What was it we were discussing?" He shrugged. "You see? It's already left me. Ah well, I suppose it wasn't important. Was it, Thornton?" Boldly, he met Pierce's gaze.

A slow smile curved Pierce's lips. "No, my friend, I don't believe it was."

"Good." Hollingsby gripped the door handle. "Take your time reviewing those papers, by the way. We'll schedule another meeting early next week." A flicker of humor. "Before you begin the sensible, charitable venture of installing the schoolhouse roof."

21

"LANGLEY, ARE YOU *CERTAIN* NO VISITORS HAVE ARRIVED AT Markham this morning?"

"None, Your Grace," Langley assured Daphne, gloved hands clasped behind his back.

Shifting impatiently, Daphne chewed her lip. "I sent the missives to Mama and the vicar more than four days ago. 'Tis the fifth day, and it's nearly noon. Where on earth could they be?" She inclined her head. "Possibly you didn't hear their carriage?"

"Most unlikely, Madam, given that I've not left the entranceway since shortly after dawn."

Daphne blinked. "Whyever not?"

"With all due respect, Your Grace, I haven't had the opportunity. I've been surveying the drive for approaching guests since your first request at sunrise."

"Oh, Langley, I apologize." Daphne was torn somewhere between laughter and embarrassment. "I've abused you shamefully. Please, go enjoy some of Cook's wonderful scones and a cup of tea. I'll take up the vigil."

"Indeed you will not, Madam," the butler countered emphatically. "His Grace left strict instructions that, given the delicacy of your health, you were not to take part in your customary ritual of assisting the staff."

"The delicacy of my health?" Daphne echoed. "I'm carrying a child, Langley, not a fatal illness."

Langley flushed at the forthright referral to her pregnancy. "I'm only following orders, Your Grace."

"Oh, for heaven's sake." Daphne rolled her eyes. "Very well. I'll have Cook bring you some refreshment."

"That would be greatly appreciated. In the interim, I shall continue scrutinizing the entranceway. Should either your mother or the vicar arrive, you can be sure I will locate you at once."

"Thank you, Langley." Daphne gave him a grateful smile, then headed down to the kitchen.

Cook scowled when she saw Daphne. "Out, Your Grace," she commanded, mincing no words. "The duke left strict orders."

"I know. I know. I'm not to lift a finger owing to my delicate condition." Daphne sighed. "Well, fret not. I've merely come to request that you provide Langley with some sustenance. The poor man has been keeping vigil at the front door for over five hours. If he doesn't eat something soon, he will probably swoon."

As soon as she realized Daphne was going to abide by the duke's demands, Cook relaxed, filling a plate with warm scones, and readying a pot of tea. "You should eat a bit of this yourself, ma'am. You scarcely touched your breakfast."

Daphne's stomach lurched. "No, thank you, Cook."

"You need to keep up your strength, and the babe's. Here." She handed Daphne a plate containing two of the flaky treats. "At least eat these." Clucking away Daphne's protests, she shooed her from the kitchen, plate in hand.

Making her way down the hall, Daphne searched for a discreet spot in which to deposit her unwanted aromatic snack. At the same time, she tried desperately to hold her breath, certain that to inhale would be disastrous at that moment. With each step she became more convinced her plight was futile.

"Oh! Pardon me, ma'am." Mary, the head gardener's

youngest daughter, scooted out of the schoolroom just as Daphne passed by. The girl came to a screeching halt, just brushing the full skirt of Daphne's gown. "Forgive me, Yer Grace. I didn't see ye."

Waves of nausea were undulating through Daphne's system. "Mary. No apology is necessary." She swallowed.

The awkward twelve-year-old blanched as she saw Daphne's distressed expression. "I just finished my lessons. I didn't know ye were out here." Slowly, she backed away. "I didn't mean to bump into ye."

"You didn't." Despite her unsettled state, Daphne realized she had to convince Mary she had done nothing wrong. "Mary—here." Abruptly, she thrust the dish of scones at the startled child. "Cook made extra. Enjoy them."

"Why, thank you, ma'am." Tentatively, Mary smiled. "I—"

Daphne never heard the rest. In a flash, she bolted, racing past the schoolroom to the nearby water closet Pierce had just had installed.

She'd eaten nothing that day, yet her body seemed not to know that, heaving again and again in protest. At last the retching stopped, and Daphne sank weakly to her knees, leaning her head against the cool surface of the wall.

"Try this. It will help."

From the open doorway, Sarah handed Daphne a cold compress. "Place it against your forehead and stay still for a minute or two. The feeling will pass."

Gratefully, Daphne took the cloth, pressing it to her overheated face.

"That's it. Now take deep breaths and relax."

The queasiness vanished as abruptly as it had arrived. Lifting her head, Daphne blinked. "The sensation is gone."

Sarah gave her a wry grin. "Not to worry. It will visit again. As early as tomorrow, perhaps." She reached out, helping Daphne to her feet. "Come into the classroom and sit down. You haven't eaten breakfast, have you?" she guessed, guiding Daphne from the water closet into the sunlit chamber beside it.

Blinking in surprise, Daphne shook her head.

"I suspected as much. You're more apt to be ill when your stomach is empty. Eat simple foods, but never neglect your meals, even if you aren't especially hungry," Sarah advised.

"Is the cause for my sickness so obvious?" Daphne asked, settling herself in a chair.

"Only to those who have endured it. I saw the greenish cast to your complexion when you dashed into the water closet. I've worn a similar one these past weeks."

"I suppose that makes sense," Daphne murmured with a twinge of disappointment.

"Why? Did you wish to keep your condition a secret?"

"Oh, no." She smiled faintly. "Not that I could if I chose to. The entire staff has been alerted by my anxious husband. But, in your case, well—I did hope to tell you myself."

"And why is that?" Sarah asked curiously.

"Because you and I are connected in an intangible way. We seem destined to repeatedly touch each other's lives. First at the House of Perpetual Hope, then at Benchley, and now here, both of us carrying our first babes. 'Tis silly, perhaps, but I suspect fate is guiding us along parallel paths. For our sakes, and for our children's." Daphne smiled. "Somehow it comforts me to know that we are both bringing new lives into the world at the same time."

"Thank you," Sarah replied, visibly moved. "That's a lovely thought."

"'Tis an honest one." Daphne studied Sarah's face. "Are you happy at Markham?"

"Oh, yes." Sarah's eyes glowed. "I never realized how much I would enjoy teaching children until you and the duke offered me the opportunity to do so. To be given a chance, without censure or scorn—" Sarah paused. "I wonder if you can imagine what that means to me."

"I can and I do." Daphne inclined her head. "But I wish you would realize how very much you give others in return. Not only the children, who have come alive after many days of your teaching, but me." Rubbing the folds of her gown between her fingers, Daphne added, "My father is a horrible man, Sarah, as I'm sure you recall. I've never been allowed companionship. Father even forbade me to visit our local vicar, who is truly my only friend. Having another woman to laugh with, to chat with, to share confidences with—that would be miraculous. Would you consider such a friendship?"

"You're asking me to befriend you?"

"Is that so astonishing?" Daphne asked with a quizzical expression.

"In all candor, Your Grace, we have nothing in common."

"I beg to differ with you. In my opinion, we have everything in common. All but our social position, which is a mere accident of fate. I invite you to name another disparity between us."

A flicker of a smile. "You win." The smile faded, and Sarah lowered her gaze, carefully weighing her next words. "I would like to be your friend, truly I would. But frankly, I'm not certain I'd know how. I've never shared laughter or confidences with anyone."

"Perhaps you've never met someone worthy enough to share them with."

A sad smile. "I don't easily accept people into my heart. And truthfully, no one's ever taken me into theirs."

"Not even James?" Daphne questioned softly.

"James." A film of tears veiled Sarah's eyes, and she quickly brushed them away. "I suppose he was the exception. But when it truly mattered, the feelings between us weren't strong enough."

"Are you sure?"

"Quite sure. He turned sheet white when I told him I was with child. Then he muttered something about needing to think. That was the last time I saw him."

"Perhaps he was dazed. The reality of becoming a father, especially since it was unanticipated, must have left him reeling."

"Unanticipated," Sarah echoed. "I suppose it was. But, as I told you at Benchley, he made his intentions clear from the onset of our involvement. His restless spirit would not be tamed, nor would his independence be compromised."

"Did he love you?"

"In his way, yes."

"Did he tell you so?"

Again, a sad flicker of memory. "On occasion, yes."

"Sarah." Daphne rose to her feet. "Does James know where to find you?"

Sarah turned away. "Don't you understand, Your Grace. He doesn't want to find me."

"My name is Daphne, and that doesn't answer my question."

"No—Daphne. He has no idea where to find me. Unless, of course, he inquired at Black's, the tavern in London where we met. When I accepted the position as a serving maid and left for Benchley, I provided Black's tavern keeper with the location of my new residence."

"I see." Daphne ingested that thoughtfully. She wanted to inquire further but refrained, sensing Sarah's reticence. Moreover, an idea was forming in her mind, and she was impatient to find Pierce to explore it. "Well," she cleared her throat, "I'd best make certain Langley has eaten some of Cook's scones." A grin. "I'm sure his reaction to them was more flattering than mine."

Sarah snapped out of her reverie. "First go to the kitchen and fetch some weak tea and a bland biscuit. And eat them. Else you'll spend the day either swooning or retching."

"You've convinced me," Daphne laughed. "And Sarah? Please consider my offer. I'd be proud to call you my friend."

A hesitant nod. "Thank you—Daphne."

With a warm inner glow, Daphne closed the door behind her, more determined than ever to carry out her plan.

"Langley!" She hastened to the entranceway.

The butler gave a tolerant sigh. "No sign of them yet, Your Grace."

"I didn't intend to pester you again," Daphne assured him. "I just wanted to make certain you'd eaten."

"I have. Three scones and two cups of tea. I'm now strong enough to continue my vigil well past noon."

"You're a treasure, Langley. Thank you."

"My pleasure, Madam."

"Have you any idea where Pierce is?"

"I believe the duke is in his study, Your Grace. He said

something about writing out final instructions for the work-men."

"Excellent. I'll find him." Daphne took three steps, then swayed, blinking to clear her head. "Langley, would you mind asking Cook to send a pot of weak tea and some plain biscuits into Pierce's study?"

"Not at all. I'll see to it at once." Langley frowned. "However, first I shall assist you to the study. You're looking far too peaked to manage on your own."

For once Daphne agreed, grateful for Langley's arm as she made her way down the corridor.

"Come in," Pierce responded to the knock.

"Forgive me, Your Grace," Langley began. "But the duchess—"

"Daphne." Pierce was on his feet before the butler finished, crossing the room to wrap his arm about Daphne's waist. Anxiously, he took in the pallor of her skin. "What is it?"

"Nothing," she assured him. "I just foolishly skipped breakfast. Langley has kindly offered to arrange for Cook to bring me some food."

"I'm on my way, sir," the butler confirmed, hurrying off.

Pierce scooped Daphne up and carried her over to a tufted chair. He started to put her down, then changed his mind, turning abruptly and seating himself, his wife clasped tightly to his chest. "Now I can make certain you stay put. Damn it, snow flame, what am I to do with you?"

"The answers to that question are limitless," she teased, snuggling against him. "A fact you yourself taught me. I'm fine," she added, smoothing the lines of worry from his face. "Merely in need of nourishment."

"I'll feed you myself. Then I'm taking you to your bedchamber where you are going to indulge in a nap. You've been pacing since dawn."

"I'm eager to see if anything has occurred between Mama and the vicar."

"Langley and I will send for you the moment they arrive. Won't we, Langley?" Pierce questioned pointedly as the butler re-entered, tray in hand.

"Most definitely, Your Grace." Langley flushed a bit when he saw Daphne curled in Pierce's lap, but he said nothing further, merely placing the food on the nearby table. "Will there be anything else, sir?"

"No. Thank you."

"My pleasure. Now, if you'll excuse me, I must resume my watch." The slightest flicker of amusement. "A dedicated sentry never deserts his post."

The door closed behind him.

There was a full moment of silence before Daphne turned incredulous eyes to her husband. "Did Langley just make a jest?"

A rumble of laughter erupted from Pierce's chest. "Yes, Snow flame, I believe he did. He also scarcely blushed upon finding you in my arms. It appears our Langley is thawing. Why, by next month I fully expect him to unclasp his hands from behind his back when I enter a room." Still chuckling, Pierce leaned forward to scoop a biscuit off the plate. "Eat," he commanded, bringing it to Daphne's lips.

"Yes, Your Grace." She gave him a mock salute, then complied. "Pierce, I want to discuss something with—"

"Not until at least two of those biscuits are gone," he interrupted. "And just as many cups of tea."

"Very well." Dutifully, Daphne chewed, amazed to find that Sarah was right. A bit of the right food made all the difference. "I feel wonderful," she announced a quarter hour later.

"Good. Then it's time to have your nap."

"Wait." Daphne lay a restraining hand on Pierce's arm. "Before you relegate me to my bed, you promised to hear what was on my mind."

"Yes I did, didn't I?" Sighing, Pierce resettled himself. "All right, Snow flame, I'm listening."

"It's about Sarah. Pierce, she misses James so much. And the way she speaks of him, I'm certain they were deeply in love."

"Yet he deserted her when he found out she was with child." Pierce's jaw set. "You know how little use I have for that type of abandonment."

"I know." Daphne caressed his nape. "But suppose James has had a change of heart? Suppose he's realized how unfeeling he was, and how much he misses Sarah?"

"What are you getting at?"

"Sarah told me that when she left Black's, the London pub in which she worked prior to Benchley, she gave them her forwarding address. But that address is no longer valid. Nor has Viscount Benchley any clue that Sarah is currently employed at Markham."

"Viscount Benchley?" Pierce gave a hollow laugh. "That bastard wouldn't assist James if he did know Sarah's whereabouts. Provide information to a common man? Inconceivable!"

"Then you'll help me?"

"Help you do what? I won't coerce the man to claim his child. If he hasn't the character to do so on his own, then Sarah is better off without him."

"Yes she is," Daphne concurred. "I'd never ask you to do that. All I ask is that you send one of your numerous contacts to Black's to leave word where Sarah can be reached. This way, if James does have honorable intentions he can carry them out."

"Fair enough."

"And one thing more." Daphne raised appealing eyes to her husband. "If James should come forward, can we find a position for him here at Markham? Sarah is so happy here. The children adore her and so do I. I want her to stay."

"Done." Pierce ran his knuckles over Daphne's cheek. "How can so delicate a woman have so tremendous a heart?"

She kissed his fingertips. "To be worthy of your love, it could be no other way."

Scurrying footsteps from the hallway reached their ears, followed by the distinct sound of horses' hooves.

"Your Grace." Langley knocked purposefully. "An approaching carriage."

Daphne leapt off Pierce's lap and flung open the door. "Is it Mama and the vicar?"

Langley blinked. "I'm not certain. I raced here the

moment I saw the carriage appear. 'Twas too far off for me to discern its occupants."

"Then let's do so together." She turned to Pierce, who had come to his feet and joined them. "My nap will have to wait."

"A short while," he conceded.

Daphne reached the entranceway just in time to see Chambers assist her mother from the carriage. "Welcome, you two. At last."

With a look of immense pride, Elizabeth hurried forward to embrace her daughter. "Oh Daphne, I can't believe it. A babe." She cupped Daphne's face, carefully scrutinizing her. "You look wonderful. A bit peaked, perhaps, but glowing and happy."

"As do you." Daphne returned her mother's inspection, amazed to see that, having shed her lines of suffering, Elizabeth looked a good ten years younger than she had scant weeks ago.

"Your missive said you've been feeling poorly," Elizabeth murmured anxiously. "Is it severe?"

"Erratic. And sudden. The sickness and the lightheadedness strike abruptly, and disappear in the blink of an eye. In between, I feel splendid."

"Well, I'm glad you sent for me. For us," she added, smiling at the vicar.

"Snowdrop." Chambers took Daphne's hands in his. "I'm delighted. May your child be blessed with good health and joy. He's already blessed with two extraordinary parents who will love him or her with all their hearts."

"Oh, Vicar, I'm so glad you're both here." Daphne hugged him. "I've been awaiting your arrival for days."

"I had to properly decorate the manor at Rutland before leaving," Elizabeth explained. "Since I plan to spend Christmas with you, I wanted the staff to have their own festivities. They've all been so good to me." She grinned. "I confess, we arrived at Markham nearly an hour ago, but a friend of yours detained us."

"A friend?"

"Yes. He watched us from a safe distance as we drove

through the gates, but evidently he recognized me and approached the roadside, staring hopefully. I couldn't disappoint him, especially not during so joyous an occasion as the celebration of my forthcoming grandchild. So I had Alfred stop before we even sighted the manor. Your friend is now feasting on Rutland's wild strawberries and blackberries, which I had originally intended to become a pie."

Daphne rolled her eyes. "Russet knows precisely who will indulge him, Mama. Doubtless, he is enthralled by your arrival."

"As if you don't spoil him," Pierce commented dryly. "That fox eats more than I do." He kissed Elizabeth's hand. "We're even more pleased than Russet to welcome you."

"For different reasons, I hope," she teased back.

Slipping unobtrusively by them, Langley assessed the number of bags in the carriage.

"Mama, I'm sure you remember Langley from your previous stay." Daphne tugged him forward proudly. "He is an indispensable member of our family."

"How are you, Langley?"

The butler swallowed several times before replying. "Well, my lady."

On the heels of his greeting he bowed, but not before Daphne detected the uncustomary expression of emotion on his face.

"You've also met Mr. Chambers," she reminded him gently.

"Good to see you again, Langley," the vicar acknowledged.

"Welcome, sir." Another bow, after which Langley straightened, fully composed. "If you'll excuse me, I'll summon some footmen to carry in your bags."

The vicar stared after Langley's retreating form. "You've rendered your magic again, Snowdrop."

Daphne's delicate brows drew together. "What do you mean?"

"Magic made all the more beautiful by its inherent existence and unconscious offering," Pierce noted aloud, his expression tender.

"Indeed," Chambers concurred.

"What are the two of you mumbling about?" Daphne demanded.

"Nothing, Snow flame." Pierce tucked her arm through his. "Shall we take our guests on a tour? This is, in a way, both your mother and the vicar's first real visits to Markham. Your mother's previous stay was a scant day and a half spent in hiding. As for the vicar, the evening he came to dinner we'd scarcely finished dessert before you brought the visit to a rapid close by fainting." Pierce grinned at Chambers. "As you can guess, we've since deduced the cause of Daphne's swoon."

"Indeed. Your forthcoming heir was announcing his creation."

"A tour sounds lovely." Elizabeth cast a worried look at Daphne. "Are you certain you're up to it, darling?"

"I'm fine, Mama. Truly."

"Daphne will be with us only for the first few minutes," Pierce stated in a voice that defied argument. "We'll begin with the room Daphne takes the greatest pride in—our new schoolroom. After that, we'll move to the second floor, at which point we will escort Daphne to her bedchamber for a much-needed nap. Agreed, Snow flame?"

"Have I any choice?"

"None."

The sun was an orange haze in the west when Elizabeth carried a tray into Daphne's room. "Are you awake, dear?" she asked, approaching the bed.

Daphne stretched and sat up. "Goodness! What time is it?"

"Half after four. You were exhausted." Elizabeth placed the tray on the nightstand and lowered herself to the edge of the bed. "And now you must be famished. I've brought you some plain broth, a bit of chicken, and fresh-baked bread."

"It sounds heavenly." Daphne took the tray and began eating voraciously. "I cannot imagine why I'm so hungry," she managed, between mouthfuls.

"You're eating for two now. 'Tis natural to require more."

Require more.

Elizabeth's phrase recalled Daphne's original purpose in sending for her mother.

Thoughtfully, she lay down her fork. "Mama, do you remember the morning I confided Pierce's proposal to you?"

"Of course."

"You said some things to me—things that implied you'd experienced a situation in which you allowed your heart to be silenced, and that you now regretted that decision. Do you recall?"

Elizabeth lowered her gaze, stroked the edge of the bedcovers. "Yes, I recall."

"'Tis none of my business, but I must ask anyway. Did that situation involve Mr. Chambers?"

Startled, Elizabeth's gaze lifted. "How did you know?"

"I didn't. Pierce guessed. He's an incredibly insightful man." Daphne leaned forward. "Did you love him, Mama?"

A painful nod. "Yes. Very much."

"And he loved you." Daphne needed no confirmation. "What happened? Why did you marry Father? How could you—" She broke off.

"How could I choose a hateful man like your father over a fine man like Alfred?" Elizabeth sighed, staring off into space. "I wonder if you know how many times I've asked myself that over the years. Perhaps the Lord meant it to be this way so I might bring you into the world."

"Thank you," Daphne whispered. "But that's not an answer. When you wed Father you had no notion what children the marriage might produce. So why?"

Slowly, Elizabeth rose, went to stand by the window. "I was fifteen when I met Alfred. He was three and twenty. There was a small gathering in our village to honor the new parish church. I attended with my parents. He was present, not as an established official, but as a young clergyman who was deeply committed to people and to God. I believe we fell in love the instant we met." A pause. "Unfortunately, my parents had no intention of allowing their only daughter to throw her life away on a poor vicar whose ambitions were rooted in ideals rather than gold. If Alfred had been willing to further himself through the right channels, if he'd been seeking a future as a high-ranking Church official, then, perhaps they would have reconsidered. But he wasn't, and they didn't. Your father was introduced to me the next summer, during my first London Season. He was wealthy, titled, and successful. He asked for my hand; my father gave it."

"But what about the vicar?"

"Alfred held me while I cried, soothed me when I confessed my fear of defying my parents. And then he let me go." Elizabeth dabbed at her eyes. "It was the single most selfless gesture I've ever seen."

Daphne swallowed past the lump in her throat. "Had the two of you plans to marry?"

"Without question. We'd spent hours visualizing our life together: the cottage we'd share, filled with our children; the gardens we'd plant, flourishing with yellow roses. Yellow roses," Elizabeth's voice quavered, "were Alfred's special gift to me. He brought a bouquet of them each time he visited. They came to signify the beauty of our love."

Another reality struck. Raising her left hand, Daphne studied the delicate scrap of silver adorning her fourth finger. "This ring, the one the vicar bestowed upon us so Pierce and I might seal our vows—"

Elizabeth's smile was tremulous. "That was Alfred's sensitive way of passing on the miracle of our love. Whatever we were denied, he prayed God would grant you and Pierce."

"Oh, Mama. Then initially he intended it for you."

"Yes." A choked sound. "Daphne, I loved him deeply, as he did me. But I just couldn't—I wasn't strong enough." Elizabeth buried her face in her hands.

"I'm so sorry." Daphne slipped off the bed and went to her mother, embracing her as if to absorb her pain.

"I shouldn't be crying. 'Twas so long ago."

"But it wasn't. You love him still. And he loves you."

Silence. Then, Elizabeth raised her head, dashing tears from her cheeks. "Some feelings never alter, I suppose, no matter how much better 'twould be for everyone if they would. You're right. Alfred's and my love has never faded. But neither have the restrictions that for more than a score of years have kept us apart. I was, and continue to be, Harwick's wife."

"Once, perhaps," Daphne amended. "But now? You're Father's wife in name alone. You're no longer even living in his house."

"That doesn't change the fact that he and I exchanged vows. And neither Alfred nor I will cheapen our love by betraying those vows. In the sight of God and man, I belong to Harwick."

"Not if Pierce has his way."

Elizabeth sighed. "I see your husband has told you of his improbable plans for my future."

"Rest assured, Mama. With Pierce, nothing is improbable. He has the most incredible way of making the impossible possible. And he is determined to procure this divorce for you. So please don't lose faith."

A small spark of hope flickered in Elizabeth's eyes. "How can I? Pierce is not the only one who is certain he can accomplish this unlikely feat. Alfred is equally confident. Between Pierce's belief in himself and Alfred's belief in Pierce, 'tis hard to remain a skeptic."

"And in the interim—" Daphne seized her mother's hands. "You are happy, aren't you Mama? I can see it all over your face. You're away from Father's brutality, safe and secure at Rutland." A teasing light came into her eyes. "Where, I understand, the vicar has been paying you visits."

Elizabeth's glow was like a schoolgirl's. "Yes, he has. He stays but a few minutes, and all we do is chat. But the magic is still there. Just as it was all those years ago." A reluctant blush stained her cheeks. "He brings a bouquet of yellow roses each time he calls."

"How romantic! Nearly as romantic as the fact that, after more than twenty years, Mr. Chambers has found no other woman on whom he chooses to bestow his heart. 'Tis still you, just as it always has been, and always will be."

Elizabeth smiled at her daughter's words. "I never thought I'd hear you extolling the virtues of love, growing up the way you did. I suppose my greatest fear was that you'd never trust a man enough to care. But all that has changed now, hasn't it?"

"Totally."

"I'm glad," Elizabeth said with understated simplicity. She cupped Daphne's chin. "Being in love becomes you. So does prospective motherhood. I needn't ask if Pierce is everything you hoped he'd be."

"Everything—and more," Daphne responded, grinning privately as she contemplated the unexpected exhilaration that had accompanied her marriage, things her mother could never fathom. The heartstopping beauty of Pierce's lovemaking, the breathless daring of spending her life with the Tin Cup Bandit, and, as she had to honestly admit, the incomparable thrill of robbing by his side.

Everything Pierce had promised the day he proposed had come to pass, Daphne realized with a flash of awed insight. He'd vowed to release her from the prison of her life, and that meant far more than wresting her from her father's brutal hands.

It meant—and she could still hear Pierce's words, fervently whispered in the woods at Tragmore as he'd enumerated all her facets he intended to free—*Your magnificent spirit, your fire, your innocence, your passion. All of you.*

Well, he had succeeded. Sometime over the past two months, Daphne Wyndham had blossomed into Daphne Thornton.

"You're lost in thought," Elizabeth murmured, bringing Daphne back to the present. "And with a most captivating smile on your face. What are you pondering?"

"Pierce," Daphne whispered, her voice hushed with emotion. "He's freed me, Mama, precisely as he vowed." Automatically, her palm shifted to her abdomen. "And, with God's help, this babe and I will free him as well."

22

"NOW REMEMBER THE PROMISE I COERCED FROM YOU LAST week," Pierce cautioned, buttoning his shirt.

"Prom*ises*," Daphne amended with a twinkle. "And I'm certain you shan't let me forget a single one." She crossed the bedchamber, reaching up to complete her husband's task. "I recall every word," she added hastily, seeing Pierce's angry scowl. "I'll stay far away from the schoolhouse while the roof is constructed, remain in my makeshift seat, and call you if I need anything at all. How's that?" She smoothed the shirt with a flourish.

"The shirt is fine. I wish I were nearly as confident of the promises. Had I not said you could come—"

"But you did. Besides, involving the children in this project was my idea. I'd be devastated if I weren't permitted to watch. Please, Pierce, I won't endanger either myself or the babe. You have my word. I'll make no attempt to help. Why, I won't even approach the cart holding the slate and the wood. I'll just sit sedately by and observe the children's joyous faces. All right?"

A sigh. "All right." He scooped up his coat. "Let's go have some breakfast. The workmen won't be arriving at the schoolhouse for several hours, and you're not leaving Markham unless you've put something in your stomach."

"I ate a piece of dry toast before I stepped out of bed," Daphne protested.

"That was four hours ago. Cook was advised to prepare a light mid-morning meal, suitable for expectant mothers. So stop arguing, and join me in the dining room."

"Very well." Reluctantly, Daphne nodded. "Although if we're late—"

"We won't be."

Rounding the second-floor landing, Pierce guided Daphne down the staircase. Halfway, she paused, nudging him and gesturing toward the foot of the steps. He followed her gaze, grinning as he saw the object of his wife's scrutiny.

Standing in the alcove, oblivious to the servants scurrying by them, were Elizabeth and Chambers. They were absorbed in quiet conversation broken by an occasional wash of muted laughter. And, though nearly a foot of space separated them, the affection hovering between them was a palpable entity no distance could belie.

"I'd best find the time to travel to London and meet with Colby, that barrister Hollingsby's engaged," Pierce muttered for his wife's ears alone. His lips twitched. "My infallible instincts tell me we'd be wise to expedite the divorce process."

"In this case your instincts are wasted," Daphne returned, tender amusement sparkling on her face. "Your eyes alone could tell you as much."

"Indeed." Pierce tucked Daphne's arm through his. "I almost hate to intrude."

"Good morning, you two." Elizabeth chose that moment to look up, smiling warmly as she greeted them. "We've been waiting for you. Cook's clucking has gotten louder and louder. Evidently, our meal is getting cold. So let's dash in and eat. Then we can all leave together for the schoolhouse."

"You're accompanying us, Mama?" Daphne blinked in surprise.

"Well, of course." Elizabeth met Daphne's gaze, her own pervaded by an inner peace until now unknown. "These past years I've been able to offer you assistance in only the most covert ways. Your cause means as much to me as it does to you. I relish the thought of translating my feelings into something more tangible, something that can truly help the children. Moreover," she exchanged a teasing look with Pierce, "who else would ensure that you behave, if not I?"

"Mama . . ."

Chambers beamed. "I wouldn't dream of trying to dissuade your mother, Snowdrop. I haven't seen her so determined in two and twenty years."

"I have no intention of dissuading her," Daphne replied, seeing beyond her mother's quip to the significance of her transformation. "Welcome, Mama." Hugging Elizabeth, she whispered, "Evidently, I'm not the only Wyndham woman who's been released from prison."

"Evidently not."

Daphne seized her mother's hand. "Come. I suddenly find myself ravenously hungry."

A quarter hour later a knock sounded, interrupting their meal. Daphne glanced quizzically at Pierce. "Are you expecting anyone?"

"No." He broke into his second teacake. "Whoever it is, Langley will handle it."

A moment later, the butler entered the dining room. "Pardon me, Your Grace. I hate to interrupt your meal, but you did ask me to advise you if a Mr. James Chapman should arrive. Well, the gentleman in question is in the hallway."

Before Langley had completed his announcement, Daphne's bowl of fresh raspberries had been abandoned. Like a bullet, she came to her feet. "James? Is that Sarah's—"

"Yes." Pierce rose as well, frowning at his wife's unchecked ebullience. "Daphne, please, let me handle this. We still don't know precisely why Mr. Chapman is here."

Daphne bit back her reply, forcing herself to remember why Pierce's attitude toward James was so severe. Having endured his own father's abandonment, Pierce was staunchly trying to protect Sarah from hurt.

"What did Mr. Chapman say, Langley?" Pierce was questioning.

"He asked to see Miss Sarah, sir."

"Did he?" Tossing his napkin to the table, Pierce headed for the door. "First, he shall see me. After which I'll decide whether or not to tell Sarah of his arrival."

"I'm going with you."

Restraint cast aside, Daphne followed Pierce's path, raising her chin as her husband turned to confront her.

"I know you don't believe I'm objective," she told him quietly. "And perhaps you're correct. But, Pierce, you are no more objective than I. And, since our inclinations in this case lead us to draw opposite conclusions, and since we both care about Sarah's future and the future of her babe, I believe we should both be present to hear what James has to say."

For an instant, Pierce hesitated.

"'Tis you who created this forthright wife," Daphne murmured. "Did you not encourage me to emerge from my stifling cocoon?"

Pride warred with frustration and won. "Yes, Snow flame, I did," Pierce conceded. "Very well, then." He extended his arm. "Shall we meet with Mr. Chapman?"

Never had Daphne felt more proud—or more loved. "Yes. At once."

James was pacing the length of the entranceway. When he saw Daphne and Pierce approach, he halted, hat clutched nervously in his hands.

"Mr. Chapman?" Pierce opened.

"Yes, sir. Are you the Duke of Markham?"

A nod. "I'm Pierce Thornton. This is my wife, Daphne."

"Mr. Chapman," Daphne acknowledged. He was much as she'd expected: tall and dark, with sharp, intelligent features, not classically handsome but overwhelmingly charismatic. "I assume, from your arrival at Markham, that the tavern keeper at Black's advised you of Sarah's whereabouts." She waited.

His reaction was immediate. "Then she is here?"

"Yes, she's here."

"Thank the lord." James raked his fingers through his hair. "I've been combing London for her, stopping in every pub and coffeehouse I pass."

"Really?" Pierce tapped his chin thoughtfully. "What made you think she was in London?"

"At first, I didn't. Originally, that fellow at Black's gave me the address of some big country estate. Said she'd left Black's to take a better job as a maid." He frowned, rubbing the brim of his hat. "Well, I went there—Benchley it was called—and the Viscount slammed the door in my face after curtly declaring that no one by the name of Sarah Cooke had ever worked at his estate."

Pierce's jaw tightened fractionally but he said nothing.

"Anyway, I thought maybe Sarah had purposely left a phony address at Black's to mislead me. So I returned to London, and my search."

"Why would Sarah intentionally mislead you?" Pierce prompted.

"Because she might not want me to find her." James averted his head. "The last time we saw each other she was terribly angry. And with good reason."

"Really? What reason was that?"

James stiffened. "With all due respect, Your Grace, Sarah's and my relationship is between the two of us. I don't want to jeopardize her job at Markham, whatever that is, but I won't stand here and discuss our arguments with you either. I presume you left that note at Black's supplying me with Sarah's true whereabouts so I could find her. Well, I'm here. And, if you'll forgive my impertinence, I'd like to see her now."

"Why?"

Even Daphne started at Pierce's sharp tone.

"Why?" James repeated.

"Precisely. Why? Is it because of her new, elevated position?"

James gaped. "I don't even know what the hell she does here."

"She teaches children. Damned well, by the way. Her position, incidentally, pays quite a bit better than the one at Black's did."

"Is that supposed to mean something to me?"

"I don't know. Does it?"

"No. I don't want her bloody money. I want her." James inhaled sharply. "Look, I don't know what Sarah's told you. But I'll be frank. When Sarah and I parted, I didn't deserve her or her love. As of now, I intend to change that. I'm not a poor man, Your Grace, only a restless one. I've been trained as a clerk. I've apprenticed under several fine solicitors over the years and accumulated a respectable sum of money and good credentials. I intend to open my own soliciting offices in whatever town Sarah chooses. Then I intend to make her my wife."

"I see." Pierce cleared his throat. "Mr. Chapman, I realize I'm being harsh and intrusive. I agree that your situation with Sarah is your business and no one else's. But Sarah is a much valued member of my household. Consequently, I do not want her hurt or upset."

"Neither do I. In the name of heaven, she's carrying my—" James broke off abruptly.

"We know about the babe, Mr. Chapman," Daphne said quietly. "That's one of the reasons we're being so protective." With unbiased compassion, Daphne took in the dark circles beneath his eyes, the lines of suffering about his mouth. Then she turned to Pierce. "I think we should send for Sarah."

Pierce inclined his head, his gaze meeting his wife's.

"My exceptional instincts," she said softly, simply. "Please. This time in particular, heed them."

The tension drained slowly from Pierce's taut frame. "All right, Snow flame," he concurred. Then he looked about, calling, "Langley."

"Yes, sir?" The butler hastened to their side.

"Please summon Miss Sarah. Tell her she has a visitor."

"Very good, sir."

"Thank you, Your Grace," James murmured gratefully. "You won't regret it."

"No, I don't believe I will. As for thanks, thank my wife. In the end, it appears she was far more objective than I." Pierce studied James thoughtfully. "You're a lucky man, Chapman. My advice is that you never again wager so invaluable an asset as the woman you love." With that, Pierce retraced his steps to the dining room.

Daphne and James stared after him. Then, Daphne turned back to their guest. "I agree, Mr. Chapman. Savor this opportunity to regain Sarah's love. 'Tis the last chance you'll be given."

"Daphne?" Sarah's voice interrupted whatever James had been about to reply. "I'm in the midst of lessons. Is there some—" She halted, all the color draining from her face. "James."

Tactfully, Daphne moved off. "If you'll excuse me, I'll rejoin my husband for breakfast." She gave Sarah a reassuring smile. "Should you need me, you know where I'll be."

"Your Grace?"

Daphne was halfway down the hall when she heard James summon her. She paused, glancing over her shoulder. "Yes?"

Sarah's hand was clutched tightly in his. "You have my unending gratitude," he called. "You and your husband."

Even from a distance, Daphne could see the joy trembling on Sarah's lips. "Be happy, both of you," she returned warmly. Her lips curved. "All three of you."

Light of heart, Daphne strolled into the dining room. "Do you think Mr. Hollingsby might require an assistant?" she asked Pierce brightly as he stood to ease back her chair.

Pierce's chuckle was rich. "My thoughts exactly, Snow flame." He grew sober. "Sarah is pleased, then?"

"Elated would be a better choice of words."

"And why not? She's with the man she loves," Elizabeth interjected, sipping her tea. Noting Daphne's questioning look, she explained. "Pierce told us about James and the delicacy of the situation. I, for one, think it's wonderful."

Daphne clasped her husband's hand. "As do I." She gazed pointedly from her mother to the vicar. "Isn't it wondrous when fate sees fit to grant those who are deserving a second chance at happiness?"

"Yes, Snowdrop." It was the vicar who replied. "'Tis truly a miracle."

Pierce brought Daphne's fingers to his lips. "Tell me, do you think Chapman's restlessness can really be abated?

After all, he's never stayed in one place long enough to set up his own soliciting practice, much less to build a home and support a family."

"Definitely." Daphne popped some raspberries into her mouth, her eyes alight with mischief. "Fatherhood has a way of inspiring great changes in men, wouldn't you say?"

A corner of Pierce's mouth lifted. "Indeed I would, Snow flame. Indeed I would."

Spirits were high when the Markham carriage arrived at the schoolhouse two hours later. Waiting only until Pierce had handed down her mother, Daphne practically leapt to the ground, eagerly surveying the bustling scene unfolding around her.

Workmen scurried about, calling to each other as they organized their materials and good-naturedly sidestepped the inquisitive, exuberant children. Over the clattering wood, Miss Redmund's stern voice rang out, admonishing the students and demanding that they behave.

She might just as well have been ordering the wind to be still.

"I'd better assist Miss Redmund," Daphne determined, exchanging amused looks with the vicar. "Else she'll have apoplexy before the construction even begins."

"Daphne!"

Having spotted her, Timmy snatched up a small box, yanking off its lid and simultaneously racing over. "I brought 'enry," he announced proudly, shoving the lizard under Daphne's nose. "I was 'oping you could watch 'im fer me while I'm working."

"I'd be delighted." Daphne was torn between chortling and retching as the thick smell of mud and grass accosted her. Breathing through her mouth, she peered closer, seeing a flash of dark green slither through the reeds.

"There 'e is! Ye see 'im? Isn't 'e great?"

"Yes, and yes." Inadvertently, Daphne inched away. "He's splendid. Only what exactly is his bed made of?"

"Oh, lots of stuff I found in the barn. Yucky stuff. Lizards like yucky stuff, especially when it's wet."

"Lizards are also notoriously shy," Pierce interjected,

biting back a roar of laughter. "So why don't we put his lid back on and give him some privacy among all these strangers."

"Ye're right, Pierce." Instantly, Timmy covered his pet. "Daphne said she'd hold 'im while I'm 'elping the men."

"A wise idea. That way there's no chance of Henry escaping and getting into trouble. A construction site is a very dangerous place for small creatures like lizards." Pierce raised his voice until it boomed pointedly across the grounds. "In fact, a construction site is dangerous for anyone who doesn't follow directions. Therefore, any of our helpers who can't do as they're told will spend the remainder of the day watching Daphne watch Henry."

A round of groans.

"Good." Pierce grinned. "I see we understand each other. Now let's gather round and approach the schoolhouse safely, as a group rather than helter-skelter, like a chaotic mob. At that point the workmen can give us our instructions."

Reluctantly, the children stopped dashing about, making their way, one by one, over to Pierce.

Gazing after them, Miss Redmund beamed at Pierce, her pudgy cheeks lifting in an adoring smile.

With a cough that sounded suspiciously like a smothered laugh, Chambers averted his head, intently studying the men as they unloaded the last of their materials.

"Who are ye?" William suddenly demanded, cocking his head at Elizabeth.

"I'm Daphne's mother. My name is Elizabeth."

"Daphne 'as a mother?" He looked incredulous. "But she's old."

"True." Elizabeth's eyes sparkled with humor. "But her advanced years are a recent occurrence. She used to be about the same age as you. So she does indeed have a mother."

"Ye're pretty," Prudence declared, hugging her new doll. "Are you a snowdrop, too?"

Elizabeth's gaze met the vicar's. "Do you know, I believe I am." She touched the doll's bright head. "What is your name and who is your beautiful friend?"

"My name is Prudence. My doll's name is Daphne." Prudence's earnest little face screwed up thoughtfully. "When Daphne bought 'er fer me, she said to give 'er a name that was special. So I did."

"Oh, Prudence." Daphne squatted beside her, tears glistening on her lashes. "That is perhaps the nicest thing anyone has ever done for me. I'm honored. Thank you."

"I gave ye my lizard to hold," Timmy protested. "That's an honor, too."

"Of course it is. What Prudence did is just a different kind of honor. Right, Prudence?" She gave the little girl a conspiratorial smile.

Prudence smiled back. "Right."

"Mr. Chambers, are we gonna be able to 'oist the beams and nail the slate?" William questioned.

"Let's go find out." The vicar gestured for them to follow.

"I'll set up some benches for you and Elizabeth," Pierce told Daphne. "Then I'll go give the workmen a hand." His eyes twinkled. "I'll leave you ladies to tend to Henry."

Within the hour, the shingles were ready to go, and the heavy wooden beams soon to anchor the new roof were lying side by side on the ground. Two powerful plow horses were brought in, tossing their heads as a foreman tied one end of the thick rope to their harnesses, the other to the first beam he intended to hoist.

Pierce tugged Timmy away from the horses, then turned to roll his eyes at Daphne.

From a dozen feet away, Daphne laughed. "I wish Pierce wouldn't hold me to that silly promise," she complained to her mother. "I want to help."

"Oh, we shall." Elizabeth settled back on the bench Pierce had made for them under a cluster of trees. "One more incident such as that and Timmy will be joining Henry. My instincts tell me he won't be alone. In fact, I suspect that most of the children are going to spend more time watching Henry's antics than they'll spend assisting the builders."

"Doubtless." Daphne looked around. "Where is the vicar?"

"Assembling nails for the slate." Elizabeth pointed. "See? Alongside the building."

"And Miss Redmund? I thought she'd be delighted to sit here with us."

"Miss Redmund is evidently more delighted to stand by the schoolhouse and gaze worshipfully at your husband," Elizabeth returned with a sideways look at Daphne.

Simultaneously, they dissolved into laughter.

A speeding carriage tore onto the scene, screeching to a halt beside the construction materials.

Daphne's laughter froze. "Oh my God." She seized her mother's hand, feeling it turn to ice.

"It's Harwick." All the color drained from Elizabeth's face, and she began to tremble uncontrollably. "What in the name of heaven is he doing here?"

"Thornton!"

Tragmore's voice erupted like a gunshot, splintering into sinister fragments all about them. He stalked Pierce in harsh, uncompromising strides, emitting a coiled, bone-chilling aura of triumph.

Slowly, Pierce turned. "Tragmore. What do you want?"

"Quite a bit." The marquis laughed. "Everything, in fact. My entire life—and yours."

"Get out." Instinctively, Pierce took a protective step in Daphne's direction as if to shield her from her father's presence. "Get out before I throw you out."

Unconcerned, Tragmore glanced in the direction of Pierce's movement. "Ah. My traitorous daughter and my adulterous wife. Your servants didn't mention I'd find them here as well. And where is the deceitful vicar? I assumed he would complete this cozy picture."

"Cease this tirade, Harwick." The vicar dropped the nails he'd been holding, coming to stand beside Pierce. "You've done enough damage to last a lifetime. Go back to Tragmore."

"Ah, there you are, Chambers. I feared you'd disappointed me. As for my going back to Tragmore, I fully intend to. But when I do, it will be as a rich and powerful man." The marquis flourished his portfolio, a vicious gleam in his eye. "Or, if not rich and powerful, then at least thoroughly vindicated."

"You? Vindicated?" Pierce laughed harshly. "'Tis you

who contaminates the rest of the world, Tragmore. Not the other way around."

"Is that why my wife is bedding down with the pious clergyman?"

Chambers went rigid. "Don't soil Elizabeth's name, you unworthy scoundrel. Not in my presence."

"How gallant!" Tragmore applauded. "'Tis no wonder Elizabeth prefers your bed to mine. Tell me, Chambers, are you sharing her room during your prolonged and intimate stay at Markham?"

"Don't dignify that vile accusation with an answer, Vicar." Pierce's eyes glittered with hatred.

"Your Grace?" the foreman called out tentatively. "Shall we wait?"

"It's not necessary, Mallor," Pierce replied, his gaze glued to Tragmore. "The marquis will be leaving shortly. Start hoisting the beams. Miss Redmund, watch the children."

"Of course, Your Grace," Miss Redmund agreed, gathering the children together.

The sounds of construction resumed.

"All right, Tragmore," Pierce ground out. "You've spoken your filthy mind. Now get out."

"Not quite yet, Thornton." With cold deliberation, Tragmore extracted five or six sheets from his portfolio. "You see, despite the overwhelming presence of your burly guards, my investigator managed to acquire a significant amount of evidence at Rutland. Enough to prove there is more involved here than my filthy mind, as you put it. Pages of evidence, in fact." He turned to the vicar. "Would you like a recounting of each and every visit you made to see Elizabeth these past two months? Of the long moments you and she were alone, unchaperoned, in the manor in which Thornton ensconced her? Just the two of you and those thoughtful, romantic yellow roses you brought her on your visits. Not to mention your unexpected and cozy carriage ride from Rutland to Markham, where you're residing under the same roof, doing lord knows what."

"We're talking, Harwick. Something you are incapable of doing except with your fists." Chambers could scarcely speak beyond his rage. "Not even your devious investigator can fabricate sins that never took place. And deep inside your black heart, you know very well that Elizabeth is incapable of deceit. That so long as she bears your name, she would never be unfaithful to you."

"Ah, but she's in the process of ridding herself of my name, is she not? Or so Hollingsby told me when he dropped by Tragmore to sever our association."

"Yes," Pierce bit out. "She is. And with just cause, as we both know. You brutalized her, you bastard, just as you brutalized my wife."

"I? A bastard?" Another bitter laugh. "I believe you're confused, Thornton. 'Tis you who are the bastard, not I. You were born of a whore who was cast into the streets where she belonged. Had the fates been kind, she would have died there, with you still in her belly, rather than taking up taxpayers' money in that filthy Leicester workhouse."

Something inside Pierce snapped.

"You son of a bitch." His fist shot out, sending Tragmore reeling backward.

"Don't, Pierce." The vicar grabbed his sleeve. "That is precisely what he's goading you into doing. For whatever reason, he wants to appear the martyr." Chambers indicated the gaping crew and children.

"You're wasting your breath, Chambers." Regaining his balance, Tragmore dabbed at his nose with a handkerchief. "You can't stop him from fighting like an animal. It's in his blood; reinforced by years of living on the streets. Let him demonstrate the truth for all to see—that, title or not, he is and always will be a workhouse gutter rat. If Markham had possessed a whit of sense, he never would have acknowledged Cara Thornton's bastard urchin as his son."

"Shut up, Father." Unnoticed, Daphne had left the bench and now stood, eyes ablaze, beside the men.

For the first time, Tragmore looked taken aback. "Well, well, what has happened to my meek little Daphne?"

"She escaped your poisonous grasp," Daphne shot back. "And so did Mama. Now get away from my family and don't return."

Reflexively, Tragmore's hand balled into a fist.

"Do it and you're a dead man." Pierce's tone was lethally

quiet. "And I don't give a damn if the entire House of Lords convenes to watch me choke the life out of you."

"You don't, do you?"

"No. I'm a gutter rat, remember?"

"Harwick." Elizabeth approached on quaking legs. "What is it you want? Why did you go to the trouble of hiring an investigator?" She glanced from Daphne to Pierce, her frightened gaze coming to rest on the vicar. "If my going back to Tragmore is the necessary price to keep you from harming the people I love—" Her voice broke. "Then so be it."

Tragmore threw back his head and laughed. "Don't flatter yourself, my dear. Your attributes are utterly replaceable. Frankly, I don't give a damn whose bed you share. I don't, of course, intend to tell that either to the Church or to Parliament. What I will tell them is that I've been abandoned by my beloved wife, the woman I've cherished for more than a score of years. Think of their outrage when they read my documents and learn you've taken up with a lover from your past—and under the roof of a *truly* violent and devious man." Tragmore's lips curled. "How quickly they will award me my divorce. And how sad for you and for Daphne." He leveled his triumphant stare at Pierce. "Not only will I snuff out any chance Elizabeth has of initiating this divorce, but I'll procure one on *my* terms, leaving Elizabeth with nothing."

"Mama doesn't need your money," Daphne bit out.

"True. But does she need the vicar?" he returned smoothly. "Because she will never have him. You see, I quite agree with Chambers. Elizabeth is far too moral to bed down with a man who is not her husband. And remarriage will not be an option, not when I'm through." His smile was malevolent as he delivered his final blow directly to Pierce's soul. "And Daphne? Daphne will no longer be my daughter. In fact, the divorce will nullify her existence. And then, Thornton, your wife will be a bastard, just like you."

A vein throbbed in Pierce's temple. "How much?"

Tragmore's brows arched in mock surprise. "Thornton, are you implying that you're willing to negotiate with me?"

"I said, how much? You've had your fun. Now tell me

what it is you *really* want. It isn't your wife. Nor is it your daughter. It's money. So how much will it take to convince you to abandon this sick scheme?"

All taunting vanished from the marquis's face. "I want every one of my notes, marked paid in full, placed in the palm of my hand, along with that outrageous agreement Hollingsby drew up, shredded into pieces. And then, I want a reasonable allowance, say, twenty thousand pounds a month, to ensure my cooperation and my permanent withdrawal from your lives."

"And what guarantee do I have that, once I've done as you asked, you won't proceed with your contemptible divorce suit?"

"I'll sign a document stating as such. Plus I'll turn over all the reports my investigator provided me of Elizabeth's meetings with Chambers."

"What sort of fool do you take me for, Tragmore?" Pierce countered. "Your bloody henchman has copies."

"Indeed he does. I'll turn those over to you as well." Tragmore gave Pierce a contemptuous sneer. "You have no choice but to take me at my word, Thornton. 'Tis true you run the risk of my reneging on my part of the agreement. But you also know that, given my incentive of twenty thousand pounds a month, that is highly unlikely. Conversely, what if you refuse my demands? Will you be able to endure the consequences? To live with yourself knowing it was you who'd condemned Daphne to the role of a bastard?"

Pierce's fists clenched and unclenched at his sides.

"How does it feel to be cornered, Thornton? To be locked in a cell for which only I hold the key, to be tormented as you once tormented me?"

The dam burst.

"You filthy scum." Lunging forward, Pierce grabbed Tragmore by the throat. "What do you know of prison and torment? I merely bled your money. You bled my soul. Mine and all the other children you terrorized and thrashed every chance you could."

"What children? What the hell are you babbling about?" Tragmore sputtered, struggling to free himself.

"The House of Perpetual Hope. Remember? 'Twas your

thorough investigator who informed you of my roots. To you, it was a great revelation that the bastard who held all your notes was indeed a bastard, one who'd spent the first dozen years of his life in a workhouse. And not just *any* workhouse, mind you, but the one to which you'd paid so many lucrative visits. It never occurred to you that I'd remember you, did it? You assumed that you'd been as anonymous to me as I was to you. But you were wrong, Tragmore. Dead wrong. I remember you vividly—your beatings, your cruelty." Pierce's fingers dug into Tragmore's throat. "And, of course, your private meetings with Barrings. The arrangement you thought was so cleverly covert. The money you pocketed in return for keeping that monster in office. I remember it all, you vicious lowlife. Every week I watched you and my *father,* the distinguished Duke of Markham, slip into Barrings's office when you thought all the workhouse trash were in bed. Every week I eavesdropped as Barrings handed you your money. And every week I vowed to make you pay for your cruelty."

Tragmore's eyes had widened, and he'd stopped struggling. "All this time you knew? So that's why you've stalked me as a predator stalks his prey." With renewed arrogance, he shoved Pierce's hand away. "I always thought my little exchange with Barrings was most ingenious. The opportunity presented itself unexpectedly, to be sure, but all in all it evolved into a brilliant scheme. A surprising fact, given that Markham indirectly inspired it."

Pierce swallowed. "So I have my father to thank for Barrings's continued reign as headmaster."

A crack of laughter. "Don't be stupid, Thornton. Markham wasn't devious enough to invent so splendid a plan. He was a weak man whose heart and conscience were in perpetual conflict with his head. What he proposed was a mere skeleton of my ultimate arrangement. He offered to pay me handsomely if I could devise a viable business venture that would necessitate his making frequent trips to the House of Perpetual Hope. Presumably, his real motive was to grant a favor to an anonymous friend by secretly keeping an eye on his bastard son—a son I recently realized was Markham's. You." Tragmore shrugged. "I always suspected there had to be more to the story than what he told me, but, quite frankly, I didn't care. I did my part, inventing the idea of bleeding Barrings, something I knew Markham's ethics would never permit—unless I were the one doing the bleeding. So I proposed doing just that. I would accompany Markham on all his visits and personally handle the whole sordid matter with Barrings, thus providing Markham with the diversion he needed to verify the well-being of his friend's bastard son. That suited Markham fine. As long as his true purpose remained unrevealed, he didn't give a damn what Barrings paid me, nor that I was collecting funds from two sources, himself and Barrings. After all, Markham had more money than he could ever spend in a lifetime. So we all got what we wanted and no one was the wiser."

"Yes, you all got what you wanted," Pierce spat. "And in your case that meant more than money, it meant blood. In between the visits you made with Markham, you made some on your own, for the pure pleasure of beating and taunting us."

"I put you in your wretched place where you belong," Tragmore snarled. "And when your father forgot his place, I did the same. In a more subtle manner, of course."

"What the hell does that mean?"

"Let's just say that when Markham's interest waned, I rekindled it by pointing out the benefits of our association."

Pierce's lips thinned into a grim line of enmity. "You blackmailed him."

"You must admit, I do it well." Tragmore's mocking words reminded him of the business at hand. "Enough," he pronounced, dismissing Pierce's upcoming question with a wave of his hand. "Our little reunion is at an end. Now, what is your answer? Will you meet my terms, or do I contact my barrister and begin divorce proceedings that will relegate your wife to the role of a bastard?"

"Don't, Pierce," Daphne said quietly, coming to stand by her husband's side. "He's inhuman enough when he's destitute. How many lives will he destroy with wealth and power behind him?"

Pierce drew a slow, inward breath, looked from the vicar

to Elizabeth to Daphne. "I'll contact Hollingsby as soon as I return home tonight."

"No!" Daphne grabbed his arm, shaking her head vehemently. "Don't do this. I'll feel less of a bastard if he denounces me than if he does not. I don't want him as a father."

Turning his head, Pierce stared down at his anguished wife. "I vowed to protect you. I intend to do just that."

"You also vowed to destroy my father."

An ironic light dawned in Pierce's eyes. "At the time, I didn't realize he'd already destroyed himself."

"I agree with Daphne," Elizabeth abruptly concurred. She raised her chin, drawing strength from the vicar's loving nod. "Harwick can't hurt me any more than he already has. But he can hurt others. Don't allow it, Pierce."

Contemplating Elizabeth's heartfelt words, pondering the absolute selflessness demonstrated by both Daphne and her mother, Pierce felt a fierce, overwhelming surge of pride. "Take all my money, Tragmore. It matters not, for I'll still emerge the winner."

"What nonsense are you spouting?" Tragmore demanded. "Are you changing your mind? Are you refusing to—"

"Sir?" Prudence, who had slipped away, unspotted, tugged at Tragmore's coat. "Don't be angry." Her voice was a whisper of sound over the shouts of the adults and the pounding construction.

"What?" Tragmore jerked around, staring down at Prudence as if she were filth.

"Don't shout," she murmured again. "'Specially not at Daphne. She's a snowdrop." Her little face brightened. "You can 'old my doll," she offered, extending her flaxen-haired treasure to him. "She'll make ye feel better."

"How dare you approach me, you dirty urchin!" Tragmore bellowed, shoving Prudence and the doll away. "Remove your vile plaything from my presence."

"Ye don't understand." Patiently, Prudence repeated herself, again proffering her beloved toy. "She'll make ye feel less angry. She makes my sister stop cryin'—and me, too. Take 'er."

With a roar of anger, Tragmore slapped the doll from Prudence's hands, sending it tumbling, face down, in the dirt.

"My Daphne!" Prudence shrieked, snatching it from the ground. Her eyes widened with fear as Tragmore bore down on her.

"This will teach you to disobey me!" he roared, slapping her so violently he propelled her backwards directly into the plow horses.

Whinnying their protest, the horses reared, wrenching at their harnesses and stretching the connecting rope beyond its endurance.

Tragmore was oblivious to their frenzy. All he saw was the wretched child on whom he intended to vent all his pent-up rage.

His hand raised again.

"No!"

Daphne didn't realize she'd screamed. The world converged into one scene: her father striking Prudence's doll, thrashing Prudence, and it was twelve years ago again, at the House of Perpetual Hope, and Prudence was Sarah.

Back then, Daphne could do nothing.

Now, she could.

"Leave her alone!" Springing forward, Daphne snatched Prudence in her arms, darting away from her father's impending assault.

The rope snapped.

"Look out!" a workman shouted.

It was too late.

The heavy wooden beam crashed down, smashing full force onto Tragmore's head.

Silently, he crumpled.

23

"I SHOULD MOURN HIM. BUT I DON'T."

Daphne stared out over Markham's gardens, gripping the rail of the morning room balcony.

"No, sweetheart, you shouldn't." Pierce wrapped his arms about her from behind. "We only mourn those who are deserving. Tragmore was a monster. Death cannot alter that fact."

Turning into her husband's arms, Daphne closed her eyes. "I'll never forget how horribly he died," she whispered. "His skull crushed beneath that beam."

"No, you won't," Pierce agreed, grateful that he'd shielded Daphne from viewing her father's mangled body firsthand. The memory of his gruesome death would dim that much faster with no hellish image to haunt her. "You won't forget," Pierce murmured again, pressing her closer, "but it's been a mere week. In time the pain of remembering will ease. Trust me. There are things I never dreamed I could recover from, and I have."

Daphne tilted back her head. "Father poured out horrid admissions to you that day, and yet, rather than becoming enraged, you seemed vindicated. As if all the anger were draining from within you."

"It was." Pierce threaded his fingers through Daphne's hair, a look of wonder in his eyes. "I never would have believed it myself. For years I've plotted, envisioning that final confrontation, the day I would reveal to Tragmore all I knew while bringing the scoundrel to his knees. I mentally enacted the scene hundreds, perhaps thousands, of times. Had you asked then, I would have sworn I'd die before conceding to his demands. But when that day of reckoning finally arrived, when I confronted my past head on, I suddenly discovered it no longer mattered. Because I now have something more powerful than hatred to live for. And that something is right here in my arms."

Daphne rose up to kiss him, her gaze filled with pride and love. "Your boundless courage never fails to astound me. Of all the magnificent deeds you've performed as Pierce Thornton and as the Tin Cup Bandit I think relinquishing your past is the most heroic." She lay her hand against his jaw. "Our babe might not yet realize it, but his father is an extraordinary man."

A shadow crossed Pierce's face.

"You're thinking of your own father," Daphne ventured.

"It's the only piece of the past I have yet to come to terms with, perhaps because I don't fully understand it," Pierce admitted quietly. "And after the things Tragmore said last week—" Wearily, he rubbed his temples. "I don't know what to think."

"It did sound as if your father was perhaps not quite the monster you believed him to be," Daphne suggested.

"He turned his back on me, damn it!"

"That indicates weakness, not cruelty." Daphne clutched her husband's forearms, determined to complete his healing process, to offer him the peace he craved. "Pierce, you told me yourself the late duke seemed disinterested whenever he and Father met with Barrings, that Markham spent most of his time wandering about the workhouse—'merely looking,' were your exact words. My father's boast just before he died confirmed what you and I had already concluded. Markham's visits to the House of Perpetual Hope were solely to assure himself of your well being. Compensation was certainly not a factor—not when he was losing money by paying Father to conduct the illegal dealings with Barrings. Nor was cruelty a factor." Seeing Pierce's puzzled look, she added, "When you accused Father of thrashing the workhouse children, did you not contend that he'd returned to do so on occasions other than his weekly meetings with Barrings?"

Slowly, Pierce nodded.

"Was the late duke present during those beatings?"

"No."

"So there's every reason to assume he knew nothing about them." Daphne counted off on her fingers. "Consequently, it appears your father accepted no payments, struck no children, and had no active interest in keeping Barrings in the headmaster's office. Nor was he aware of Barrings's and Father's brutal treatment during his absence. He only wanted a reason to see his son. No, Pierce, that is not the behavior of an uncaring man. Only a vulnerable one."

"True." Pierce inhaled sharply. "Which brings to mind the one unanswered question that continues to plague me. Tragmore claimed he blackmailed Markham to keep him involved in the workhouse scheme."

"I remember." Daphne nodded thoughtfully. "Father said Markham lost interest, presumably when you ran away from the workhouse, and he found the means to rekindle that interest."

"Yes, but with what did he blackmail him? What threat did he use? Damn!" Pierce released Daphne and turned away, a tormented look in his eyes. "Over and over we continue to speculate. But that's all it is, speculation. I wish I knew what Markham had been thinking. Perhaps then I could find some peace."

"I believe I can help you on that score."

Both Pierce and Daphne turned to see Hollingsby standing in the doorway.

"Forgive me for intruding. And don't blame Langley. He did his job flawlessly, insisting that you were not yet receiving any visitors." The solicitor's lips curved into a grin. "But I've been sharpening my timing. I waited until Langley took one of his infrequent breaks, then showed myself in. And evidently, my timing is better than I realized." He strolled over, laying his portfolio on the desk. "I have a letter here that I believe will provide you with the peace you seek."

"You're not a visitor, Hollingsby. You're a friend," Pierce responded at once. "And you're always welcome in our home." His brows drew together. "A letter?"

Hollingsby extracted two envelopes, simultaneously inclining his head in Daphne's direction. "I'd like to express my sympathy on your father's untimely death."

"Thank you, but it isn't necessary." Daphne crossed the room, pouring two glasses of brandy and handing them to Pierce and Hollingsby. "We all know what kind of man Father was. I wouldn't wish so violent a death on anyone, but to feign mourning would be absurd. In truth, what I'm feeling is a combination of deep sadness and deep relief. Sadness at the ugly waste Father made of his life, and relief that Mama, and all the others who were subject to Father's cruelty, are finally free."

"You're an astonishing woman," Hollingsby replied admiringly. He stared into his drink, then raised his gaze to meet Daphne's. "I'll be blunt. What I have to show Pierce involves your father. If you'd prefer not to be present—"

"No." Staunchly, Daphne went to her husband's side. "I'll stay."

Waiting only to see Pierce's nod of agreement, Hollingsby extended the first sealed envelope. "The late duke left specific instructions that I deliver this letter to you only upon and immediately following the Marquis of Tragmore's death."

With a start of surprise, Pierce set down his drink and accepted the envelope, tearing it open and smoothing out the handwritten sheets it contained. Then he sank down onto the settee, gesturing for Daphne to sit beside him. She complied, and together they read his father's words.

My dear son Pierce:
  You have no idea how long I've wanted to address you as such, to shout to the world that you—and your mother—are mine. But some realizations come too late, as it is only at the end of one's life that one can

truly assess what is important and what is trivial. Apologies are meaningless, for no words can recapture what has already been lost, nor mend pain too deeply inflicted to heal. Just know that I have suffered greatly by my own stupidity and weakness, for I denied myself a life with the woman I loved, as well as the chance to know the child we shared.

How proud I am that you have inherited your mother's compassionate heart and strength of character, for your children will never know the agony of desertion I allowed you and Cara to bear.

Enough empty regrets. The fact that you're reading this letter means that Tragmore is gone, and his threats can no longer harm us. In looking back, I realize what a fool I was to trust him. My only defense is that, in my colossal naiveté, I truly believed him to be a friend.

Let me explain my imprudent actions of three and twenty years ago, in the hopes that you will comprehend, if not understand.

The letter went on to reiterate the details Tragmore had flaunted before he'd died: that Markham had approached him out of a desperate need to visit the workhouse and under the guise of overseeing a friend's child, that Tragmore had conjured up the idea of accompanying him in order to himself conduct illicit dealings with Barrings, and that, once Pierce had escaped the confines of the House of Perpetual Hope and Markham had wanted to extricate himself from the whole situation, Tragmore had refused to allow it.

Eagerly, Pierce turned the page, searching for the answers he so desperately craved.

Tragmore didn't give a damn if I continued accompanying him to see Barrings or not. All he wanted was my ongoing payments for his initial assistance and my ensured silence about his illegal activities. He revealed to Barrings that I was considering backing out of our arrangement, embellishing on my notification by adding that I planned to report their unlawful transactions to the authorities—something I'd never threatened, nor even considered. Of course, Barrings panicked, as Tragmore knew he would. The two of them confronted me, announcing that, should I refuse to agree to their demands, Tragmore would go to the House of Lords and disclose the entire scheme, except that he would proclaim me its perpetrator and he and Barrings the shocked and innocent parties who had denounced my illegal dealings and now sought justice. Barrings would, of course, support Tragmore's claim. With such weighted evidence, my family and my reputation would be destroyed.

It wasn't worth the risk, Pierce. It was far easier to just pay Tragmore his cursed money and be done with it. And not only to protect my family name. You would also be in peril, should I refuse. You see, by now I understood the way Tragmore's mind worked. He wouldn't stop at condemning me before the House of Lords. If I refused to comply with his wishes, he'd dig into my past until he discovered my true reason for visiting the workhouse. And then, you'd be exposed to his blackmail—something I refused to permit. So I agreed to their terms, and started my private search for you all over again. Had I located you immediately, I assure you, you would not have spent those long years on the streets. I would have found a way to help you, no matter the cost. But by the time I unearthed your whereabouts, you were no longer a crafty pickpocket, but a shrewd young man, well on your way to success. The manner in which you assessed your investments, carefully and accurately selecting the lucrative ones and dismissing those that were unprofitable, reminded me a great deal of myself. You were a force to be reckoned with. You still are. Consequently, son, you didn't need my help.

Nor did you need me.

Ironic, isn't it, that it is now I who need you?

At this point, Pierce raised his head, realization jolting through him like gunfire. "Hollingsby, the day you read me the codicil, I recall your saying my father had kept a perpetual, though discreet, eye on me after I'd left the workhouse and that he therefore knew of my keen mind and suitability to run his estates and businesses."

Hollingsby nodded. "And he did, as you can see for yourself. I also told you he planned to approach you personally, but his illness thwarted him. Read on, and you'll find that to be true, as well."

Pierce lowered his head and resumed.

I can't give you back the years, Pierce. Nor can I bring back your beautiful mother and beg her forgiveness for being the selfish, weak man who cast her aside. All I can give you is the knowledge that I was a heartless fool, and that I deserved neither Cara nor you by my side. Also know that I recognized these facts long ago, and that what kept me from riding to Wellingborough all this time and acknowledging you as mine was shame. Not shame for you, but shame for myself and for my cowardice. You see, I hadn't the courage to face the hatred in your eyes when I told you who I was. And now, when I'm even willing to risk your enmity so that I might once stand before you and call you son, I fear it's too late, for each day I grow weaker, less able to leave my bed. So heed my words, Pierce, lest I die before having the chance to say them aloud.

You're an extraordinarily fine man, son. One who's survived the depths of hell and flourished, both in spite of it and because of it. Never doubt your worthiness, for if any man can call himself noble, it is you. Be armed with that knowledge, for I'm proud that my blood flows through your veins. And now, in the event that you are seeing this letter before your two-year term as the Duke of Markham is complete, read my final note to you, left in Hollingsby's capable hands. But remember, whether or not you choose to remain the Duke of Markham, you will always remain my rightful heir—an honor, indeed, not for you, but for me.

With great affection, Your father, Francis Ashford

For an endless moment Pierce stared down at the pages, his fingers trembling as he folded them.

"Pierce?" Daphne touched his face. "Are you all right?"

"I've lived thirty years believing he didn't care enough to acknowledge me," Pierce replied in a choked voice. "Even after I'd heard the terms of the codicil, I assumed he'd only made those stipulations because he wasn't alive to be humiliated by heralding his bastard son."

"He was terrified you'd reject him," Daphne returned softly. "He was also terrified of my father's blackmail, not only for himself, but for you. The duke was protecting you, and in his way loving you. Those were the reasons he never came forward, not cruelty or disdain. My God, Pierce, surely you see how proud he was of you. It's evident in every word he's written."

"Yes. It is." A muscle worked in Pierce's jaw. "What final note is he referring to?"

"This one." Hollingsby proffered the second sealed envelope. "The day I revealed the terms of the codicil, you asked me if your father had made provisions in the event that you remained childless or produced a daughter rather than a son."

"I remember. You told me the duke had left a sealed envelope for me to open after the two-year period had passed."

Hollingsby nodded. "This is that envelope. It is your final communication from your father."

"But two years haven't elapsed."

"True. But Tragmore's death makes the waiting period unnecessary, as your father stipulated when he entrusted the letter to me." Silently, Hollingsby pressed the envelope into Pierce's palm. "Open it."

Dazedly, Pierce tore open the envelope.

Pierce, it began:

> If you're reading this letter, I must presume that either two years have passed since you've assumed your rightful title, or Tragmore is no longer alive to threaten your well being. Whichever is the case, I can at last rest in peace. With you at the helm, Markham has doubt-

less thrived, as have my businesses. Quite possibly, you have a child of your own now, and a wife who loves you as you deserve. For the sake of your happiness, I hope so. For the sake of the codicil's terms, however, it matters not.

You see, son, the provisos I alluded to are fictitious. I invented their existence merely to satisfy your curiosity and to pique your interest enough to ensure you accepted your title. Having observed you for years, albeit from afar, I know you well. And you loathe turning your back on two things: a challenge and an opportunity to aid the poor. By offering you the dukedom, I provided you with both. I did this for two reasons, only one of which was selfish—that being the hope that you would carry on the Markham title and the Ashford family name. My other reason holds true whether you remain at Markham or resume life as Pierce Thornton. It is my fervent hope that, during this difficult time when you've been forced to assume a role you despise, you've discovered what I learned too late: that nobility is born in the heart and nourished in the mind.

I pray this discovery grants you the peace you seek. Teach it to your children, Pierce, and the agony we've endured will be given purpose.

All I have is unconditionally yours: my name, my fortune, my thanks.

Father

Pierce raised his head, his eyes damp with emotion. "He knew," he murmured incredulously. "He willed me his title knowing it was the very essence of all I loathed—*because* it was all I loathed."

"Loathe*d,*" Daphne repeated, emphasizing the past tense. "Pierce, think of what you told me not five minutes before Mr. Hollingsby arrived. You said that when your day of reckoning finally came, when you confronted your past head on, you suddenly discovered it no longer mattered, because you now have something more powerful than hatred to live for. Oh, Pierce, don't you see?" Daphne dashed tears of joy from her cheeks. "This is precisely what your father sought. He wanted you to find peace—and you have. What a miraculous gift he's given you."

"Indeed." Hollingsby removed his spectacles, frowning at an imaginary speck of dust on one lens. "Now the question is, what will you do with this gift?"

Still dazed, Pierce inclined his head quizzically. "What do you mean?"

"Your title. Will you keep it, or renounce it?"

The issue hung precariously for a moment, dissipating, along with Pierce's confusion, in a blaze of discovery.

Capturing Daphne's hand, he smiled, a definitive gleam in his eye. "As my beautiful wife once said, there are all varieties of dukes. I will merely enhance that number by one."

With a grand sweep, Hollingsby seized his glass, raising it in solemn tribute. "To your father's gift, then. And to all the Dukes of Markham—past, present and future."

Epilogue

"YOUR HEIR IS INQUISITIVE LIKE HIS FATHER," DAPHNE REported, leaning against the nursery wall and pointing to their son. "Even at six weeks of age."

The black-haired infant—named Ashford Thornton in honor of both Pierce's parents—was a wondrous blend of Daphne and Pierce, boasting his father's dark coloring and his mother's kaleidoscope eyes, eyes that, at the moment, were wide open and intently fixed on a patch of sunlight dancing along the wall.

"He's scarcely blinked all afternoon, lest he miss something." Daphne shook her head in amazement. "Not a motion or sound escapes his notice."

"He obviously possesses cunning," Pierce determined with a smug grin. "And instinct. We have only to supply the skill." He wrapped his arm about Daphne's waist. "Not that our daughter is lacking in either." He glanced at the second crib and its cooing, honey-haired occupant with an expression of intense satisfaction. "Juliet is every bit as intelligent as her twin brother. She's radiant and precious, which is as it should be. After all," Pierce's eyes twinkled as he recalled the reason they'd christened their daughter Juliet, "as only you and I know, 'twas not your doll alone that inspired Juliet's name. Her name is truly Jewel-iet."

"In which case, you're losing your touch with gems," Daphne commented dryly. "Because, in Juliet's case, it is she who has stolen from you. Your heart is most definitely in her custody."

"Only a portion of it." Pierce caressed Daphne's cheek. "A portion belongs to Ashford. As for the rest of it—" he brushed his wife's lips tenderly, "the rest of my heart belongs exclusively and entirely to our twins' incomparable mother." Drawing Daphne closer, he deepened the kiss until he felt his wife's heated response. Then, abruptly, he ended it, his breathing ragged. "I miss you so bloody much, I'm going insane. Christ, how the hell long has it been?"

Daphne laughed, a whisper of sound against his lips. "Patience, my darling. Timing is everything." She tipped her head back to study Pierce's face. "Tell me the truth. Were you even a touch bothered when Juliet made her entry into the world?"

"I *was* terrified." Pierce's jaw tightened. "You were so weak when that midwife threw me out." He shuddered. "Seeing you in pain and not being able to do a damned thing to ease it—"

"Stop." Daphne pressed her fingers to his lips. "I'm perfectly fine now. Besides, that's not what I meant. I only wondered if you were disappointed when you thought your first—your only—child was a daughter and not a son."

Pierce blinked in astonishment. "Disappointed? Not for a second. I told you, Snow flame, indulging a daughter was as real a dream to me as siring a son." He threaded his fingers through Daphne's hair. "Still, I must admit, I was thrilled with the idea of acquiring a son and a daughter simultaneously. At least once I was convinced you were all right." He flashed her a cocky grin. "I did a remarkable job, didn't I?"

"You?"

"Very well, *we*. We produced two extraordinary infants."

"Proclaimed by their unbiased father." Daphne eased away, folding her arms. "So, what are today's gifts for the children?"

"What makes you think I bought them gifts?"

"Because you did yesterday and the day before and the day before that. And then last week—"

"All right, you've made your point," Pierce chuckled, not a bit deterred by his wife's admonishment. "Very well, I spoil them. 'Tis my right, after all. Two of those beautiful infants belong to us and one to Sarah and James. Who else should spoil them, if not I?"

"Quite a question. Now, let's see." Daphne tapped her chin thoughtfully. "Cook practically lives in the nursery, when she's not arguing with Mrs. Gates over whose turn it is to feed the babes. Langley rotates between two posts now, the front door and the nursery. Then there's Lily and Bedrick, not to mention Mama and the vicar, who alternate between their wedding plans and their nursery visits. Need I go on?"

"There are quite a few people vying for our children's attention, aren't there?" Pierce concurred. He paused, considering his options. "Actually, Ashford's gift is too cumbersome to bring into the manor. He'll have to wait a bit to see it."

"I'm afraid to ask. What is this gift?"

"A splendid filly I've had my eye on for a fortnight—perfect for our son."

"Pierce, a horse? The child is a babe!"

"So is the filly. They'll be ready for each other soon enough."

"Lord." Daphne rolled her eyes.

"But the girls' gifts are quite transportable—and very special. Wait here." With a mysterious look, he slipped away.

Alone in the nursery, Daphne strolled about, stroking her infants' fuzzy heads and thanking God for all the love with which they'd been blessed. She paused beside the third crib, where little Alison slept. Born just two weeks before the twins, she had strengthened the ever-growing bond between Sarah and James, and made them precisely what Sarah had prayed for, a family.

"Daphne?" Sarah poked her head in, concern darkening her gaze when she saw where her friend was positioned. "Is there a problem with Alison?"

"No," Daphne reassured her. "In fact, your daughter seems to be the only one in this nursery who's cooperating. My two imps evidently never intend to sleep."

Sarah laughed aloud, the lonely and unhappy young woman she'd been forever gone. "Where's Pierce? Rarely is he away from the twins. Has he gone to inspect the new schoolhouse?" She raised teasing brows. "Miss Redmund must be devastated at their prolonged separation."

"I'm sure she is," Daphne concurred good humoredly. "Unfortunately, Miss Redmund will have to accustom herself to seeing less of Pierce, especially now that the construction is complete. After all, her charms, potent though they are, are no match for these three babes here." Daphne gave a tolerant sigh. "No, Pierce has gone to collect today's purchases. He'll be back any moment."

On cue, the nursery door opened, then kicked shut.

"Oh, Sarah, good. You're here." Pierce's hands stayed firmly behind his back. "I have gifts to give our daughters, but they involve you and Daphne as well." Seeing their puzzled expressions, he explained, a wealth of emotion in his voice. "It's been more than a decade since your work-house meeting—two young girls who were completely different and yet so very much alike. Little did you realize that one day you would span the world separating you to become friends. Because of your courage, our daughters can begin their lives as equals, with none of the censure of the past. And now, to signify their new beginning . . ." Pierce brought both arms forward, each hand clutching an identical doll with golden hair, huge blue eyes, and a pink satin dress. "For Alison and Juliet," he proclaimed, offering the dolls, both new and untainted, to their mothers. "In honor of the special women who gave them life."

"Presenting us with those dolls was a beautiful gesture," Daphne told Pierce that night in his bedchamber.

She unbuttoned her robe, shaking out her hair and glancing sideways at her husband as he sat down to read the *Times,* his nightly ritual since the twins' birth had spawned his forced celibacy. Daphne bit back a smile, determinedly hiding the flush of excitement on her cheeks. "Most heroic. Thank you."

"My pleasure." Pierce frowned, purposely opening the pages of his newspaper to block Daphne and the revealing cut of her nightwear from view. "Tell me when you're abed. I can't bear watching you undress and knowing I can't have you."

"Very well." Nonchalantly, Daphne climbed beneath the bedcovers and extinguished the light. "I'm abed."

"So I gathered."

"The room is pitch dark, Pierce. You can't possibly read."

"It doesn't matter." A pause. "Why the hell did you wear that diaphanous nightgown?"

Daphne propped herself on one elbow. "Because our endless wait is at an end."

"What did you say?" Pierce shot to his feet.

"Come to bed and I'll show you."

Pierce's body was already rigid. "Isn't it too soon?" Even as he asked, he was shedding his robe, crossing the room to the bed.

"No. It's been well over a month. I'm healed." Daphne reached for him, wrapping her arms about his neck.

"God, I've missed you, Snow flame." He buried his lips in the scented hollow of her throat.

"And I you." Shivering, Daphne gave herself up to her husband's magic. "Let's see if your instincts are as keen as ever," she whispered.

She felt the rumble of laughter vibrate through his chest. "Very well, Snow flame." He lifted his head, covered her mouth and her body with his. "And, should you deem it necessary, I promise to spend the entire night honing them to perfection."

Long, delicious hours later, Pierce cradled his slumbering wife in his arms and settled both of them amid the disheveled bedcovers. He was utterly exhausted yet too exhilarated to sleep, inundated by a happiness he'd never in his life anticipated. His heart and soul were at peace, his body sated from a night-long reunion with Daphne. He was also a

ANDREA KANE

father, and his beloved children were asleep down the hall in their beds.

At long last Pierce Thornton had a home.

Raising his eyes, he gave silent thanks to the heavens, vowing never again to doubt what he now knew to be true.

Prayers could indeed be answered.

Shifting a bit, Pierce spied the copy of the *Times* he'd cast to the floor the instant Daphne had offered him the paradise he'd been denied for six weeks. Still wide awake, he reached for it, angling the newspaper toward the window and the illuminating glow of the moonlight.

An article on the front page caught his eye:

> Lord Weberling returned from his three-month journey to India yesterday, bringing with him what he claims to be the largest, most perfect pair of diamonds ever to grace English soil.

"'Neither stone possesses either a flaw or a chip,'" Daphne read aloud over her husband's shoulder. "Fascinating."

Pierce's head snapped around. "I thought you were asleep."

"I thought you weren't interested in reading."

"I wasn't. But now that I've exhausted you, I am."

"Hmm. I see." Naked, Daphne rose, slipping thoughtfully into her robe. "Lord Weberling. Are you acquainted with him?"

"No. Are you?"

"Oh, yes. He was a friend of my father's. One of his best informants, in fact. Every time I visited the vicar, Lord Weberling spotted me, and took great pleasure in reporting my indiscretions to Father."

"Did he?" Pierce inclined his head, watching Daphne from beneath hooded lids.

"Both diamonds are large and flawless—the article does specify that, does it not?" she asked, tapping her chin.

"It does."

"I wonder what their total value is."

"Lord knows. Probably tens of thousands of pounds."

Daphne's expression was the picture of innocence. "'Tis hard to envision the number of children that could feed."

"Countless."

"Such a pity." Daphne sighed. "Lord Weberling is a greedy and unfeeling man. He'll probably squander the funds at White's or have the diamonds made into rings for his garish, coldhearted wife."

"I fear you're right," Pierce agreed, his eyes beginning to twinkle.

Crossing over to the double chest, Daphne eased open the drawer housing Pierce's cravats. She reached to the back, groping about until she extracted the glittering sapphire they'd secreted there for safekeeping. "Do you think the diamonds could be larger than this?" she asked, fingering the stone.

"Definitely. Several times larger, if they're half as grand as Weberling boasts."

"Perhaps we should make sure—examine them at close range."

"A splendid idea." Pierce climbed out of bed and strolled over to his wife. "Do you know, I just realized I have yet to initiate that handsome black cloak you gave me for Christmas."

"True. And I have yet to accustom my husband to seeing the mother of his children adorned by a mask."

"Just this once," Pierce qualified in a dark whisper.

"Just this once," Daphne concurred, the essence of sincerity.

Their gazes locked.

And the Tin Cup Bandit smiled.

Author's Note

As with all my heroes and heroines, Daphne and Pierce came alive for me during the time I was writing *The Last Duke*. Like dear friends, they carved out an indelible place in my heart and made it nearly impossible to say good-by. I hope you share some of that warmth and reluctance, and that as a result you'll feel compelled to read their story again some time.

In the meantime, I'm already immersed in the writing of my next Pocket Books historical. *Emerald Garden*, set in the beautiful Cotswold Hills of Regency England, is a destined-to-be-together love story that's been clamoring inside me for quite some time, just dying to be told!

Enjoy the preview Pocket Books has provided of *Emerald Garden*. And thank you again for all your wonderful letters. They mean more to me than I can ever express, and I promise to continue answering each and every one.

If you'd like a copy of my latest newsletter, just drop me a legal-sized SASE at:

P.O. Box 5104
Parsippany, NJ 07054-6104

Andrea

Pocket Star Books
Proudly Announces

EMERALD GARDEN

Andrea Kane

Coming from
Pocket Star Books

The following is a preview of
Emerald Garden . . .

"I thought I'd find you here."

Lord Quentin Steel mounted the steps of the white lattice gazebo, pausing beside the bench's occupant. "I stopped by your estate first. But, as I expected, your father said you'd left Townsbourne just after dawn. So I rode directly to Emerald Manor."

"Where else would I be at a time like this?" Head bent, Brandice Townsend's mournful reply was swallowed by her lap. "Emerald Manor holds my happiest memories. 'Tis only fitting for it to hold my saddest ones as well."

Tenderly, Quentin ruffled her cloud of cinnamon hair, smoothing it back to coax her chin from her chest. "Smile, Sunbeam. The world hasn't ended."

"Yes. It has." Without raising her head, she scooted over, silently inviting Quentin to sit beside her.

He complied, unbuttoning the decorated coat of his uniform to settle himself, gently taking her hand in his. "I won't be gone forever."

"That depends upon your definition of forever."

"Look at me, Brandi." Hooking a forefinger beneath her chin, Quentin forced her gaze around to meet his. "I'll stay in Europe only until we've defeated Napoleon and ended the war."

Brandi's dark eyes misted. "That's hardly a comfort. The war is interminable and throughout its countless days you'll be right alongside Lord Wellington, at the very heart of the fighting."

"That's where I'm needed," Quentin acknowledged quietly. "The Lieutenant-General cannot lead us to victory if no one is able to successfully decipher French messages."

Brandi nodded, her slender brows knit with worry. "For once I wish you were not quite so brilliant. Then you could remain in England, safe, rather than lord knows where, endangering your life with every battle." She caught her lower lip between her teeth. "I'll miss you."

"You'll scarcely notice my absence," Quentin assured her, his knuckles caressing her cheek.

"You have a legion of others to spoil you—your father, my parents."

"Desmond," she added with pointed derision.

A shadow crossed Quentin's face. "I realize that my brother's more," he paused, searching for the right word, "traditional nature upsets you."

"Traditional?" Brandi reiterated. "Desmond is a relic!"

Quentin's lips twitched. "I shudder to think what that makes me. After all, Desmond is but three and thirty, a mere seven years my senior. Do I border on antiquity as well?"

"Never." Her denial was immediate and fierce. "You and Desmond are as unlike as a knight and a dragon."

"Ah, but which am I, knight or dragon?"

Brandi shot him a don't-patronize-me look.

"Very well, Sunbeam." Abandoning all attempts at diversion, Quentin reverted to a candor he seldom required, save with Brandi. "I won't deny your statement. Desmond doesn't understand you, nor can he fathom your unorthodox behavior. But, in his defense, he *is* concerned about your future, albeit in his own way."

"Everyone is concerned about my future!" Brandi burst out, vaulting to her feet. "Everyone means well. Everyone is anticipating my impending coming of age—everyone but me." She crossed her beloved gazebo, clutching its entrance post and gazing restively over the vast, manicured gardens of Emerald Manor, the fairy-tale cottage that, though built and owned by Quentin's family, had become Brandi's haven over the years. "As for understanding me, no one understands me but you. Not Papa, not your father, not even your mother. I adore them, Quentin, truly I do. Heaven knows they try to make allowances for my unruliness. But your parents are the Duke and Duchess of Colverton, and Papa, the Viscount Denerley. For generations, their families have thrived on the same rigid values. So it follows that they share Desmond's opinion that, as a soon-to-be grown woman, I'm to adopt the role of a proper lady."

Quentin stifled a chuckle. "Well, you are nearly sixteen. 'Tis only natural for your father to expect—"

"The Season after next he plans to bring me out," Brandi interrupted, her small hand tightening its grip. "Then my life truly will be over."

"Aren't you being a touch dramatic?"

"No." She pivoted to face Quentin. "I'm not. And you know it. The moment I make that magical Court appearance, all I adore most will be wrested from my grasp. No more fishing in the cottage stream without stockings, tearing through the woods astride Poseidon, or honing my shooting skills. Instead, I'll be transformed into a pianoforte-playing, needlepoint-stitching ninny, a procurable prize to be flourished before the *ton.*"

Throwing back his head, Quentin shouted with laughter. "You certainly make it sound dismal, Sunbeam. Although, if your description is accurate, you'll need every moment of these next two years to prepare. Currently, your needlepoint is abysmal and your pianoforte playing, obscene."

"Neither of which I plan to rectify." Brandi's retort was adamant. "I've dreaded my coming-out for as long as I can remember. My only consolation, until now, has been the knowledge that you'd be here to comfort me in my misery."

Quentin rose, sobering as he met her gaze. "I'll return to the Cotswolds the moment I'm able. I wish I could promise—"

"Don't," Brandi interrupted. "Don't promise. We've never broken a pledge to each other, Quentin. Don't alter that by offering me a vow you might be unable to keep."

Whatever Quentin intended to say was cut off by the sound of his carriage driver calling out to a coachman, and the horses whinnying their impatience.

"Is it time?" Brandi asked, a lump forming in her throat.

"Soon." Abruptly, Quentin reached into his

coat pocket and extracted a pair of intricately carved pistols. "But not quite yet."

"Quentin!" Her anguish temporarily forgotten, Brandi's eyes widened with surprised delight. Impulsively, she darted forward, reverently touching one polished barrel. "How exquisite! Did you just purchase them? You must have. I've never seen them before. Where did you ever find them? The workmanship is magnificent!"

With an indulgent grin, Quentin offered her a closer look. "I discovered them last week when I was in London and, keeping us both in mind, I purchased them on the spot." He pressed the pistol Brandi was caressing into her outstretched hand. "Go ahead, take it."

Brandi needed no second invitation. Her trained fingers closed around the ornate handle, exploring the weapon while carefully avoiding its sensitive trigger. "It truly is splendid," she breathed, stroking the gleaming wood and brass.

"Might I interest you in a farewell shooting match?" Quentin inquired with a knowing twinkle.

Instantly, her head came up. "You might."

"Choose our target."

Cheeks flushed with excitement, Brandi stepped into the garden, pivoting to survey the surrounding woods. A resolute tightening of her jaw told Quentin her decision was made. "That towering oak," she instructed, pointing. "The one standing alone."

"Quite a distance, Sunbeam," he drawled, strolling down and squinting to assess the designated target. "You're proficient at spans of nearly fifty feet, but that tree must be ninety feet away. Are you certain you don't want to reconsider?"

"I'm certain," Brandi returned, eagerly embracing the challenge. "Whichever one of us cleanly strikes the center of the oak's trunk— shall we say, just below the first row of branches —will be declared the winner."

"Agreed." Grandly, Quentin gestured for her to proceed. "Ladies—" A twinkle. "Pardon me. Hoydens first."

"On the contrary," she teased back. "Soon-to-be great war heroes first."

"As you wish." Quentin cocked and raised his pistol. An instant later his shot rang out, whizzing through the air and striking the oak a mere inch or two from the designated spot.

"Excellent," Brandi commended. She appraised the tree before raising her own weapon. "But I'll surpass it."

"Such faith in your skill, Sunbeam."

She tossed him a saucy grin. "No, my lord. Such faith in my instructor." Taking careful aim, she fired.

Her bullet flew to its mark, piercing the oak a fraction to the right of Quentin's shot—dead on target.

Triumphantly, Brandi turned to her opponent. "Well?"

Quentin whistled his appreciation. "It seems your instructor is worth his weight in gold."

"Oh, he is." With a sunny smile, she offered him her pistol. "In fact, he appears to be a better instructor than he is a marksman."

Laughter erupted from Quentin's chest. "Touché, my victorious pupil." Still chuckling, he began cleaning his own gun, ignoring her outstretched hand. "What will you claim for your prize?"

All humor vanished from Brandi's face. "Your well being. 'Tis all I ask."

Quentin ceased his task, raising his head to regard Brandi with gentle understanding. "I'll be fine, Sunbeam. You have my word, contest or not." His gaze fell to her proffered weapon. "Now, as for your prize. It must be worthy of that imposingly accurate shot of yours." He pretended to ponder his dilemma until, abruptly, he appeared struck by a brilliant notion. "Your pistol!" he proclaimed. "'Tis the perfect prize." So saying, he pressed Brandi's fingers more tightly about the handle, urging the gun toward her. "It's yours."

"Mine? To keep?"

"Yours. To keep. As I shall keep its mate."

Brandi turned captivated eyes to her gift. "Oh, Quentin. I don't know what to say."

"Say nothing. You won our match—and the pistol." Savoring Brandi's exhilaration, Quentin was abruptly seized by a sense of impending loss, an innate perception that all he loved would be somehow changed when next he walked English soil. Silently he admonished himself, fighting off the unsettling premonition, dismissing it as a reaction to the imminent bloodshed that loomed ahead.

Still, it persisted.

"Keep the pistol close beside you," he instructed, focusing on something he could control. "Then *I* can be assured of *your* well being during my absence."

"Oh! That reminds me." Oblivious to Quentin's emotional turmoil, Brandi sprang to action, scooting over to the bench and carefully laying aside her cherished prize to gather up a small parcel. "This is for you." She placed the box in Quentin's hands. "A going-away gift."

"You didn't have to—"

"Yes I did. And you'll soon see why." Brandi's grin was impish. "I have a feeling my motives and yours are much the same." She gestured impatiently toward the package. "Open it."

With a puzzled expression, Quentin complied. A moment later, he lifted out a thin, exquisitely crafted knife.

"You're an incomparable marksman, my lord," Brandi explained with a maturity as disconcerting as it was atypical. "But guns alone cannot protect you. What if you should be caught by surprise, attacked at close range? No pistol is small enough to remain unerringly concealed. A proper blade is. Especially one as thin as this. I had it fashioned just for you. Keep it with you at all times, hidden in your boot. Then, no one can harm you, whether in battle or out."

"'Tis the finest blade I've ever owned." Quentin stared intently at the onyx handle. "Thank you, Sunbeam."

"Now both of us will assuredly be safe, will we not, Captain Steel?"

He found his smile, sliding the knife inside his Hessian. "Indeed we will, my lady."

"Lord Quentin?" The coachman stood at a discreet distance, calling out to Quentin and pointing at his timepiece. "Forgive me, sir, but your ship leaves the London docks at half after three. We really must be off."

"Thank you, Carlyle," Quentin acknowledged with a wave. "I'll be along straightaway." He turned back to Brandi, twining a lock of cinnamon hair about his finger and tugging gently.

"Adieu, Sunbeam. And remember, safeguard your new pistol. For I intend to demand a rematch immediately upon my return, even if you've already traversed the dreaded portals of womanhood."

Blinking back tears, Brandi nodded. "Agreed. And *you* remember, always keep your blade close beside you lest you need it." She rose to her toes, giving Quentin a fierce hug. "God-speed."

He brushed his lips to her forehead, then released her, descending the gazebo steps and crossing the lush, rectangular garden for which Emerald Manor was named. Halfway across the sculpted lawns, he turned, seized by a compelling need to capture a memory, to take with him something neither time nor change could erase.

Leaning against the gazebo's ivied post, Brandi waved, her burnished hair blowing in soft wisps about her shoulders, a blanket of violets and wild geraniums at her feet.

Resplendence stretched before her; a lifetime loomed ahead.

Heavy hearted, Quentin returned Brandi's wave, smiling as she held up her pistol, its polished barrel glinting in the sunlight. In return, he patted his boot, indicating that his blade was securely in place.

At half after three Quentin's ship left London,

transporting him to the European mainland and its awaiting war.

With him he carried Brandi's knife and an unrelenting premonition.

One that four years later was destined to become a reality.

———————————

Look for

Emerald Garden

Wherever Paperback Books Are Sold
Coming from
Pocket Star Books